THE
PRINCIPLES
BEHIND
FLOTATION

Also by Alexandra Teague

Poetry:

Mortal Geography
The Wise and Foolish Builders

THE
PRINCIPLES
BEHIND
FLOTATION

A NOVEL

ALEXANDRA TEAGUE

Skyhorse Publishing

First Edition

This is a work of fiction. Names, places, characters, and incidents are either the products of the author's imagination or are used fictitiously.

Skyhorse Publishing books may be purchased in bulk at special discounts for sales promotion, corporate gifts, fund-raising, or educational purposes. Special editions can also be created to specifications. For details, contact the Special Sales Department, Skyhorse Publishing, 307 West 36th Street, 11th Floor, New York, NY 10018 or info@skyhorsepublishing.com.

Skyhorse® and Skyhorse Publishing® are registered trademarks of Skyhorse Publishing, Inc.®, a Delaware corporation.

Visit our website at www.skyhorsepublishing.com.

10 9 8 7 6 5 4 3 2 1

Library of Congress Cataloging-in-Publication Data is available on file.

Cover design by Erin Seaward-Hiatt

Print ISBN: 978-1-5107-1728-2
Ebook ISBN: 978-1-5107-1729-9

Printed in the United States of America

"A belt of mud . . . prevented Arkansas from having a port as well as a metropolis, a civilization, and a history. A people who were willing to foot it a hundred miles through the muck to get nowhere founded Arkansas and achieved their aim."

—C.L. EDSON, IN *THE NATION*, 1920S

"*Dreyfus once wrote that on Devil's Island he would see the most glorious birds. Many years later in Brittany he realized they had only been seagulls. To me they will always be glorious birds.*"

—MAUDE, *HAROLD AND MAUDE*,

BY COLIN HIGGINS

1

Kyle's Aquariums is crowded with tanks and pumps and shell wind chimes, and A.Z. presses against the tetras to let a family of pilgrims pass. They're headed for the emerald catfish, which are silver and sickly, and which Kyle is trying to unload with a sign that says SEA OF SANTIAGO SOUVENIR CATFISH.

The catfish are actually from South America, but the pilgrims don't know this. They buy them for their kids' tanks back in Tulsa or wherever, and the kids carry the rubber-banded, three-quarters-water, one-quarter-air plastic baggies around until they forget about them. A lot of dead fish end up under chairs at restaurants or on tour buses. It's not very humane, and Sahara, who was A.Z.'s best friend until she turned out to be such a hippie, started a boycott over it two years ago in seventh grade.

A.Z. could never boycott Kyle's because it's the only aquarium store in town. And since the Gordings don't allow anyone beyond the swimming lagoon in the Sea of Santiago, it's the closest thing she has to scuba diving. From what she's seen on TV, this is sort of almost like it: air bubbles rising around her and tetras flickering their fins, snuffling in gravel and swaying plants, which are plastic but still sort of lifelike. If she's stressed about something, like Mrs. Ward almost catching Scotty copying her test, she likes standing between those lit-up tanks. It makes breathing feel sort of miraculous.

Larsley thinks fish are lame. She's over by the ornaments—pastel ceramic castles and pagodas no one buys—looking at a pink humpback whale the size of a stapler. "Check this out," she calls past the pilgrim family. "We should totally steal it."

A.Z. glances around for Kyle, who is fortunately in the back stocking fish food or something.

Larsley isn't serious anyway; she's just trying to freak out the pilgrims. During junior high, she and A.Z. spent a lot of time perfecting this, including running in front of pilgrim cars when Coach W. sent everyone on the loop past the Ark Park. Unlike locals, who speed down the middle of the roads and veer aside when another local speeds around the curve, pilgrims drive on the correct side, braking intermittently, even on flat stretches. When you run in front of them, they get confused and check their maps like you might be a miraculous landmark.

These pilgrims don't look freaked out. The kids are smudging their fingers on the aquarium glass, squealing, "Catch it, catch it!" and the dad is swishing a little green net, trying to scoop the right catfish, which is probably really a bunch of different fish.

"Shit. Dagnabbit," he says, netting a fish his little girl doesn't want. The mom holds the plastic bag of water, and the fish plops in and turns around, like it's trying to figure out where the rest of the tank went.

"It has worms on its face," the little girl says as she starts to cry.

A.Z. starts to say those aren't worms—they're barbels to sense food at the bottom of the water—but then the family might think she works here, and besides, she's trying to stop saying geeky stuff.

Last week, when no one asked her to dance at the Spring Splash Dance—which was dumb and in the cafeteria, so she shouldn't have felt sad—Larsley said guys are just intimidated because she knows so much. This isn't fair. It's not her fault her mom is Compolodo's librarian, and she grew up with books, or that she's teaching herself oceanography, which is the coolest career in the world because you get to study everything about the real nature of the Sea—which no one has researched because the Gordings unscientifically believe God doesn't want people to ask questions about the Sea of Santiago's miraculous waters.

"Speaking of whales," A.Z. calls back to Larsley, "did you see Scotty copying off me in English? He was leaning over with his neck all sideways, and Mrs. Ward walked over like *The Shadow*."

"What's *The Shadow*?" Larsley says.

"That radio show from the '40s." A.Z. sometimes forgets that since her mom is way older than regular moms, normal people in 1989 don't know these things. "I thought she was going to fail us both." She doesn't admit she sort of let Scotty copy.

Mrs. Ward had paired them for the review session on *Fahrenheit 451* on Friday, which Scotty spent leaning across her desk to talk to Rob.

Scotty and Rob are the two fastest runners in Compolodo and always wear do-rags and shiny grey pants that say COMPOLODO WHALES, and they never have to do any algebra because Coach W. is the teacher. They have to do English, though, so finally, Scotty turned to her and said, "Hey, I've got this sweet idea. I'll just copy from you." This was pretty smart, by Scotty standards. And A.Z. should have told him no, but she didn't.

"So?" Larsley shifts the whale back and forth between her

red-and-black-chipped-nail-polish fingers and glances at it like she's really thinking of stealing it.

Larsley never worries about getting into trouble because her parents, the county's two ambulance drivers, are too busy to notice her. And she doesn't have to worry about losing her 4.0 and not getting into Sea Camp because she doesn't have a 4.0 and doesn't want to go to Sea Camp. She says it's probably fascist like the Boy Scouts.

Larsley is wrong: Sea Camp is completely not fascist. It's not even exactly a camp. It's an oceanography program where you get to live on boats in the Florida Keys and study with real oceanographers, and A.Z. is applying to go this Christmas break. Unfortunately, it's also expensive without scholarships and really competitive. Most people who get accepted come from schools with actual classes in oceanography and not just a summer independent study and library books that your mom has let get all outdated.

Standing between the aquariums and thinking about the failed test and her Sea Camp application, A.Z. suddenly doesn't actually feel calmer. She feels like the fish slipping past on every side of her are all the ways she might not quite get in—all the data she has to collect from the Sea of Santiago for her independent study this summer, flickering just out of reach. "Never mind," she says. "We should get out of here."

After the dimness and churn, the world in the parking lot seems bright and sort of transparent—like she and Larsley have also been scooped out of their element into plastic bags. It takes A.Z. a minute to notice her father's brown-paneled Oldsmobile parked in the lot. Her dad is in the car, scribbling notes in his steno pad, which is propped against the steering wheel.

As the only reporter and editor for *The Compolodo Daily News*, the county weekly, it's been her father's one-man role since before A.Z. was born to try to fill the news hole around the ads for the county's two biggest employers—Chuck Chicken and the Miracle Play—with stories about broken tractors; Compolodo's first proposed stoplight; the anniversary of the Compolodo murder (which involved a cook at the Anchor's Away Inn, an axe handle, and his girlfriend); ratings of the best salt water taffy (before the funnel cakes, one of the two pounds A.Z. has gained this spring); bulletins before and after the Greenville Fourth of July Fish Fry; and stories about the Miracle Play opening night, each year on the second Friday in May.

The Miracle actually occurred in March, but Compolodo is sometimes still icy then, and even devout pilgrims don't want to huddle under rented blankets to watch a two-hour outdoor play.

Her dad looks up when he sees them and waves with his pen. "I'm glad I found you; I wanted to head out to the Miracle Play early to interview some pilgrims about opening night."

"It's opening night?" Larsley says.

"Mid-May miracles," A.Z.'s dad says. Alliteration is his signature style; he says it tames the tempest of every possible thing he could say.

A.Z.'s dad loves *The Tempest*. He used to be an actor, and his deferred dream is to stage it on Mud Beach, which the Gordings would never allow because *The Tempest*'s magic doesn't come from God, and they probably wouldn't make much money.

"Hop in," he says.

A.Z. hasn't actually admitted to Larsley that she's agreed to go to the Miracle Play. She and her dad go every year to opening night, which they've probably seen more times than anyone in town except maybe the Gordings who work there. It's super long and boring, and pretty much the same every year. A.Z. wouldn't keep going if it weren't for the last two minutes—when the backdrop falls.

"Cool!" Larsley says, even though it isn't. She opens the back door of the Oldsmobile, which she always says looks like it's aspiring to be an RV.

At the Miracle Play, the bleachers are cheap, rattly aluminum, like the ones at the Greenville track, but taller. During peak season, they fill with pilgrims from all over the Midwest and Texas and the East Coast. A.Z. and Larsley walk back and forth on the empty bottom row, which is reserved for some tour group, and A.Z.'s dad climbs to the top to interview pilgrims for "Pilgrim Profiles." In the off-season, there's not much news and he has to recycle old columns, so he tries to find really repeatable stories now: pilgrims who got married on Mud Beach or promoted at work after swimming in the holy water.

"This is boring," Larsley says, which is a bad sign since they've only been here one minute. "We should ask your dad to borrow his press pass so we can go get free Dr Peppers."

"Yeah," A.Z. says, doubtfully. Her dad probably needs his pass to show to pilgrims, and anyway, it's not a real press pass; he typed it himself like he's always typing up everything.

Fortunately, the tour group arrives, clomping up the bleachers with popcorn and cameras and blankets. Larsley steps into the aisle, trying to be casually in the way.

"They died," she tells a guy who is shielding his eyes like he's scanning for his family. "Rogue wave."

"Who died?" Greg says. He's appeared from somewhere—maybe a secret passage in the bleacher wall. He's wearing a uniform with a gold embroidered conch shell and looks weird without his baseball cap.

"Everyone cool," Larsley says. "Except A.Z. and me. What are you doing here?"

"Parking cars." He's got a light wand in his hand, but it's off. "What are *you* doing here?"

"Her dad's writing a story," Larsley says. "We're getting everything free."

"Hey A.Z.," Greg says, "want some squirrel jerky?"

It's been his joke since fourth grade, when she did a speech on the sailor's diet. She'd just read *Lives of the Great Explorers* and was planning her own future entry: *Anastasia Zoe McKinney, Great Exploreress: First Person to Sail Around the World from Arkansas.* That was back when she wanted to be a sailor—before she realized that sailing is about the surface, and what matters more are all the currents and ecosystems and saline levels underneath.

Greg doesn't wait for A.Z. to answer. A double-decker tour bus is pulling in, so he switches his light stick on like he's some parking Jedi and strides over, waving it left and right.

"Germans. A bunch of families and one cute boy with bleached hair," Larsley says. "Like Billy Idol, but all German and stuff."

"Blue-haired ladies from a retirement home in Tennessee," A.Z. says. Of course, they can't see who's inside the mirrored windows, but the first woman out has short permed hair. In the twilight, it could be white or blue, but A.Z. claims victory. "You owe me a Dr Pepper."

Larsley walks backward to the concession stand like she's still watching for a German Billy Idol. It's not impossible. Germans sometimes come on tours from Oberammergau, which has a religious play that is probably just as boring as this one.

"Hey, there's a blind dude," she says. "Can you imagine coming all the way to the Sea and not really seeing it? Your boyfriend is helping him across the parking lot." She always gives A.Z. shit about Greg liking her. "I can't believe he's working here."

"Me neither," A.Z. says.

Greg is Nell Gording's nephew, but it's still a really lame job. A.Z. knows because her dad first came to Compolodo to work in the Miracle Play. He'd seen an ad in his stepmother's church bulletin in Texas and was looking for a way, besides the Dairy Queen drive-through, to use a BA in theater. He got hired as a townsperson, which sounded good, but turned out, like everything at the Miracle Play, to pay minimum wage.

It also turned out not to be a speaking part. Sometime in the late '60s, the Gordings had pre-recorded the entire script. That way, the microphones wouldn't pick up the sound of gulls—and none of the actors would need to act.

At the concession stand, Larsley tells the girl working there that they're reporters for the school paper, which would be a better lie if Compolodo Elementary-Junior-High actually had a paper.

"We're doing this article about ice," Larsley says. "We've heard that some crushed ice has rat shit in it and we're testing all the soft drinks in town."

"The Gording Foundation doesn't allow us to give free concessions," the girl says, smiling stiffly bright, like the cheese sauce they goop next to nacho chips.

Larsley spreads her red-black fingernails on the counter in that "so, here's the thing" way. "I guess we'll just have to put you on the rat-shit list."

"We have cans in the vending machine," the girl offers, "by the Miracle Museum."

The museum is a circular concrete-block building like a highway rest stop, and the vending machine is by the gift shop, which sells Miracle story books, coloring books, and cow statues covered with glued-on shells. There aren't any cows in the Miracle Play, but before the Sea took over their pastures, the Gordings had the biggest herd in northwest Arkansas. A.Z.'s mom still sometimes unfairly refers to the Sea as "that cow pond."

A.Z.'s mother, who was forty when A.Z. was born and had already lived this weird, tragic life, isn't a fan of large bodies of salt water or God or miracles. Once—when A.Z. was young and obsessed with sailing—her mom pulled the red *National Geographic Atlas* from one of the library's shelves. In the northwest corner of Arkansas lay the Sea of Santiago: a tiny, beautiful, blue splotch, its borders faint and uncharted.

"See all this land?" her mom said, pointing at Missouri, Mississippi, Louisiana, and Texas. "The Sea of Santiago is landlocked. You can't sail from here to anywhere."

But A.Z. wasn't convinced. If the Gordings only allowed rented paddle boats as far as the Mud Beach buoys, and no one had ever charted the Sea, they couldn't know where it ended, or didn't end.

And besides, explorers always did impossible things. What about Jeanne Baret, who stowed away on de Bougainville's ship and became the first woman to circumnavigate the globe?

A.Z. spent years secretly singing the Naval Prayer, which she'd learned when her dad was researching "Hummable Hymns"—"O Christ! Whose voice the waters heard and hushed their raging at Thy word, Oh, hear us when we cry to Thee, for those in peril on the sea"—and praying, for good measure, to both Poseidon and God to help her sail around the world.

But then in seventh grade, she took Careers, where she became friends with Larsley, who pointed out religion is a drug for the masses, and where she learned about the infinitely cooler science of oceanography.

"Opiate," A.Z.'s mom corrected when A.Z. announced her epiphanies.

Larsley only has two quarters, so they buy one Dr Pepper. There's no line for the museum, and for some reason, no one working the door. "We should go in," Larsley says.

"Yeah," A.Z. says, even though she's nervous a guard will appear. The Gording Foundation guards are sometimes mean. When A.Z. was little, a guard at Mud Beach yelled at her for feeding seagulls, which turned out to actually be chickens that had blown off Chuck Chicken trucks.

A.Z.'s mom almost yelled at her, too. She quoted that hawk and handsaw part of *Hamlet,* and made A.Z. study *The Encyclopedia of Ornithology* for the rest of the week.

The museum is dim and has mildewy-smelling blue carpet, and it shouldn't be cool but sort of is. The walls are painted with the story of the Miracle: beginning with Nell Gording's near-death sickness in the spring of 1955, her instantaneous recovery when she found a rowboat floating on her family's cow pond, and finally the miraculous appearance of the Sea, which began with rain rippling the pond in March 1955. Within a month, it covered the Gordings' pastures all the way to the Missouri border.

In front of the murals is a replica of the wooden rowboat, studded with shells and tiny white barnacles from drifting across millennia and oceans. In some way that only Nell can fully understand, the boat belonged to the Apostle James, whose bones once showed up in a similar boat in a cow pasture in Santiago de Compostela, Spain.

Of course, since that was a Catholic miracle, the Spanish people only got a boat with bones. For the New Ark Church, the boat was just the first sign. The real wonder was when God sent an entire inland saltwater sea.

Actually, as A.Z. has read, this part of the Ozarks was, millennia ago, covered by an even bigger inland sea. The earliest maps of North America show a vast sea stretching across this whole area, and the limestone still holds fossils of trilobites and hemithecellid or segmented mollusks. Scientifically, it sort of makes sense that a sea would return.

"We should steal that boat," Larsley says, even though there aren't any pilgrims around to freak out. "I saw this thing on TV about this guy who got past all kinds of security and broke the fingers off the Mona Lisa before anyone stopped him."

"Wasn't that the Pieta?" A.Z. says. It seems like Larsley should know this since her family is technically Catholic.

"Yeah, whatever," Larsley says.

The lights are flashing above the bleachers by the time they get back, and A.Z.'s dad is talking to himself like he does when he's brain-storming headlines. "Family finds faith. Family finds firm faith."

"You're just in time," he says. "I just talked to a man who used to be an alcoholic until his wife threw a frying pan at his head and he realized God wanted him to come here."

A.Z.'s dad doesn't tell the pilgrims this, but he considers himself agnostic, which means he's not sure how the Sea appeared, but, like pretty much everyone in Compolodo, his job depends on it. And he wouldn't mind going swimming in it if he ever had a day off.

In the darkness before the stage lights, Nell's bedroom is being wheeled out. The actress playing Nell is under a quilt, looking weak. Actually, from the bleachers, you can't tell how she looks, but the voice-over is booming, "*After three months in bed with a fever, Nell Gording was weak. The birds were singing outside, but poor Nell could barely hear them.*"

"Chirp, chirp," A.Z. whispers, as chirping pours from the speak-ers, but Larsley doesn't laugh. She looks as if she's actually watching the play.

"*But this morning, there was no one but her to feed the cows, so she dragged herself out of bed.*"

The music swells, violiny and foreshadowy, and pink spotlights flicker.

A.Z. wishes she had a flashlight so she could finish *Fahrenheit 451*. She picks up her backpack but doesn't unzip it, because the next bright part won't happen until the Apostle James appears. And besides, Larsley will call her a geek. The quiz today was on chapter two, and A.Z. is on chapter nine, and anyway, Mrs. Ward only cares about the symbolism. So far, fire symbolizes rebirth, which is obvious on pages two, five, and fourteen, and is not open to interpretation.

A.Z. and Larsley don't need a book to tell them about fire and rebirth. Last month, Larsley found a lighter and can of Aqua Net in the locker room and discovered she could spray letters on the cinder block walls and light them. Now when everyone else goes running in PE, they write flaming messages. It's like sending up flares if you're lost at sea, except with cement instead of water.

The scene ends with more pink lights, the bedroom is wheeled away, and the pasture becomes Spain a millennium ago when the Apostle James was alive. This part of the play goes on forever and doesn't have much to do with the Miracle, but it takes up time before Nell Gording tromps around in hip waders watching it rain. Apparently the rain was crazy that spring, and even A.Z.'s mom, who doesn't believe in miracles, said she'd never seen anything like it.

A.Z. untangles some threads around the fraying holes in the knees of her jeans, then starts slowly unzipping her backpack. But before she can get the book out, Larsley mouths something. "What?" A.Z. says.

"Boring."

"No kidding," A.Z. says.

"*There's been a terrible injustice,*" a voice cries.

A.Z.'s dad says the words, too, because this used to be his part, even though he'd hoped to play his namesake, the Apostle James.

The townsperson flails his arms and throws himself to his knees, like he's possessed by a vision or blinded by spotlights. "*Rise up,*" the Apostle James says, "*and tell me more.*"

The townsperson explains that an innocent boy was hanged five weeks before and leads the Apostle James to the boy, swaddled in a sheet.

"Wouldn't the body be all rotted and oozing and stuff?" Larsley whispers. She tightens the hair fountain on top of her head by pulling the hair out to both sides of the rubber band. Larsley's hair is really coarse and wavy, and before she invented the hair fountain, it bushed out in a way that wasn't nearly as cool.

"Totally." A.Z. wishes she'd thought of this. The Kenny-G-style saxes are going crazy as the boy levitates, dangling on mostly invisible cords until the lights finally fall.

When the lights return, the townsperson tells the father his son has been resurrected. The father shakes his head. "*If only it were true.*" The townsperson insists, and the father pounds the table, where the glasses don't shake because they're glued down. "*Nonsense! My son is no more alive than that roasted fowl.*" He points dramatically at the casserole dish, but when he lifts the lid, a chicken is pecking around under its feathers. The lights fall again, and the music gets even louder to indicate more and better miracles after intermission.

Ending with the chicken helps sell concessions, especially Chuck Chicken bites, which A.Z. doesn't eat because her dad toured the processing plant in Greenville and told her about the hoses they use to suction out the brains and blood. Her dad couldn't write that part because Chuck Chuck, who owns Chuck Chicken, also owns *The Compolodo Daily News.*

When A.Z.'s dad goes in search of more profileable pilgrims, A.Z. and Larsley wander off to find something to do.

"Maybe we can sneak backstage," Larsley says.

"There isn't really a back to the stage," A.Z. says. "The Sea's right behind the backdrop."

"We should go swimming."

"Totally." A.Z. can't imagine anything better or more unlikely. She's cold from sitting on the metal bleacher in the dark, and the seawater must still be icy—not literally, but shooting straight to your bones, a whole-body ice cream headache. There are sometimes pockets like that even on June first when Mud Beach opens.

From the parking lot, A.Z. can't see the Sea, on account of the stadium lights, but there's a damp, fishy wind blowing in. "A fisher in your memory," A.Z. says. It's a line from "You Are the Everything."

Actually, they're not sure what Michael Stipe says, but it sounds like that.

"A fisher in *your* memory," Larsley says back, all serious and ominous.

"There's been a terrible injustice!" A.Z. says.

And for a minute, it doesn't feel so bad to be at the stupid Miracle Play, at only intermission. There's something right and fated about walking with Larsley across the parking lot—like sometimes at Food 4 Less, when you're rolling the cart down the cereal aisle, and a cheesy song comes on like a soundtrack, and for just a second, you feel like you're in a movie about a girl grocery shopping in which interesting things could happen.

They stop at the chain-link fence, their fingers through the links. On the other side, tangles of juniper roots and clay give way to the Sea, a faint dark splash against the shore. Once, according to local legend, Katie Wilson's brother and his friend got caught trying to climb over and were banned from the Sea, which is the most impossible thing A.Z. can possibly imagine.

The first time she saw the Sea, she wasn't even born yet.

It was March 19, 1975, the twentieth anniversary of the Miracle, and of course her dad was covering the celebration. Even her mom came, because she was two weeks overdue and might need to be rushed to the hospital. March tends to be rainy, but the sky had cleared, and Nell Gording, in an Easter dress and pearls, was making a speech on Mud Beach. Above, bright streamers of green and gold and red fireworks fizzled into the Sea. And maybe it was the explosions, which were startling the gulls and making them dive toward the water, or maybe—as A.Z. likes to think—the time for her birthday had just arrived, but, right then, A.Z.'s mom's water broke. Right there on the beach.

A.Z. shouldn't be able to remember this but she swears she

does—the distant, low booms, and the shriek of gulls, like she's hearing it from inside a shell: her synchronous birth, her destiny to be the Sea of Santiago's first oceanographer and learn everything about how it really came to be—the story that no one, not even her mother or her father, knows.

"I wish we had a car," Larsley says, glancing back at the parking lot. She's been obsessed ever since she got her learner's permit. Since both her parents are ambulance drivers, she's convinced she learned to drive fast and safely *in utero*.

"Or a boat," A.Z. says. She thinks about the boat locked in its glass case at the museum, but of course that's impossible. "Maybe there's an extra boat for the play in dry dock or something?"

"What's a dry dock?" Larsley backs up and throws a rock over the fence, but they can't see it fall. They can't hear it or the waves because the angelic choir, which has started back up, is drowning out everything.

"You know, where they repair boats," A.Z. says.

"Busted," Greg says, pointing his light stick at them. "You're not supposed to be here."

"No kidding," Larsley says. "We were on our way to blow up the stage. There's this recipe in *The Anarchist Cookbook* for this crazy powder."

Larsley hasn't actually seen *The Anarchist Cookbook*, but Angie's brother told them about it. He hasn't seen it either. According to the library card catalog, there used to be one, but maybe it went missing like the Bible.

"You don't need anarchy powder. Gunpowder would work." Greg keeps a rifle in his pickup in case he needs to shoot squirrels or mailboxes. He's old enough to drive by himself because he started school late or got held back in kindergarten.

"Totally," A.Z. says. "That's what they packed into the cannons on old ships. I mean, they looked like cannons, but they weren't because those have to be on land and have balls."

"I've got balls," Greg says. He grins and grabs his crotch, in case they missed something.

"Perv," Larsley says. "Let's go."

When they get back to the bleachers, Nell is wearing hip waders and carrying an umbrella. It's been raining for weeks, and the ripples have become knee-deep lasers lapping the backdrop cows. "*We've been chosen,*" Nell exclaims rapturously. "*God has chosen us!*"

According to A.Z.'s mom, who was newly stuck in Compolodo and her first marriage at the time, the Sea's arrival wasn't nearly so simple. A lot of people thought Nell had gone crazy from the fever, and there were rumors about diverted water and earthmovers, plus protests by the First-First Southern Baptists of Greenville, led by Reverend Bicks Sr., who said the Sea was clearly the work of Satan because it was nowhere in the Bible and also in sudden competition with the Bickses' Civil War Museum, the county's one previous tourist attraction.

Even a faction of the New Ark Church denounced Nell—who had incorporated as the Gording Foundation to keep private control of the Sea—since clearly the New Arkers' collective prayers had prompted God's active work in her cow pasture.

New Ark Church used to stand for "New Arkansas Church," but the church saw the Sea as their God's latest wonder. In the New Ark world, animals didn't just line up two by two, and there wasn't a dove or receding waters. Instead, the flood came and stayed, and people rented conch-shell floaties and beach towels and lay in the sun eating tater tots.

And eventually, most of the dissenters stopped arguing. The Miracle meant pilgrims were suddenly willing to drive across the country to stay in motels and eat buffets and buy souvenirs made of shells or rocks that kind of look like shells.

"*And so, it rained and rained and rained and rained,*" the voice-over announces. This gives A.Z. the shivers, although she won't admit it to Larsley.

"Is it almost over?" Larsley whispers just before the voice thunders, "*And then, there was the Sea of Santiago.*"

The backdrop falls, and the spotlights drench the actual waves. They look different under lights, like something newly carved, like the obsidian ring A.Z.'s mom's first love, Arthur, gave her in that romantic story.

A.Z. imagines, the way she has so many times, herself as the Sea's first oceanographer: sailing across those waves to whatever is beyond—where the stage lights disappear, and the blackness envelops her, like she's that blind guy in the parking lot and she can only rely on the touch of lines, the wind, the water, and the distant stars for live reckoning.

2

From the high school to Mud Beach is four miles. It's hot in the sunny stretches, and humid in all the stretches, and the billboards saying COME SEE THE WORLD'S NEWEST WONDER: 1 ½ MILES. ONLY 1 ¼ MILES TO GOD'S GREATEST SEA! seem less like progress markers than proof they'll never get there. Larsley says they should catch a ride with some pilgrims and pretend to be psycho killers, but when she sticks out her thumb, no one stops.

"We should have a party for the Fourth of July," Larsley says. "When my parents are at the Emergency Response Conference in Little Rock."

"I thought that was in a couple weeks," A.Z. says.

"Whatever. Early Fourth of July. We should get Jägermeister and peach schnapps."

A.Z. and Larsley once tried peach schnapps from Larsley's parents' liquor cabinet and replaced it with water, but A.Z. doesn't know what Jägermeister is. She doesn't admit this.

Anything cold and drinkable sounds good. It's one of those

years that's gone straight from cool-damp spring to boiling summer, and already her jean shorts feel like a hundred layers of fabric sewn together, and her back is itching like she's wearing the wool swimsuit her mom wore in northern New York before her father died and she ended up at boarding school, which is why she's strict about things like A.Z. getting back by seven to study for her French final.

This is totally unfair. A.Z. should not have to leave the Sea—which she hasn't even arrived at yet—before it closes. And she should not have to study verb conjugations for a class she already has a 103 percent in.

She should get to swim for as long as she wants, and fill her vials with water for her independent study, and label their saline parts per thousand, and take notes about the Sea's salinity on the paper she can't actually carry out in the water because she forgot a ziplock bag.

And then she should get to lie for hours—all wet and in her element with saltwater all around her—on the dock at the far edge of the swimming lagoon because it's June first, the first day Mud Beach is open, the best day all year.

The Gording Foundation was planning to get rid of the dock in case a pilgrim slipped on the algae and sued, but Greg volunteered to build a new one. He's hoping to get promoted to head parking attendant.

A.Z. knows because she's had to sit beside him in algebra since someone narced about the flaming hairspray, and Coach W. separated her and Larsley, banishing A.Z. to the far side of the room with the shop guys and the guys who don't talk, like Stephen, who draws intricate aliens all over his notebook.

Stephen has amazing eyes—like the sky after an ice storm through the hard bright crystal casing of the trees. It's really challenging to see this, though, because he lets his hair fall over his face—in this sort of mysterious, sort of greasy way—and he doesn't look up very often.

A.Z. keeps imagining Stephen will pull up and offer them a ride, which is unlikely since he doesn't have a car. If she and Larsley had found a ride from school like they'd hoped, they would have been at the Sea for an hour already, and A.Z. wouldn't be so worried about the time that she's taken off her watch. She can still feel it ticking in her pocket: each tick a reminder that her mom is going to be—in two hours or whatever—waiting at the newspaper office to meet her.

They pass, finally, under the sign that says Welcome to the Miracle Sea! You've Made It! and they pay the entry guy two dollars each, and A.Z. hurries under the white plaster archway and peels off her million pounds of sweaty clothes and runs into the water.

The Sea is just like she's been imagining for months. Exactly. Perfectly. She swims a fast Australian crawl, and it feels effortless because she belongs here. She gets to the dock way before Larsley and does a flip, rising with salt stinging her eyes. And then she swims along the string of deep-water buoys that don't really mark very deep water, and back to the dock, and out along the buoys again a few more times until she's wonderfully salt bleary and a little tired. Finally, she drags herself up on the dock where, apparently, Greg forgot to build a ladder.

The dock is, as always, the best place besides the water. The Sea is a little deeper than near shore, and fewer pilgrims swim out here. Today, she and Larsley have a few feet of Sea all to themselves: blue sky and blue-brown ripples, and A.Z.'s skin shrinking against the salt wind, like she's an X-ray of herself, all bones and important organs.

Larsley sits up beside her and hugs her knees to her chest. She can do this because she has a naturally flat stomach. "We should make a list of who to invite to the party," she says. "Angie and Liz."

"And maybe Stephen." A.Z. rolls over to get evenly burned, closing her eyes so she won't have to see her body. On the rack at Wal-Mart, her bikini seemed cool with its blue sailor piping. And in the dressing room—in the bad fluorescents, when she imagined a tan—it seemed kind of cool. But now she suspects her pale, slightly freckled skin and the cloth are competing shades of doughy.

"Stephen Franklin?" Larsley wrinkles her nose. "He's socially retarded."

A.Z. wants to point out that Stephen is shy and that even though she isn't interested in aliens, his are really good. He seems to know all the details, the way Mrs. Reuter makes them draw every part of the frogs they dissect. The way—after she finishes her independent study and gets accepted and goes to Sea Camp—she'll know how to study all the details of the Sea.

"We should invite Scotty and Rob," Larsley says.

"No way. No do-rags."

"Yeah, but we want people to come. You should invite Greg. Maybe he'll give you a boat." Larsley shields her face before A.Z. can splash her. She's been giving A.Z. a hard time ever since A.Z. asked Greg, really casually, where they repaired stuff at the Miracle Play. As she should have known, there isn't a dry dock because most of the props are styrofoam.

"I don't need some dumb boat from Greg," A.Z. says. On her stomach, she can smell the new, sort of chemically wood of the dock, and she rests her head on her arms to try to get away from it. Now that she thinks about it, if Greg could build an entire dock in a couple of weeks, it can't be that hard. And a dock is pretty much just a tied-down raft.

"Thor Heyerdahl built his own raft," she says. "You know, out of rope, and balsa wood, and pine, and sailed from South America to Polynesia in 107 days."

"Wouldn't it have been quicker in a motorboat?" Larsley slides off the dock, dog paddling toward the buoys.

"Yeah," A.Z. calls, "but he was testing how ancient people might have made the trip. It was a scientific mission."

"Oh," Larsley calls, leaning back and resting her feet on the buoys, like you're not allowed to do because it drags the rope under, so nothing divides the swimming lagoon from the rest of the Sea.

And it's like a sign. Like Thor Heyerdahl must have felt sitting on the coast of South America. Or Sir James Clark Ross when he figured out how to do modern sounding of the ocean floors with reflected sound waves. A.Z. can picture herself and Larsley floating on a newly built raft across that invisible line. Coming back with samples that will give her so much data that her Sea Camp application will need extra postage when she mails it on September first. Data that will amaze Mrs. Reuter, so she'll get an A not only on her independent study, but maybe in next year's biology class, too.

A.Z. can see it now: the isohaline graph that will prove something totally groundbreaking about the salinity, like maybe where the outlets are, or how the Sea of Santiago is similar to other seas, or how the currents work. All the things that, if she were Nell, she would have studied as soon as the Sea appeared. She doesn't need to wait for Sea Camp for permission; she needs to prove to Sea Camp she already knows how to be a real open-water oceanographer.

Admittedly, the Gordings would arrest anyone who tried this, and A.Z. hasn't actually taken shop class because it's where the gross, Skoal-chewing guys like Greg hang out, and she's never constructed anything bigger than model ships. But her mother's father built an ice boat with wings that skimmed across Lake Titus in the Adirondacks. She's seen the photo of him piloting it in a wool-lined, chin-strap, aviator-sailor hat. With a grandfather like that, surely she's inherited enough skills to secretly build a raft.

"We're about to be sophomores," she calls ecstatically to Larsley, sitting up and not even caring if a few inches of her 122 pounds pooch above her bikini bottom. "We can't wait around for anyone's permission to do what we want. We need to build our own raft."

"Totally," Larsley calls back, sort of lifting her head from the water enough to probably have heard her, just as, on shore, the lifeguard blows his whistle: that high, piercing cry that's not like any sea bird.

"Fascist," Larsley says.

"Yeah," A.Z. says. But she's sort of happy: it's like her research raft vision was so powerful the lifeguard has seen it, too, and he's pre-emptively trying to call them back from the unexplored center of the Sea—and its maybe way deeper and saltier or less salty water.

"Anastasia Zoe McKinney, you're an hour and ten minutes late," her mom—who is waiting, exactly where A.Z. knew she would be, on her dad's couch, reading—says, without looking up from her book. "Your father has been worried sick about you."

A.Z. glances across the office at her dad, who doesn't look worried. He looks busy, as always, typing a deluge of green letters into his new computer screen.

"It must have taken longer to walk out to the Sea and back than we realized," A.Z. says, like she's sort of been rehearsing. "Angie was going to give us a ride, but then she had to take her brother to the dentist, and we couldn't find anyone else. It took forever to walk; we barely even got in the water." She's been feeling—with each step closer to her mom—sort of more drippy and late than euphoric.

"Yeah," Larsley chimes in. "We didn't know the Sea was closing. We thought the lifeguard was blowing the whistle because I was hanging on the rope."

This is probably the wrong thing to say, and Larsley should probably not have insisted on coming in. A.Z.'s mom, who considers herself a good judge of character, doesn't approve of Larsley. She thinks Larsley lives in an unsupervised house because her parents are never awake or home at the same time, which Larsley says is the only reason they get along. If A.Z.'s mom knew about the flaming hairspray, she wouldn't even let A.Z. and Larsley hang out.

"And then we had to walk all the way back, too, because we

couldn't find a ride," A.Z. adds. She doesn't mention that they were soaking because they didn't get out until the lifeguard's final warning whistle and they'd forgotten towels, but her mom can see that part. "I tried to keep track of time, but it's light really late now."

"You have a waterproof watch," her mom says flatly. She's still looking down, her eyes intent, like she's reading deeper inside the words than normal people.

When A.Z. thinks about the Swatch her parents gave her last Christmas—which is still in her pocket—she imagines setting it back, like Daylight Savings: the little peg pulled out and time all malleable. She imagines the compass pointing toward some north where her mom isn't.

"All the pilgrims were jerks," Larsley says. "And that lifeguard was a total fascist."

A.Z. wants to agree again, but her mom lived during World War II and probably doesn't think the word *fascist* applies to lifeguards.

Her mom sighs, her chin still tilted down, but her eyes finally raising. "Anastasia Zoe, you promised me you'd be back by seven, and it's 8:16 p.m., and you have a final tomorrow. You're not going anywhere until Saturday."

"But I have research to do," A.Z. says. "And I'm fourteen now. And tomorrow is the last day of school. So then it's summer. You can't ground me at the start of summer."

Her mom lays *Wakefield* face down, the clear plastic cover crinkling ominously.

"Watch me," she says.

The library is a terrible place to read. Not only is there no privacy— because A.Z.'s mom can, at any moment, climb the stairs to the

second floor, which is only a loft overlooking the reference section—
but the library is almost never quiet.

Whenever someone asks for the *Women's Guild Cookbook*, or the
National Geographic with the space shuttle, A.Z.'s mom ends up telling a story. She refers to herself as a "reference librarian," which means
any reference is cross-indexed to New York and Arizona, exploding
ships and trains, and boarding school. Her mom's stories are so long
that people sometimes forget to check out the books they came for.

Since A.Z. got here from school, her mom has been talking to a
pilgrim woman who probably stopped for directions but is hearing
the story of Russell Hayes trying to drown A.Z.'s mom at summer
camp in Arizona in 1950.

"I only knew his name because they had written our names on
the front of our song books so we wouldn't lose them," her mom is
saying. "Russell Hayes. I remember thinking even before he said anything that there was something untrustworthy about him."

Like all of her mom's stories, A.Z. has heard this one a million
times, and right now she's not feeling sympathetic. It's her first hour
of being officially a sophomore, and she has important research to do,
and she's being held hostage in a library by her own mother.

"I was swimming laps in the pool before dinner, and Russell
showed up," her mom is saying. "I didn't want to get out of the water
with him there, so I pretended I didn't see him. Just as I was raising
my arm, I felt his hand on the back of my neck. He kept pushing my
head under and saying, 'Just say you love me.' I would have died if
one of the counselors hadn't happened to walk by."

"He actually claimed he loved you?" the woman asks.

She doesn't know that everyone used to fall irrationally in love
with A.Z.'s mom, who looked twenty when she was fifteen, with
auburn curls and a bust that pushed against her button-up shirts like

Judy Garland in *The Wizard of Oz*. Once, a Navajo guy she met on a bus asked her to marry him. And Arthur, her first love, spent weeks playing "The Petite Waltz" for her on the jukebox at the diner where she waitressed before giving her an obsidian ring and then dying. Even when she was in her mid-thirties and already had a teenage daughter, A.Z.'s half-sister Catherine, and should not have been pretty, the first time A.Z.'s father came to the library, he sang her "Marian the Librarian" from *The Music Man*, even though her name is Sophie.

A.Z. doesn't have her mom's bust, and she has straight brown hair instead of auburn curls, and she's only had two boyfriends. Will, in sixth grade, was out of her league, with red parachute pants and an off-white Don Johnson suit coat. He only dated her for two days because Sahara called him using a script she and A.Z. had written: *What would you say if I asked you to go with A.Z.? Just say yes.*

A.Z.'s second boyfriend, Chris, didn't actually ask her of his own volition either. Last January, Sean told Chris to ask her because she'd told Sean she had a crush on Chris, partly because she had a crush on Sean, too, and needed an excuse to talk to him. Chris and Sean have bleached-blond hair that angles over their eyes, and they're too busy doing ollies to date anyone, which is why the relationship didn't lead further than the back lot of the Conch Motel.

Chris asked her for a piece of Bubblicious, but she didn't have any—other than what she was chewing—and neither of them had change for the vending machine, so she offered him hers. He said, "That's disgusting. I can't put your gum in my mouth." But then he did. And then he spat it out and kissed her with his tongue, which was much, much better than the gum and also tasted like artificial peaches.

The smell of peach gum still makes her sad because Chris broke up with her on February twenty-eighth. He said it was awkward that they were both such good friends with Sean. A.Z. is not really *such* good friends with Sean. And now Chris always acts normal around her, like they never dated. It's nothing like the Navajo guy who offered her mom two donkeys and a house.

The pilgrim woman is saying, "Oh my goodness; I don't think I'd ever go in the water again if someone tried to drown me."

This is what a lot of people say, although, as A.Z. wants to point out, it wasn't the water's fault. The logical thing would be to never get near another person.

A.Z. wonders if the woman was asking directions to the Sea, and she has the crazy idea to climb out the window and find the woman's car and hide in it—like Irene, the Navajo girl her mom was friends with in boarding school, who climbed out the school window to run away.

But the second-floor window doesn't open, and besides, she'd be grounded until she's twenty. So she does the one thing being trapped in a library is good for; she subtly gets *Kon-Tiki* from its shelf and starts a list of supplies for her raft: balsa wood, hemp ropes, mangrove, pine (splashboards and centerboards), bamboo.

She has balsa left over from the science fair project where she tried to build the Bay of Fundy, but the only bamboo she's ever seen is in a ceramic pot by the Buddha at Seven Happiness. At least last season, it was bright green and spirally and not big enough to carve into a pair of chopsticks, much less decking.

When the pilgrim woman finally leaves, A.Z.'s mom goes to the reshelving cart. A.Z. is hoping now that her mom has finally stopped talking, she'll notice A.Z. isn't speaking.

Instead her mom calls, "How was the last day of school? Your dad says he didn't get to talk to you at the pep rally."

A.Z. doesn't say anything, so her mom says another irritatingly logical thing: "You can not speak to me, but it isn't going to make the time pass any faster."

A.Z. wants to point out that she didn't even have to take her French final because of the pep rally. The whole school missed two periods to celebrate Compolodo's unprecedented regional track meet victory. Finally the Greenvillites—who don't like Compolodo because they have to live in a valley with the Chuck Chicken Processing Plant and no Sea—weren't going to be able to gloat, "Stomp their whale tails! Watch them go slow, slow, slow!"

Actually, as A.Z. knows, killer whales and blue whales swim thirty miles per hour, which makes them among the fastest marine mammals. And since water is 750 times denser than air, it really shouldn't have taken more than thirty years for the Whales to beat the Mountain Lions. Even if A.Z. and Larsley don't care about sports, it was hard not to clap after Scotty's cheerleader-captain sister, Gwennie, handed out trophies.

And then Angie, who was sitting cross-legged in her thrift-store suit coat, looking natural like A.Z. maybe will when she's a senior who's so cool she doesn't think it's uncool to talk to sophomores, invited A.Z. and Larsley to the beach.

"Everyone is at the beach," A.Z. says, without fully deciding to speak to her mother. "Everyone but me."

"If you worry about what everyone else does," her mom says, "you're going to find yourself gravely disappointed." It's the same point she made years ago when A.Z. decided to go by her initials.

"Anastasia Zoe," her mom had said, sighing, "I didn't give you a beautiful, historical, polysyllabic name just to have you abridge yourself into a *Reader's Digest* version of a person."

And A.Z. had said, "But it's way better and easier to say. Everyone agrees."

"Of course they do," her mom had said. "People always want whatever's easiest. And if you worry about what everyone else does, you're going to find yourself gravely disappointed in life."

As far as A.Z. can tell, her mom is responsible for the only gravely disappointing thing in her life. And now that she's speaking, she can't help pointing this out: "I barely got to spend any time at the Sea yesterday and now I'm stuck in this stupid library."

"We're about to go home," her mom says from somewhere around the 400s.

"Then I'll be stuck at home," she says, yelling to make sure her mom hears. "It's my first day ever of being a sophomore, and you're making me sit here while all of my friends are out at the Sea or doing something that's not entirely boring and pointless. It's unjust."

Of course, A.Z.'s mom knows all about injustice. Her father was drafted and killed on an ammunition ship in World War II when she was ten. No one ever found the bodies, so A.Z.'s mom believed for years—after her own mother moved them to that awful house in Arizona with the stepfather who drank and the cockroaches—that her father would still come back and save her. She made a deal with God: she'd tell her father where to find her if God would just help him be alive. But God didn't keep his half of the deal.

And then Arthur died tragically, and A.Z.'s mom married a man she didn't love in order to run away. She and Curtis made it as far as Arkansas before the muffler fell off, and while they were waiting for a new one to be shipped to Compolodo, A.Z.'s mom found out she was pregnant with A.Z.'s half-sister, Catherine. She ended up spending twenty years as a housewife with an insurance adjuster husband who didn't even like reading.

Arguments about injustice never really work on her.

But A.Z. has started and before she knows it, she's adding, "Just because you were raised back in the Victorian age, you don't understand. No one gets grounded anymore. Larsley's mother never grounds her."

"I'm not Larsley's mother, thank god," A.Z.'s mom says. "And you're not Larsley. And the 1940s were not the Victorian era."

"It isn't just Larsley," A.Z. yells, starting down the stairs. "You're trying to ruin my life. You're trying to make me unpopular. People already call me 'the Librarian,' and now I'm stuck in this stupid library with my stupid mother." She doesn't even bring up her dad, stomping on the bleachers at the pep rally and chanting, "Whay-uls, Whay-uls," until she wanted to drop through to the darkness with the old Blow Pop wrappers and dust.

"If you don't stop yelling," her mom says, "you're going to be grounded until your grades come. You're lucky I didn't ground you for setting hairspray on fire in the locker room."

"What?" A.Z. says.

Her mom just looks at her. Actually, stacks of books are between them, but A.Z. can feel her eyes. This is when A.Z. ought to say, "I'm sorry." Or go back upstairs. But she's already on her way down.

"See if I care," she yells. The waves are slapping against her, and the raft she hasn't even built yet is sinking, and for a second, it feels almost good.

3

Seven Happiness is the only Chinese restaurant in the county, and Thu is the only Chinese person, although actually she's Vietnamese. Most people don't realize this because they don't know the difference, and Thu doesn't correct them because it might be bad for business. A.Z. worked for her last summer and she's just stupidly agreed to work for her again.

A.Z. was searching for shrimp in the shrimp fried rice on the buffet when Thu came out of the kitchen carrying egg rolls and a rag to wipe up sweet-and-sour sauce. Thu is always in motion because she's the prep cook and cook and cashier, which is supposed to be her boyfriend's job. Sam is the reason Thu ended up in Arkansas, and you can tell sometimes, when he snaps the pages of the sports section and Thu pours hot chili oil in the woks and turns up all six burners, that they're bickering about how lazy he is and how bossy she is, and when is he ever going to marry her like he promised in Vietnam?

"Very, very busy," Thu said. "Lots of dishes in the back. You start today? I'll give you a free lunch."

"I'm already getting a free lunch with my dad," A.Z. said. Her dad was there researching for his new series called "Bountiful Buffets," even though Seven Happiness is right by his office and he eats their takeout all the time, and even though he and A.Z. had just come from the Sunday pancake buffet at the Anchor's Away Best Western.

Thu looked at her in that way she sometimes does, like A.Z. is seeing her through the wrong end of a periscope.

"And I'm grounded," A.Z. added. She wasn't sure if grounding applied to work, but it seemed like it should apply to something useful. "But I guess I can start once I'm not." She tried not to think about Larsley making herself free chocolate shakes at Creamy Days, where A.Z. would have applied, too, if she hadn't gotten grounded.

"Do you want more egg rolls?" her dad asks when she sits back down. He's scribbling his version of shorthand in his steno pad: *enrmous, elegnt, enrgizing eggrlls.*

"No," A.Z. says. "I'm totally sick of buffet food. I don't even know why I came."

Her dad furrows his brow, but she can tell he's thinking about adjectives—not about the button on her jean shorts that's pressing her stomach because she's sampled too many pancakes and egg rolls, or that she's going to spend all summer scalding her arms in dishwater full of waterlogged bamboo shoots to earn money for Sea Camp, which she'll never get into because she's already way behind on building a raft and starting research because she's been grounded for nine whole days because the school apparently forgot to even mail the grades.

"What about these wontons?" he asks.

"Wet," she says. "Watery. Wobbly."

"That doesn't sound very appetizing," her dad says. "Do you mind if we stop at the Starfish Inn on the way back? They're building the foundation in the shape of a starfish. I've got this idea for a series:

'Starfish: Start to Finish.' It's the first non-rectangular hotel since the Ark Motel in the '70s. The Unitarians are protesting. Maybe Sahara will be there."

A.Z. wants to point out that she and Sahara haven't really been friends for two years, but parents are slow about these things. The last time she and Sahara really talked was at that party of that guy from California, who Sahara is dating now. A.Z. can't remember his name because she and Larsley always call him "The Intense Guy."

He's their age, but he lives by himself downtown because his parents haven't shown up yet. He's always staring you in the eyes and saying, "I'm really intense, aren't I? Don't you think I'm intense?" There really isn't anything intense about him, and she and Larsley think he's a big poser and his parents probably sent him to Arkansas to get rid of him, which might be cool in some situations, but isn't in his.

"That doesn't look anything like a starfish," A.Z. says, as her dad pulls into the parking lot. "It just looks like a pit."

"It might be different from an aerial view," her dad says hopefully. "I was going to climb a tree to take some pictures, but I guess they've cut them. This should just take a minute."

The protest is the kind of controversy her dad likes because it's so noncontroversial that no one stops advertising. Sahara's parents, Abe and Dragonfly, protest all the new motels, which always get constructed anyway.

Outside the car, the air doesn't feel any cooler. The trees that haven't been cut are a hyper, hazy green, and everything seems to be moving slower, like time itself is gummed together with pine sap and sweat and the stench of chicken houses. It's one of those days when it would be best to just go sit in the Sea and not get out.

Sahara is sitting on a log, looking bored. She's wearing a crystal on a long piece of leather and she's gotten her nose pierced with a little cubic zirconium since A.Z. last saw her. "Hey," she says. "What are you doing here?"

"My dad's doing a story. He's going to interview your dad. What are you up to?"

"I *was* here to protest for the trees, but Mr. Franks thought we were having a service, and now this is going on like for forever, and everyone is losing focus. That's exactly what's wrong with the world."

"Yeah," A.Z. says, looking at the logs behind Sahara. They seem really useful.

She wishes Larsley were here so they could make a plan to steal them for their raft. Obviously no one cares very much or they wouldn't have cut the trees down.

Mr. Franks, the printer, is really old, so his voice rattles like a cup of Yahtzee dice as he speaks into a microphone. Or maybe A.Z. just thinks this because he's reading, "God does not play dice with the universe."

"What's up with the microphone?" she says.

"Big Bob set it up for the protest. *He* cares about the trees," Sahara says.

A.Z. looks for Big Bob, and sure enough, he's standing by her dad and Abe, eating whole wheat animal cookies, which the Unitarians always serve. Big Bob, who isn't actually very big, shows up at services sometimes because the Unitarians are non-exclusive, which means that they don't treat people differently if they wear a pink sweat suit and a coonskin cap when it's ninety degrees or carry a purple back-pack stuffed with speaker wires and duct tape.

According to stories with timelines that don't match the develop-ment of computers, Big Bob used to be a brilliant programmer. Or a physicist. Or an engineer, with inventions patented under pseud-onyms. Since the early '70s, however, when something went wrong during an acid trip, he's been living in the woods on the Coreys' land. Despite being crazy, Big Bob knows a lot about electronics and sets up the sound for school dances and things.

A.Z. used to spend every other Saturday night at Sahara's, so she went to a lot of Unitarian services. Except when Big Bob said something random or wired the telephone post to the light socket and shorted everything out, the services were deathly boring. Someone read aloud a large section of some book that wasn't the Bible, and the grown-ups talked on and on about what it meant, which A.Z.'s mom approved of slightly more than regular church.

"Remember that time Big Bob said that peeing inside a woman after sex meant she wouldn't get pregnant?" A.Z. asks.

Sahara widens her eyes. "That was sooo gross." Then she adds, dreamily, "He must have had a really bad trip." She sounds like she might actually know what she's talking about, which freaks A.Z. out. Other than that time at the Intense Guy's party when Larsley got stoned and kept talking on the phone to someone who wasn't there, A.Z. doesn't know much about drugs, except that, according to her mom, Big Bob is *not* the exception. Doing drugs inevitably leads to losing your mind and living in a cave or—in the case of A.Z.'s half-sister's ex-husband, Dan, the local taxi man—driving a taxi.

"Do you know they cut down over a hundred trees for this dumb motel, and now they're going to pave all this land for another parking lot?" Sahara says. "It's so intense."

A.Z. wonders if the logs really add up to a hundred trees. That should build ten or twenty rafts—sturdy, long-distance ones. But then she looks at Sahara staring at the trees like they're piles of dead kittens, and she feels guilty. If someone were paving the Sea, she'd definitely protest. Even if Sahara has gotten dippy lately, she cares about stuff. For as long as A.Z. has known her, she's wanted to be a veterinarian. When they were little, they used to save food for the chickens at Mud Beach, and Sahara totally understood why A.Z. used to think they were a type of gull.

Sahara lowers her voice. "Josh and I are planning to sit on a log until we stop the construction. They do that out in California. It's very intense."

"Wow," A.Z. says, because she's not sure what else to say. "Oh, hey, did you hear that Larsley is having a Fourth of July party this Friday?" She doesn't mention that she's been grounded this whole past week and has only actually gotten to talk to Larsley once—during one secret phone call before her omnipresent mother got home from the library. She also doesn't mention how worried she is that her grades will somehow not arrive in time, and she won't even get to go to the party.

"Yeah," Sahara says. "That's wild about her and Scotty. I can't imagine them going out. I mean, he's like a total jock."

A.Z. has no idea what Sahara is talking about, but she can't admit this. Larsley is her best friend so—even if A.Z. has been kind of out of the loop for nine days—she knows there's no way Larsley would ever go out with Scotty, even if that time the VJ on MTV was talking about some new song called "Love in an Elevator" and she and Larsley listed boys they wouldn't mind being stuck in elevators with, Larsley listed Scotty as one of those "good gross" guys who was cute but not.

Fortunately, Mr. Franks is still reading, slowly and shakily, so A.Z. pretends to be interested: "Although I am a typical loner in daily life, my consciousness of belonging to the invisible community of those who strive for truth, beauty, and justice has preserved me from feeling isolated. The most beautiful and deepest experience a man can have is the sense of the mysterious. It is the underlying principle of religion as well as all serious endeavors in art and science. He who never had this experience seems to me, if not dead, then at least blind."

"That's crazy," A.Z. says, finally, which she hopes will be sufficiently ambiguous and apply to everything.

A.Z.'s grades, which would have traveled faster on an old-fashioned around-the-world packet boat than through the local post office, finally arrive late Tuesday afternoon. They're a column of As, which, she resists pointing out to her mom, means that being grounded was extra unjust.

She runs up the driveway from the mailbox to call Larsley.

"What's going on?" Larsley says. She must be watching MTV because A.Z. can halfway hear Michael Stipe chanting "Stand . . . where you . . ." in the background. Larsley has MTV because her parents were born in this century and don't have weird ideas about it "building character" to live without it and air conditioning.

"Not much," A.Z. says. "I'm finally not grounded. Want to try to find a ride out to the Sea?"

"Yeah," Larsley says. "But I can't tonight. Tomorrow after work?"

"Yeah," A.Z. says. "Cool." She realizes she needs to call Thu and say she can work tomorrow's lunch shift. It takes a lot of four-hour $4.25 lunch shifts to earn the $250 for a flight to Sea Camp, plus tuition, which is another $500 if she doesn't get a big scholarship. "Want to meet up at Seven Happiness around three? I kind of told Thu I'd work again."

"Sure," Larsley says, over people squealing on what sounds like some giveaway contest.

And then, casually, like A.Z. hasn't been thinking about it for two days, she says, "So is something going on with you and Scotty?"

"What? Who said that?"

"I don't know, I just heard it somewhere."

"He comes in for ice cream sometimes," Larsley says, "on his loop through town. Oh my god, you totally need to see what's starting. It's the sneak peak of the video for 'Love Song.' There's this cave, and Robert Smith is crawling around. His hair is all standing up, and he's all puffy and fat and alcoholic, but it's really kind of hot. I mean, you can tell he's dying because of love. He's in total agony."

The Seven Happiness lunch buffet is super busy, which Thu thinks is because of A.Z.'s dad's "Bountiful Buffets" article, which came out this morning.

"If this keeps up, I'm going to bring my brothers over from Vietnam," she says. She's come back for more bok choy, which she pulls out of its wilty cardboard and chops on the metal prep table with a military-precision *thwack-thwack-thwack.*

Thu has been talking since last summer about saving money to bring her brothers over to help instead of making shoes in Saigon. A.Z. isn't totally sure why working at Seven Happiness would be better, but she doesn't say this. She's happy for Thu, even though she suspects the extra business is a fluke. Pilgrims move like schools of fish—tour buses pulled by some rumor of plankton. The only consistent business is the Miracle Play.

"I need to see about paperwork," Thu says. "Very long process to bring them, but a good summer like this, and I have evidence that I need them." She's eyeing the woks in the kitchen while she chops carrots now with that special knife that turns them into serrated ribbons.

A.Z. empties another bus tub into the dishwater. The problem with the tubs is that everything mixes together and ends up covered in the same sweet-and-sour-sauce, sesame-oil grease. She has to scrub even the tea cups, which slip to the bottom of the deep sinks that Thu fills with scalding water first thing each morning, and which take most of the day to cool. Maybe faucets work differently in Vietnam or something.

Today, A.Z. doesn't mind as much as usual. Being at work is just more proof that she's finally not grounded, and she's feeling buoyant, like after being sick, that new-kind-of-health feeling you get, like your body is glowing.

Every time she plunges her arms into the water, she has a strategy, or maybe it's a daydream. She imagines she's swimming in the Sea, and the water has heated up from the week and a half she's been away from it, but it's the nice kind of hot, like the sun has become part of the water—dissolved like some glowing mineral.

It's one thirty, and in just two hours, she'll really be swimming.

The air outside Seven Happiness, when she finally gets off work, doesn't feel much different than the rice-cooker humidity inside. She stands in the parking lot, swatting mosquitoes, which apparently love the smell of egg rolls, and looking down the highway for Larsley. After almost thirty minutes, she's starting to worry that Larsley wasn't paying attention on the phone last night.

She wanders around the parking lot and thinks about going to her dad's office to get out of the sun, but she doesn't want Larsley to think she isn't here, so she stands for another fifteen minutes with a growing cloud of mosquitoes dive-bombing her arms.

Finally, she hears Larsley calling "Ayzee!"—that cool way she does, like it's all one word. But her voice is coming from the wrong direction.

When A.Z. turns, she sees why. Larsley isn't coming from Creamy Days; she's coming from up the highway, and she's running. And Scotty is running beside her. He's wearing shiny grey shorts and a white T-shirt and a red do-rag, and his head is lolling sideways in that stupid zombie way. He reaches A.Z. before Larsley does and puts up his hand to high-five her. A.Z. doesn't want to respond, but it's a reflex, like when the doctor hits your knee with a hammer.

"We creamed those English tests," he says. "Go team."

"Totally," Larsley says, stopping beside him, out of breath. "He got a better grade in English than I did."

"My parents are going to get me a car," Scotty says. Larsley smiles at him.

A.Z. wants to point out that she's the one who should be getting a car because she's the one who knew the right answers and stupidly kept letting him copy. But of course that's not how things work, and her mom won't let her get a learner's permit 'til next year, because of Arthur dying by driving into the unlit side of a train. And of course she doesn't really want a car.

"Listen," Larsley says. "I know we were maybe going to the Sea and everything, but Scotty says no one is using his parents' pool right now. I guess they're building some new motel next door and the construction is really loud. Plus, it's free, instead of two stupid dollars." She rolls her eyes, like this totally wasn't her idea.

A.Z. doesn't want to agree, but she doesn't feel like she's really being given a choice. Now she and Larsley won't be able to talk about the whole last week, or her research raft supply list—which is in her jean shorts pocket accumulating lint but no actual supplies—or see the Sea, or do anything useful, because of stupid Scotty.

At least Larsley is right that no one is in the pool. Scotty's parents' motel, the Seahorse Inn, is right next to the Starfish Inn construction site, and it makes sense that pilgrims don't want to hear earthmovers first thing in the morning while they're trying to sleep.

Most of the rooms are vacant, despite the sign that says BIG DISCOUNT: $30/NIGHT. Actually, right now, the sign says BIG DISCO because someone snuck up and removed the other letters.

A.Z. is still pissed about the change of plans, so she dives into the deep end of the awful chlorine with her T-shirt on and swims thirty laps. Swimming with your clothes on is good practice in case you're shipwrecked.

Larsley gives up after five laps and lies in the sun beside Scotty.

Then Rob shows up, chugging Gatorade. "Hey Lars," he says, which is stupid because it's Larsley's dad's name. "Hey Librarian. What are you doing here?"

"Swimming," A.Z. says, frog-kicking as she hangs on the edge.

"Yeah, the Librarian can *swim*," Scotty says.

A.Z. wants to say, *Of course I can swim*, but then she realizes that Scotty means *really* swim—like kick some ass at it, which at least is true. If the Gordings allowed swimming beyond the lagoon, or all the motel pools weren't too small or kidney-shaped for real practice, or the school had a swim team, she'd definitely be on it. She took lessons when she was little because her mom—who hasn't swum since Russell Hayes—was scared A.Z. was going to drown. Apparently as a toddler, A.Z. used to run toward the Sea with her arms out, like she was trying to hug it.

"Did you steal us fortune cookies?" Larsley calls to her.

"Between the sheets!" Scotty says, even though no one has said a fortune yet.

"I have fortune for you," Larsley says. "You will wear new boobs to the best party ever."

A.Z. wishes she hadn't told Larsley about Thu saying "I like your boobs" instead of "I like your boots." Thu's English is usually pretty good, although she also says "crotch pot."

Scotty and Rob go watch the front desk while Scotty's dad runs errands, and A.Z. swims another twenty laps. She would keep going except a pilgrim family shows up: the dad in an awful orange Speedo and the mom in a flounced, flowered suit, and their two little girls.

A.Z. gets out, rubbery and light-headed, and lies next to Larsley, ratcheting the chair flat so her stomach will look flatter.

"Sorry," Larsley says. She mumbles it into her towel, but A.Z.'s pretty sure that's what she says.

"Whatever," A.Z. says. She takes off her T-shirt and rolls over and closes her eyes so all she feels is the sun on her back, and the water trickling from her bikini top, and this occasional breeze, which is really nice except for smelling like dead chickens from the chicken houses upwind. Finally, she turns to face Larsley and says, "I thought there wasn't anything going on with you and Scotty."

"He was just trying to be nice," Larsley says, "I mean, I was telling him we were going swimming, and he invited us up here, and I thought it'd give us more time. He comes into Creamy Days a lot because he has to eat like four thousand calories a day or something. It takes a lot of calories to be the fastest runner in the county."

A.Z. cannot believe Larsley has just said "fastest runner in the county," like she's at a stupid pep rally. "He's sooo terminally preppy," A.Z. says.

Larsley doesn't say anything, so A.Z. says, "Did you notice all the logs over at the Starfish? We could steal some to build our raft."

"Yeah," Larsley says, but not like she's fully listening. Scotty is opening the gate: balancing a stack of three cans of Dr Pepper and carrying a Moon Pie package with his teeth.

"I've got a key to the machine," he says. His calves, which are level with A.Z.'s head, bulge in this clumpy way that reminds her of diagrams of mis-tied knots. He hands the Moon Pie to Larsley without wiping off his spit.

"Oh, yeah?" she says. "Then you won't care if I do this." She jumps up and runs around the pool and throws the Moon Pie into the deep end.

"You dweeb," Scotty says, and he chases her and throws her in, and she squeals, and then he jumps in beside her—splashing water like a little kid all over the pilgrim mom.

A.Z. sits up, sucking in her stomach, and stares over at the construction site to see if Sahara is on the log. She isn't. There are a bunch of workers standing around, and a backhoe, but no one is doing anything. Pretty soon, someone in a hard hat makes the rounds, and the workers start leaving. A.Z. can't imagine the shutdown has anything to do with the protest, and she's trying to come up with other explanations when she notices a boy standing beside a bicycle.

He's stuffing leather work gloves into his backpack, but he doesn't look like the other workers. He's a boy her age in ripped black jean shorts and a faded black T-shirt and black boots with mud streaks. A boy with silver hoop earrings, more than one; she can't count from this angle. A boy with an angular nose and high cheekbones, like he's Native American or maybe Mexican.

Lately, a lot of Mexicans have been moving to Greenville to work at Chuck Chicken. A.Z.'s dad wanted to do an article, but then he got Mr. Finley to interview a few and discovered they didn't want to talk—maybe because Mr. Finley's Spanish is so bad, or because they're here illegally. A.Z.'s dad realized that if Chuck Chuck was hiring illegal immigrants, it wouldn't make a good story, so instead he wrote about the new chip aisle at Wal-Mart.

None of the Mexicans A.Z. has seen have been as tall as this boy, though. He must be six feet, and thin, like a tall ship—all mast and taut canvas and ropes below the skin. He's wearing a black bandana, not one of the dumb do-rags jocks wrap over almost-shaved heads, but a necessary bandana that holds back his bangs and ponytail. She knows because he pulls it off and long dark curls fall over his eyes, and then he ties it back on, really casually, and drinks from a two-liter bottle of Mountain Dew. Then this boy climbs onto his bicycle and pedals away from her.

4

"I forgot to tell you," A.Z. tells her mom. "Larsley invited me to spend the night tomorrow because there's this really good Jacques Cousteau special on HBO."

She's practiced this a bunch of times until, she hopes, she doesn't sound nervous. What she's saying is totally true. What isn't true is the implication that she and Larsley are going to watch the show—and a bunch of people with Jägermeister won't be there.

"Oh? Will Scotty be there?" her mom says. She's dicing onions, which don't make her cry like normal people, so unfortunately, she can see A.Z. very clearly through her bifocals.

"Why would Scotty be there? We're watching Jacques Cousteau." She hasn't told her mom about Scotty and Larsley, but apparently her mom knows. She might have even known before A.Z. Maybe Scotty's mom came to the library, or Scotty came to the library (which seems unlikely), or her mom just knows like she knows everything—like the world is one of those crossword puzzles in the Little Rock paper that

Chuck Chuck won't pay to include in *The Compolodo Daily News* and that A.Z.'s mom is ridiculously good at.

Her mom raises her eyebrows. "Be at the library no later than nine on Saturday," she says. "I want your help with nonfiction."

"What's going on with nonfiction?" A.Z. can feel her voice shaking, like her legs after swimming. She washes an eggy whisk, even though she's about to wash dishes all afternoon.

"It's in shambles," her mom says. "I've been meaning for years to take everything off the shelves and reorganize."

A.Z. wants to point out that not enough people check out nonfiction books for anything to get disorganized. And that she might be busy on Saturday—like riding the bike she doesn't have somewhere with the boy who doesn't know she exists yet. But of course she's not going to say this, or anything, that might make her mom change her mind. "OK," she says.

A bike really *would* be useful for getting back and forth from the beach to do research and maybe carrying raft supplies. The problem is that the only bike she has is an awful hulking metal thing from the 1960s that Catherine left when she moved out years ago.

According to their mom, it's a "beach cruiser," but a bike that heavy would just rip up the imported sand and stick in the mud underneath, and besides, the Gordings don't allow bikes on the beach, and the last time A.Z. tried to ride the bike, it tipped over and almost crushed her.

She's thinking about this as she rides in the car with her dad, who is headed to the Ark Park and has offered to drop her off at the beach for a couple of hours before work. Mornings are a good time to do research because a lot of pilgrims sleep in, so it's not as crowded. And Larsley has promised to come meet her before work, maybe to make up for yesterday and Scotty's dumb pool.

"What happened to the orangutan?" she asks her dad, picturing herself pedaling down the curve beside the car.

"I'm not sure," her dad says. "Maybe it was old? I just know they've got a new flamingo to replace it. A flaming flamingo."

When the Gordings first opened the Ark Park in the '70s, they kept pairs of animals, but maybe the cages were too small, or the Gordings didn't feed them enough. Now the cages just hold one or two different animals at a time, and those change really frequently, which worries Sahara and means A.Z.'s dad can fill a lot of column space with animal articles.

"I just have to stop by the office for the camera," he says, turning into the lot.

He parks beside his usual space, which right now is occupied by Chuck Chuck's big white pickup with its chicken decal.

Chuck Chuck usually has a hands-off policy about the paper, but when he does drop by, he's hard to get rid of, and A.Z. can see her dad considering backing up and leaving. He doesn't though. It's only 8 a.m., but it's already sticky in the car, so A.Z. gets out, too, and follows.

Chuck Chuck is sitting on her dad's desk, his fingers through his belt loops on either side of the gold buckle that says *Chuck Chuck*. His real first name is Howard, but no one calls him that except A.Z.'s mom, who doesn't believe in nicknames.

"Jimmy," he says. "I was just leaving you a note. We've got a little problem. Just between you and me and Reverend Bicks. Now I know you can understand this, being a family man yourself. There's just some things a man doesn't expect to see at his lunch buffet."

"What things?" A.Z.'s dad says. He's still standing by the door, like he might leave.

"The devil statue," Chuck Chuck says.

A.Z.'s dad swallows like he's just taken a mouthful of seawater. "What devil statue?" he says.

"They have it sitting right there by the cash register with a sign saying rub the belly," Chuck Chuck says. "Can you believe that? Six Happiness. That's the number of the devil, too. Don't you think that Reverend Bicks hasn't noticed."

"Umm," her dad says, glancing at her, like maybe she'll be wearing a Seven Happiness T-shirt, which only the waiters actually wear. "It's actually *Seven* Happiness, and I think the statue on the front counter is a happy Buddha, not Satan. I mean, I think it's a symbol of happiness. Like the bamboo or the goldfish."

"It's evil, that's what it is," Chuck Chuck says. "And they've got it up there grinning like a pickaninny. Mind you, I didn't see it myself. I don't go in for that spicy kind of food, but Reverend Bicks told me. He tried to complain, but the woman doesn't even speak English."

A.Z. pictures Reverend Bicks in the lunch rush yesterday: Thu working the register, worrying about the food burning, and telling people, "No to-go boxes for buffet," as she rang up his meal beside the new bronze Buddha. Thu is really proud of the Buddha, which she got winter before last when she visited Vietnam, her first time back in nine years.

Thu probably didn't respond to Reverend Bicks because Reverend Bicks doesn't make sense, even if you speak the same language. He's called A.Z. "Anna Stacy" ever since she was born and always says she reminds him of his youngest daughter, Stacy, who unlike A.Z. is blond and eleven and sings in the First-First Baptist Church choir. Fortunately, A.Z. doesn't see her very often because Reverend Bicks doesn't usually come to Compolodo, except to eat its buffets.

Chuck Chuck shifts his weight, bunching one of her dad's steno pads under his pant leg. "You know Reverend Bicks thinks highly of your taste in food and always follows your recom'dations. And I'm not asking, of course, that you don't write 'bout whatever buffets you see fit. But maybe it'd be better if you stuck to the more usual ones. Just think if one of our older ladies or a little child without Reverend Bicks's defenses to fight against the devil went to that buffet."

Her dad swallows again and glances at the other door. "I'll give Reverend Bicks a call this afternoon," he says. "Or maybe I can stop by to see him."

"Now that's a fine idea." Chuck Chuck stands. "Good talking with you, Jimmy." He slaps her dad on the back.

Her dad flinches and smiles. He hates being called "Jimmy," but has never corrected Chuck Chuck out of fear of losing his job, which he got in 1972 when, laid off from the Miracle Play for the winter, he wrote on an application that he was good at "line management."

After Chuck Chuck leaves, her dad sits down at the desk, like he's forgotten the flamingo, and starts typing really fast.

"Don't tell Thu"—*click, click*—"about the Buddha"—*clickclick- click*—"because I don't want to worry her." *Click. Clickclickclick.* "Maybe I can write a feature on church food for next week"—*click- click*—"instead of 'Bountiful Buffets.'" *Click, click.* "Church chow. Holy hamhocks."

"Enjoy the flamingo," A.Z. says when they finally pull up, an hour later, at Mud Beach. But her dad turns off the car and just sits there staring at the water.

"Bye," she says.

"Maybe I'll get in for just a minute." He reaches into the back for his briefcase, which he never carries, and in which he keeps random things, like apparently his swim trunks. He goes to change in the con- crete cubicles as A.Z. strips from her T-shirt and shorts to her bikini.

The Sea is glassy, almost like a lake, but when she runs into the water and tucks her legs under and lets herself sink, she tastes salt, a million times better than chlorine. Actually, the Sea seems extra salty, which is exactly what she's going to test.

Based on what she's read in *Oceans of the World*, she's thinking the Sea of Santiago may be a poikilohaline environment, which means the saline levels vary dramatically, and probably seasonally, but which may be hard to prove because she doesn't have access to the Sea in any season besides summer.

She sits on the soft sand bottom and watches her dad jog down toward the water, startling a couple of chickens and a gull, which flap sidewise and settle in the water-fountain runoff.

"Race you to the dock," he says, splashing up beside her.

A.Z. really doesn't want to be seen racing her dad, but Larsley is obviously running late, and her dad has already taken off, so she pulls as hard as she can with the crawl, not even breathing every other stroke. She sees the blur of him beside her and kicks for all she's worth. She touches the dock before he surfaces, several feet to the right. He always veers when he swims.

"I'm out of practice," he says.

"You did well," A.Z. says. "I just swam a bunch of laps yesterday."

She glances toward shore at two pilgrim girls, maybe a few years older than her, who are paddling toward the dock, keeping their heads above the water. They climb gracefully up the new ladder in leopard-print bikinis and sit, dangling gold-braceleted ankles. They also have gold pendants shaped like naked fairies, and stiff-sprayed, poofed-out bangs like a lot of preppy and pilgrim girls: what Larsley named the "hair flower."

"How do you know his dick is crooked?" the blonder one says loudly.

Her dad glances over, but not, thank god, like he's listening.

"Maybe you could come with me to the First-First Baptists," he says. "You could help me sample their Sunday potluck."

"I promised Mom I'd help reorganize nonfiction this weekend," A.Z. says.

The pilgrim girls laugh. "'Cause I seen it," the other one says. "Like a bent banana."

A.Z. feels herself blush. She wants her dad to swim back to shore but she also feels as if it's the girls who are invading her Sea. It's like when Scotty's slutty older sister, Gwennie, sat behind her in speech class and talked about practicing blow jobs on a frozen hot dog, which A.Z. couldn't quite imagine because she doesn't fully understand what a blow job is because her sibling who is supposed to explain these things is almost twenty years older and lives in Little Rock, and her mom doesn't keep books on sex in the library because teenage boys will just steal them.

To drown out the girls and because she's sort of been wondering, A.Z. says, "Are you still working on the article about the Starfish, too? I mean, are you interviewing the workers?"

"'Starfish: Start to Finish' is finished," her dad says. "They're having permit problems."

"Permanently?" She tries to sound unfazed. What does she care about conveniently cut logs, and the boy with the bandana and work gloves he isn't wearing, because he doesn't have to work, which means he'll maybe find another job and she won't ever see him again?

"For the foreseeable future," her dad says. "Fragile foundation. It turns out the points are problematic." A.Z. isn't sure if he's quoting a headline or isn't aware he's alliterating. That happens sometimes.

When her dad finally leaves—veering right, and correcting himself, and veering left—A.Z. waits a little longer for Larsley and finally swims back to get her test kit, which she holds subtly by her side on her way back to the dock. The lifeguards are strict about what people take into the Sea.

She pulls the stopper off a vial with her teeth and fills it, but writing on the label while holding everything is impossible, so she lays the test kit by the girls' feet. She fills another vial from closer to the Sea floor and tries not to pay attention to the girls smearing on Hawaiian Tropic and flirting with Frank and his friend, who have pedaled up in a dumb paddle boat.

"Need a hand?" Frank says, which isn't funny or original, despite getting voted Funniest Senior last year. The girls giggle and introduce themselves as sisters from Stillwater. Besides the bikinis and jewelry, they don't look like sisters. A.Z. and Larsley used to tell pilgrims they were sisters, too—identical twins who didn't look alike because of a genetic disease.

A.Z. imagines having a private raft instead of this dumb public dock. She imagines the dock coming unmoored, the girls squealing and swimming back toward shore. She glances back for Larsley, who maybe overslept or something.

Finally she sees her. She's dog paddling like she does and yawning. She hangs off the ladder beside A.Z. and yawns again. "I'm so sleepy," she says. "After you left last night, Scotty and I went to a motel room and this show about Prefontaine came on, and then he came to my house, and we watched MTV all night."

"Who?"

"Scotty."

"No. Prefon-whatever."

"You know, the runner. He had the national record in five different categories and he probably would have gone on to world records, but then he died really tragically in a car wreck."

"Wow." A.Z. thinks about Scotty and Larsley lying on the carpet in front of Larsley's bed the way A.Z. and Larsley always do. She thinks about Prefontaine dying in a car crash like her mom's first boyfriend—the night he drove to her house to leave her the obsidian ring, which was clearly supposed to be an engagement ring.

"Hey," she says super casually. "Did you see those workers at the Starfish the other day? That one really cute guy with the earrings and the bandana and the bicycle? I mean, I don't know if he's working anymore because I guess the construction is over, but I was thinking maybe we should ask him to help us with a raft or something."

Larsley yawns again, wider. "I didn't notice," she says. "What's that by your head?"

"Some water I stole." For some reason, even before Larsley doesn't react, A.Z. sort of feels like crying.

"I'm getting sooo dark. I'm gonna look Mex'can," the dark-er-haired girl says.

"*Sí*," Frank says. "*Estás muy fuego*. It means 'You're really hot.'"

Larsley rolls her eyes—in that good way, not the googly-eyed way she was doing with Scotty, like those dolls that blink if you pick them up. She takes Spanish—the hour Mr. Finley wears his sombrero instead of his beret.

"You should tell that to the construction guy," she says, starting to laugh in that irrepressible way that makes A.Z. start laughing, too, before she even knows what's funny. "Tell him we're having a party and say, 'Hey, you're very fire!'"

5

Larsley keeps changing lipstick, so her lips are kind of swollen orange-red-pink-purple. She looks good, though, in rolled-up stonewashed jean shorts and a new purple tank top, which is brighter and maybe cooler than A.Z.'s Tall Ship Elissa T-shirt. Or maybe the problem is A.Z.'s hair, which is chlorine-salt dried out and pulled into a really boring ponytail. A.Z. is worried about this, but also she isn't.

Larsley is handing her the almost-empty Jägermeister. At first it tasted like burning licorice, but it's getting really good: herbally and sweet.

A.Z. takes a drink and passes it back to Larsley, who throws her sparkler into the sink full of plastic cups. Earlier, she was telling people not to light sparklers in the house but now she's carrying them everywhere.

"They keep losing their sparkle," she says, sort of walking and sort of stumbling from the kitchen toward the deck.

"Did you see Skip?" Angie says. She's talking loudly over the Depeche Mode cranked in the living room. Skip is a junior who always looks somehow wonderfully Irish—like Bono and The Edge at the same time. He has on a cap like those old-fashioned paper-boys and a long-sleeved button-up shirt, even though it's over ninety degrees.

"Yeah," A.Z. says. She wants to tell Angie about the *muy fuego* guy, who is way cuter than even Skip—but who she's never seen again, and therefore never invited to the party, or anywhere, not that she'd probably be brave enough. But Shelley drags Angie off to the living room. So A.Z. wanders to the deck where Scotty and Rob, wearing jeans and T-shirts instead of tracksuits, which makes them seem strange and somehow older, are setting off pinwheels.

She doesn't see Larsley, so she goes back inside and up the stairs, where the house is quiet, like a whole other soft, blue-carpeted world is happening. She finds Larsley in her bedroom putting on dark red lipstick.

"Isn't this the best party?" Larsley says. "Can you believe we're almost fifteen? Remember when we said we wouldn't even kiss a guy 'til we were seventeen? Or have sex 'til we were twenty? God, we were so young then."

"Yeah," A.Z. says, trying not to think about the fact that she's fourteen and not-even-a-half and has still only kissed Chris—and just that once. She reassures herself that if Larsley has had sex with Scotty, she would have told her.

A.Z. stares in the mirror: at her unraveling jean shorts and the sails on her T-shirt, which match her spiral-knot earrings but also look out of place, like a ship in a bottle. Or maybe she's just thinking that because of the Jägermeister.

"You've got to come down," someone calls. "Rob just dared Scotty to streak down Shell Street."

But when they get downstairs, Scotty is still on the deck, fully dressed, and someone has opened Larsley's parents' liquor cabinet.

"That was their fancy wine," Larsley says, linking her arm through A.Z.'s like they're best friends, which of course they are. "They'll just blame each other for taking it."

"I wish my parents didn't get along," A.Z. says, and then she wishes she hadn't. Mentioning her parents makes her nervous—like her mom is somewhere in the crowd in the kitchen yelling, "Chug, chug, chug!" But that doesn't make any sense, and it feels good that the idea of her mom is nonsensical.

In the living room, Angie is sitting cross-legged on the arm of the couch talking to two pilgrim girls, who heard about the party from a girl in Greenville. "I couldn't find you," Angie calls to her and Larsley. "Skip got more Jägermeister." She holds up the bottle like a trophy.

A.Z. takes a drink, which makes her feel floaty until she realizes she can't feel her legs. She's standing on them, but it's like they're not there. Apparently she says this out loud.

"They're probably just asleep," Angie says. "They're just sleepy."

"You're sleepy?" Larsley has her arm linked through Scotty's now.

"I can't feel my legs."

"We'll get you water," Angie says. She and Larsley walk toward the kitchen, and Scotty sits on the couch where Angie was.

He lifts the Jägermeister. "To the swim team."

"My legs are messed up," A.Z. says. "They're not there."

"To the Special Olympics swim team!"

"Remember when she told everyone she was going to sail to the North Pole?" Rob says.

"Yeah," Scotty says, laughing. "And that speech about eating rotten fish?" He waves his hand and says, in that Grey Poupon voice, "Can I interest you in some rotting fish?" and then, in his own voice, "Lars told me you still want to build a raft. Like Huckleberry Finn!"

Rob laughs; Larsley laughs. She's back from the kitchen but she doesn't have any water.

"What?" A.Z. says. The lines are mixed up, like those multiple-choice tests where you draw lines from question to answer. Rob and Scotty probably didn't even read *Huckleberry Finn*. Scotty probably copied off someone. And A.Z. isn't anything like that stupid river-kid. She's an oceanographer. She's going to be an oceanographer. And Larsley is laughing with them about her research raft, like it's her fourth-grade speech all over again, like it's some stupid joke.

Even without legs, she stands up.

"Where are you going?" Larsley says.

"Away," A.Z. says.

"Sail away, sail away, sail away!" Rob pretends to paddle the air by the couch—even though sailors don't paddle—and starts another round of that awful Enya song that admittedly A.Z. loved when it came out this spring, before it started blaring from every single shop in Compolodo. "Sail away, sail away."

Then, before she thinks about it, A.Z. is running. She's out the front door and on the porch, the heavy wood thudding shut behind her. Somehow, she runs without legs all the way to the highway.

With the bright darkness of the streetlights but no one out, she's in a photograph of a place called Compolodo. She's seen it in an old book in the library, taken before the invention of fast shutters: horses and people blurring into an empty street. Maybe she's surrounded by people she can't see because she's moving at a different speed than they are. She's around the world in a distant port, teeming with people and the noises of wharves, the smell of seaweed and salt and the blood-iron of ship yards. She's with all these people—these sailors, these explorers—and also she's walking alone. She can suddenly feel not only her legs, but her lungs, and face, and arms swinging at her sides. Everything tingles and is light, like she has feathers on her skin.

It must be very late because no one is out—except someone standing on a box below the sign for the Sands Motel. The sign says

COLD POO. The person is moving the letters, like A.Z.'s mom moves Scrabble tiles back and forth. Her mom is a very good Scrabble player, and A.Z. feels irrationally certain the person is her mom.

The person is reaching into the sign and pulling the "a" and then the "t" out of FREE BREAKFAST, then the "r," "e," and "e" and then it says FAT BRE KFAS, and then the "e" and "s" are gone, and then some letters are arranged, rearranged, quickly: FREE BARF. COLD POO. The person stuffs the other letters into his backpack. He slings the backpack over one shoulder and, holding the box he was standing on, climbs onto a bicycle. He bends over as he rides, not like a racer, but casually, out of necessity from his height. It can't be—but is—the boy.

His bike makes a high-pitched squeal, like distant seagulls. He's pedaling faster, and she loses him before the junction to Gording Lane. She tries not to think about Larsley and Scotty laughing back at the party. She tries not to think about her legs, which aren't merely there, they're making up for their absence: feeling eight times as much like legs as they ever have.

She walks as fast as she can, despite her legs. She'll catch him at the next sign; she'll stride up nonchalantly. She'll stand beside him, and he'll ask her to hand up an "e" or a "t"—like Vanna White, only a million times better. He'll know without asking that his secret is safe with her. Only a girl with her own deep secrets would be walking alone down the highway at night.

The Ark Motel has a huge wooden sign shaped like an ark, with pairs of painted animals. There's also a smaller changeable sign that says HBO and FREE LOCO CALLS. She's trying to find a word with a missing "o" when she hears the bicycle. He's on the other side of the road, coming toward her. He must have turned around.

"Hey," she calls. "Do you know what time it is?" She's impressed she's thought of this. She really isn't wearing her watch.

"What?" He leans back, coasts toward her. He's even taller up close.

"Do you know what time it is?"

"Late."

"Yeah. I sort of knew that."

He's standing over his bike with both feet on the ground, which for some reason doesn't really seem stopped. She's worried he'll roll away, disappear.

She needs to think of something more to say, quickly. She wants to tell him she likes the signs but she doesn't want to sound as if she's been following him. She says it anyway.

"Thanks," he says. He doesn't ask how she knows the signs are his. He doesn't look Mexican up close, although he could be part Native American, with high cheekbones. "It's conceptual art."

"Oh," A.Z. says. She isn't sure if she knows what that means.

"It's a radical underground movement. I'm the only member. Or maybe you're also a member." He laughs—a quick burst of sound that doesn't quite fit into the space after his words but makes her feel good—and sits down on the seat, with his feet on the ground. The bike is too small for him.

"Cool!" She's feeling kind of flushed, maybe from the Jägermeister or walking or being, suddenly, a member of the boy's radical underground movement. She's a radical underground oceanographer. She tries not to think, *This is the boy, the boy, the boy, and you're meeting him. You're talking to him. He's real. He's sitting on a bicycle.*

"Where's your bike?"

"What?"

"Did you ride out here?"

"No. I was on my way from a friend's party and I thought I'd walk out to the Sea." She only figures this out as she says it. Of course that's where she was going.

"You should get a bike."

"No kidding. I mean, I sort of have one, but it's like a hundred years old and weighs a million pounds. It's like a tank from the '50s."

He laughs again, that same laugh, like water that has been under pressure being released. "Bicycle-tank."

She laughs, too. "I never got another one because my mom is weird about bikes because she got surrounded by a pack of wild dogs when she was on a bike once in Arizona. They almost bit her, except someone came up and started throwing rocks." She realizes even as she's telling the story how stupid it sounds. In another state, years ago, a pack of dogs didn't actually bite her mom. But the boy doesn't point out how dumb this is; he looks kind of interested.

"My mom's a bitch," he says.

"Oh," A.Z. says. She's never heard anyone call their own mother a bitch before. She didn't really know it was possible.

"She got this job at that chicken place, and now she always smells like brains."

"Really?"

"Yeah, she vacuums the brains out with a hose."

"At Chuck Chicken?" A.Z. has heard about the bloody conveyor belts and people power-washing chicken guts off their boots in the Greenville Car Wash, but she's never really talked to anyone who works in the plant or has a mom who does. Even her father hasn't been inside for years. Chuck Chuck says it's bad for business and dinner if people think about how a chicken gets to the frozen food aisle.

"Yeah," the boy says. "You smell like Jägermeister." This is undoubtedly true, but seems rude to mention, like telling another person they have bad breath. She's talking to the boy, the boy, the boy, and she smells like she's drunk. She realizes this is a problem for a lot of reasons, including that she can't go to the library tomorrow until she brushes her teeth for several hours with the toothbrush she left at Larsley's.

"The party I was at was really lame," she says. Without talking about it, they've started walking toward the beach, the boy wheeling his bicycle beside her, beside her, beside her. "Are you going to change more signs?"

He laughs again. A.Z. doesn't really understand what's funny about this. "I don't know," he says. "It's not the kind of thing you can really know until it happens. Language is inherently arbitrary."

The boy, the boy, the boy, who tells her his name is Kristoff, says a lot of things like this.

When she asks about language being arbitrary, he tells her he believes in radical nihilist causation, which means there isn't any cause and effect.

He says he's a radical conceptual underground nihilist artist, although during the day, he does things like lay rebar for the Starfish because his mother spends her entire paycheck buying useless crap at Wal-Mart, and they're always broke. In their last apartment, the electricity was shut off for two months. Kristoff keeps calling his mom a bitch, but he has no choice but to love her because she's the only parent he has. He's never met his father; he doesn't even know his name, but maybe it was also Kristoff. This could explain why his mom calls him "Little Shit" instead.

Kristoff sounds like a famous German artist, A.Z. says. She waits for him to ask about her name, but he doesn't. He doesn't ask a lot of questions.

When she asks how old he is, she finds out he's a junior, despite his height just a year and a half older. He dyed his jean shorts himself and added the safety pins, which he also used to pierce his ears four times. It didn't hurt. And he didn't even use ice because the power was off and there wasn't any. It was the middle of the night, which is when he does a lot of things because he doesn't sleep very much.

He tells her it doesn't matter if he just lies in the dark in the trailer in Greenville and thinks about ideas, or if he goes out and creates them. "That's the point of conceptual art," he says. "It doesn't even have to happen."

This sort of makes sense to A.Z., but also right now it doesn't because the most wonderful concept is happening. They're at the gate to Mud Beach, which is of course locked with a padlock, but Kristoff stands on the chicken crate he's carrying and swings one of his long legs over. The gate isn't really that tall—just imposing because of the arch.

And then he reaches out his hand to her, and she's pulling herself up and over. After, she can still feel where his hand touched hers; like it's warmer, but also cooler than the rest of the air.

A.Z. has never been on Mud Beach at night before; no one has. She's only imagined it—and once, when she was a kid, her mom drove away at sunset because she wouldn't quit feeding the gulls, which was scary until A.Z. realized she was probably going to end up raised by them, the way Romulus and Remus were by those wolves.

Right now, the sand feels different than during the day—cooler through the soles of her shoes and more shifting. She's sure that a security guard is going to appear and arrest them. She's going to end up in jail with a criminal record for trespassing and underage drinking, and she'll never see Kristoff or the Sea again. But she can't say this. She can't think of the words. Maybe he's rearranged them.

"Have you come out here before?" she asks finally.

"I've ridden past," Kristoff says. "The other night, I was thinking about riding all the way to Florida."

"To Florida?" A.Z. says.

"Yeah, we used to live there when my mom was married to my asshole stepdad."

"You lived in Florida?" A.Z. says. "You've seen the ocean? The Atlantic Ocean?"

"Yeah," Kristoff says. "When we lived in Miami, we went to the beach a couple of times. I went wading once, I think."

"But isn't Miami right on the beach?"

Kristoff laughs and says it's a big city and people don't go to the beach all the time, which A.Z. thinks is definitely a radical, nonsensical idea.

"Did you go to the Keys?" she asks.

"No," Kristoff says, "but we went to Disney World once. There were dyed blue waterfalls and this Jungle Cruise with animatronic elephants and hippos and stuff. Sort of like Compolodo." He sits down a few feet back from the water, so A.Z. sits down on the warm-cool sand beside him.

"Like the Ark Motel?" she says.

"Yeah, like everything."

A.Z. tries to imagine animatronic animals in the Sea but she's not sure what animatronic means, except obviously not real. She isn't sure how Compolodo is like Disney World, but she's trying not to think too logically about stuff, because apparently that's not the point of radical conceptual thought, and besides, her head is starting to hurt behind her eyes. So she closes them, but then she has to open them because she feels like she's spinning and like the boy might not really be there.

"Have you heard about Sea Camp?" she says. "It's in the Keys."

"No," he says.

"It's this place where you live on boats and study oceanography. I'm applying to go this Christmas. I'm doing a study right now on the salinity of the Sea, and how it varies in different areas and depths. No one has ever studied it."

"Cool," he says, and it really does sound like he thinks so.

"Did you ever think you'd end up here?" she asks.

"If you think about it," he says, "we could really be anywhere. It's all the same place."

"Yeah," she says. "I know what you mean."

And she kind of does. Kristoff has lived by the Atlantic Ocean. He's waded in it, and now he's sitting beside her. He has his knees drawn up to his chest, rocking back and forth. And she's sweeping her hand through the sand, making one deep wing of an angel. "I'm planning to build my own raft this summer to research," she says. "I mean, I can't just study the shore; I have to know what's really out there."

"OK," he says, almost as if she's asked him to help her. And A.Z. is scared to say anything else that will rearrange the words and silence of this moment, so they sit there staring at the water, with him rocking back and forth slightly like there are already waves underneath them.

6

"I hope you realize, Anastasia Zoe," her mom says, dropping books onto the reshelving cart, "that you're never going to Larsley Wilkens's house again. In fact, you're not going near her or Scotty Brashears. If Scotty and Rob think they're still going to college on track scholarships after being caught underage drinking, they're going to be gravely disappointed." She stares at A.Z. through her bifocals, like there's a top half and bottom half to her disappointment.

A.Z. can feel pieces of her brain jarring against each other. But she also feels strangely happy. First, there's Kristoff, riding away this morning after saying, "See ya," as if he was going to see her again, as if he already planned on it. And second, her mom has just forbidden her from doing what she doesn't want to do. Just fifteen minutes ago, she stood above Larsley, who was lying on the fuzzy rug by her toilet, and said, "I'm just here to brush my teeth. I'm only speaking to you to tell you I'm not speaking to you."

"Other people may not care about their futures," her mom says. "But you know better."

A.Z. tries to nod, but her head is on one of those centrifugal-force rides at the county fair.

"At least you had the good sense to leave with Angie before Officer Gibbs came. Even if you didn't have the good sense not to lie about what was going on at Larsley's." Her mom carries an armload of books to the counter. "You can start unshelving where I left off."

A.Z. has no idea why her mom thinks she left with Angie, and she's scared this is evident. Angie is super cool, but they don't usually hang out, just the two of them. She's sure her mom is going to say something next about her being on Mud Beach with Kristoff, but she doesn't, maybe because Sahara's mom, Dragonfly, comes in.

Dragonfly is wearing a white sundress with an elasticky tube top that might belong to Sahara. She's one of those moms who could be an older sister until you notice the grey in her hennaed hair.

"Someone paid off the permit office to start construction again at the Starfish," Dragonfly says. "They're back at work this morning. Do you have any books on handwriting tests? I just read this article about handwriting analysis, and I'm starting a petition to have our city officials tested to make sure they're still honest."

"Testing politicians' writing certainly has precedent," A.Z.'s mom says. "Nixon's signature at the start of his presidency was perfectly normal, and then before Watergate, it's almost illegible, and after, the letters have disintegrated to squiggles. I can find you the examples."

She looks toward the stacks, but doesn't move. "But, of course, criminals can have gorgeous handwriting. There was a boy named William Henry Ireland in the eighteenth century who came to Stratford-upon-Avon when it had just become a tourist site and started selling forgeries of Shakespeare's plays. Even after the whole fraud was exposed, he kept selling forged plays because people *want* to believe."

A.Z. has sat down on the floor between the stacks, and maybe it's all the books above her, but the air feels super heavy. She's on a planet with super strong gravity, like Stephen would draw for his aliens— only she doesn't care about Stephen. She's on a planet with random causation and radical nihilist underground conceptual gravity.

But apparently she's also in the library because—pausing her story for a second—her mom calls, "You can bring the next stack to the counter."

A.Z. has to hold onto the reshelving cart to stand, and it rolls slightly, which makes her super seasick. The 300s are supposed to be social sciences, but for some reason, these books, where her mom told her to start, are about alcoholism.

"Oh, I didn't see you here," Dragonfly says. She leans in, closer than A.Z. wants anyone to lean, and hugs her. "I miss having you around."

A.Z. wonders suddenly if Sahara remembered about the party, and if Dragonfly knows—if everyone knows—A.Z. was there.

Although, of course, she also wasn't there. That's the amazing thing: everywhere is kind of the same place.

"You can take this dust cloth," her mom calls, "and wipe down all the empty shelves." Then she turns to Dragonfly. "I don't know if I've told you this story, but my first love ended up in jail for forgery. He wasn't criminal by nature, he just had the most beautiful handwriting. He used to write me letters in boarding school. And then he needed money and forged a check from his boss. It's hard to live without structure, and he didn't have any family."

It's weird for A.Z. to be hearing this story right now—with a pounding head and waves of nausea—because Kristoff also doesn't have much family. Although, she's worrying now, he didn't play a song for her on a jukebox like Arthur did for her mom, and she's only hung out with him once, by accident, and even though he said, "See ya," maybe it's just an expression.

"My mother never trusted Arthur even before he went to jail," her mom continues. "She used to call him a drifter and say I'd end up pregnant. We were actually just sneaking away to read Zane Grey to each other. You can't get pregnant from reading."

Dragonfly laughs, like people always do at this part, and she and A.Z.'s mom finally walk toward the stacks.

"I just rearranged my bookshelves, too," Dragonfly says. "I made categories by color. I just have to think, *I want the blue book on composting*, and there it is."

A.Z.'s mom doesn't say anything, probably because she thinks this is dumb. She believes in the Dewey Decimal System, even though, now that A.Z. thinks about it, it's really just as arbitrary.

And maybe because her brain is splintering, A.Z. says aloud, "We should come up with a new system for the library. You know, colors aren't any more arbitrary than numbers really."

Her mom turns with a look that makes A.Z. feel magnified, like her sweating palms and dry throat and nausea are totally visible. "Not if the numbers are assigned by category," she says. "You wouldn't know anything about the motel signs around town being rearranged, would you?"

"The what?" She's pretty sure her mom is going to tell her everything she did last night.

"The Ark Motel and the Seahorse and the Sands have all been having problems with signage vandalism. Officer Gibbs was going out to investigate this morning."

"Weird," A.Z. says. "I don't really read the motel signs. I mean, they all say the same thing. *HBO* and *pool* and *vacancy* or *no vacancy* or whatever." The words sound strange.

Her mom clears her throat, but miraculously, it doesn't sound like her I'm-about-to-call-your-bluff throat clearing. It sounds like she's breathed too much book dust.

"What a great idea," Dragonfly says. "You could combine signs into all kinds of political messages."

Signage vandal, A.Z. thinks. *Kristoff and I are signage vandals, and now maybe we'll have to run away on a raft together.*

The First-First Southern Baptist Church is over-air-conditioned so Reverend Bicks can wear his burgundy polyester suit and thump the Bible without having a heart attack, and A.Z. is freezing in her sundress. She wanted to look nice. It's been twenty-nine and a half hours since she's seen Kristoff, and even though Greenville is admittedly a town of 7,000 people, and probably she won't run into him, also, possibly, if he didn't have to work at the Starfish today, she will.

In the fidgety time before the service starts, an old, heavily-rouged woman hands A.Z. and her dad big white envelopes.

"Welcome," she whispers gushily. "We sure are glad to have you pray with us today."

A.Z. sort of wants to point out that they're really here to eat the potluck, not to pray, but of course she doesn't. She looks down at the curly letters on the envelope, which say *Welcome, Youth!* Which, after a few minutes, she realizes could also spell *cow mouth.*

A man who looks like an overstuffed armchair announces the canned food drive and the Fourth of July Fish Fry. Then everyone stands for the first hymn, which is about sin and the heavens, which are for some reason flaming and rolling like a parched scroll.

A.Z.'s dad sings loudly—not because he believes, but because this is the closest thing he has to being in a musical.

A.Z. doesn't believe in heaven either, but the lyrics are kind of cool when she pictures the sky and earth rolling like storm waves at sea, crashing around a ship where maybe Kristoff is helping her with the highest rigging.

As soon as everyone sits back down, Reverend Bicks comes up to the podium and starts bellowing: "The Lord has instructed you, and because you are hungry, you will rage and curse your king and your God. You will look up to heaven and down at the earth, but wherever you look, there will be trouble and anguish and dark despair. You will be thrown into the darkness. You will be thrown into the flames of He-el-ll."

He lifts the Bible and smacks it against the podium. "Darkness," he cries again. "It is a sin to worship false gods. It is a sin to worship idols. And sinners will pay with eternal fi-ir-re."

A.Z. is pretty sure he's going to tell everyone to march out of the church and burn down Seven Happiness and its Satan-Buddha—but he doesn't. Instead, after a long time of this, he smacks the Bible again like he's swatting demonic flies, and then everyone stands and sings: "I Have a Song I Love to Sing." Apparently this is true because the hymn has a million verses.

When the service finally ends, Reverend Bicks hurries over. "Sure is good to have you'uns here, Jimmy," he says. "And Anna Stacy, be sure to get yourself a slice of the red velvet cake in the fellowship hall. Jan puts in extra love and Crisco."

Then his wife, Jan, asks A.Z. how her mama is doing and says it's such a shame she couldn't come. She says this every time she sees A.Z., even though it's obvious A.Z.'s mom doesn't come to anything church-related. She hasn't since she and Jan and Chuck's wife, Vera, were part of the same sewing circle in the '50s, when A.Z.'s mom was an unhappy housewife and didn't have a choice.

"She's at the library," A.Z. says.

"Always working," Jan says. "Tell her 'hi' for me, will you? I still think about her meeting Gorgeous George. Can you believe he pulled right up to her stepfather's gas station and gave her two gold bobby pins from his hair? He was one of the most famous wrestlers back then. Such a heartthrob." She looks at A.Z. with that expression that means she's lucky to have a mom who had such an exciting life and still keeps two gold bobby pins in her jewelry box.

A.Z. thinks of explaining that gold bobby pins are not half as cool as silver hoop earrings, or that she's only here because her mom is punishing her for drinking at a party where she actually ran off with a radical nihilist artist, but she just smiles. "Yeah, I'll tell her."

The fellowship hall doesn't have windows—just white, con-crete-block walls with three long tables pushed end to end. Even with both her and her dad, there's no way they can sample all the food: Jell-O, potato, tuna, and macaroni salads; macaroni and cheese; hot dogs; hot dog casserole; rolls; cornbread; watermelon; mashed pota-toes; corn on the cob; fried chicken; roast chicken; tuna casserole (at least that's A.Z.'s best guess); apple, pecan, lemon meringue, banana cream, and strawberry pies; strawberry shortcake; chocolate cupcakes; chocolate chip cookies; brownies; and lemon, white, chocolate, and red velvet cakes. A.Z.'s dad takes dutifully impressed notes: *copious corn-on-cob, cake, casseroles.*

A.Z. agrees she'll try all the salads, and her dad will try the cas-seroles, so she fills her plate and pours a Dixie cup of very yellow lemonade. Then she follows her dad to a seat close enough to Chuck Chuck to seem friendly, but far enough for her dad to concentrate. She forks a few macaroni out of the pool of mayonnaise and tastes the potato salad, which is also mayonnaisey, but good. She's suddenly hungry and finishes both. She's eaten half the tuna salad and is mov-ing on to the orange Jell-O ambrosia when Reverend and Stacy Bicks show up.

"Stacy just couldn't wait to see you, Anna Stacy," Reverend Bicks says, "I know you two have a lot to talk about." Stacy smiles in a forced, wired-together-teeth way. She has bits of roll stuck in her braces, and she's wearing a seafoam-green dress with one of those removable crocheted collars that used to be in back in 1985.

"Hi," she says, in her soprano voice. There isn't room for her to sit, so she's standing above A.Z., which makes A.Z. feel weird.

"I'm going to get more lemonade," A.Z. says.

"OK," Stacy says, like this has something to do with her.

At the beverage table, Stacy pours Kool-Aid, and A.Z. pours lemonade, and they stand there awkwardly—Stacy glancing at the youth table, where her friends probably are, and A.Z. glancing at her little flowered cup. She considers saying something to make Stacy go away—like the lemonade tastes like the rum she drank before the Jägermeister—but her dad is here, and, anyway, the lemonade tastes like liquid Jolly Ranchers.

"Are you coming to the Fourth of July Fish Fry?" Stacy asks. "I'm singing a solo."

"I doubt it," A.Z. says. Maybe it's thinking about the fish fry, but she suddenly feels nauseated, like her stomach is swirling against itself, like she's somehow still super hungover. "I'm feeling kind of sick," she says. She's worried Stacy will follow her, but Stacy just nods and smiles with her teeth gummed with disgusting bread clumps.

A.Z. doesn't remember where the bathroom is, and she turns the wrong way down the hall, and doesn't make it. She doubles over, right below the Bible Study bulletin board, retching mayonnaise onto the carpet as a tacked-up Jesus pets a lamb above her head.

7

There's no one working at the Starfish when A.Z. and her dad pull up on Tuesday—just a few pickups and shovels sticking up like flagless flagpoles. "They must be at lunch," her dad says. "I was worried about that."

"Sorry," A.Z. says. She feels like she might start crying—about getting ready slowly and making her dad late and the uselessness of putting on makeup to not look sick when Kristoff's not even here, and how awful she feels being out of the house for the first time since the poisonous potluck.

On the curves of the highway, the emptiness in her stomach started churning, and the hot wind reminded her strangely of dog breath. She almost had to ask her dad to turn around. What if she threw up on Kristoff? What if it seemed really obvious that she'd come with her dad like some stupid kid reporter?

But of course now Kristoff isn't even here.

"We should get you some ginger ale," her dad says. "I'll stop at the P.M./A.M." He's obviously still feeling guilty about taking her to get poisoned. Yesterday, he went to work late and sat by her bed, reading aloud articles he was proofing, although she made him stop at the headline "Baptists Break Bounteous Bread."

"Maybe," A.Z. says. "I don't know if I can really drink anything."

Her dad is signaling to turn into the newspaper lot when someone honks and then lolls his head out the window. It's Scotty—grinning that dumb zombie grin and driving one of those sports cars that taper at the front. He waves because he's too dumb to remember that A.Z. isn't speaking to him or Larsley.

"Hey Librarian!" he calls. "I'm going to Fayetteville for stuff for the pool part-ee!" He roars away before A.Z. can not say anything.

She's about to tell her dad that maybe she'll just sit in the car and feel miserable for a while, when she looks across the highway at the P.M./A.M. Beyond the gas pumps and the big sign that says PRE-MIRACLE/AFTER-MIRACLE, a group of workers are smoking by the concrete-block wall. And beside that is a bicycle.

"Maybe I do want some ginger ale," she says. "I think the walk would be good for me."

She has to wait for a break in the traffic to cross the highway, and although she'd usually run, she can't. When she gets to the pumps—feeling light-headed but triumphant—Kristoff is walking around the corner from the outdoor bathrooms to the front door, the bell jingling just above his head. She pretends not to see him and heads straight for the ginger ale. But Kristoff is there too, getting a two-liter Mountain Dew.

"Hi," she says. She suddenly feels nervous. Maybe it's just because she hasn't eaten much for two days, but she somehow has this irrational fear that she imagined the whole other night, that Kristoff won't even know who she is.

"Hiya," he says, grinning. "I got the last bottle."

A.Z. isn't sure if he's grinning at her or at his luck, but it feels so good to be standing next to him, for him to obviously remember her, that she doesn't care. "I'm getting some ginger ale," she says. "I've had food poisoning." She wonders if he's wondered why he hasn't seen her.

"Barf!" Kristoff says. "That happened to me once. The power had been off for a week, and I ate this fuzzy cheese."

The idea of fuzzy cheese makes A.Z.'s stomach clench, but then Kristoff laughs, which makes her laugh, too. She can't tell if he's serious or not, and it doesn't matter. Nothing is serious. Maybe she never had food poisoning at all.

"These ham sandwiches suck," Kristoff says, pulling one from the cold case. "I just ate one." A.Z. thinks he's going to put it back, but he carries it to the counter and pays.

"Hey, did you know that it's illegal to name a pig 'Napoleon' in France?" she says. "There's a law about it." She'd read this in one of the books her mom made her reshelve. It seemed like the kind of thing Kristoff would think was funny.

Sure enough, he leans forward and laughs with a snort, like he's imitating a pig. "That's the funniest thing I've heard in days." He takes a bite of the sandwich. "Too much mustard and not enough Napoleon."

Then he does this amazing thing: he unscrews the cap of the Mountain Dew and takes a swig and hands it to her—like she hasn't been throwing up for days, like this is totally normal.

A.Z. has never tried Mountain Dew because her mom believes soft drinks destroy character and tooth enamel. She only makes an exception for ginger ale after sickness, and Dr Pepper, which she first drank in its birthplace, Waco, Texas, in 1947, when her father had died and her mother was moving her and her younger brother from New York to Arizona. A.Z.'s mom always says that bottle of

Dr Pepper tasted like the best thing in the world: like snow and cold maple syrup.

But Kristoff's Mountain Dew is much, much better. It tastes like electric lights and that glow that comes up from underneath glaciers that A.Z. used to imagine she'd see when she sailed to the poles.

Maybe it's the Mountain Dew she's been secretly buying to keep her stomach settled, but by Thursday, A.Z. feels well enough to stand in a small room that smells like steamy garlic and pork and water chestnuts. Or she hopes she feels well enough. She's walking through the kitchen at Seven Happiness on her way to the sinks when Thu stops her.

"I've been waiting for you," Thu says, wiping her hands on her apron. "I got a weird letter on the door this morning. You know what this means?" She takes down a piece of paper from the stainless steel shelves above the stove, where she keeps the big mixing bowls and extra soy sauce.

In big block letters, the paper says: *TAKE YOUR HEATHENFILTH BACK TO CHINA OR YOU WILL ANSWER TO THE WRATH OF THE LORD.*

"I looked in the dictionary, but there's no word like that," Thu says.

"Umm. I don't think it's really a word."

A.Z. wants to say more, but she's not sure how to explain—even if she hadn't promised her dad not to. "Baptists Break Bounteous Bread," with its potluck praise, came out yesterday morning, so Reverend Bicks should have stopped preaching against Buddha-Satan and gone back to threatening people with some other kind of Hell. "How about I show it to my dad?"

She feels bad for Thu but also excited to tell Kristoff this crazy word *heathenfilth*. But she hasn't seen Kristoff for over a day, which is starting to worry her, like he's avoiding the P.M./A.M. because he decided she was gross after all.

She's hoping to drop the note off at her dad's office and then get another Mountain Dew at what should be Kristoff's lunch break, but Seven Happiness is really busy; even Sam leaves his newspaper and works the register. Another tour bus comes in right when they should be closing, so A.Z. has to stay late.

Finally, Thu brings back the last bus tub and leans against the freezer. "Sam said some boy came by looking for you, but it's very busy out front, so Sam told him it's better to go away."

"What? Someone came by looking for me?" She tries to remember if she told Kristoff she works at Seven Happiness. She must have. And he came to see her, but Sam was too lazy to tell her. She feels anxious suddenly—like the bright glacier-glow energy that has made her extra fast at dishwashing is all pooling in her chest.

"And there was another man who looks like George Michael. You see him?" Thu loves celebrities. After work, she reads about them in the Little Rock paper. Sometimes she asks A.Z. questions like, "You hear Madonna wear that pointy bra on stage? Where do you think she bought a pointy bra like that?"

"No," A.Z. says sort of crossly. "I didn't see him. I never see anyone back here."

"Too bad," Thu says. "Very good looking, like Sam before he get all bald. You know the paper says George Michael is maybe gay? I don't believe that."

A.Z. tries to wash the last few dishes extra fast in case Kristoff is waiting, but the water has cooled so the grease won't wash off. She finally sets the last cup in the drainer and hurries into the dining room, but no one is there, so she goes to her dad's office and leaves the *heathenfilth* letter and a note tucked under a paperweight.

Then she walks slowly to the library—where her mom is making her work even though she's just worked all day.

Sahara is at the front counter, talking to her mom, who is dusting a stack of books, turning them over one by one like she's drying plates.

"Hey, did Josh find you about the drum circle?" Sahara asks, turning to A.Z.

"What?" A.Z. says. She feels suddenly embarrassed—like she announced to everyone, or at least really loudly in her mind, that Kristoff had come to see her. "Did he come by Seven Happiness?"

"He was supposed to. He took the highway, and I'm talking to people downtown. We're holding it at the Starfish tonight. They've started construction again, and we're going to use civil disobedience to stop it. Your mom was just telling me how she helped her friend Irene escape from boarding school. I can't believe the Catholic Church took Irene from her mother and put her in the school because her mom reported being raped by the reservation priest."

A.Z. hates it when people retell her her mom's stories. "I can't come tonight," she says. "And anyway, don't you think the workers at the Starfish kind of deserve to keep working? I mean, what if they have moms who don't pay the bills and no dads or whatever?"

Her mom and Sahara both look at her weirdly.

"I mean, we can't all work for free," she says quickly.

She climbs onto the step stool in the 400s, where her mom has cleared most of the top two shelves, and gathers a huge armload of books to further demonstrate how hard she's working as an indentured library servant. This is obviously what Sahara, or someone, ought to be protesting, but Sahara mumbles something about needing to tell other people about the drum circle and waves goodbye.

"Is something wrong?" A.Z.'s mom asks from the counter. She's sorting the books now—laying them out in rows like playing cards for solitaire.

"Yes," A.Z. says. "Even after Dad's article about the stupid potluck, the First-First Southern Baptists just wrote this threatening letter to Thu. What if they boycott her and she goes out of business and I don't even get to save money for Sea Camp? What if I'm just working here for free?" She doesn't mention how busy Seven Happiness actually was this afternoon.

"The Bickses have been trying to boycott the Sea since it didn't dry up in 1956," her mom says in that irritatingly explanatory way she does, "and look how far that's gotten them. Nell is still doing perfectly good business."

"But that's the Miracle Play and the Sea," A.Z. says. She wants to add, *Maybe it's going to be different this time. Maybe you don't know everything, and you're forcing me to work all the time, and I haven't seen Kristoff since Tuesday, and I thought he came to see me, but he really didn't*, but instead, she slams more books into a pile, raising dust.

She's not going to admit it, but nonfiction is clearly disorganized. These are supposed to be dictionaries, but she's just found an old etiquette book, *Date Talk: How to Talk to a Boy, to a Girl*, from 1967. The cover shows a guy wearing a sweater-vest and tie, and a girl wearing one of those off-white polyester blouses that adults pretend aren't see-through. It's obviously totally irrelevant but so is organizing books, so A.Z. opens it.

"What if you know more about missiles than *he* does?" it starts. "Let it be your secret. Remember, this is a *conversation* you're considering, not a midterm test. A lost ski party in the mountains would look for a boy to lead the way out. It's his job. Let him lead in *talk*, as well. Don't lead *him*. (Would you lead on the dance floor?)"

A.Z. isn't sure how to answer. Her relationship with Chris didn't overlap with any dances, so she spent "Wind Beneath My Wings" watching couples circle in the cafeteria. It never looked like anyone was leading, just like they were bobbing together: two buoys in the slightest waves. If she thinks about it, though, she can only imagine Kristoff leading. He's so much taller it'd be hard for her to navigate him.

"You wouldn't believe the things Curtis used to talk to me about," her mom says. She's somehow moved from the counter to right beside A.Z. Her mom isn't a small woman but she has this way of moving silently.

A.Z. tries to jam the book back into the pile, but obviously her mom has already seen it. "He'd drive all the way to my mother's house every Sunday and he still couldn't find anything better to talk about than actuary tables. I could tell even then the muffler was going to fall off that car."

"I can't believe you married him," A.Z. says. "You didn't even love him."

"It wasn't that simple; after Arthur died, I didn't have anything to stay there for. And I didn't want to spend another year at boarding school." Her mom climbs onto the other stool and sighs, like the air is thinner up there. "You can put that one in the giveaway box."

"Yeah," A.Z. says. "It's totally outdated. And so are these dictionaries." To make this point—and to further prove how unfairly hard she's working—she picks up the whole too-tall-to-hold toppling stack. Foreign-language dictionaries crash to the floor around her.

"Anastasia Zoe McKinney," her mom says, just as the bell above the front door rings, which means Sahara is back to tell them more about the stupid drum circle. Her mom climbs off her stool with a stack of books and heads to the front counter.

But then the inner door swings open, and a voice says, "Hiya."

Maybe the acoustics are weird up on the step stool because the voice sounds like Kristoff's.

He's walking toward the back like he knows where he's going. He's wearing his red Converse, and bright yellow jean shorts, and a black T-shirt. A.Z. can see the top of his head above the 700s. She can feel her heart beating in her ears; even though Kristoff is two rows away, and her mom is two rows the other direction, the library feels really small.

"Anastasia," her mom calls, "When you're finished throwing books around, could you find 214.67?"

"OK," A.Z. calls, trying to sound totally natural. She's watching—while trying not to seem like she's watching—Kristoff get a big coffee table art book from the 700s and sit on one of the reading tables you're not allowed to sit on. He pushes his long bangs—the kind she and Larsley named the *hair dog* to distinguish it from the *hair flower*—from his left eye, where they fall right back. They hang all the way to his chin—the way A.Z. has wanted her hair dog to do but it never does because her hair is too straight and her mom won't let her cover one eye because it will lead to bad vision and a lifetime of difficult reading.

She's glad Kristoff doesn't look over because she's pretty sure she's blushing. She climbs off the step stool and walks past the racks of *National Geographic* and finds 214.67 and concentrates on breathing. Then she walks back, really casually, past the reading table.

This time Kristoff notices. He looks up and grins. He doesn't seem surprised to see her, but it's hard to tell.

"This Rothko stuff is amazing," he says.

A.Z. leans in closer, but not so close that it seems like she's trying to lean close. She doesn't feel like she's blushing anymore, but maybe too much blood is still in her brain because she's having trouble focusing. The picture looks like a dark purple rectangle, darker at the edges, a little lighter in the middle, but pretty much purple. "Wow," she says, "that's really purple."

"They're called multiforms," her mom calls from the card catalog. "In the early ones, he used brighter colors, but by the year he killed himself, the paintings are almost all black."

"What?" A.Z. says.

"Yeah," Kristoff says. "She was telling me about it the other day. Rothko was a genius. He said that abstraction is the realism of our times."

A.Z. wants to say, *What do you mean she was telling you about this the other day? How many times have you been here? What are you doing talking to my mom? Does she know who you are? What are you doing here? What am I doing here?*

"It looks kind of like a bruise," she says.

"The world of the imagination is violently opposed to common sense," Kristoff says. "That's part of his manifesto."

Her mom is walking toward them in her peasant blouse and broomstick skirt, pushing the reshelving cart, which squeaks ominously. "Did you find the book?" she asks. "I told your father I'd bring it up to the office. He called earlier for an article about good luck symbols." She sighs. "Not that I should be furthering his attempts to appease people who would think the Easter Bunny was the devil if they hadn't appropriated its pagan symbology in the first century." She brings the cart to a halt beside them and leans in, too.

"At the end of his life," she says, "Rothko created a whole chapel in Houston. The viewer stands in the middle of a circular room of multiforms, which is incredibly moving."

"You've never been to Houston," A.Z. says.

"You don't have to go places to know about them," her mom says. "That's one of the principles of a library." She pushes her bifocals up her nose, even though they haven't really slid down. "Can you watch the library for a few minutes?"

When the bell rings, signaling that her mom has left, A.Z. resists the urge to make sure she's really gone. This has to be a trap; her mom almost never leaves the library, and there's no way she's left A.Z. alone with Kristoff, who is reading aloud from the manifesto: "'Art is an adventure into an unknown world, which can only be explored by those willing to take risks.'"

"That's beautiful," A.Z. says. Obviously Rothko would have wanted to study the Sea, too; he would have built his own raft and gone out to explore the unknown saline parts per thousand. "Why'd he kill himself?"

"Because he was a genius," Kristoff says. "Hey, you smell like egg rolls."

She feels herself blushing again. "I came straight from working at Seven Happiness. This crazy preacher from the First-First Southern Baptist Church in Greenville thinks my boss's Buddha statue is Satan. And he just wrote this note telling her to take her *heathenfilth*—all one word—back to China. She's not even Chinese; she's Vietnamese."

Kristoff laughs like she hoped he would. "Satan Stir-fry," he says. "My stupid mom just bought a set of Snow White lawn ornaments instead of getting us groceries."

"Snow White and the Seven Satans," A.Z. says. "I'll warn Reverend Bicks."

"I think that dude came to our house," Kristoff says, laughing. "We live right down the road from that church. You know, that ugly avocado-green trailer. I told him I'd just moved from Salt Lake City and all three of my moms were at work." He laughs. "That place is weird, too. It's got that big lake like Compolodo."

"Yeah. But that's a lake. This is a sea. You know, early explorers thought the Great Salt Lake was an arm of the Pacific Ocean, but it isn't. It's just the remainder of a larger lake. That's different from a new inland sea."

She realizes, too late, that she sounds like a dumb conversation from *Date Talk*.

"You're really into the Sea, huh?" Kristoff says. "There's this painting I should show you. I found it in a book here the other day."

"Cool," A.Z. says. "How many times have you come in here?"

"I don't know. Two. Three. The librarian won't give me a library card because I don't have a Compolodo address. But the Greenville library sucks."

"So you've been talking to my mom about art?"

"Oh, is that your mom? She seems pretty cool."

A.Z. can't imagine that Kristoff missed all the stuff about her mom taking the book to her dad, but maybe he was concentrating on Rothko. "She's kind of a control freak."

"But she knows a lot about art. My mom just bought a velvet painting of a deer. She paid twenty dollars for it at some garage sale. Hey, check this out: 'It is our function as artists to make the spectator see the world our way not his way.'"

"Totally," A.Z. says. It's exactly what she's been trying to do: get everyone else to see that the Sea isn't just a way to make money or a one-time miracle; it's a living place with currents and algae and salts and plants no one understands because they haven't tried to.

Kristoff goes to find the painting book in the 700s, and he takes a while, so she gathers up the spilled books, then climbs on the step-ladder. She takes down two more books and steps off, and then steps back up for the next two. Down and up. Up and down. She feels like she's on that dumb aerobics show with Richard Simmons, but also like those women in that cabaret play in Fayetteville, who wore fishnet tights and danced on chairs and tables. She's on one of the up-steps when Kristoff comes around the corner with a big art book open. He stands right next to her. From the stepstool, she's just at eye level with him.

The painting shows a raft with a sail—just like she's imagined building, except with emaciated, shipwrecked bodies on it. One man is waving a shirt as a flag, but the distant ship doesn't see. The sky almost looks like it's on fire with these billows of clouds, and waves are churning all stormy green-blue-gold up the sides, and people are falling off and reaching desperate hands out.

It's the most beautiful, tortured image she's ever seen. Like *Man on a Raft*, except more tragic. Like Reverend Bicks's sermon, except a million times better.

"That's amazing," she says, in what must be a whisper because Kristoff says, "You don't have to whisper. The librarian isn't here."

"I wasn't whispering," she whispers. She can't help it. She's looking at Kristoff and that raft, which should be terrifying, and is, but also isn't because maybe they're about to be rescued, and in any case, they're in the middle of the sea. And even though they're maybe dying, they must also feel, somehow, that it's better to be in danger there than safe on land.

Then Kristoff reaches up like he's going to help her get a book from the top shelf but he puts his hand on her shoulder, and maybe it throws her off balance, or maybe he's leaning toward her, but somehow she has her arms around him, and he has his arms around her, and the book is jabbing into her ribs, all awkward between them, but she doesn't care. His eyes are sadder up close, brown shading into other browns, like a Rothko. She thinks about saying this, but she doesn't because somehow they're kissing. Their lips are against each other, dry and kind of awkward, too, and wonderful. And then

Kristoff is just standing beside her, and everything is normal and not normal at all, and she has this terrible fear her mother has walked into the library. But she hasn't. It's just the two of them and the painting of the raft in the aisle of books.

8

There aren't any bicycles in the Greenville Wal-Mart parking lot for the July Fourth Weekend Big Top Blowout Sale, and the tent feels like the outside heat condensed into one white-hot vacuum. A.Z. thinks bikes should be in Automotive, but they aren't, and when her dad asks, the guy tells them Toys. A.Z. thinks this must be a mistake, but he's right. Behind the pink boxes of Barbie tea parties and the Super Soakers are bikes leaning on kickstands and hanging on racks. Only two are on sale: a kids' one and one with red-white-and-blue stripes like the tent.

"It's festive," her dad says.

"It's for retards," A.Z. says.

"It reminds me of a barber's pole," her dad says.

The only kind of cool bicycle is hanging on a rack and costs $125. It's silver with a black seat and a bunch of gears that A.Z. doesn't know how to use.

"Try it," the sales guy says.

The bike is obviously about a million pounds lighter than the beach cruiser, but A.Z. isn't sure what to do with the gears. She's over in Lawn Mowers—pedaling in zero gravity—and has to swerve to avoid crashing into a metal crate of beach balls. She finally coasts to an unsteady stop beside her dad, who's holding a dorky grey helmet.

"Your mother reminded me," he says. The sales guy nods, like he talked to A.Z.'s mom, too.

There's a line, as always, in the express lane, and the cashier is paging Housewares for a woman buying ten rolls of flag-printed paper towels. A.Z. wonders if it's Kristoff's mom but decides Kristoff's mom would be taller, with beautiful black hair.

The line takes forever, and A.Z. starts worrying the bike is too expensive and she won't get better at changing gears and will fall miles behind if she ever goes biking with Kristoff. Or that it'll seem really obvious if she rides from the fish fry to try to find his trailer down the road. Is she really going to knock and say, "Hey, I'm trying out my new bike on your road"?

But then it's her turn, and she pays, trying not to think about what percentage of her savings for a flight to Sea Camp she's spending. It helps a little that her dad buys the helmet and hands her twenty dollars. Maybe he's feeling bad about dragging her anywhere near the First-First Southern Baptists. She's already told him she's not going to eat anything.

In the church parking lot, she looks away from the door that leads to that dim Jesus-vomit hallway. She leaves her helmet—sort of accidentally—in the back of the car and climbs onto the bike, riding unsteadily out onto the gravel road, which smells like burning trash mixed with frying catfish from Sykes Creek.

Despite her nervousness, biking is kind of fun, and she switches gears until it's not impossible to pedal as she rides through a cooler shady patch, and back through a roasting patch, holding tighter to the handlebars for the washboardy parts that she's worried are going to puncture the tires. Maybe she was supposed to get some special kind of tires for dirt roads.

Apparently she's moving faster than she realizes because she's barely ridden at all when she sees an avocado-colored trailer. In the yard is a rusted trash barrel with flames flaring up. And beside that is Kristoff, spray-painting something. She can hear the fizzling, like sputtering fireworks. And then the trailer door opens, and a voice—raspy, like she hasn't talked yet today—comes through the screen: "You're going to set the house on fire, you stupid shit."

Kristoff doesn't look up. He's wearing a Walkman.

"Hey, Shit, I'm talking to you." The screen door opens, and a woman nearly as tall as Kristoff, but not nearly as skinny, comes out. She's wearing cut-off grey sweatpants and a saggy yellow tank top, and her short orange-red hair is sticking up. "You're going to set the friggin' house on fire." She throws her cigarette onto the gravel by the car, which is dark green, with one mismatched black door.

Kristoff finally takes off his headphones. "What?"

"You're not even watchin' the friggin' barrel. And there's some girl here to see you."

Strangely, A.Z. has forgotten that the whole time she's been able to see Kristoff's mom, Kristoff's mom has been able to see her. She has the sudden panicked urge to ride away, but of course, that'd be even weirder. "Hey," she says.

Kristoff's mom slams the door behind her. "Bitch," Kristoff says. Then he smiles—that great smile that comes from nowhere, like he's so tall it has to travel farther. "Check it out." He presses the button on the can, releasing a spray of black, and A.Z. realizes what he's painting.

He stands the dwarf—Grumpy?—upright next to three others and starts on its back. "Multi-dwarves," he says. "I'm making a chapel."

"Cool!" A.Z. says. "I just came from the fish fry—you know, for Fourth of July. Up at the church." She realizes she maybe should have brought him something, but she can't imagine riding with a plate, and besides that might look like charity or like she planned to stop here.

"You go to all the food stuff, huh?"

"Just sometimes." She wonders if she's obviously gained weight since he last saw her.

"Is it free?"

"Yeah, of course."

"Cool. We should go. I'll get my shoes. And Sneezy." He doesn't motion for her to follow but he leaves the door open, and after a few minutes, she walks up the cinder block steps.

The trailer is dim and even hazier than outside, like there's one of those smoke machines the school rents for dances. Kristoff's mom is lying on the couch watching TV.

"I'm going to get some chow," Kristoff says. He sits on the arm of the couch to put on his Converse. "Watch the fire."

His mom stubs out her cigarette and reaches for the pack. She's still staring at the TV, where on *People's Court* a woman is yelling about her no-good husband and waving turquoise lace underwear that obviously don't belong to her because they're about four sizes too small.

"My feet are swollen. I told you," his mom says. She has Kristoff's same almost-drawl. She was probably pretty at one point—before the dyed hair, and sweatpants, and extra weight.

"It's your trash," Kristoff says. "I already watched it all morning and I'm hungry because your fat ass ate all the cereal again."

A.Z. keeps hoping Kristoff will introduce her, and his mom will say, "I've heard so much about you." But his mom is still staring at the woman waving the underwear and Judge Wap-whatever banging his gavel, like he's drumming in unison with her.

Kristoff's mom runs her hand through her hair and coughs for a minute, and then, finally, she glances at A.Z. "I'm sorry he's such a dumbass," she says.

A.Z. isn't sure what to say. There's something conspiratorial about the way Kristoff's mom says it—like she and A.Z. are responsible for putting up with Kristoff. So A.Z. laughs.

And just like that—like this is the most normal interaction in the world—Kristoff opens the door and bounds down the steps. "I hate it when she's off work," he says.

"At least your parents aren't always following you around."

"Yeah, she'd have to get off the couch to follow me." He swings his leg over his bike, which is old and black, with peeling stickers. It doesn't seem to have gears, but somehow he pedals hard and then coasts with his feet off, which looks fun, but impossible.

"I'm still kind of getting the hang of this," she calls, pedaling not as smoothly behind. The first time he doesn't hear her, but the second, he coasts to a stop. He leans over and laughs. "This is for going straight uphill. Here." He reaches down and shows her the right gear.

"Cool. Thanks." She's embarrassed, but she also likes him leaning closer, like he's going to kiss her again, which would be great except that they're within sight of the fish fry.

"We should go biking sometime," he says—as if they aren't already kind of doing it.

She really wishes they could ride the other direction, that she didn't have to work later.

"Yeah," she says. "Do you want my number?"

"Six," Kristoff says, laughing. But then he holds out his hand for her to write on it with a Sharpie he has in his pocket, which is really permanent—almost like a tattoo.

When they get in line by the fish fry kettles, A.Z.'s dad waves; he's talking to Chuck Chuck and the rougey welcome lady. "How's the bike?" he calls, coming over.

"Good," A.Z. says, feeling suddenly really self-conscious. "Uh, Dad, this is Kristoff. Kristoff, this is my dad. Kristoff was helping me with the gears."

She hopes, as her dad balances the foil-covered plates he's holding and shakes Kristoff's hand, that he doesn't notice their telephone number in black Sharpie.

"Hiya," Kristoff says.

"Hi," her dad says. "I used to ride a unicycle."

"Unicycles seem cool," Kristoff says.

"They're great once you get the hang of it. Fortunately, I had all semester to learn. I was playing Feste in a modernized *Twelfth Night*."

A.Z. can't decide if this is awkward or kind of cool. She's pretty sure most dads don't know how to ride unicycles. "Kristoff was hoping to get some fish," she says.

"Oh good," her dad says, handing Kristoff both plates. "Jan insisted I take extras."

"Thanks," A.Z. says. Her dad goes back over to Chuck Chuck, and Kristoff sits on the sidewalk with the black ants, where he eats a whole plate of fish and hush puppies and coleslaw. A.Z. has to look away from the mayonnaise.

"We went to church once," Kristoff says. "My stepdad was trying to ask forgiveness for beating up my mom, so he made us all go."

"Your stepdad beat your mom up?"

"Yeah. He was a jerk." Kristoff runs the fork tines along the denim of his shorts, where the fabric is thinning. He peels the foil off the second plate and bites into another piece of fish, which dribbles oil down his chin.

"Wow," A.Z. says. She tries to think of something more sympathetic and appropriate to say, but before she can, her dad comes back.

"How's the fish?" he asks. He's acting really normal, as if there's nothing strange about her showing up with Kristoff.

"Fried," Kristoff says. He takes another bite, just as, down the road, something explodes with a deep boom.

It shakes the awning of the church—like the aftershock of a bomb. Of course, A.Z. has never heard a bomb, but she's seen the pictures of her grandfather's ammunition ship: smoke pluming for miles. She glances up anxiously.

"Fireworks?" her dad says.

"It's the end of the world as we know it," Kristoff says. He bites into a brownie.

"I hope no one was hurt," her dad says. He looks down the road—clearly hopeful there's a good but not too time-consuming story at the end of it—and gets out his keys.

The fire truck and ambulance are parked in the shade of a black-jack oak by Kristoff's driveway when A.Z. and Kristoff ride up. A small crowd—Kristoff's mom, a Greenville fireman, a guy in a cowboy hat, Larsley's mom, and A.Z.'s dad—are standing by the concrete-block steps. A.Z. is relieved that Kristoff's mom doesn't look hurt; she looks the same as she did an hour ago—tired and pissed off.

"Speak of the devil," she says.

"Had ourselves a little explosion," the cowboy-hat guy says. "Could see it clear over yonder at my place. Fireball big as a Chevy."

A.Z. looks to see if the trailer or car or trash barrel are blown to pieces, but they're all still there.

"What kind of fireball was it?" A.Z.'s dad asks. He has his steno pad out.

"Huge," the neighbor says. "Like one of them mushroom clouds but all orange-yellow."

Kristoff's mom shrugs and shakes a cigarette loose from her pack. "It was up in the sky by the time I seen it. I was going back in the trailer, 'cause it's too damn hot to be standing around outside."

"Yeah," Larsley's mom, Emily, says. "It's roasting out here." She lights a cigarette, too, even though she quit smoking last New Year. "You're lucky the fire didn't spread."

"Yeah, my lucky day," Kristoff's mom says. A.Z. is surprised that no one is really focusing on this: Kristoff's mom could have been trapped in a burning trailer.

"So the explosion came from the barrel?" A.Z.'s dad asks. It's sort of strange to hear him being a reporter in Kristoff's yard—like Kristoff and his mom could be anyone.

"Your dumb cans blew up," Kristoff's mom says, glaring at Kristoff. "You left them lying around the yard."

"Yeah," Kristoff says crossly. "But the yard wasn't on fire." He's sitting on his bike still.

"I didn't call no one," she says. She glares at the cowboy-hat neighbor and then the fireman in a way that's sort of scary but also brave and cool.

"So you threw my paint cans and dwarves in the barrel?" Kristoff's jaw is hardened in a way A.Z. has never seen before—like someone has sketched a firmer line around it. A.Z. glances at the spray-paint-blackened grass and realizes that's why the lawn looked so empty: not only the cans, but also the four dwarves are gone.

"I was cleaning up trash," his mom says. "Landlord's coming on Monday."

"That wasn't trash," Kristoff says. "I was working on a sculpture."

"Looked like empty cans and junk," his mom says. She laughs again, and the cowboy-hat neighbor laughs, too. He obviously really enjoyed the fireball.

"Fuck you," Kristoff says. "Those dwarves were mine. I paid you for them." And then he stands on his pedals and rides fast down the road—away from the church and the highway—churning dust behind him. A.Z. expects him to motion for her to follow him, to leave everyone else in the scorchy front yard. She's ready to climb on her bike and ride, in whatever gear, down the gravel. But she isn't fast enough to start pedaling by the time he disappears. And he doesn't turn around for her.

9

After dinner, A.Z. sits in her bedroom like she's done for the past five nights and makes deals with her speckled trout, Cousteau. If he crosses above the sunken treasure chest, the phone will ring. But Cousteau stays in the corner with Ballard, and nothing happens.

Finally, she turns on the radio and picks four—that old game she and Sahara used to play—and the fourth song is so clearly her message—"Right Here Waiting"—that she listens to another four, which is a waste of time because it's "Opposites Attract."

She imagines Kristoff working on a new sculpture so intensely he hasn't had time to call her. She understands. If someone threw away all her research data, she'd want to get it back. But of course, she hasn't gotten much data yet because she's been sort of distracted.

So she reaches under her bed for the seawater refractometer Mrs. Reuter loaned her and the vials of water she collected at the swimming dock, and carefully calibrates the refractometer using a drop of freshwater. Then she drops seawater on the prism and holds it to the light—angling until she's getting a clear reading.

This should be an epic moment—her first time using the refractometer for her major independent study—but right now, it feels anticlimactic. The refractometer reads just over 35 ppt, average for seawater. And the drop from the other vial—deeper near the sea floor—is thirty-six, slightly more salty—which doesn't make sense if salt evaporates and therefore concentrates near the surface like she's read but could make sense if the salt is highly concentrated and there's not much circulation from currents.

She lies on her bed and thinks about the raft she doesn't have, and Kristoff, who hasn't called, and all the research she has to do, and tries to read *Window in the Sea* until she remembers to feed her fish, realizing midway that she's already done this. She's trying to net the food, which has mostly disintegrated, when the phone rings.

She stubs her toe, running.

The ringing sounds exactly like it would coming from a pay phone, which Kristoff's call would be because he doesn't have a phone because his mom never pays their bill.

"Hello," she says, trying not to sound breathless.

"Hi," her dad says. "The Gordings are rounding up chickens. I guess the ones that have blown off the Chuck Chicken trucks have been making a molting mess on Mud Beach. I thought maybe you'd want to come."

"You thought I might want to come watch chickens get caught?" She can't believe her dad is tying up the line for this.

"Yes," her dad says. "I'm doing a front-page story to go beside 'Fireball Fish Fry.' Greg says chickens can't see in the dark, so the Gording guards are going to net the chickens without flashlights and take them to the Ark Park."

"Why don't they just take them back to Chuck Chicken?"

"I guess there's room now that the flamingo's gone. And Nell says they're her chickens now since they've bred on the beach. I can pick you up. I just need to finish the ad for 'Egg Roll Extravaganza.' Thu's running a special."

"She is?" A.Z. says. She doesn't remember a special during the lunch shift.

"Yes," her dad says. "I was just eating dinner over there, and I told her *heathenfilth* means some people like her egg rolls better than her Buddha, so she should move the Buddha to the kitchen and put out coupons on the front counter instead."

A.Z. wants to point out that this is kind of a violation of Thu's religious freedom, and also Reverend Bicks isn't likely to stop back by, and also now A.Z. is going to have to wash a million extra greasy plates with hot mustard and goopy plum sauce. But she doesn't have a better solution.

Right now, she just feels sort of sad about everything: imagining herself washing egg-roll plates and then coming home to feed her fish and going back the next day to wash more.

"OK," she says. "I guess I'll come with you."

She's stuffing research vials in her backpack—because the darkness of the chicken capture should be useful to sneak away for water samples—when the phone rings again.

"Yeah?" she says, sounding obviously bored so her dad will catch on and quit calling to tell her dumb chicken facts.

"Hiya," Kristoff says.

"Oh," she says, feeling like she's dived off a dock while inhaling and exhaling and holding her breath all at the same time. "Hey! What are you up to?"

"The power got shut off, so I went on a ride. It's really hot outside, too, though, and it's really, really hot in this phone booth."

She doesn't like this fact; probably he'll want to go soon. She has to think of something good to say. "So have you been working on a sculpture with the other dwarves?"

"Sculptures are dumb," Kristoff says.

"Oh," A.Z. says. "Yeah." She feels like she should have thought of this; sculptures are kind of dumb.

"Before the TV shut off, I was watching this crazy show about this woman named Anna Anderson who claimed she was Princess Anastasia, you know, from that Russian family."

"Uh, yeah. That's who I'm named for. My mom was reading this book about the Romanovs when she found out she was pregnant. The *Zoe* part is from my dad, who ate at Furr's Cafeteria in Texarkana while he was waiting for the bus to Compolodo. He was nervous about crossing the border, but this waitress named Zoe said she saw great roles in his future." She realizes she's sort of telling a long story like her mom but she can't help it; it's like if she keeps talking, Kristoff can't disappear off the phone.

"Maybe that's why I thought of you," Kristoff says. "There was this funny part when she was talking about the firing squad, and she said, 'It was all shit, shit, shit.' And the interviewer was looking at her like she was some crazy old bag lady. No one could tell if she really was the princess. I don't even think she knew."

"Wow," A.Z. says. Kristoff has just said he was thinking about her—like when she wasn't around—and even though he maybe didn't know her first name, also, somehow, he did.

"I'm gonna ride out to Gording Way," Kristoff says. "Big Bob says there's this great junk pile by this cave he used to live in."

"On Gording Way? By Nell's house?"

"Who's Nell?"

"You know, the woman the Miracle happened to. She lives by the Sea and doesn't come out much anymore because she's really holy or stingy or whatever. I've never talked to her, but she's the first person who saw the Sea, which is cool."

"Yeah," Kristoff says. "Your mom showed me this *Art in America* about this dude who convinced some rich people to pay him for the idea of digging a ditch across their driveway. He didn't even have to really dig it. They just paid him for the concept."

A.Z. isn't sure how this connects to the Sea. She also wonders when Kristoff was at the library. What if he was there in the past four days while she was at work, and she didn't even know? What if he was looking at *The Raft of the Medusa* all the times she wasn't?

She's been taking breaks from reshelving to memorize the really amazing facts about it: like it was painted by a man named Géricault and based on a real shipwreck off the African coast. There wasn't enough room in the lifeboats, so 150 people packed onto one little raft and almost everyone died, became dehydrated, or went insane— which isn't very romantic or hopeful, but is still amazing. Like Rothko said, it's the sort of risk people have to take to know the world.

"You want to come with me?" Kristoff says. "We can go see some shit, shit, shit, shit."

A.Z. is nervous about riding toward Nell's house, which is probably the last place they should be trespassing. But also she's really happy— even with her burning, knotting legs; her numb butt; her gears that keep slipping when she tries to ratchet them; and her helmet, which she shouldn't have brought, clattering in her backpack. She feels like an oceanographer who is also maybe a princess who is also maybe a person pretending to be a princess who never got shot in the head. She feels like her calves are going to burst, like she's going to hyperventilate and roll backward down the hill, like—when Kristoff stops finally at the top of the next one and calls, "Come on, Anastasia"— she's going to float to the top without even pedaling.

By the time they reach the edge of town—her trailing behind and then catching up each time Kristoff stops for a drink of Mountain Dew—the sky is getting dark.

"Hey," she calls. "Do you have a bike light?" She's not sure how they'll see anything in the woods.

"No," Kristoff calls back. "Light gets in the way of the darkness."

It's true; they can see better when no cars are passing—or at least they can see, just ahead, the curved outline of the Ark Park sign, and four people waving signs and chanting, "Chickens are people, too! Chickens are people, too!"

It's Sahara and the Intense Guy and two junior high girls with flowing skirts and pretty but maybe-not-washed-very-recently hair.

"It's sooo nice of you to come," Sahara says. She hugs A.Z. without setting down her sign, which means A.Z. is hugging poster board that smells like patchouli. If Sahara is surprised A.Z. is riding around with a tall, skinny guy, she doesn't act like it. "You've heard about the chickens, too," she says. Then she hugs Kristoff, too, which isn't necessary.

"Yeah," Kristoff says. "They have really tough brains."

"I know," Sahara says. "No one appreciates that." Then she lowers her voice: "I guess your dad told you. They're bringing the chickens here tonight. It's completely cruel."

"Yeah," A.Z. says. She hopes her dad found her note, taped to the door, saying she'd meet him at Mud Beach. She's worrying about time—that she's been biking so slowly and they're not even at the cave. Gording Way is at least a mile from Mud Beach, down a whole different road, and looking at a junk pile in the dark might take a while.

"We're not sleeping if the chickens can't sleep," Sahara says.

"I haven't slept in three days," Kristoff says.

"You haven't slept in three days?" A.Z. says. This seems as if it would have given him a lot of time to call her.

"We're out of poster board," Sahara says, "but you can use this sign." She hands A.Z. a pizza box top with CHICKEN TORTURERS markered around congealed cheese blobs.

"Thanks," A.Z. says. She half-heartedly waves it because she feels like she has to—even though all the pilgrims are at the Miracle Play, and there's not much traffic. She glances over at Kristoff, who has wandered off by the cages where the chickens are going to be.

"There's an alligator over here," Kristoff calls. "With some pink feathers in its cage."

"Yeah, right," A.Z. says. Her dad would definitely have mentioned if the Ark Park had gotten an alligator.

"You really shouldn't be over there," Sahara calls. "You could get us arrested. Gus Gording told us we have to stay by the road or he'll turn us in for trespassing."

"We should go anyway," A.Z. says. "I mean, we'll try to come back later but we sort of have to be somewhere. Hey, if my dad stops by, can you tell him I'll be out at Mud Beach in a little bit?"

"Sure," Sahara says. "Here—take this flashlight. You can shine it for the chickens to see. You know, they can't see in the dark."

"Yeah," A.Z. says. "I heard."

For a second she feels guilty about not going straight to the beach to try to help the chickens, which really are practically aquatic and everything. But she has important junk to look at.

She's always pictured Nell's land being fancier—not rusted barbed wire, which she's climbing over with shaky legs, and thickets of black walnut and oak, and groundcover of brambles and burrs, and probably a million little deer ticks. The woods feel crawly and dark, like being inside a log. She tries to reassure herself that Nell doesn't have a locked gate—just a cattleguard—so she must not really care about trespassing.

"This way," Kristoff says. "I think." They've left their bikes on the other side of the barbed wire, in a ditch by the road, and he's walking fast through the woods, flickering the flashlight over the tree trunks and branches.

"So Big Bob used to live out here?" A.Z. says, almost running to keep up on her wobbly legs.

"Yeah, when the Sea first appeared, he thought it was an acid flashback." Kristoff laughs. "He didn't realize for a couple of years that there was real water."

A.Z. has never heard this story before, but it makes sense. "Yeah, he's kind of crazy."

"He's a genius," Kristoff says.

"Maybe. He's good at setting up the speakers for dances at school and stuff."

"He sets up all the stuff for the Sea, too."

"For the Miracle Play?" A.Z. says.

"Yeah, and the waves."

"The waves are from wind," she says. "That's what forms waves."

Kristoff laughs. "Reality is arbitrary. Einstein says so."

A.Z. doesn't really see how the wind forming waves can be arbitrary—there's a whole science to it that she's going to study—but, also, she *does* understand. It's like Terrance and the unicorn.

Terrance was twenty when he finally graduated last year, and before that, he was the only kid with a moustache because he'd had to repeat so many grades. He drew his own design for his unicorn tattoo, and he had a T-shirt of a silver unicorn that would have been wimpy if he hadn't been so tough. Once, a kid said, "Do you believe in unicorns?" and Terrance said, "I don't believe there are any right here, but I haven't been everywhere."

Not that A.Z. believes in unicorns—but she understood. There's a lot more to the world than people think: a whole Sea of salts and algae and currents. And even though she knows that Big Bob has nothing to do with waves, she also understands that no one understands exactly how waves form on the Sea of Santiago. Or no one yet.

Kristoff has stopped, and when A.Z. catches up, she realizes they're at the edge of a cliff. The next ground is about ten feet below, and down the hill from there is the Sea: a silvery-black moonlit shimmer between the trees.

"Oh my god!" she says. "It's right there." She's never seen the Sea from anywhere but the Miracle Play and Mud Beach.

Kristoff is peering over, like he's thinking about jumping, but instead he walks along the edge, scrambling down the hillside, which is steep, so A.Z. has to hold onto trees and roots when she follows him. Underneath the overhang is a shallow cave—curved like a natural amphitheater or a shell. The air feels sheltered and cool, and the walls arch around them on three sides—pitted and dark and damp, as if the seawater has just been here.

She sits on the cool stone floor of the cave with her legs dangling and looks out at the water. "This is amazing," she says. "Did you know the caves in this area were created by an ocean that used to cover Arkansas and Missouri millions of years ago? That's what made the area karst."

"I wondered why it was cursed," Kristoff says. A.Z. isn't sure if he knows the word *karst* and is joking, or if he really doesn't know, but it's funny either way.

He's shining the flashlight over the side of the ledge. "Hey, there's a mattress."

She scoots over and peers down. There's not only a dirty, lumpy mattress in the leaves, but also an old washing machine and a bunch of tin cans and boards with nails sticking up. "You could find all kinds of things for art down here." She starts to say "sculptures," but remembers in time.

Kristoff doesn't say anything. He jumps down, which seems sort of dangerous, and then he does this amazing thing: he turns and holds his arms out. For a second, she's weightless, like in *Flashdance*, only without the stupid unitard.

Beyond the mattress, in the moonlight and the flashlight beam, she can see rusted box springs, tin cans with lids hanging off, the fender of a car, and some small bottles that look old-fashioned and medicinal. A.Z. walks carefully around the upright nails to keep from slicing through her Converse, like that girl in her mother's story who stepped on a two-by-four and the nail went all the way out the top of her foot. But then she realizes something obvious.

"We could make a raft down here!" she says. "You know, with all these boards, and maybe a couple bigger logs you could get when you're working at the Starfish."

"I quit," Kristoff says. "Real artists can't work on anyone else's schedule."

"You quit?" A.Z. says. She's about to ask what kind of real art he's going to make instead, when he unzips his backpack and pulls out a rolled-up magazine. In the flicker of the flashlight he's holding in his teeth, A.Z. can see the Compolodo Public Library sticker below *Art in America, 1982*. She tries not to think about how much her mom hates for magazines to be rolled up. She tries not to think about her mom at all, how late it is.

"Check this out," he says. "It's Christo."

A.Z. thinks he's making a joke about his own name, but then she reads the caption: "Christo's Pink." It looks like a sculpture, but maybe she's confused about the line between concept and sculpture.

And anyway, it's one of the most beautiful things she's ever seen: a group of oval islands ringed in bright pink cloth, which folds out into the ocean like a huge, surreal jellyfish, or that algae bloom she saw one time on Jacques Cousteau. Where the beaches would be, a wave of pink ripples out from the land: everything that isn't water distilled into a single electric bloom.

"Wow," she says. "Where is this?"

"Miami."

"It's so gorgeous. Did you see it when you lived there?"

"It was already gone." Kristoff rolls the magazine back up. "That's part of the point. Real art shouldn't be permanent."

He bends over again, leaning into a clump of pokeweed in the middle of the clearing, and picks something up.

When he stands, A.Z. can see it's one of the cow statues from the Miracle Play gift shop, with a leg broken off and cowrie shells dangling from its head where they used to form ears.

"Hey, there's a boat in there," Kristoff says.

"In the cow?" A.Z. says, laughing.

"No," Kristoff says. "In those bushes."

"Yeah right," A.Z. says. She's getting used to Kristoff saying random stuff—like about the alligator, or the Sea of Santiago's waves—because language, like art, is impermanent and arbitrary.

10

"It looks old," Kristoff says. He's stepped farther into the pokeweed, and between the stems, the flashlight beam bobs and swims like a school of translucent fish.

"I bet," A.Z. says. She doesn't want to sound like she thinks he's serious, but playing along is obviously part of conceptual art. "It's probably the boat the Apostle James came in."

"Yeah, it's sort of fucked up."

"Yeah," A.Z. says, squatting to inspect some two-by-fours in the junk pile. "I've always thought the Apostle James part of the story didn't really make sense. A boat wouldn't have had a way to get here before the Sea."

She holds one of the boards up, squinting at it, and then walking it toward the flashlight's haze.

And it's like the Cheshire Cat appearing in *Alice in Wonderland*. One second, there's a two-by-four she's holding, and then the dark stems and clusters of darker pokeberries, and then her eyes adjust and she sees, beside Kristoff's leg, something triangular and white.

Something way bigger than a cow statue or any of the junk. Something prowlike.

"Oh my god," she says—louder than she should without knowing exactly where Nell's house is, how the wind might carry her voice. "You're not serious, are you?"

When she was a little girl, she used to have that dream of a ship appearing from England or China or India—a tall ship that would sail into the Sea, that she'd climb aboard, that would prove the Sea of Santiago was connected to everywhere.

Only this isn't a tall ship. And it's definitely not one of the plastic paddle boats at Mud Beach or the aluminum canoe she and her dad took on Sykes Creek for "Summer Splashes." It's a rowboat with boards so weathered that when A.Z. runs to it and slides her hands along its strakes, they feel splintery and insubstantial, like they don't fully exist.

Although they absolutely do. The paint peels off onto her hands, little white curls and flecks, soft but also stiff, like feathers. "Oh my god," she says again. "Where do you think it really came from?"

"God," Kristoff says. "Or Satan. Or Big Bob."

"Maybe it washed in from some inlet. Or it's an old boat from the Miracle Play. But it really doesn't look like a prop."

"Yeah." Kristoff bends over, pinning the flashlight between his elbow and ribs and pulling the bow, which scrapes clunkily across tin cans and brambles.

"Be careful," she says. "We need to repair it."

"I've got duct tape," Kristoff says. "Duct tape fixes everything."

A.Z. has never heard of using duct tape to repair boats. "We probably need epoxy," she says. "And oars." She only sees one, and it's split all the way up the paddle through the handle.

"Yeah," Kristoff says, pulling again as the bow scudders, nerve-rackingly.

"We have to be careful," she says again.

"It's OK," Kristoff says, "I used to be a carpenter." He yanks, and the bow slams into a rock with a cracking sound. The flashlight bounces from his arm—shining straight into A.Z.'s eyes.

"Ow," she says. "Really, let's stop here." She kneels portside, bailing debris—rusted cans and leaves and pine cones—as Kristoff pulls a roll of duct tape from his backpack and tears a strip with his teeth. He sticks it to the hull, and A.Z. can see, when she shines the light, the fibrous underside between the strakes. "Maybe you should put another strip inside."

He leans in and lays a strip parallel and then another crosswise, then crosswise of that. Technically, this should be sort of sturdy, but the tape doesn't look as if it's sticking so much as floating on the peeling paint. "We should drag it down to the water," he says.

"We have to actually fix it. You know, sand it down and repair the cracks with epoxy and get it seaworthy."

Kristoff doesn't answer. He's pulling the boat again, which lugs toward him with a shuddery but not as scrapey sound. He keeps dragging until he's down on the clay and roots by the shore. Out from under the trees, the moon is brighter, and the boat, even with its weathered paint, glows against the black water—like the first phosphorescence Pliny discovered rising from damp wood.

"We should pull it back up a little," she says, but Kristoff wades the other way—into the Sea—in his boots. "What are you doing?"

"Duct tape fixes everything." He leans over the starboard and hoists himself in, pushing off at the same time, so the boat rocks toward him and then out into the water, almost capsizing.

"Oh my god!" she yells before she realizes she shouldn't yell. "It can't support you."

"It's a boat," Kristoff says. "It's supposed to hold people." And he's right: it's already righting itself—the wide, flat bottom coming to rest again in the water. "Get in."

The water seems different at night, cooler, but also deeper, like even with her shoes against the seafloor, she's drifting. Maybe that's why it's so hard to climb over the side—the boat pitching toward her and away. The first time, she slips back sputtering. The next, Kristoff tries to grab her hand and almost tips them the other way, and then her arms are tired, and she's nervous about spilling more of the Sea over the side, but finally, and not very gracefully, she drags herself up. It's way harder than climbing onto the dock, and she's soaking.

Kristoff starts rowing with the one split oar, which creaks in the rusted oarlock, and they turn in a circle, the Sea and the moon-outlined trees spinning slowly into view and back.

She closes her eyes in the buoyant, turning darkness; she opens them again and looks out across the Sea, which is like the obsidian she imagined, but also not obsidian at all—not solid, but living and shifting below them. The moon scatters silver across the water—sparkling, shifting flashes—like the Sea is sending messages in codes of light. A.Z. has this crazy feeling that if she squints she'll be able to read them; she'll know exactly what the water is telling her.

Even though, obviously, they need to head back to shore, and even though they don't have any way to really row, she sort of wants Kristoff to row them away forever. The waves are swelling and sloshing below them. They're being held—like the boat is part of the water, like a lung in a body.

"There's a fish in here," Kristoff says. He has the flashlight off, and A.Z. isn't sure how he can see this or if he's kidding.

But then she notices the water sloshing against her feet, around her Converse and up her ankles. "Shit," she says. "I don't think the duct tape is working. Maybe you should get out and swim and pull?

We won't find it if it sinks. We might never find it." She suppresses what feels like panic: the darkness taking the boat back as quickly as it appeared.

"I can't swim," Kristoff says.

She laughs, which makes her feel better for a second. "Yeah, right."

"No, really."

"What?" She feels sort of bad for laughing, but she's also worried; they're not too far from shore, but the boat is taking on water fast. She has to stay calm, be the captain. "I'd better climb out and push while you row."

She jumps overboard, a little more gracefully than she got in, sidestroking awkwardly with her right arm while she holds on with her left. For a second, it works.

But when Kristoff starts rowing, the bow swings back around and she loses hold—reaching toward something that is maybe the boat and maybe air, and then the bow swings back again, slamming her. "Maybe you need to get out, too," she calls, "and help me pull."

With neither of their weights, the boat rides higher, the Sea rising to nearly her shoulders. Kristoff is tall enough that his chest is out of the water, and he can shove toward shore with the next wave. With him standing and pushing and her swimming and pulling, they gain some ground, and eventually, the bow scrapes against a root. She lies in the silty water beside it, shaky but euphoric.

"I didn't think it would float," Kristoff says. This kind of doesn't make sense because it means he thought the boat would sink but he got in anyway, but it kind of does make sense because A.Z. thought it might sink, and she got in, too.

"I know," she says. "You know, boats have to sink a little in order to float. That's one of the principles behind flotation." And even though this is a really geeky thing to say, and even though it doesn't really apply to boats with holes in them, it seems sort of profound right now.

And Kristoff must think so, too, because he smiles and leans away from her, so, if they could see anything, they could really see each other. "You know, you're not limited like other people," he says.

11

The guy at Wal-Mart tells her they're out of penetrating epoxy sealer.

"Are you sure?" she says. "Could you ask a manager?"

"Hey," the guy yells. "We got any of that penetratin' epoxy?"

"Back order," the manager yells back.

"Until when?"

"Till when?" the guy calls—like he's got to translate between them.

"Week. Two weeks. Your daddy building a deck?" He nods at the gallon of outdoor latex paint. The metal handle is cutting into her hand, and she should have set it down. She's also holding sandpaper—fine- and heavy-grit because she isn't sure which is better. She's worried the heavier grit will strip the boards themselves away.

She's also carrying, strapped to her backpack, her dad's saw, which she's a little concerned someone at Wal-Mart will think she's stealing. She actually borrowed it, sort of without asking, from the garage this morning, trying to avoid questions from either parent.

She's still reeling from her luck two nights ago: her father was still at Mud Beach when she and Kristoff got there, three hours late—after sitting by their boat and maybe kissing, their lips salty, right there in the water of what might as well be their secret cove that only Big Bob, who doesn't count because he's crazy and lives on the Coreys' land now, and maybe Nell, who doesn't count either, even know about.

The chicken capture had fortunately been a big, slow mess of feathers and nets, and her father believed her when she explained her soaking clothes were from Sahara's protest: obviously everyone had to go swimming in the Ark Motel pool to show that chickens deserve to be in the water.

"Breaststroke for breastmeat," her dad said, scribbling it down.

"Maybe you shouldn't write that," A.Z. said.

She pays for the boat supplies, which are sort of expensive but obviously necessary for her research, and pedals fast—but carefully—with her over-full backpack to Kristoff's house.

He comes to the door after she's barely knocked and picks her up from the top step and kisses her. "I just signed the sky!" he says.

"Cool!" she says. "What?" She wishes she didn't have a job either. She imagines living on the boat together—staying up all night charting phosphorescent plankton.

"Whee!" he says. He spins her around so they're facing the couch, the door, the TV. The trailer is hazy from dust or old smoke or the way the light isn't really coming through the closed venetian blinds. There's a little kitchen to one side beside a bookshelf that's empty except for two Dean Koontz novels and the Greenville phone book. The other books must be in Kristoff's mom's room or something.

The hall is windowless and even dimmer, carpeted the same brown. It feels narrow and flimsy, like the walls aren't quite real. Kristoff's room is also narrow, just wide enough for a single bed and a chair covered in clothes. The floor is covered with stuff, too, including empty Mountain Dew bottles that would be really useful for bailing or as pontoons.

She sets down her heavy backpack. "Did you just say something about signing the sky?"

"Yeah. Yves Klein was this French Dada genius. He and his friends divided the earth and the sky, and he signed the sky, which was the start of his going to the far side of the infinite."

"Wow. That's really cool." She's not quite sure how someone would sign the sky—except with those smoke things that write messages behind airplanes. "Kind of like Christo signing the ocean?"

"He's a poser," Kristoff says. "He's nothing compared to Yves Klein. Yves Klein had a whole exhibit in Paris about the void. There was nothing in it." Kristoff laughs—his eyes dark and shining, even in the dimness.

She tries to imagine an exhibit of nothing: like the empty metal shelf where the penetrating epoxy was supposed to be. She wants to say this, but missing epoxy doesn't seem nearly as cool as a Parisian void.

"He created his own color of blue. People came to the void and drank blue cocktails and looked at nothing."

A.Z. tries to picture a *nothing* blue, but all she can see is the Sea when the water looks super blue in the middle of the afternoon—which is pretty much the opposite of nothing.

"I was going to paint my new sculpture blue," Kristoff says, "but I only had white, and anyway white is the real void. It reflects all colors, so it's really no color at all."

A.Z. sort of wants to ask when, in the past forty-eight hours, Kristoff decided sculptures were cool again and Christo wasn't, and she thinks about mentioning the way refractometers measure the refractive index of water by comparing it to the speed of light through a vacuum, which is basically a void, but instead she says, "I got white paint for the boat, too. And wood glue because they didn't have any epoxy."

"Cool. I got more duct tape. It's in the living room. The sculpture's in the kitchen."

He takes her hand and pulls her in there, opening the blinds so light sifts onto the counters scattered with dirty dishes and Diet Slice cans.

In front of the stove is what looks like a giant angular spiderweb with electrical wires coiling through chicken wire, and a lightbulb dangling off. The whole thing is super bright white.

"Wow," she says. "That's amazing. It looks like octopus tentacles."

"Yeah," Kristoff says. "Big Bob gave me some wires. It took me all night." He closes the blinds and goes back to the living room, sitting on the arm of the couch, the way A.Z.'s mom never lets her because it makes the arm saggy. But Kristoff doesn't care. And his mom doesn't either. The couch was here when they moved in, which is why Kristoff says it smells like dog pee.

A.Z. sits beside him, and Kristoff starts Depeche Mode on the boombox and then he puts his arm around her, and somehow they slide down onto the brown velvety cushions, which have a pattern of little water wheels and barns and don't really smell *that* much like pee.

Lying beside him, A.Z. finally feels like one of those effortlessly waify girls she's dreamed of being since she became almost her current five foot four and a half inches and 120 or 122 pounds in that awful growth spurt in sixth grade. Their faces are centimeters apart: Kristoff's long, dark eyelashes and perfect, sharp nose, and the thin black cloth of his T-shirt against her bare shoulder—soft, but also rough where the hem is torn. His tongue is slippery and tastes like water.

After they kiss for a while, they lie there, and the tape, which isn't Depeche Mode now, switches to a song about two lost souls swimming in a fish bowl, which is exactly how it feels to lie together in the not-quite-clean-fish-tank haze.

"This is so beautiful," she says. "Who is it?"

"Pink Floyd."

"Oh, I should have recognized his voice. I love 'Learning to Fly.'"

"This is back when they were good," Kristoff says. He kisses her again, sliding on top of her. This should crush her, but for some reason, she feels as if she can breathe better than ever—like she's a marine bird with super buoyant lungs. She almost doesn't care if they don't make it to the boat, even though she traded shifts just so she'd have the whole day to work on it.

Kristoff is pulling her T-shirt over her head, and even though she's still wearing her bra—34A, not a bra size you want to think about—she feels naked. Kristoff still has his shirt on, and she wants to take it off but she's nervous. She's never taken anyone's shirt off; she's never had her own shirt taken off.

Kristoff is trying to unfasten her bra, but the hooks are sticking, so finally she helps wiggle it over her shoulders, sitting up, which makes her stomach swell above her shorts. But Kristoff isn't looking at her stomach; he slides the bra over her head, catching it on her chin and her hair. And then the bra is on the coffee table by the ashtray and the copies of *Art in America*. She tries not to think about the mailing labels addressed to her mom.

Instead, she's imagining Kristoff asking her to be his girlfriend. She's chanting in her mind something like, *he loves me, he loves me, I love him*—when she hears a car engine cut off outside the trailer.

"Oh my god!" she says.

"Relax," Kristoff says, with his hand still on her breast.

"There's someone here." She scrambles to sit, pulling herself up on the slippery fabric. How could they not have heard the tires on the gravel? She grabs her bra and runs to the bathroom, which smells cheaply sweet, like air-freshener roses. Her bra hooks don't line up; the little teeth just slide past each other. And then she realizes her shirt is on the couch in the living room, where Kristoff's mom is saying—loudly, so A.Z. has no trouble hearing through the thin, thin door—"Don't make no noise. I've got a migraine."

A.Z. has the terrible realization that his mom is going to need the bathroom. And then what is she going to do? She can't walk out in just her bra and she can't wrap herself in a towel, because why would she be wearing a towel? She tries to send Kristoff desperate brainwaves to bring her shirt, but how can he do this with his mom right there?

But his mom doesn't head for the bathroom. She walks down the hall and shuts her bedroom door. A.Z. gets her bra hooked—finally—by turning it around and staring down at the hooks. She opens the bathroom door, as quietly as she can, and hurries to the living room. Kristoff is sitting on the edge of her shirt, like he didn't even notice it. He looks up and laughs when he sees her.

"Give me my shirt," she whispers. "Hurry."

She's never been so happy to get dressed, and as soon as the shirt is on, she can feel her heart slow. She's safe. She's invincible. Or mostly. She's trying to ignore the swampy feeling in her underwear, which she hopes isn't noticeable and doesn't smell or anything.

"I can't believe your mom showed up," she whispers.

Kristoff is still laughing, which makes her start laughing, too. She buries her face in his arm so the sound won't escape. She's kind of shaky, maybe from relief, or the intensity and nervousness of what was happening. But there's another feeling, too, almost disappointment, like she wishes they could have kept going, just a little further, or that Kristoff would have told her she was the most beautiful person he'd ever seen, that he loved her.

The sanding is easy—the paint is so old it flakes away with the fine grit—and she finishes the bow and sands the starboard, along the grain the way you're supposed to, while Kristoff saws the boards she's gathered to sister to the strakes. She's never seen him do construction up close, and he looks natural: balancing the wood on its end and sawing with smooth, angled strokes.

When he finishes, he helps her sand. A.Z. wishes they'd brought a rag to wipe off the sawdust, but it probably doesn't matter because the glue is like super-adhesive vanilla pudding. The wood they use for smearing it sticks to the boat and then their hands, which stick to the dirt and Kristoff's bandana, which they try to use to wipe them clean. The bottle says it dries in fifteen to twenty minutes, but it's really more like thirty-five in the humidity.

"Water water everywhere and not a drop to drink," A.Z. says. She really wishes they'd brought water from Kristoff's house in addition to Mountain Dew.

They repair the biggest crack in the bottom of the boat, using two pieces of wood just to be safe, but when they move to the crack on the slanted hull, the glue mysteriously loses its stickiness, and the wood slips, like a little waterslide. A.Z. has to lean awkwardly to hold it.

"This is really boring," Kristoff says.

"But we're making progress." She glances at her watch. It's 1:23, the same time it's been the last two times she's checked. "Sort of."

"We should go look through the junk."

"Yeah, but we just got started. I want to do all the gluing today so we can start painting tomorrow and put on a second coat if we need to."

"It's too hot for coats," Kristoff says.

She presses another piece in place while Kristoff goes to look for material to make oars. He comes back, thirty-five minutes and eight seconds later, with an armload of baling wire.

"What about the oars?" she says.

Kristoff shrugs. "My mom bought eight fucking TV tables. They were on sale at Wal-Mart. I'll saw them up." A.Z. doesn't remember seeing TV tables at Kristoff's house and she isn't sure they'll be long enough for oars. But she's also not sure if Kristoff is serious. "We can't watch TV anyway," he says. "The electricity's still off."

"Oh." She should have realized that's why the trailer was so dim. "That sucks." She can't imagine not only no air conditioning but no power at all.

Kristoff shrugs again. He finishes the Mountain Dew, his head tilted back so his black curls fall against his silver hoop earrings, and his wonderful Adam's apple glides in his wonderful neck. For a weird, distracting moment, she imagines running her tongue down it.

Apparently Mountain Dew really isn't thirst-quenching if it's all you're drinking. By the time they bike to the highway, her mouth feels like when the dentist vacuums it with that little hose. She motivates herself to pedal by fantasizing about Tastee Twirl—not French fries or shakes—but a big cup of ice water, the waxy-coated side sweating from the aqueousness of it.

They're just past the High Tidey Laundry when a car pulls up and Angie leans out. "Are you coming to Scotty's?" she calls.

"No," A.Z. says. "We're going to Tastee Twirl."

"We just got more beer! And pizza's on its way."

A.Z. is not going to Scotty's party. She's going to drink a glass of water. And Kristoff is going to eat onion rings. And they're going to talk—very quietly—about the boat and the saline samples they're about to get from way out in the Sea.

But Angie doesn't pull away. She raises her eyebrows and looks from A.Z. to Kristoff in that way that means *nice going* and *aren't you going to introduce me?*

"Hey, Angie, this is Kristoff. Kristoff, Angie."

"Cool," Angie says, smiling. "We're in the back. 107 and 108. See you there!"

"The party is going to be stupid," A.Z. says as soon as Angie leaves. "There's going to be all these jocks. I mean, they're not really my friends, except Angie."

She realizes she and Kristoff haven't really talked about their friends; maybe lost souls in fish bowls don't have them.

"Free pizza," Kristoff says. "I could definitely chow down on some of that."

"I guess," A.Z. says. "I could definitely drink some free water." She pictures those plastic-wrapped, thin-plastic glasses that motels always have. Filling one and standing there drinking it as she talks to Angie and Kristoff.

Maybe the Starfish construction is still hurting business, and Scotty's parents have gone on a trip, because from the back of the motel, the party is super obvious. The doors to two rooms are open, and Scotty and a bunch of other runners are standing on the sidewalk holding beers. A.Z. sees Larsley talking to Liz in the doorway to 108, so she heads to 107.

Inside, the table by the window is covered with empty cans and Dorito bags. There's some nacho cheese dip, but nothing to dip in it, and anyway, the dip has a weird layer of liquid floating on top.

"Gross," A.Z. says.

"Yeah," Kristoff says. He's standing beside her so their arms are almost touching. Even though she doesn't really want to be here, she realizes it's also kind of cool to be at a party with Kristoff.

"You made it!" Angie says, appearing from the crowd. "There's beer in the bathtub." She grabs A.Z.'s hand and pulls, and A.Z. has the presence of mind to reach back for Kristoff's and pull him, too. His hand is warm and a little sweaty, and she feels better holding it.

The bathroom isn't big enough for five people, but two of Angie's friends are also there. Angie fishes Bud Lights out of the icy bathtub, and A.Z. looks on the sink shelf for those glasses, but the only one she sees is unwrapped and full of cigarette butts. Kristoff is already drinking his beer, so she opens hers. She's never tried beer. It's always smelled musty and disgusting, but right now, it's wet and nice.

"It's sort of like water," she says, and one of the guys says, "Yeah. How is American beer like making love in a canoe?"

"I don't know," A.Z. says.

"It's fucking close to water!"

Everyone laughs—including Kristoff—who doesn't look freaked out about being at a party with strangers in a motel bathroom. A.Z. realizes it's the second time she's been in a bathroom today under really weird circumstances. Her head is swimmy and warm, and in the mirror, she sees a big dirt smudge on her chin, which Kristoff really should have told her about. She tries to rub it off, but maybe it's glued on.

"We went on this bike ride today," she tries to explain, but no one's listening

Larsley and Liz have appeared with their arms linked, swaying. "Wow!" Larsley says, doing this really obvious double take, "It's A.Z. and *Muy Fuego!*"

A.Z. hopes Kristoff doesn't know Spanish. It's the first time she's seen Larsley since the other party.

Liz sits on the edge of the bathtub, and Larsley reaches for a beer and almost falls in. And then Gwennie and two friends—wearing stonewashed jean shorts and bikini tops—push into the bathroom, chanting, "Beer run, beer run!"

"Oh my god!" Gwennie squeals. "Kristoff! I didn't know you were coming."

"Me neither," Kristoff says.

None of this makes any sense; there's no way that Kristoff knows

Scotty's dumb cheerleader sister. But Gwennie just said his name. And Kristoff just answered. And he didn't say, "A.Z. brought me." He didn't even explain why he was here.

"You should swim with us!" Gwennie flutters her fingers in a way that looks nothing like swimming.

"Hey, Kristoff," A.Z. says, "Didn't you want to go find food?"

"I've got the key," Larsley says. This sounds metaphoric until A.Z. realizes she's holding the little silver key to the vending machine.

"Cool," Kristoff says, maybe to Larsley but maybe also to Gwennie.

Outside, the machine has obviously been opened several times, and A.Z. gets the last pack of gum, and Kristoff gets two peanut logs and a bag of salted peanuts.

Gwennie, who has also stopped, for no apparent reason, says, "I'm still sooo stuffed from those chips," and wrinkles her nose, the way skinny preppy girls who eat one potato chip talk about it for hours.

A.Z. rolls her eyes at Larsley, which is a reflex from back when they were friends, and even though Larsley probably has to be nice to Scotty's stupid sister, she rolls her eyes, too. But then she goes with Gwennie and her friends toward the pool.

"Come on!" Gwennie calls back loudly. She's standing at the edge now, with her string bikini tied in bows at her skinny hips.

"We should go," A.Z. says. She chews a piece of gum hard, willing it to make her mouth less dry and beer-dusty. She's always loved the idea that human bodies are more than 50 percent water—like seas inside skins—but right now, she feels like 2 percent.

Kristoff is walking beside her, but then he stops and looks back toward the pool.

"What are you looking at?"

Kristoff shrugs. He crumples the wrapper from his second peanut log. From the pool, A.Z. can hear squealing and splashing.

"You never told me you knew Gwennie."

"I don't."

"Yes you do. She knows your name."

"She saw me changing the sign one night. She thought it was funny."

This doesn't make any sense because there's no way that Gwennie is smart enough to get Kristoff's radical nihilist conceptual signs, and anyway, no one is supposed to know that Kristoff was the one changing the signs, and anyway-anyway, that's how A.Z. and Kristoff met. "So you hung out in the middle of the night and talked about signs?"

"Pretty much."

"What do you mean, 'pretty much'?"

"Then we went in the pool."

"You went in the pool?" A.Z.'s voice isn't as soft as she means it to be, but fortunately no one else is on the sidewalk. "But you don't even know how to swim."

"I just stood there. She was drunk, so she just held onto me." He laughs, his great under-pressure laugh that A.Z. thought was special for her but apparently is also for drunk cheerleaders.

No wonder Kristoff still hasn't asked her to be his girlfriend. She's like Gwennie or anyone, except not as skinny or popular. Gwennie isn't limited either. Gwennie with her cheerleading and frozen-hot-dog blow jobs. She's even *less* limited.

And even though there is absolutely no moisture left in A.Z.'s body, she starts to cry. She can't help herself. It's like that impossibly long paper chain the magician pulled from his throat at the show in Branson—all the things she shouldn't say taped to each other and untangling from her mouth: "I thought you liked me," she says. "I was so stupid. I bought a stupid bike to go riding with you, and wasted my Sea Camp savings, and wasted all this time, and kissed you, and went out on the boat with you and everything, and you don't even care. You don't care about the Sea or me or anything. I'm just like a cheerleader to you. I don't even know who you are."

"No one knows who they are," Kristoff says.

"I know who I am," A.Z. says.

12

"Are you OK?" a voice is saying above her. A.Z. can hear the person bending closer, earrings or bracelets tinkling like water. A.Z. wants to open her mouth and drink the sound.

Water: Kristoff splashing in the pool with Gwennie like *Debbie Does Dallas*. A.Z. hasn't seen it but she's heard. She keeps her eyes closed and tries not to picture it, but it's there.

She reaches to rub the gravel from her face, but her arm hurts—her elbow, her hand. She landed on it. She remembers that: the burning, skidding, her bike wheel on the gravel, the horn blaring. She was riding out to the boat. She was crying so hard she couldn't see. And her head was light and strange—like it wasn't quite attached to her body. And her body wasn't quite attached to the bike. She wasn't even slowing for the hills. She was beyond gravity, beyond resistance, beyond Kristoff, who wasn't—she kept checking—following her.

And maybe she overreacted when she heard the horn. Maybe she braked too hard, skidding on the shoulder in front of the Salty Pines Motel, her bike leaning farther and farther.

"I'm fine," she says, "I'm just really thirsty." But when she tries to sit, pain arcs like a Tesla Coil across her palm to her knuckles. She opens her eyes. Sahara is leaning over her. Sahara by the highway, barefoot, ankle bracelets rattling tiny bells as she lifts A.Z.'s backpack into the back of Josh's car.

In the red from the taillights, A.Z.'s hand looks all bloody. Or maybe it is all bloody. She bites her lip, wills herself to sit. She tries not to look at the strips of skin dangling like a bloody version of Christo's stupid pink fabric or like a jellyfish she'll never get to study because she's a one-handed oceanographer with a half-repaired boat and no boyfriend.

"Those chicken trucks should be illegal," Sahara says. "They take up the whole road. You know, I think they're shipping chickens secretly back to Chuck Chicken at night."

"It's really intense," Josh says. He's sitting in the open hatchback.

For once, Josh is right. As A.Z. stands, she can feel her knee intensely burning, intensely refusing to bend.

Sahara looks back over, concerned. "Are you sure you didn't hit your head?"

"No," A.Z. says. "I mean, yes, I didn't hit it." She realizes that she's crying, the tears and snot running down her face, like a pathetic, sniveling child.

A.Z.'s bike doesn't fully fit in Josh's hatchback, so he leaves the back wheel sticking out, and A.Z. holds onto the frame with her good hand. She tries to stop crying in the backseat as Sahara and Josh sing along to Tears for Fears.

At A.Z.'s house, Josh waits in the car, but Sahara insists on coming in. She carries A.Z.'s backpack, from which, fortunately, A.Z. has had the one-handed presence of mind to pull her helmet.

It's 10 p.m., but A.Z.'s mom is not only awake but sitting on the stepstool in the kitchen, talking on the phone; she's shaking her head and saying less than usual, which means it's Catherine, with some crisis about A.Z.'s niece, Abigail, who goes to a magnet music school in Little Rock.

"Rachmaninoff can be challenging for a five-year-old," her mom says, but then she sees A.Z. "Hold on a minute."

Apparently A.Z.'s hand and arm and knee really do look dramatic because her mom tells Catherine she has to go and then hugs A.Z. in a way that is comforting but means A.Z. has to hold her breath and hope the smell of blood and wintergreen gum covers beer and swampiness, the very thought of which makes her want to start bawling again.

"Honey," her mom says. "We need to get the gravel washed out. What happened?"

"She wrecked because of a chicken truck," Sahara says. A.Z. had sort of forgotten Sahara is still standing there. "I'm going to add that to the petition."

A.Z. isn't sure which petition, but she nods. But then she realizes she couldn't sign: her hand is all puffy, skin dangling in ways that seem even more terrifying under the kitchen light.

Her mom goes for a washcloth and hydrogen peroxide, which she streams over A.Z.'s palm like some Halloween dry-ice horror trick. "Ow!" A.Z. says, chewing her gum harder.

"You can't let it get infected," her mom says. "I knew a boy in Arizona who had to have his toe amputated because he didn't clean a cut. You're lucky you were wearing your helmet." She looks right into A.Z.'s eyes—sympathetic but searching.

A.Z. has a flash of fear that Sahara is going to tell her mom the truth, but then she almost doesn't care. She pictures Kristoff splashing in the pool while Gwennie wiggles her fingers.

She winces as her mom lathers soap across her hand and starts to scrub. The washcloth feels like sandpaper—like A.Z. is being stripped to raw wood.

Sahara cringes, too, while trying to look like she's not. "I should go," she says. "Josh is waiting. I'll see you at the protest tomorrow maybe?"

A.Z.'s mom nods, like she's the one planning to protest. "Well, she definitely can't wash dishes or go swimming in that cow pond for a while."

"You could have been killed riding without a bike light," her mom says as soon as Sahara leaves. "When Arthur left my house the night after my mother lied and said I didn't want to see him, he was driving across the desert, probably crying. And the workers who were moving a train across the highway on a siding had only hung a lantern on the other side. They weren't expecting anyone on the highway that late. There was no crossing gate, and absolutely no way for Arthur to know that train was even there until he drove right into it. He broke every single bone in his body on impact."

Of course A.Z. knows this by heart; it's one of her mom's major stories: the tragic death of her newly-out-of-jail-but-not-really-criminal first love. Right now it makes A.Z. cry, not just because of Arthur and her mom but because she doesn't have anyone to cry over.

"All because of one missing light," her mom says, pouring peroxide over A.Z.'s knee.

It stings at first, but then her mom kneels down and scrubs. And maybe A.Z.'s knee isn't as hurt as her hand, but there's something almost gentle and nice about having her mom clean the parts she'd have trouble reaching, like she's a little kid again and will never kiss a boy who likes cheerleaders and doesn't know who he is.

A.Z. is too thirsty to sleep but when she finally gets up for water, she's too hot and her head is pounding. And then she's sleeping. And then she's awake because she's had a nightmare.

She's at Tastee Twirl, and the white plaster cone is spinning, flames coming out the sides. Reverend Bicks is in the parking lot yelling that she's going to Hell, hungry and thirsty, which is true because Gwennie and Kristoff are behind the counter, wearing a bikini and swim trunks. They're reading the paper—laughing over a story about a bike wreck.

"The water's been turned off," Kristoff says when she tries to order some.

At the edge of Nell's field, A.Z. cuts straight for the fence where she and Kristoff used to leave their stupid bikes. It takes her a minute to orient, but she finds the first landmark: two oaks growing from a single trunk; then the triangular moss-covered rock; the grove of blackjack oaks; the hollow, singed trunk that must have been hit by lightning.

She pictures herself kneeling on her good knee by the boat, which she'll somehow manage to carefully turn over, one-handed, even though it's heavy and unwieldy. She pictures herself painting the bow: the white maybe not precise, but shaded, like a Rothko.

Only not like a stupid Rothko. Like nothing connected to Kristoff.

She is not thinking about Kristoff.

She is also not thinking about Angie, who she just saw taking a smoke break outside the She Sells Sea Shells Grill. Angie who smiled like everything was normal and asked where she'd gone at the party. Who put her arm around A.Z.'s shoulder as A.Z. sniveled, like A.Z. vowed she wouldn't.

"You think he went swimming with the caterpillars?" Angie said. "Really?" She stuck her arm out to imitate what Larsley named "gloved caterpillar," which the cheerleaders do at every pep rally: lining up behind each other and extending their arms to peel off their gloves, which for some reason the guys always whistle for.

A.Z. was not, and is not, thinking about that whistling.

"He seemed totally into you," Angie said. "But guys are dumb. You know, Skip asked me out the other night, but now he's all serious about some girl in Fayetteville." She sighed, blowing smoke toward the sky.

Angie had never smoked, as far as A.Z. knew, but it didn't seem strange. The smoke smelled like the Catholic church, incensey.

"I'm sorry," A.Z. said, still sniveling.

Angie shrugged. "I don't have time for a relationship anyway. I have to save money to get out of here." She looked around, like she literally meant the parking lot.

A.Z. *is* thinking about Angie waving goodbye, lighting another cigarette, saying the cloves are supposed to burn holes in your lungs, "but they give us longer breaks if we smoke." A.Z. is thinking about how lucky she is to have not just a few minutes, but days off from washing dishes. Even if she's sort of handicapped, even if she might need to apply to Sea Camp on some special scholarship, at least she can focus on her boat.

She's not going to be like Larsley or Sahara or Catherine, before she divorced Dan the taxi man: all wrapped up in being some dumb couple. She doesn't have time for work or a relationship either. She's a solo oceanographer. And the gallon of paint in her backpack feels—even if it's objectively behind her—like a weight pulling her forward.

She's scrambling the last steep part of the hill, about to jump to the leaves beside the cave, when she sees Kristoff.

He's lying on the lumpy, dirty mattress, reading some book that looks like it came from a shipwreck—water-warped, with rippled pages.

"Hey," he says. "This bed is pretty comfy, except for the mush-rooms."

He's wearing the same yellow jean shorts and red shirt from the day before. Maybe he's been here since the party. Maybe he came back here—to their cave—with Gwennie.

"What are you doing here?" A.Z. says, even though she doesn't care.

"I was painting the shore pink, but I ran out of spray paint."

"I thought Christo was a poser."

"He is."

"So did you have a good swim with Gwennie?" She doesn't mean to say this.

"I don't know." He sets the book on his head, shielding his eyes from the sun.

"You don't know what?"

"I didn't go. I was tired." He yawns, as if to demonstrate this.

"So is that why you didn't follow me?" She really doesn't mean to say this either.

"You rode off. You seemed like you wanted to be alone."

"You seemed like you wanted to be with Gwennie."

Kristoff laughs. "You're really obsessed with Gwennie."

"*I'm* not the one obsessed with Gwennie. You're the one who went in the pool with her in the middle of the night and then kept staring at her in her bikini like you wanted to get back together with her."

"I was seeing if the vending machine was still open." He yawns again.

"Oh." She wants to say something way better. But she feels stupid. What if he really was just looking at the vending machine? What if he was still hungry after all their biking and his mom never buying groceries? "But you went in the pool with her before."

"Yeah, just for a few minutes. She was really drunk and passed out and snored after she tried to kiss me." He imitates the snoring, like this is in any way funny.

"You didn't say she tried to kiss you!"

"Yeah, I didn't get that far. You walked away like you're doing now."

"I'm not walking away," A.Z. says, although really, she was starting for the boat, which she realizes is also bright pink. Kristoff has painted it this awful, visible color.

"Now everyone can see the boat from shore," she says. "You've screwed it up. Now no one will mistake it for a flock of birds or anything."

"Escaped flamingos," Kristoff says, laughing his gurgly under-pressure laugh. "I don't see why you're so upset about everything."

"I just thought we were kind of dating or something." She definitely doesn't mean to say this either-either.

"Yeah." He unshields his eyes. They look extra dark right now, like the water in deep-sea trenches. Or sadness. "Do you ever have stuff show up in your head and you don't know where it's come from?"

"Uh, sort of." She isn't sure if Kristoff is changing the subject, or if this has to do with them dating, which he's just sort of said they are.

"Sometimes, I get this feeling like I'm falling, like there isn't anything solid in the world, and everything is all black and swirly, and if I don't hold onto something I'm going to get sucked into it. Sometimes I'm not sure I'm real at all."

"Of course you're real," A.Z. says.

"Yeah," Kristoff says, almost like a question. She has the sudden urge to put her hand on his shoulder. Apparently she starts to move her hand that way, because Kristoff says, "What's up with your hand?"

"I got in a bike wreck."

"Shit, shit, shit," Kristoff says more cheerfully. "Did you fly over the handlebars?"

"No. I just skidded." She feels kind of good with Kristoff looking at her hand, making their Anna Anderson joke.

"That's lucky. The last time that happened to me, I thought I was going through the woman's windshield."

"The last time?" She's seen the scars on his legs but she didn't know he'd gone over the handlebars more than once. Don't people die like that?

"The time before that, I was in Salt Lake City, and someone's blown-out tire was in the road. I tried to go around it, but this car didn't see me. That wasn't actually too bad. It hurt worse the time I wiped out on gravel." He lifts his shirt and shows her the raised white lines, which are fainter than on his legs, like a map of currents.

"Wow," she says. She wonders if she'll have a map like that on her hand—if she and Kristoff will have sort-of matching scars. Right now this seems really beautiful and real. Not like a stupid ordinary couple; like a couple who's not afraid to take the risks that Rothko talked about even if it sometimes hurts them.

"It's like the propeller scars on manatees," she says.

"Those weird elephant things?" Most people in Compolodo don't know what manatees are. But of course Kristoff lived in Florida.

"Yeah, I've always wished there were ones in the Sea of Santiago. They'd be safe here because there aren't any motorboats. Did you know they're related to elephants, but they stayed in the water? You know, because it's better in there."

"It probably is," Kristoff says—sitting up and looking out at the water.

"It definitely is," A.Z. says.

"Yeah," Kristoff says. "We should swim like Yves Klein to the far side of the infinite."

A.Z. wants to point out that Kristoff doesn't know how to swim, but it's sort of nice he's saying they should swim together, which he didn't do with Gwennie because he isn't dating Gwennie; he's dating her. "Yves Klein swam to the far side of the infinite?" she says.

"Actually he leapt off a wall into the infinite void," Kristoff says.

"Oh," A.Z. says. This doesn't exactly seem like swimming, but also maybe the void is the same whether it's water or air: a space you can go into if you're brave enough. If you row far enough and then swim far enough toward all the unanswered questions—even if sometimes it's dark and swirly, or seems so infinite you'll never get there.

"We should definitely swim there," she says.

13

A.Z. has been doing a good job keeping her arms crossed when she's around her mom and not discussing her hand, which has become sort of greenish under the bandage, which doesn't make sense because the salt in the seawater should be kind of sterile and healing.

She probably shouldn't keep swimming, but Kristoff has been making good progress. After only three days, he can dog paddle and sort of do the breaststroke—although he likes to pretend he's sinking even when he's not, and come up laughing in that gurgly way that also sort of sounds like drowning.

As soon as they find wood long enough to make oars, they'll be ready to row out with their research vials into deeper water.

Actually, right now, they're ready to eat at the She Sells Sea Shells Grill for clam alfredo night with A.Z.'s parents. It was her mom's idea. She invited Kristoff, which is nice, but nerve-racking, in case Angie is working and says something about A.Z. crying over Kristoff, or in case her mom says pretty much anything, or Kristoff accidentally mentions their swim lessons, or really a lot of other subjects.

"I can't believe Mud Beach is closed because of chickens," Angie says when she drops off the basket of cheese rolls, raising her eyebrows at A.Z. in a way A.Z. hopes her parents and Kristoff don't notice. "We've been slammed with all these pissed-off pilgrims since we opened." She glances at the other tables.

"Mud Beach is closed?" It seems impossible that A.Z. doesn't already know this, but of course she hasn't been going to Mud Beach or hanging out with her dad as much as she used to.

For a second, she pictures Sahara's chicken protest shutting down Mud Beach. But the chicken protest ended days ago. The chickens are all in the Ark Park and her dad already published "Chock-Full of Chickens."

"I guess," Angie says. "I keep getting stiffed because what they really want is somewhere for their snotty kids to make sandcastles."

"But Mud Beach never closes during pilgrim season," A.Z. says.

After Angie scribbles their order and disappears through the swinging doors, A.Z.'s dad leans toward the table to take a cheese roll and stays leaned in. "I'm not supposed to say this," he says quietly, "but the beach isn't closed because of chickens. I got an anonymous call this afternoon." He's almost just mouthing the words at this point. "Apparently the alligator is missing from the Ark Park."

"What?" A.Z. says. "There was really an alligator?"

"Apparently," her dad says, still super softly. "I guess it came after the flamingos."

"The alligator went to Mud Beach?" Kristoff laughs, his mouth full of cheese rolls.

A.Z. can't imagine an alligator loose between the Ark Park and Mud Beach, which is pretty much where the cave is. She's never considered watching for alligators in the water or the underbrush. She and Kristoff could have been eaten together, which is really romantic and terrifying.

"I guess the cage wasn't very well locked, or that's what my anonymous source said." Her dad obviously likes saying "anonymous source." As far as A.Z. knows, this is the first one that has ever called.

"They had an alligator at the Flagstaff zoo," her mom says. "Arthur and I went the summer he was working on a ranch there."

"Who's Arthur?" Kristoff says.

"My first boyfriend," A.Z.'s mom says in a way that makes A.Z. feel weirdly as if she's pointing out that A.Z.'s first real boyfriend is asking.

"I thought I was your first boyfriend," A.Z.'s dad says. He makes this joke sometimes.

Her mom smiles perfunctorily and continues. "He was breaking horses. It's such dangerous work. He'd broken his leg the summer before I met him, but of course that was nothing compared to the way he died." She looks as if she's about to continue that story and maybe embarrassingly lecture A.Z. again about her bike light—which she made A.Z. buy yesterday at Aqua Hardware, which is conveniently in Compolodo but inconveniently way more expensive than Wal-Mart—even though A.Z.'s hand isn't well enough to bike yet.

But before her mom can continue, Kristoff says, chewing into his third cheese roll, "Yves Klein broke his leg, too. He was jumping into the infinite void."

"I've seen some photographs," her mom says. "There's a biography I could interlibrary loan for you."

"Cool," Kristoff says.

"I don't see how it's infinite if he broke his leg," A.Z. says. She doesn't want to question the void, but, from a scientific perspective, landing implies finitude. And she's feeling sort of frustrated with her mom and Kristoff talking about what she thought was hers and Kristoff's story. "I mean, if he landed, isn't the void technically just the air before he hit the ground?"

"Yeah," Kristoff says. "But it was infinite before he landed."

Fortunately, Angie arrives with their side salads, and A.Z.'s mom launches into a story—that at least doesn't have to do with voids—about a new book that speculates Monet had a retinal disease that caused the blurring in his Impressionistic paintings. This is sort of a cool scientific explanation, but her mom goes on about her uncle having the same disease, which got him out of being drafted, while her father had better eyes and wasn't spared.

"I used to think my father was dead," Kristoff says. "Actually, my mom used to tell me he was dead, but then I found out she just hated him."

A.Z.'s mom nods as if it's totally normal to spend dinner talking about dead boyfriends and broken legs and fathers. "Is your mother still working at Chuck Chicken?"

"Yeah. She hoses the brains out." Kristoff laughs, but not his happy gurgly laugh.

"It's hard being a single mother," A.Z.'s mom says. "When Curtis and I divorced, if Rose Barnett hadn't wanted to retire from the library, I would have been in dire straits."

A.Z. is picking at her salad, left-handed, the cherry tomato rolling around like the ball in one of those little plastic maze games. She's always thought cherry tomatoes were stupid.

"I used to walk to the library every day, just as a patron," her mom says—and then as if this relates: "Alligator or not, be careful where you're going on walks. People can be very defensive about trespassing. My brother got shot once in Arizona just for climbing a fence."

"We haven't been trespassing," A.Z. says.

"Private property is overrated," Kristoff says.

"This is impossible to eat left-handed," A.Z. says quickly.

"I'm sorry, honey," her mom says, "but it's actually good to learn to be ambidextrous. Arthur could write with either hand." She clears her throat, like she's gotten a clam stuck in it. "He was so artistic and so misunderstood. You remind me of him," she says, looking at Kristoff.

"How big is the alligator?" Thu asks. She's alternating stirring the chow mein and gesturing so enthusiastically with her long stirring chopsticks that A.Z. is sure they're going to poke either her dad or the grease-splattered Buddha on the shelf above the stove.

"At least six feet," A.Z.'s dad says, "or that's what Sy Gording thought. He spotted it this morning out in the swimming lagoon near the dock."

Her dad has just picked up a Gording Foundation press release, which confirms yesterday's anonymous call. He's gearing up for an emergency edition. He's going to use what reporters apparently call the "second coming" font: letters so big they fill the front page between the header and the fold. It's reserved for unbelievably unique events—like World War III or the return of the Bubonic Plague or an "ALLIGATOR ADVISORY ALERT!"

"Everyone says they're delicious," Thu says. "They have them in Cat Tien, but not Saigon." She pokes the chopsticks in the air again as punctuation.

"I need to go back to the beach," A.Z.'s dad says. "And to the library for 'Magnificent Muscled Mouths.'" He hurries out with his to-go box.

He'd come for egg rolls because he didn't have time to eat breakfast, and A.Z. has come to tell Thu she can't wash dishes for a few more days, until the Neosporin starts working on her hand. Having more time off should be useful, but the alligator means she and Kristoff obviously can't keep swimming, and they're going to have to make extra sturdy oars in case they're out on the water and the alligator tries to attack them like that whale shark did with the *Kon-Tiki*.

"I'll run a special on alligator egg rolls," Thu says. "Many pilgrims will want to come eat them."

"You'd need alligator meat," A.Z. says. "There's just one alligator."

"Green dye and chicken," Thu says cheerfully, setting her chopsticks across the rim of the wok and smiling in that way that changes her face from I-have-to-get-this-stir-fried-in-a-hurry to really pretty. "Sam can make a sign. Alligator wonton, too."

"The alligator is somewhere out in the Sea for sure," A.Z. says when she gets to the cave to meet Kristoff. "Sy saw it by the dock, but now it's disappeared. It must have swum under the buoys."

"Cool," Kristoff says flatly. "Maybe it'll eat someone."

He's leaning against a tree, sketching something that doesn't look like a plan for an oar, unless you can make an oar out of a series of 3-D triangles.

"Except they're keeping the beach closed until they find it. That could take ages. What are you drawing?"

"Art can't be explained."

"I thought you were working on oars." She glances down at her bandaged hand and then at the still-pink boat, feeling kind of anxious. "We still haven't really gone out on the water."

She doesn't admit how worried she is about her research. Maybe she's been one-handed dropping too much or too little water on her refractometer, but the last saline samples she got from swimming tested as 18 and 16 ppt, which is really brackish.

She's thinking maybe the Sea of Santiago is like the Baltic Sea, stratified, with more salt near the bottom. But if she still doesn't have any samples from the deeper bottom, she has no way to prove this.

"Water is overrated," Kristoff says.

"What?" A.Z. says.

"It's overrated."

"Regular water maybe. And pool water and stuff, but seawater is amazing, and it's already July eleventh, and we're still waiting to really research it."

"Research is overrated," Kristoff says.

"Research isn't overrated," A.Z. says. "It's important. It's how you understand the world."

"The world is overrated."

"Is something wrong?"

"Hey!" Kristoff says.

"What?" A.Z. says. But then she realizes Kristoff is looking at something behind her. She jumps—looking desperately for the nearest tree to escape the alligator, which is clearly in the underbrush, about to eat her.

But then a voice says, "Hey!" back, and when she turns, Big Bob is standing by the cave. He's wearing his sweat suit in the sticky heat, with grass stains and dirt stains and better-not-to-think-about stains, and the legs are rolled up like he's been wading, although he isn't wet. He looks different than she remembered: rounder-faced, with a fringe of white-blond hair. It takes her a second to realize she's never seen him without his coonskin cap.

"You smell that fish?" he says.

"What fish?" Kristoff says cheerfully.

"All the fish in the Sea," Big Bob says, smiling and showing his few teeth, which don't actually look like teeth so much as pecan shells. As he walks closer, A.Z. can't imagine him smelling anything over himself: sour and animaly, like the cages at the Ark Park. "Back in Frisco, I only ate what I caught for one whole year. I was building a yacht. That's the life. Twenty thousand miles and the sky for free."

"That's the life for sure," Kristoff says.

"Caught myself a girl, too," Big Bob says. "On New Year's Eve.

This fine Korean girl asked me to dance the dragon dance, and I couldn't say no."

"Cool," Kristoff says. "Are you living down here again?"

"Just passing through for a swim." Big Bob makes a wavy motion with his hand.

"You know there's an alligator out there?" A.Z. says. She's sort of hoping this will make Big Bob leave.

"Yup," Big Bob says. "All sorts of snakes in these woods." He smiles again. This time, A.Z. is positive his teeth really *are* pecan shells. "Nell wants me to make her an underwater sensor."

"Cool," Kristoff says. "We were just about to make oars for this boat."

It's nice that Kristoff is talking about their oars, but A.Z. also wishes he hadn't drawn attention to the boat—even if it's totally visible. She has the irrational desire to throw her body across to try to hide it.

But before she can move, Big Bob turns and lays his grimy hand right on the bow. He pats it, like it's a dog or something. "Nice to see this old thing up and running." He looks out at the Sea and then back. "Now if Nell really wants to catch that gator," he says. "All she's got to do is get a lady alligator and put her up on shore. All the animals in the world understand that language." He sways his pelvis forward and back. "The croc'll come right out."

"Yeah," Kristoff says, laughing.

"You hear me, brother," Big Bob says, heading, finally, toward the water. "Hope you don't mind if I wash my ass!"

A.Z. turns away but not fast enough. He splashes for a minute, and climbs out, drying his hairy white ass with his dirty clothes.

"Sayonara," he calls.

"Sayonara," Kristoff calls.

"That was totally freaky," A.Z. says, once Big Bob disappears up the hill, pulling on his sweat suit as he walks. "I can't believe he just did that."

"What?" Kristoff says.

"What do you mean? Everything. Him taking his clothes off. And that joke about the alligators. It's disgusting. And what if he tells Nell about the boat and that we're down here?"

"He won't," Kristoff says, as though he knows Big Bob really well and Big Bob is actually predictable.

"He might," A.Z. says. "And you're acting like he's your friend and agreeing with everything he says. He's totally creepy and crazy and touching our boat."

"Maybe it's his."

"It's not. Nell has never let anyone out on the water, and he's too crazy to build a boat."

"He built a yacht."

"Maybe," A.Z. says. "But we fixed this boat. It's ours. We just need oars so we can really get out on the water and won't just turn in a stupid circle."

"Everything turns in a circle," Kristoff says.

"No it doesn't," A.Z. says.

"Logic does," Kristoff says.

"Only circular logic," A.Z. says.

"Exactly," Kristoff says.

14

Kristoff must have forgotten what time they were meeting at Seven Happiness the next afternoon. He's an hour late, so A.Z. is standing in the parking lot, finally freed from her new big purple plastic gloves, eating chow mein left-handed. The one good thing about her hand is that she hasn't been eating much.

Finally, she walks over to the P.M./A.M. Kristoff's bike isn't outside, but she wanders around the two aisles just to make sure. Then she walks back to Seven Happiness.

"You want an egg roll and hot mustard?" Thu says when she comes inside. "Very good for clearing out sinus."

It sounds more like "very good for clearing out science," which makes A.Z. anxious. Sea Camp applications are due September first, barely a month and a half away, and with Big Bob appearing and that stupid sort-of fight, they're no closer to oars.

"No, thanks," she says. "I'm looking for Kristoff."

Thu raises her eyebrows with obvious interest.

"This guy I'm dating from Greenville."

"Greenville boys drive very fast on motorcycles," Thu says. She looks happy.

"He rides a bike," A.Z. says. "Maybe he rode down to the library or something." Of course, this is logical: Kristoff went to look at a book about Monet or Yves Klein, or hopefully about oar-making.

She doesn't want to leave when maybe Kristoff is going to show up, so she walks to the newspaper to call the library. "He hasn't been in," her mom says. "Sahara was just here, though. Officer Gibbs is accusing her of letting the alligator out."

For some reason A.Z. has imagined the alligator independently deciding to escape. But of course Sahara did it. Alligators are people, too.

They hang up, and A.Z. stands there wishing she could call Kristoff at the cave, at his house, wherever he is.

She waits for another two hours in her dad's office, trying to read, but the phone keeps ringing with people leaving messages—including Sahara claiming Sy and Greg let the alligator out just so they can shoot it as a trophy.

"They're on the beach with shotguns," Sahara says. "It's inhumane. I'm talking to Dr. Grulkey about how to build a humane trap." Dr. Grulkey is the vet Sahara volunteers for when she's not protesting.

Then Reverend Bicks calls and leaves a long message complaining that the picture of the First Southern Baptists' pecan pie—which A.Z. knows was actually recycled from an old Thanksgiving article—was bigger than the picture of the First-First Southern Baptists' red velvet cake and suggesting that her dad maybe wants to come for another potluck.

Then her dad calls from a payphone—which must mean he's filled or misplaced his steno pad—to remind himself that he should do an article on the interesting fact that there are actually two kinds of alligator: American and Chinese.

Finally A.Z. walks all the way along the highway and down Gording Way and across the fields to the cave.

She checks for signs of Kristoff—a new book he's reading or something—and then she one-and-a-half-handedly pries the lid off the white paint and repaints the pink bow and part of the port side until the paint runs out.

Then she rummages for boards to saw into oars—because the TV stand Kristoff brought down and has been using as a table by the mattress really isn't long enough.

And finally she walks home, which takes extra forever because she keeps thinking about her boat, still oarless in the junk pile; and Kristoff not coming to meet her; and how fast the curves would pass if they were biking together.

What if Kristoff decided biking with her is overrated? What if he's given up on their oars and gone to help Big Bob build that stupid sensor? What if he's gone to do the dragon dance with some less overrated girl?

The next day, A.Z. washes a million plates stained with dyed green chicken meat, and Kristoff doesn't appear and he doesn't call. She checks the library and her dad's office and back at home.

Finally, she catches a ride as far as the beach with her dad—which at least saves her two miles of walking. The beach is technically still closed, but her dad is here to talk again to Greg's older cousin Sy, who is leading the alligator arrest.

A.Z. is planning to leave and walk straight to the cave, but Greg sees her.

"Hey, Squirrel-Jerky," he says.

He's holding his walkie-talkie to his ear, so if it weren't for calling her "Squirrel-Jerky," she wouldn't know he was talking to her.

"I'm going to shoot that gator right between the eyes." He points the antennae of the walkie-talkie like a stubby gun. "Pow! It won't be taxidermied 'til next week, though."

"It's not even dead yet," she says. "Do you even know where it is?" She looks out at the swimming lagoon, which is way more alligator-colored than she ever realized.

"I can't say," Greg says.

She can tell he has no idea.

If it weren't for talking to Greg and Kristoff being missing, standing on Mud Beach when it's closed would be cool—like she's an oceanographer the Gordings have hired to explain where the alligator's best aquatic habitat would be.

Not that she actually knows anything about alligators. And not that she even has very good data on aquatic habitats. The one isohaline she's drawn to try to graph the saline just looks like a stupid crooked line.

Maybe it's her lack of data or Greg talking about shooting things, but she's super anxious the whole walk to the cave. She keeps worrying Big Bob will be in the water washing his ass. And when she tries to convince herself Kristoff will be there instead, like that day after the Gwennie pool thing, she keeps picturing him biking away. Keeps hearing him say, *Research is overrated.*

Big Bob isn't at the cave, but neither is Kristoff. A.Z. forces herself not to cry. She sorts one more time through boards to use for oars, and even though all the wood is too narrow or rotted, she saws into one broader, red-paint-peeling piece that looks like it maybe came from a barn.

She holds it with her right hand, which still can't grip very well, and tries to saw with her left, but the saw slips after a couple strokes and veers terrifyingly down toward her right hand.

This is probably why oceanographers usually work in teams. But she doesn't have a team. *Research is overrated*, she hears Kristoff saying again.

She sets down the board and looks out toward the Sea, and then she has an even more terrible thought. What if Kristoff went in the water by himself? What if they haven't gotten far enough with their lessons, and he tried to practice and drowned? Or got dragged under by the alligator? Why hasn't she thought of this? Right now he's dead in Davy Jones's Locker, drowned in the infinite void, and she's been stupidly here on shore, oblivious.

She runs to the Sea and wades in—risking both legs and hands as she reaches for what keeps not being Kristoff but fortunately also never the alligator—and then she wades back to shore, feeling lonely and uselessly wet, like some sea snail dragging murk and sadness all the way on the long walk back to the highway.

At the Ark Park, no one is protesting, but there's a new, correctly arranged sign: FORMER HOME OF THE MIRACULOUS COMPOLODO ALLIGATOR!

"He'll show up," her mom says when A.Z. comes to the library the next afternoon. She's supposed to be helping with the reshelving now that her hand is sort of better, but she's really late because she walked all the way back out to the Sea and waded around for a second time.

"He probably got busy with a new art project."

"But it's been three days. What if he got eaten by the alligator?"

"Why would he get eaten by the alligator?" Her mom looks at her intently.

"I don't know," A.Z. says. "But maybe he did."

"Maybe he found a new job."

She wants to say, *He doesn't believe in working. He's an artist.* Instead she says, "What if he got hit by a car?" She realizes, terribly, as she says it that it's way more likely. The scars from different states. Kristoff dead by the side of the road. "Or a train."

"There aren't any trains in Compolodo," her mom says. "Don't be melodramatic."

"I'm not being melodramatic. He could have gotten thrown over his handlebars. He could have a concussion."

"I'd worry about yourself first," her mom says. "You're lucky you didn't get a concussion riding around with your helmet in your back-pack."

"What?"

"I wasn't born yesterday, Anastasia Zoe," her mom says. She holds up a book, reads its spine, puts it in place.

"I can't believe you'd accuse me of that," A.Z. says. For the first time, she understands her dad's love of acting. Saying the lines sort of makes them true. And now that she's mad at her mom, it feels good—like something to focus on. "You probably drove Kristoff away with your dumb conversations. You probably freaked him out by saying he reminds you of your dead boyfriend."

"That was a compliment," her mom says. "Kristoff is bright enough to know that."

"What you talk about is creepy. Normal families don't sit around telling creepy long stories. Kristoff and his mom don't even talk to each other."

"That sounds great," her mom says, wryly. "You're certainly loaded for bear today."

"No I'm not!" A.Z. says loudly.

She hates this expression. When she was little, she thought it meant she was acting like a bear, although apparently it has to do with bullet size. In northern New York, where her mom was born, hunting was a genteel thing—not a hick thing like Greg's squirrels and alligators.

"He'll call," her mom says. "You can't control everything. He's his own person."

"You don't know anything about him," A.Z. says. "You don't know anything about me either." And she storms out of the library.

The New Ark Church used to be a feed store before the Miracle, but the New Arkers fixed it up with a steeple, and you wouldn't know, except for the sort of grainy smell.

It's crowded for the special sunrise service, but A.Z. and her dad find folding chairs near the middle. There aren't pews because people need to be able to throw their chairs out of the way if they get caught by the spirit.

"Nell called to say she couldn't be here," her dad whispers, "but she made scallop shell cookies. You have to help me figure out how to write about them without sounding so excited that I upset Reverend Bicks but without insulting Nell."

"I don't eat things at church potlucks," A.Z. says. "Remember?" She wishes she hadn't come, but her dad caught her when she was sitting at the breakfast table at 5 a.m. because every time she tried to sleep she saw Kristoff sinking.

And every time she tried not to see that, she heard him saying, *Exactly,* sort of like he was kidding, but also like he didn't care at all what overrated things she thought.

"Right," her dad says, scribbling something as the minister starts to preach: "We have the gift of healings by spirit. We have the gift of miracles. The gift of tongues. The gift of prophecy. One and the same spirit works all these things. For one who speaks in a tongue does not speak to men but to God; for no one understands, but in his spirit he speaks mysteries."

He doesn't smack the podium and yell like Reverend Bicks, but his eyes roll back and he raises both arms to the sky like he's about to catch something falling.

A.Z. looks up, too, which is when she notices the stained glass behind the altar, which looks more like that melty stuff you do in the oven. It's a cool color of blue, though, like the Sea, and in the center is a big white triangle that is maybe supposed to be an ark, but could also be an abstract splotch or a botched wing or an island.

She wonders if there really are islands in the center of the Sea. If she and Kristoff—if he hasn't left her and also died—will find one. She imagines rowing that far: the distance into the void, which, even if it isn't precisely infinite, might take days to cross. Days during which someone—like obviously her mom—will notice she's missing. Days during which if Kristoff is gone, she'll be the only one rowing.

She doesn't want to start crying, so she stares hard at the white triangle, which could be an island, but looks—the longer she stares— like a sail. Why hasn't she thought of this? She's let the rowing part of the rowboat distract her. Thor Heyerdahl didn't take off across the Atlantic on a raft with stupid, overrated oars.

She pulls her notebook out—hoping everyone will think she's being a geek and helping her dad—and glances at her old *Kon-Tiki* notes. *Canvas and rope. Two small pines for masts?*

"For to one is given the word of wisdom through the spirit," the minister says. "To another the word of knowledge through the same spirit, to another faith by the same spirit. Brothers and sisters, do you feel the spirit?"

He reaches toward two pilgrims in the front row, laying his palms on their heads. Maybe because it's early and she's sleepy, A.Z. imagines for a second that they'll levitate, but their hair doesn't even move.

"I feel the spirit," someone cries from the back. A.Z. twists around, sort of involuntarily, but apparently the spirit came and went really quickly. She twists back. Of course she doesn't believe in the spirit, but the part about wisdom and knowledge seems pretty relevant.

"We have been given the alligator as a sign and wonder," the minister cries. "As proof of the living God among us. It has been sent by God's spirit."

A.Z. wonders if the rest of the New Arkers realize the Gordings are actually trying to shoot the alligator.

Snt sprt, her dad writes. *Signs. Wndrs.*

When A.Z. was a kid and first heard about *signs and wonders*, it seemed obvious the Sea was a wonder. But then she found out that wonders are the truth revealed and aren't supposed to be questioned.

But of course, you have to ask questions to reveal the truth. That's the basis of science. *Leeboard? Daggerboard?* she jots down. *Grommets. Needles. Sail cloth. More rope.*

And suddenly, she can see her future research sailboat clearly there in the hazy, sleepless early morning light of the church, which is bright but also fuzzy like the background in an Olan Mills glamour photo. And before she realizes it, she's crying after all, and the minister is nodding at her sympathetically—his face blurring with the blue glass void and the white sail splotch. Her rowboat-sailboat that, if Kristoff is dead, will be like the Raft of the Medusa, an homage to him, and if he's left her, won't have anything to do with him.

15

A.Z. doesn't talk to her aquarium fish or her plastic seagull—which squawks when you press its belly and is actually really realistic—because she's fourteen and almost a half. Or not usually. But as soon as she gets home from the New Ark Church, she tells them she's going to ride to Wal-Mart. She's not going to be scared. Even though she hasn't ridden in a week and a half—which is bad according to that thing about getting right back on a horse, or in this case a knock-off Schwinn.

She goes downstairs and rolls her bike out of the garage, easing her hands around the levers and riding shakily across the yard. Then she stops, and for the first time ever, puts on her helmet. The chin strap hangs loose, but the little plastic buckle refuses to budge. When she finally manages to yank the ridged nylon down, it pulls too far through the teeth, and when she tries again, it's choking her, which at least seems safer.

She tries not to worry that if ratcheting a chin strap is challenging, rigging an entire sail-rowboat may take longer than she's hoping.

She wills herself to be calm. To think clearly. The highway to Greenville isn't as winding as the one to the Sea. Gripping with her hand hurts, but not as badly as she imagined. After a couple of miles, the biking really does come back. On a few of the flat parts, she feels almost natural—almost like she's gliding or sailing.

She tries not to think about the possible problems with a mast. The added weight and instability. Whether an A-frame, like Thor Heyerdahl used, or a single mast will better withstand the three thousand pounds of pressure that wind can create on open water.

She rides slowly around the curves, the wind tugging at her T-shirt, her body rigged up and safely bracing.

She leaves her bike at the rack by the sliding door into Wal-Mart and goes into the air-conditioned entry, where the old greeter guy in the blue vest calls, "Welcome to Wal-Mart! Happy shopping!"

Welcome to sailing into the infinite void! she imagines yelling back. But of course she doesn't.

She picks out another gallon of paint and some grommets and rope in Home Repairs, avoiding questions about her dad building decks. Then she goes to Fabrics. She'd imagined finding some strong sail-sewing needles, but all the needles look flimsy, like the ones her mom keeps in a tomato-shaped pincushion in case she needs to stitch book bindings.

Finally she chooses a package that claims they can sew through leather and are called Pocahontas, with a picture of Pocahontas in a beaded leather skirt, which kind of embarrasses A.Z.: like the people at checkout will think she's making some kind of costume.

She's carrying the needles, and paint, and grommet, and rope. She's on her way to look at bolts of cloth. When right there between Fabrics and the soft drink aisle—pushing a cart full of stuff—is Kristoff's mom.

She's wearing flip-flops, sweatpant shorts, and a Mickey Mouse

T-shirt. She's holding a sales flyer. She doesn't look like she's in mourning.

A.Z. ducks behind a bolt of fabric with big tropical fruit bowls. She suddenly feels as if she might hyperventilate. Obviously, Kristoff isn't dead. Which means he hates her.

She can feel it. How overrated she is. How overrated everything around her is: as if the room is a huge fluorescent scuba tank pressurized beyond capacity by its overratedness. Bolts of soft T-shirt cotton, and polyester, and curtain linen, and squares of gingham—none of them strong enough to be a sail, to withstand thousands of pounds of wind. All of them ready to blow apart.

She forces herself not to cry. She forces herself to go back to Home Repairs and find a canvas tarp—which costs fifteen dollars, way more than she should be spending—and then she hurries to checkout and runs past the awful happy vested greeter man and pedals home fast with her helmet all crooked.

Fortunately, neither of her parents is there, and she lies on her bed and bawls into her blue-green comforter. Then, when she's cried until she feels like the pearlescent inside of a shell, everything but some tragic iridescent color drained out of her, she takes down her *Encyclopedia of Sailing*.

There's no information about converting rowboats to sailboats, but she reads about leeboards—which seem safer than daggerboards because she won't have to drill through her barely-repaired hull. She takes notes about this, and how to attach a mast, which involves fastening it in front of the thwart and knowing the hull's center of lateral resistance.

Then she goes outside—by the persimmon tree, where her parents can't see if they get home—and lays out the canvas and starts stitching on grommets, which is super challenging because apparently canvas is way thicker than buckskin. She keeps bending the needles, and both of her hands are hurting, but it sort of feels good; her fingers stiff and stinging the way sailors' hands get, the way solo oceanographers' hands get; the canvas becoming three grommets closer to being a sail.

When she finally folds the canvas and goes inside, her mom is home and talking on the phone. A.Z. tries to avoid her mom—like she has been since their fight in the library—but of course her mom is impossible to avoid.

"I was just coming to look for you," her mom calls.

"I'm really busy," A.Z. calls—cutting through the living room toward the stairs and taking them two at a time.

"Oh," her mom calls, just as A.Z.'s about to sort of slam her door shut. "Kristoff is on the line for you. He was just telling me about his new job."

A.Z. closes the door more softly and runs across her room and picks up the receiver and waits, blood pulsing in her hand and head, for the click that means her mom has hung up.

"Hey," she says as calmly as she can.

"Hey," Kristoff says. "Guess who's the new chicken reaper?"

"What?"

"Yeah. You should see the room; there's thousands of chickens hanging from shackles. One hundred and eighty-two a minute come through the stunner, and if they don't get stunned all the way, they're still moving, and they might move their necks out of the way of the guillotine. And if that happens, I have to slit their throats with a knife."

"Jesus." She feels as if she's going to be sick—partly from the description and partly from the mixed-up anger and relief. Kristoff is alive. He's alive, alive, alive. He's called her. He isn't dead, which means he should have called her days and days ago.

"Yeah, it's like your mom's boyfriend breaking horses, except with more blood."

"I don't get it," A.Z. says. "Are you working at Chuck Chicken? Did you apply there?"

"Yeah, the other morning. They hired me on the spot because the other guy quit. I've been training, and now I'm officially the chicken killer. I'm making $6.25 an hour."

"Wow." Six twenty-five is two dollars per hour more than she makes washing dishes, and for a second she wonders if she could kill chickens to pay back what she's spent on the bike and boat and sail supplies. But of course she couldn't. She can't imagine slitting the throat of anything. Hundreds of chickens hanging from shackles, being stunned or whatever. "Why didn't you tell me?" She tugs the cord, straightening the coils so she's away from the doorway and her mom can't hear but not so hard she pulls it out of the wall socket. "You were supposed to meet me the other day, remember?"

"I've been working crazy shifts. This work thing is weird." He laughs.

"I thought you didn't believe in working," A.Z. says. "I thought you were dead. That something must have happened. I was worried." Then she wishes she hadn't. She doesn't want to seem desperate—as if she didn't have anything better to do than worry about Kristoff.

"Me, too. I was so tired by the end of yesterday I was almost hallucinating. I was just telling your mom that. It's like Monet and those paintings."

"I guess." She doesn't see what her mom or paintings have to do with this. She doesn't really like that Kristoff told her mom before he told her. "So you've been working straight through since Thursday?"

"I had last night off. I think I fell asleep while I was eating." Kristoff laughs again, snorting. "I woke up holding a bowl of cereal."

"Oh." She pictures Kristoff eating cereal while she was hanging out with her trout. She tries to imagine being at Seven Happiness all sleep-deprived and having to do some really crazy job—like dismember cows for the beef chow mein—and she thinks that if she were supposed to meet Kristoff, she would still find a way to tell him where she was.

But of course, she doesn't know what it feels like to have to stay up all night working; to kill something. Not just something, but chicken after chicken after chicken.

"Hey, my mom got this two-for-one coupon for Pizza Hut. You wanna come?" Kristoff says.

"Tonight?"

"Yeah. As soon as my mom gets her fat ass ready."

A.Z. doesn't see Kristoff when she first walks in because Pizza Hut is crowded. There's a line of people at the salad bar, scooping croutons and peering at the breadsticks through the sneeze guard, and a few kids running around, climbing on the backs of the booths.

"Can I help you?" the hostess says. She's wearing that awful Pizza Hut outfit—orthopedic black shoes and black polyester pants and a burgundy shirt. A.Z. is really thankful she doesn't have to wear a uniform. She wonders if Kristoff does. Maybe a big rubber apron.

"I'm meeting someone. Two people." She scans the restaurant again and then she sees them—at a booth in the far corner of the smoking section. But it's not just Kristoff and his mom; there's some guy. A big, older guy wearing a trucker cap and overalls.

"They're over there." She takes the menu and wends her way past the salad bar. She's hoping maybe Kristoff will notice her and wave. She's suddenly nervous. They haven't seen each other for four whole days. What if her blue tank top looks too tight? The T-shirt with the Eiffel Tower fit better, but she didn't want to seem like she was wearing it because of Yves Klein.

"Took you long enough," Kristoff's mom says when A.Z. slides into the round booth. She really wants to slide all the way next to Kristoff but she feels weird with his mom there, and this guy, who is wide enough that he takes up most of one side of the booth by himself. He guffaws at Kristoff's mom's joke—which is the only way A.Z. really knows it's a joke.

"Yeah," A.Z. says. "Sorry. My mom wanted me to help with dinner."

"So you already ate?" Kristoff's mom stubs out her cigarette and lights another. The guy lights one, too, from the pack in his shirt pocket.

A.Z. wonders if Kristoff's mom is hoping she'll say she's already eaten so they'll have more pizza for themselves, but A.Z. is hungry, so she tells the truth. "No. I was just helping out."

"Sounds like a good woman," the trucker guy says. "Cooking her man dinner. Don't see anyone around here doing that." He laughs again.

"Shut your fat trap," Kristoff's mom says. "You're getting pizza."

"Pizza I'm paying for," the guy says. He waves at the waiter, who doesn't notice. "What's a man gotta do around here to get more iced tea?"

A.Z. doesn't remember Kristoff ever saying his mom has a boyfriend, and no one is introducing him. She's feeling kind of awkward. Kristoff grinned when she first slid into the booth but he hasn't said anything.

"We should have Money Bags over here pay," Kristoff's mom says. For a second, A.Z. thinks she's talking about her. "Did he tell you he's making $6.25 for that dumb job?"

"Yeah," A.Z. says. "That's really cool."

"You should have seen it," Kristoff says. "The slicer got stuck today, and it didn't go all the way through the neck and the blood was spraying all over the walls." He laughs.

A.Z. feels suddenly really thankful for Seven Happiness, where the grossest things are old bok choy and those black mushrooms and chicken dyed green to look like alligator.

"And then the drain clogged up," Kristoff says, "and the river overflowed to the top of my boots, and we had to mop up all the feathers and dead chickens and stuff."

"The river?" A.Z. says.

"Yeah, there's this trough for all the blood, and sometimes chickens and other stuff floats by. It gets clogged up a lot with feathers, though."

A pimply-faced waiter shows up with two large pizzas—Meat Lovers, with greasy pepperoni and sausage and ham gummed up in the cheese. Right now, they look disgusting.

"More sweet tea," the guy says—already reaching for the pizza and sliding three big slices onto his plate. "And some mayonnaise."

"And Mountain Dew," Kristoff says.

A.Z. doesn't have a drink but she doesn't speak fast enough, and no one notices. She waits for everyone else to take slices, and then she takes the smallest one.

"I'm trying to get Fatso over here to take the day shift," Kristoff's mom says. "But he thinks they're going to make his dumb ass manager of the plucking line."

"Been there eight years this May," the guy says.

"She's just jealous 'cause she can't apply," Kristoff says.

"Why not?" A.Z. says. "They'd probably hire you because you already work there, right?"

"Can't," Kristoff's mom says, biting into the pizza. She's lifted the whole slice off her plate, and it's dripping. "They don't let women do the killing."

"Goes against instinct," the guy says.

"Really?" A.Z. says. "They don't hire women?"

"Yeah," Kristoff says. "In case they have a nervous breakdown or something."

"That's sexist," A.Z. says.

"Yeah," Kristoff says. "But it's probably true."

"It's chicken shit, if you ask me." Kristoff's mom looks at Kristoff and then at A.Z., like she knows A.Z. is with her. It's kind of nice—being the two women against the two men at the table, and A.Z. is trying to think of something else to say when Kristoff's mom says something that pretty much sums it all up: "Just 'cause I don't have a dick."

"Not sure he's got a dick either," the guy says, nodding at Kristoff. "He's a fucking bean pole." He laughs, slurping the end of his iced tea. The waiter must have forgotten the refills.

A.Z. feels like it would be a logical time for her to say something, like that Kristoff does have a dick—which she sort of felt pressing through his pants that one time on the couch—but of course she can't say this, and she can't figure out what else to say.

She tries to make eye contact with Kristoff, but he's reaching for another slice. "You're just too fat to see your dick," he says. His mom laughs, and the guy ignores them, calling to a different waiter about iced tea and mayonnaise, which A.Z. thinks and hopes Pizza Hut doesn't have.

It's weird to hear Kristoff talking like this, but obviously his mom and the guy aren't going to talk about Yves Klein or whatever. For a second, A.Z. pictures her parents—eating spaghetti with homemade tomato sauce and talking about the alligator and the new books at the library.

"Hey," she says, "My dad says the Gordings are officially opening the beach for viewing tomorrow. So people can try to see the alligator if it surfaces." She wishes she could go ahead and tell Kristoff the more important oceanic news—about their sails—but of course she can't.

"What beach?" the guy says, like he really doesn't know what she's talking about, even though obviously it's just seven miles away, and the only real beach for more than 700 miles.

"Mud Beach," A.Z. says. "On the Sea."

"They oughtta allow fishing over there," the guy says. "What good's all that water, you can't even catch yourself a catfish?" He looks at the greasy aluminum pizza tray, where somehow, the two large pizzas have completely vanished.

A.Z. doesn't think this is the time to explain all the reasons why the water really is good, even though she agrees fishing would be reasonable. The waiter is asking if they want anything else, and Kristoff's mom is saying "no" and handing him her coupon. The guy pulls out his wallet, and A.Z. gets out hers because no one has really said they're buying her dinner. "What do I owe?"

"I'll take a fifty if you got it," the guy says. He laughs and begins the process of unwedging himself from the booth. "But I know how it is. You women usually conveniently don't got it. So it's free." A.Z. tries to make eye contact with Kristoff's mom, to reinforce the solidarity of being women, but she's rummaging in her purse for gum.

"Thanks," A.Z. says awkwardly.

But then Kristoff says, "You want to come over?" which is exactly what she's been hoping he'll say.

They climb into his mom's car, which smells like smoke, even with the windows down, and A.Z. and Kristoff hold hands in the back. The darkness and warmth feel safe, and A.Z. relaxes for the first time in days, listening to the country station that Kristoff's mom plays loud enough that no one has to say anything.

The TV is already on when they open the door of the trailer, and for a second A.Z. thinks someone has broken in but then she realizes Kristoff's mom must have just left it on. Apparently the power is working again. It's some drama with a guy shooting and jumping off a bridge, and Kristoff's mom and the guy sit down and start watching it, like they just returned from the kitchen with a glass of water. Maybe it's a rerun, and they already know what's going on.

A.Z. follows Kristoff down the hall, and when he closes the door to his room, she has this feeling they're in a submarine—the two of them in a perfect air-tight chamber, with its unmade single bed, and piles of clothes, and cow skull on the chair by the window.

"Wow," she says. "You have a skull."

"Yeah. I found it in a field by Chuck Chicken. I'm going to paint it yellow."

"Why yellow?"

"Because death is surreal." He sits on the bed and unlaces his boots, which have feathers stuck around the top of the soles. A.Z. tries not to think about what's making the feathers stick.

She sits on the edge of the bed, wondering if she should take her shoes off, too, and looking at the skull, which is creepy, but also beautiful. The snout is flat and broad and tapers to a row of lengthwise ridges, almost like a beak—like some transitional creature between birds and mammals.

"It doesn't really look like a cow," she says.

"Maybe the cow skull is actually the cow, and the other cow is just an illusion we've been conditioned to see," Kristoff says.

She slips off her shoes and scoots back on the bed. It feels different from hers—saggier and thinner. The sheets are warm and feel like Kristoff's sheets, like she can sense his body against them. With her head by his shoulder, she can smell blood and antiseptic soap. It's kind of freaky, but also right—like Kristoff doesn't need to be afraid of death like other people.

"Did your mom and that guy meet at Chuck Chicken?" she asks.

"Yeah. Gerald's a dickwad. My mom always dates dickwads."

No one really uses the word "dickwad" anymore, but Gerald does seem like maybe a dickwad. "Do you really think he's never been to the beach?"

"Probably not."

"Wow," she says. And then more softly: "I've had an idea. Instead of oars, we need sails. We can go way farther and faster. I started today, but it's sort of complicated." She slides her drawing out of her jean shorts pocket—unfolding it to show Kristoff the sketch of grommets she's attaching as cringles for the rope to slide through.

"Cool," Kristoff says. "Fruit Loops! You should add a toucan." Then he grins at her—a grin that reminds her of the best possible undertow. "I thought of a name for the boat."

"You did?" She's spent a lot of her life thinking of names for ships, but weirdly, she hasn't thought to name theirs yet. She's just wanted it seaworthy. But of course they need a name. You can't go on a real research mission in an unnamed boat. And now Kristoff is going to christen it.

"The *Evol Taob*."

"The *Evil Taob*? Like the evil Buddha?"

"But you'd need to be the cruise director, and I need a bow tie."

"What?"

"The Love Boat."

"Oh," A.Z. says, trying to sound super calm, which is hard because she can hear her heart beating in her ears. She wonders if Kristoff can hear it, too; he's leaned his head on top of hers, which is nice, even though it makes her scrunch down the wall.

"Love exciting and new, come aboard, we're expecting you!" he sings.

"Yeah," A.Z. says, still trying to sound normal. She sort of remembers hearing the theme song on TV at some friend's house. She has to remind herself that it's just a song. Just a TV show. Kristoff hasn't exactly said—although also he really has—that he loves her.

"Or we could call it *Disco Baby/Alas, Poor Dwyer/After the War/ Ticket to Ride/Itsy Bitsy*, but we'd have to paint really small," Kristoff says.

"What?"

"It's one of the episodes. My mom used to be really into that show."

"Oh," A.Z. says. "Why does the episode have such a long, weird name?"

"It's a long, weird episode, I guess. They used to have different writers for different sections of the episode, so the stories didn't even match up."

"Wow," A.Z. says. It's like that parallax experiment Mrs. Reuter likes to do where the straw in the glass of water looks like two different straws. It's like a lot of things in life, now that she thinks about it. The parts don't quite match, but also you know that they do.

16

The new sign above the archway to Mud Beach says SEE THE WORLD FAMOUS SEA OF SANTIAGO ALLIGATOR! BEACH CLOSED FOR SWIMMING.

"I have come all zee way from Par-ee to zee your gay-tor," Kristoff says, sounding better than Mr. Finley.

They should arguably be at the cave, cutting one of Nell's small pine trees into a mast, but Kristoff thought it'd be funny to come out here. He's in a really good mood because he finally has the morning off, and they're hanging out.

Apparently the alligator really has become famous. Traffic is dense, crawling into the parking lot, where guys with flags are waving people into spaces that aren't usually spaces.

"Six dollars," the entrance guy says. Beside him is another much smaller sign: VIEW AT YOUR OWN RISK. THE GORDING FOUNDATION AND SEA OF SANTIAGO ASSUME NO LEGAL LIABILITY.

"But there's only two of us," A.Z. says. "Deux personnes."

"Yeah," the guy says. "It's three dollars each to see the alligator."

This is obviously a huge rip-off, especially since no one knows if the alligator will appear, and A.Z. considers saying she has press clearance, but she goes ahead and pays for both of them. Kristoff won't get his first check until Friday.

He's standing right beside her, so close the sleeves of their T-shirts are touching, and A.Z. can't help but think about last night in his narrow submarine room after the *Evol Taob*. How light-headed she felt when he slid his hand inside her underwear. Like they were already somewhere on the other side of the world or so deep under water that the pressure around them would break all their bones if they didn't keep lying against each other.

She wishes the *Evol Taob* had an area under the deck, if it had a deck, where they could sleep at night together—anchored somewhere way out in the water.

On the beach, a crowd of pilgrims and locals are scanning the Sea with binoculars, which the Gordings are renting out from a little stand. A.Z. wonders how they got so many binoculars, but then she remembers that the Miracle Play rents them to people who want to see the lip-syncing actors.

A.Z. isn't sure binoculars would help. Even when she and Kristoff stand right behind the caution tape, the sun is high enough to make the water glimmery, which means the ripples stand out in dark relief, each one like the ridged back of an alligator: a flicker of tail, a snout.

Down by the lifeguard stand, Sahara is holding a sign. When they walk closer, A.Z. can see it says SAVE THE ALLIGATOR! HUMANE RESCUE ≠ HOOKS. No one seems to be noticing. The closest pilgrims are sitting on towels, sunbathing and scanning the water, their kids running around holding the binoculars backward to their eyes and crashing into each other.

"What's the hook about?" A.Z. asks.

"They haven't seen the alligator again," Sahara says. "So they're trying to lure it out with some huge hook from Bass Pro. It's going to die."

"Everything dies," Kristoff says. "If it didn't, there'd be dinosaurs and fifteenth-century people on the beach with us."

"It doesn't deserve this," Sahara says. "Yesterday it ate a whole trout off a smaller fishhook and then disappeared. It's obviously really intelligent."

"Or hungry." Kristoff glances at the empty box of chicken-alligator egg rolls he's holding. They were supposed to be a picnic, left over from A.Z.'s lunch yesterday, but he's already finished them.

"We need to lure it out calmly and humanely," Sahara says. "I read about this guy in Florida who uses blue lights to calm alligators so he can wrestle them. Of course, we're not going to wrestle it. You shouldn't use animals for sports they didn't invent."

"The world needs more Crocodile Dundees," Kristoff says just as A.Z.'s dad hurries over. He has binoculars and a camera around his neck, and about ten open Bic pens in his pocket. Fortunately his shirt is dark blue.

"They're going to start baiting the alligator first thing tomorrow morning," he says, running his hand through his sort of wispy hair, which leaves some of it standing up like there's a strong Sea wind. "I'm going to come take pictures. Apparently Chuck Chuck is donating chickens as bait. Sy says they may need to use two at a time since the alligator is so powerful."

"They could just run an electric current through the water," Kristoff says.

"It'd kill everything in the Sea!" Sahara gasps. "It's capital punishment for nature."

"Yeah," A.Z. says quickly. "I mean, at least they're not doing that."

"We just have to save it," Sahara says—looking out across the water as if she can net the alligator with her compassionate gaze. "It's very intense to be an alligator."

It's 5 a.m., six and a half hours before A.Z. needs to be at work, but Kristoff is working the dawn shift, so it's solidarity to be awake, too, on her way with her dad to the beach.

"Huge humongous hook," her dad says, swerving slightly. He alliterates more when he's tired, like his brain can only really think of one letter at a time. "Alligator alleviation arrives!" He swerves the other way just as a tour bus blares toward them.

A.Z. sort of thinks she should remind him to get some sleep. He was up all night working on the next "Special Sighting Sheet." The last one—with the "Amazing Alligators" feature on Chinese and American alligators—was so popular that, for the first time ever, people took all the papers from the stands. Either that or Sahara took them to line the humane trap. A.Z. didn't have the heart to mention that possibility.

The beach is still locked when they get there, and her dad peers over the fence—the one she and Kristoff climbed on their first date. Of course her dad doesn't have a chicken crate and he's wearing those slippery dad shoes that are not quite tennis shoes and not quite dress shoes, so when he tries to climb up, he just slides back down like a squished bug. He calls out, cupping his hands as if the sound will carry to the beach. Then he walks along the fence and disappears into the trees. A.Z. can't really imagine her dad climbing through the blackberry brambles and over barbed wire, but he doesn't come back.

She gets her bike out of the car and thinks about going ahead and riding to the cave, but she sort of feels like she should wait until her dad reappears. So she sits back in the car, which is hot even though it's early, and looks at her notes about how to use an oar as a rudder—which seems like a good plan if she can epoxy the old, split oar.

After a few minutes, Sy pulls up and honks. "Where's your daddy?" he calls, leaning out.

"He went to find you. I think he climbed over the fence."

"Sheet. I hope Greg doesn't shoot him."

"What? Can't you call Greg's walkie-talkie?"

"Ah, Greg won't really shoot him," Sy says. "And your dad don't look like an alligator, does he? You gonna move that car?"

"I can't. I don't have the keys." This is true, which is good because she doesn't have to admit she doesn't know how to drive.

"Guess I'll have to go around you then." Sy gets out to unlock the gate and paces beside her dad's car like he's figuring angles on a military patrol. Then he gets back in and pulls forward and backs up a bunch of times until he rattles past her with his truck, which is pulling a trailer.

A.Z. doesn't really want to end up on the beach with Greg and Sy and some weird alligator trailer, but she's also getting kind of worried about her dad, so she follows Sy.

Unfortunately, Greg is coming up the beach to lock the gate. "Security," he says. "I figured out exactly how we're gonna get the gator. We're gonna put the hook on the back of the trailer and drag it right out of the water."

"Great," A.Z. says, with what she hopes is obviously sarcasm. "So you're trying to keep it alive now?"

"Depends. If we can get it safely, we're gonna put it back in a cage so everyone can see it. But if we can't, or it surfaces away from the hook, we'll shoot it and stuff it and put it in the plexiglass case I'm building."

A.Z. feels sort of bad imagining the alligator in a cage or dead in a plexiglass case at the Miracle Museum. But she also doesn't want an alligator out in her Sea and a bunch of pilgrims with binoculars scanning for it. Sailboats aren't as low profile as rowboats.

"I've got to go find my dad," she says. She veers toward the fence and walks past the lifeguard stand and the bathrooms, and when she doesn't see her dad, she walks back, following the yellow caution tape, which is already sagging like streamers after a party.

When she gets to the middle of the beach, Sy has backed up the truck to the swimming lagoon where the pilgrim kids with floaties are supposed to be. The truck hulks weirdly by the water, and the tires have dug deep grooves in the sand, so the mud shows through. Greg and Sy and another guy she doesn't know are standing on the trailer doing stuff with ropes and pulleys and a hook maybe five times the size of a fish hook.

"We should have got a hook for the dock, too," Sy says.

"This one'll get him," Greg says confidently, holding up the hook on its metal chain. But then he pauses—looking toward the woods where A.Z.'s dad has just appeared, yelling. He's getting closer but also more out of breath, so it doesn't get easier to make out what he's saying until he's past the lifeguard stand. ". . . tail . . . rocks."

"Hot damn," Sy says. He jumps off the trailer and reaches into the cab for his gun. Greg and the other guy drop the hook and grab their guns, too, and all three of them and A.Z. run toward her dad, who is waving his pen like a magic wand—like he's Prospero.

A.Z. has never been in the woods at the end of the beach before, and they're disgusting—stuck with popsicle wrappers and diapers and feathers that apparently the Gordings are too cheap to pay anyone to clean up.

"Which rocks?" Sy calls. He's at the water's edge, which is bouldery and brambly.

"Over there," her dad says.

"There," Greg says. "I think I seen it."

"Where?" Sy says. And then he laughs. "That ain't nothing but a big old turtle."

"Maybe it was farther down. I'm sure the thing I saw was bigger. It had a tremendous tail." Her dad looks sadly at the water. A.Z. feels bad for him and also a little pissed that she's cut up her legs chasing an alligator that was probably a turtle that wandered into the water.

"I bet it was the gator," Greg says. "I bet he's hiding down by them big rocks." Then he looks at Sy. "I told you we should have searched the shore."

"Suit yourself," Sy says. "No offense, Mr. McKinney, but it was probably just a turtle. We got tricked by one of them the other night, too."

"Maybe," her dad says doubtfully. He looks like he wants to follow Greg but he doesn't.

A.Z. wishes her dad hadn't started the idea of the alligator in the woods by the shore. She really, really needs to move her boat right now. Fortunately, Greg heads down the shore in the other direction.

A.Z. follows her dad and Sy and the other guy back through the trashy underbrush to the beach. They're just passing the restrooms when there's a sound behind them: not quite like a backfire, not quite like a paint can exploding.

"Sheet," Sy says. "What's Greg firing at?"

There's a second shot and a yell, which is almost eclipsed by the shot but hangs in the air. Sy and her dad start running.

Before A.Z. even reaches the woods again, Sy sprints back past the other way. He turns the pickup around and guns it, spinning up sand and parking with the engine idling at the edge of the woods.

A.Z. is expecting to see Sy and Greg and her dad dragging the body of the alligator, all long and snouty, but instead, after a couple of minutes—during which she can hear someone saying, "Shit, shit"—Sy appears, with Greg leaning on him like crutches. Greg's right foot is wrapped in his T-shirt, which is soaking through with a big red splotch.

"The gun misfired," Greg says. "I was just about to shoot the gator between the eyes but I slipped on one of them rocks at the edge." He looks like he's trying to grin, like it's no big deal, but he winces. With his shirt wrapped around his foot, A.Z. can see his pecs, more defined than she would have imagined, between the orange flaps of his hunting vest.

"It's not too deep," Sy says, "but we gotta get him to the hospital." He and the other guy and her dad, who is still holding his steno pad, hoist Greg into the truck, hitting his foot on the door on the way up, which makes A.Z. cringe, even before Greg says, "Ow. Dammit." She can sort of relate because of her hand.

"That was terrible," her dad says, as Sy speeds off. "Misfiring mishap. I'm not sure I can put it in the paper, though. Nell might not want people knowing a security guard got hurt hunting."

"He's really a parking attendant," A.Z. says. "I can't believe he shot himself in the foot. I didn't know anyone ever literally did that." She wonders if Greg really even saw the alligator or was just pretending so it wouldn't be as embarrassing.

They're at the turnoff to the highway when Chuck Chuck, in his big pickup with its chicken decal, honks. "Glad I caught you," he calls. His window is a couple of feet above, so A.Z. can only see his jowls. "You're not leaving already, are you?"

"There's been an accident," her dad says. "I think everyone's going to be OK, but Sy and his crew have gone to the hospital."

"Gator got someone?" Chuck Chuck says, climbing down from his truck.

"No," A.Z.'s dad says. "Not exactly."

Chuck Chuck settles his shoulder against their car and looks sort of disappointed. "You know," he says, "Reverend Bicks was reading your article about the China and Amer'can gators, and he sure doesn't remember there ever being an alligator in the county before."

"No," A.Z.'s dad says, "I think it's unique and unprecedented." He glances at his steno pad, like he's considering writing this down.

"Reverend Bicks pointed out that the Bible warns about this very thing," Chuck Chuck says. "Satan himself sometimes comes in the form of a big old sea monster. A levi'than or a snake or an alligator."

"He does?" A.Z.'s dad says.

"Yup," Chuck Chuck says. "It says so in Genesis and Revelations and that other one. Reverend Bicks told us last night in Bible Study. He says if you give Satan an inch, he'll take your whole county. He says it's plain as day: that Satan statue lured this Chinese Satan alligator right here to this county."

"Chinese Satan alligator," A.Z.'s dad says, like an echo that doesn't want to be an echo.

Chuck Chuck nods, which makes his jowls bob. "I gotta get back to Greenville, but it sure would be a help if I could just unload these pullets with you. Give them to Sy when you see him, would you? We gotta catch that Satan gator fast as we can with this blessed bait."

He goes to the back of his truck and lugs an ice chest to their station wagon. "Thanks, Jimmy," he calls.

When he pulls away, A.Z.'s dad lays his head on the steering wheel. Then he shakes his head back and forth vigorously like he's trying to clear water from his ears after swimming. "Aaah," he says. "Stupid, stupid, stupid."

A.Z. thinks he means Reverend Bicks and Chuck Chuck, but then he sits up and smacks his hand against his steno pad. "Why did I ever mention the Chinese alligator? Why?" he says, sort of looking at her and sort of at the windshield. "This is probably an American alligator, not even a Chinese alligator, and I can't write that it's Satan or Nell will stop advertising and the paper will fold, but if I say the alligator's a wonder, Reverend Bicks will be mad and maybe start a boycott of Seven Happiness, and anyway Chuck Chuck could fire me at any moment because I'm not even a real journalist."

A.Z. has seldom heard her dad say this much at once, and sometimes even in an entire day. "You're a great journalist," she says. "Remember how much everyone liked 'Fantastic Funnels'?"

"Aaah," her dad says again, laying his head back down and thumping it against his steno pad and the steering wheel so hard the horn honks.

17

"Did you hear about Greg?" A.Z. asks. "He actually shot himself in the foot yesterday trying to hunt the alligator."

"It's instant karma!" Sahara says. She's outside Seven Happiness, where A.Z. just got off work, inserting flyers into the newspapers in the box, which is maybe illegal, like sticking things in people's mailboxes. "Nature is saving the alligator until we can finish the trap."

"Maybe," A.Z. says. "What part of the shore are you taking the trap to?"

"I don't know," Sahara says. "Big Bob says he knows somewhere."

"Oh," A.Z. says, trying not to feel super anxious. She can't admit, of course, that she's already worried that Sy is searching the shore; that right now, while she's outside Seven Happiness waiting for Kristoff, Sy is down by the cave finding her pink-white, sailless boat and commandeering it to look for the alligator.

"You know," she says, "it's possible the alligator isn't even still out there. I mean, maybe it's swum down an outlet. It hasn't been definitely sighted for days. Sy thought my dad just saw a turtle, and who knows if Greg saw anything."

"We have to save it," Sahara says—as if its existence is irrelevant to it being saved—as Kristoff coasts into the lot with his hands off the handlebars.

A.Z. realizes when he stops that he's holding a roll of chicken wire under his arm. He's also wearing a yellow shirt with a red splotch in the middle, like he's been shot. Obviously, she just has bullets on her mind.

"You brought it!" Sahara says.

"What?" A.Z. says.

"We ran out of wire," Sahara says, "and Kristoff said they had a lot of old cages at work. I just have to finish flyering, then I'll meet you at my house?" She waves as she climbs on her bike and rides away.

"What's going on?" A.Z. says. "We need to go out to the cave right now. This guy Greg shot himself in the foot trying to get the alligator yesterday, which is the only reason he didn't keep searching the shore and maybe find our boat."

Kristoff laughs, his water-under-pressure gurgle.

"I'm serious," she says, even though Greg's foot is admittedly sort of funny. "We need to be focusing. We still have to finish the sails and cut a tree for the mast. And then we need to sand it and attach it and make sure we've reinforced everything and lined it up with the center of lateral resistance." She's still not 100 percent sure she knows what this really is, but it makes her feel a little better to mention it.

"We should just use a flagpole," Kristoff says. "My mom bought a bunch left over from the Fourth of July."

"Oh," A.Z. says. A flagpole—if it's wooden and attachable to the hull—would be quicker and already made to withstand the wind and everything. "I wish you'd brought it," she says. "Instead of that wire. I don't see why we're helping Sahara."

"The trap is funny," Kristoff says, laughing again. "It's totally conceptual."

"It's not conceptual. She's building an actual trap to catch an actual alligator."

"But alligators eat chickens, and now the alligator is going to be inside a chicken cage."

"Oh," A.Z. says. This *is* sort of conceptual but doesn't change their needing to focus. "So when did you make this plan to help her?"

"Two a.m.? I ran into her and some dude working on the trap when I was out riding around. I couldn't sleep because I keep having this dream where this chicken doesn't die, so I have to keep killing it and killing it, and it keeps squawking. SQUAWK! SQUAWK!" Kristoff takes a drink of Mountain Dew and then grins, which doesn't seem like it matches the story.

"Ugh," A.Z. says. "That's awful." She's starting to see why the chicken killer position has such high turnover. "Is that blood on your shirt?"

Kristoff grins again. "Chicken blood tie-dye."

When A.Z. drops off chow mein for her dad the next afternoon, his office is messier than she's ever seen it—a landslide of papers on the desk and couch, including pictures of humane traps that Sahara brought, in case he wants to write an article called "Alligator Arrest Alternatives."

A.Z. tries not to look at those; she's still resentful about losing an entire afternoon to the chicken-wire trap, which doesn't seem nearly strong enough to hold an alligator.

"I was going to cancel Thu's alligator egg roll ad," her dad says—still typing his usual ninety-five words per minute as he talks—"because it didn't seem good to link her further with the Chinese alligator, but then I realized, I should just make the ad less Chinese."

"Egg rolls are kind of Chinese," A.Z. says.

"Yes," her dad says. "But not if I call them 'American-Asian finger food.' Do you think that's good? Or 'All-American-Asian finger food'? I just won't mention the egg rolls or the alligator."

"Um," A.Z. says. "Sure." She feels bad for her dad but also like trying to convince Reverend Bicks that a Satan-Buddha didn't lure the alligator here might be like trying to convince an oceanographer that the ocean has no water in it.

"And I still need to proof 'Reptile Relatives' for controversy," her dad says. "I need to be careful. Completely and cautiously careful. And I'm half a day late for the drop-dead deadline." He angles his wrist to look at his watch, without stopping typing. "You wouldn't have a minute to look at it, would you?"

"Sure," A.Z. says. She isn't supposed to meet Kristoff at the cave for nearly an hour—way longer than she'll need to edit an article her dad mostly copied from the encyclopedia. She wishes she could tell Chuck Chuck and Reverend Bicks that they should blame the encyclopedia, not Thu, for the idea of a Chinese alligator.

Her dad rifles through the papers, handing her the sort of crumpled article and swiveling around, almost knocking a pile of papers to the floor before swiveling back and typing furiously.

The first section, "Ravenous Reptiles," begins with the fact that alligators weigh up to eight hundred pounds and eat worms, fish, crustaceans, and sometimes birds and deer, all of which—except crustaceans—are plentiful around the Sea. Crocodiles, in contrast, can bite down on prey with five thousand pounds of force per square inch (which, she mentally notes, is more force than wind against a sail) and are ambush hunters. They eat birds and fish and even sharks, and capybara. The two main types are Saltwater and Nile (neither of which—A.Z. checks with herself—seems Biblical, although of course she doesn't really know much about the Bible). There's a third type called Orinoco, which immediately starts that dumb Enya song playing in her head, and which she crosses out just because it makes her feel better.

Crocodiles have a membrane in their mouths that holds their tongues back so they can't stick them out, and can close their nostrils when they submerge. And they have salt glands in their tongues, which are similar to marine turtles but absent in *Alligatoridea*.

She reads this last fact twice to make sure she understands. And then she reads it again.

"If *Alligatoridea* don't have salt glands, then the alligator can't still be alive in a saltwater Sea," she says. "It wouldn't have a way to process the water." She's feeling happy, vindicated. The stupid alligator probably died days ago from drinking saline and has sunk to the bottom, where it's decomposing. Maybe she'll find evidence in her water samples: whatever minerals decomposing reptiles leave behind.

"But I saw it two days ago," her dad says.

"Are you sure it wasn't a turtle?"

"Yes," her dad says. "It was substantially more sizeable."

"Hmm," A.Z. says. She's not sure she believes the alligator is still out there, but if it is, then it can't be an alligator. According to the data, it has to be a crocodile.

She gets the library's encyclopedia off her dad's bookshelf and flips to the section on *Crocodilia* and reads the entry, which makes her shiver. She and Kristoff really could have been mistaken for capybara—whatever those are—and eaten while they were swimming. "If it's alive, it has to be a crocodile," she says.

"Crocodile," her dad says, sort of absently, typing. Then he

swivels around. "Compolodo crocodile! Compolodo crocodile capture. Chinese alligator not Chinese or alligator!"

"Yeah," A.Z. says.

She doesn't point out that crocodiles sound way more dangerous
than alligators. Obviously Reverend Bicks won't like that any better.
She wonders if she should warn Sahara. In fact, she should tell everyone. This is a huge deal: a genuine scientific discovery. The Darwin-
esque kind, not the kind she puts on poster boards for the annual
science fair.

She sort of feels better about the crocodile now that she's discovered it: now that she can think of its salt glands processing the same
seawater she's studying. Maybe she can put this on her Sea Camp
application: experience differentiating between marine and non-ma-
rine reptiles.

She's excited to tell Kristoff, but when she gets down to the cave,
she doesn't see him. For a second, she worries that he's already come
and gone, but then she reassures herself that he's probably just running late, too. His boss keeps turning the stunner down to save electricity, which means Kristoff has to stay overtime slicing throats.

She's sewing grommets to the tarp—jamming the needle as far
as she can on each stitch and then using a rock to press it the rest of
the way, which is easier on her hands but also keeps breaking the needles—and thinking about the flagpole they're going to attach later,
and her amazing discovery, when she hears skittering pebbles.

"Kristoff?" she calls, hoping it's not Big Bob or Sy or limping Greg.

Kristoff doesn't say anything, but she can see him standing on the
ledge of the cave in that same yellow shirt from yesterday, only less
yellow and more covered in brownish splatters.

"Did you bring the flagpole?" He isn't carrying anything, but
maybe he left it up with his bike.

Kristoff shrugs, as if this isn't a yes-or-no question. "People shouldn't own stuff."

"Yeah. But your mom already owns it."

"It doesn't exist."

"What?"

"Nothing exists."

"The boat exists," she says. "And part of the sail. And more of it would exist if we hadn't spent yesterday on the trap."

Kristoff jumps off the edge of the cave and goes over to the mattress, lying back with his legs and boots dangling off. He's obviously in one of those weird bad moods.

"Should we ride back to your house to get it?"

"I don't have a house," Kristoff says.

"Trailer. You know what I mean."

"I don't have a trailer," Kristoff says.

"Your mom's trailer. Whatever. Is something wrong?"

"Yeah," Kristoff says, and then he closes his eyes, like he's going to sleep.

"I don't get what's going on," A.Z. says.

"Yeah, you wouldn't," Kristoff says, crossly. "It's not like your fucking landlord gave you a week's notice to move all your stupid cheap-ass shit somewhere else."

"What?"

"At least your fucking asslord isn't evicting you."

"You're getting evicted?"

"Yeah. We're two months behind on rent, and my fucking mom took all but twenty dollars of her fucking paycheck and spent it on crap at Wal-Mart." He looks at her now—his eyes hard like his voice, like it's somehow A.Z.'s fault or she should know this really obvious fact.

But A.Z. has never known anyone who's gotten evicted. She can't imagine it, although her mom has that story about that girl in Arizona whose mother was an alcoholic, which meant she and the kids eventually had to move into a tent with a goat. "Oh my god," she says. "A week isn't enough time to find another place and actually move."

"No kidding."

"So where are you going to go?" She has the horrible realization Kristoff is leaving. This is why he's in such a bad mood. He's moving back to Florida. She'll really never see him again.

"The moon," Kristoff says.

"Seriously—doesn't your mom have a plan or something?"

"Who cares."

A.Z. tries to imagine having a mom who doesn't pay rent and spends all their money. Even though her mom asks embarrassing questions and tells endless stories, she also does nice things like washing A.Z.'s hurt hand and not grounding her forever for not wearing a helmet. "There must be laws to protect you. Your landlord can't just kick you out with no warning."

"He already warned us." Kristoff sits up and picks up a piece of pinecone from the ground and throws it toward the pine tree in front of him.

"When?"

Kristoff shrugs. "Three weeks ago? Why do you think I got that stupid job?"

"Oh," A.Z. says. She feels like she should have somehow known this. "Why didn't you tell me? I could have helped you."

"It wasn't relevant."

"Of course it's relevant. I'm your girlfriend. I love you." She's never said it so directly and it makes her nervous, but also feels really necessary and sure.

"You shouldn't bother." He's quit throwing the pinecone. He's rocking back and forth with his knees against his chest, like he's crying but without any sound. "I make up shit for no reason. My mom didn't even buy any flagpoles. It just sounded like some stupid shit we'd have."

A.Z. can feel her thoughts stretching over and around themselves like the pink taffy in the window of Sea's Taffy. She feels mad and dumb for not knowing about the eviction and for believing Kristoff, and sad about not having a mast, and even more sad that he still hasn't said he loves her back. And she wants to put her arms around him and make him stop rocking, to balance his body with hers some-how, like chloride mixed with sodium into perfect salinity.

She sits beside him. The bed is super lumpy and sort of damp, maybe from his sweat, and she can feel the box springs really clearly—each spiral jabbing her bare legs.

"This hurts," she says.

"Yeah," Kristoff says. "Pain is reality."

"Yeah," she says. She thinks about Kristoff not able to sleep—rid-ing around hearing the squawk of dying chickens, knowing he was about to get evicted. "I wish you'd told me the truth. We're supposed to be in this together."

Kristoff doesn't say anything. He's still rocking back and forth—looking at the ground.

"Maybe you should move over to Compolodo and get a new job. You could change all the signs to say *crocodile*. I just made a discovery. The alligator is really a crocodile."

"Language is arbitrary."

"But not when it's factual like this," A.Z. says. "Not about species and things. It's like the difference between a lake and a sea."

"Yeah," Kristoff says. He leans his head against his knees and starts to cry. "I suck," he says. "And you always have everything fig-ured out."

"You don't suck," A.Z. says. "And I *don't* have things figured out.

I don't have any real theories about why the salinity is so variable and low, and I still haven't really gotten off the shore." This makes her start crying, too. Then they're crying together, and Kristoff is pulling her toward him, and they're both lying back on the mattress—which isn't as uncomfortable somehow and is also really uncomfortable.

And then Kristoff is kissing her, running his hand up inside her tank top, and under her bra, and down into her underwear, his body sort of everywhere around hers like the perfect temperature of water. Or like they're on the Raft of the Medusa together; like their bodies are life rafts. He's saying he loves her.

She can feel Kristoff's sweat through her shirt, or maybe it's the spots of still-damp blood, which should be disgusting but aren't because they mean she's pressed closer against death, but also life, than she's ever been.

And then it's like that scene in *Clan of the Cave Bear*, which Sahara loaned her in seventh grade because A.Z.'s mom said it was trash and wouldn't keep it in the library. Except instead of the bearskin rug and candlelight, there's a junk pile and a Sea with a crocodile in it, and a mattress with mushrooms growing from the sides and rusted box springs poking through against her back.

18

It's 7 p.m. and really hot in A.Z.'s room, but she's under her sheet with her head anchored below her pillow. She can't ever come out. She's not going to answer the door, even though her mom is knocking.

"Anastasia Zoe," her mom calls. "Dinner is ready."

"I'm not hungry," A.Z. calls. Her face is soaked with threads of snot and tears. She's never going to move. She's never going to face her mother.

"What's wrong?" her mom says, opening the door. "Are you crying?"

"No," A.Z. says, sobbing.

"Did something happen with Kristoff?"

"No."

"But something's wrong."

"Obviously." A.Z. pulls the pillow halfway off.

"OK," her mom says. She sits in the wooden chair by A.Z.'s bed;

A.Z. can hear the slats creak into place. "Did you and Kristoff have sex?"

A.Z. yanks the pillow tighter over her face, gripping the edges so she can't see that she has a mother, a mother who always knows everything because she has special knowledge that normal people who are living their lives for the first time don't.

Finally she says, "I can't believe you'd accuse me of that. You're just like your mother accusing you and Arthur."

"I'm sorry. I'm just trying to help you."

"Go away." She can hear her mom standing up—the slats on the chair creaking again. Her mom doesn't leave, though. She stands beside the bed. After a few minutes, A.Z. uncovers her mouth for air. "I'm scared," she says. "Everything is ruined. My whole life is ruined."

"You've thought that before," her mom says. "Remember when you thought you'd failed that pre-biology test and spent all night crying, and you'd actually gotten a ninety-seven?"

"This isn't some dumb biology test. It's really over. Go away."

"You should come down for dinner," her mom says. "Your father is already refusing to come home until he finishes three more articles. And then there will be three more after that."

"No," A.Z. says, her head still under the pillow. "I'm not hungry." She starts crying harder again, jagged sobs that make her whole body shake.

"Talk to me," her mom says.

"Kristoff got evicted. He and his mom are moving."

"That's awful," her mom says. "But that's not why you're crying."

"I can't explain. You wouldn't understand."

"Try me."

"No," A.Z. says. She's seasick. She's in a boat, but she's still on land. Kristoff is on top of her, which hurts and doesn't. The spirals of the box springs are pressed into her back, imprinting her, like Hester Prynne.

Then they're sitting beside each other. *My body feels weird*, she says. And Kristoff says, *I like the way it feels*, which is really nice, but doesn't mean he understands. She feels as if her body is miles away— like having been so close means now any regular distance between them is farther.

"I can't tell you," A.Z. says. And then she does. Maybe it's the tears that wash it out of her, like water washing over the edge of a boat: "We had sex and the condom tore."

Her mom sighs, like something heavy is pressing the air out of her. A.Z. is glad she can't see her face. "Where was the tear?" she says, sitting back down.

"What?" A.Z. says through the pillow.

"Was the tear up near the opening or down at the tip where the semen is?"

"I don't know." She does; she can picture the tear but won't let herself. The condom, limp and sticky and awful, like a piece of ripped-off skin. Apparently Kristoff got it in sex education in Miami, and maybe it was too old. He found it under his bed. "I don't want to talk about it."

"You need to talk about it. I need to understand. Where was the tear?"

"Down the side. Maybe it tore when he was taking it off. But it could have been torn the whole time. I could be pregnant."

She's never said this word to her mom before. Her mom never sat her down like Dragonfly did with Sahara and showed her that picture book with drawings of bodies. A.Z.'s mom didn't have to because A.Z. had "common sense." She wasn't going to have sex and wind up pregnant like Catherine did with Abigail at nineteen, or her mom did with Catherine at seventeen, which is why she didn't leave Curtis even though she was miserable. And now A.Z. has ruined everything.

Her mom sighs again, but the sigh sounds different, relieved. "You're really young," she says, "and you should have waited to get birth control pills. But if it didn't tear until he was taking it off, then you're probably all right."

This is what Kristoff said, too, but of course Kristoff and her mom aren't the ones not going to Sea Camp, or having an abortion—like Julie Owens, that senior last year, who Larsley said ended up with cramps and strange bleeding, scared and leaking her insides.

"When is your period supposed to start?" her mom says.

"This weekend."

"We'll see what happens, and then we'll go to Planned Parenthood in Fayetteville. You're fortunate to live in a time when the pill is accessible. No one talked about birth control in the 1950s, especially not in a town where people thought God was responsible for creating seas."

A.Z. sort of hopes her mom is going to keep talking. Even though it's all embarrassing and weird, her voice is comforting—like all of this is just another story that has already worked out to be whatever it is. Instead she says, "When did this happen?"

"Today," A.Z. says.

"At Kristoff's house?"

"Yes." She can't tell her mom the truth. "I was helping him pack."

"That was nice of you," her mom says wryly. She sighs again. "I'm sure it's hard for Kristoff to live in such an unstable home. He's had to grow up so fast." Then she pauses and says, "Why did you do it?"

"What?"

"Have sex. Did you feel sorry for him? Did he pressure you? Do you love him?"

"I love him," A.Z. says.

"Good," her mom says. "I barely even kissed Arthur. I thought I'd have all my life."

After both of her parents leave for work and A.Z. finally climbs out of her tear-soggy bed, she goes downstairs and stands in front of the mirror and puts on eyeliner, mascara, and bright green eye shadow—more makeup than she's worn since seventh grade. And then she washes it off because she looks like a slut, because she is a slut. And then she starts crying. She wants to call Kristoff, but he doesn't have a phone, and soon not even a house. She puts the makeup back on, because her face looks weird otherwise, like she doesn't recognize herself, and gets out the comedy and tragedy mask earrings her dad gave her.

Back in junior high, she'd wear the smiling one on the right if she was happy, and the frowning one on the right if she was sad. Today she puts them on without checking, and when she looks in the mirror, she's sad, which makes her cry so hard her eyes puff up.

When she gets to Seven Happiness, she tries to slip back to the sinks without anyone seeing her, but of course Thu is in the kitchen she has to walk through.

"Your father was crazy this morning!" Thu says, lowering the basket of wontons into the fryer with one hand and turning a burner down with the other. A.Z.'s mom must have told her dad about A.Z. and Kristoff having sex. And her dad told Thu. Everyone knows. And Thu is excited: a slutty, pregnant sort-of-almost-fifteen-year-old dishwasher is wonderful gossip—better than Madonna's pointy bra.

"What?" A.Z. says. She feels like she's going to throw up into the wok.

"I told him about the chicken shortage, and he got really upset and ran out."

"What chicken shortage?" A.Z. says. She's confused but also relieved. Thu doesn't know. Maybe her dad doesn't even know.

"The delivery truck didn't come last night, and when Sam called about it, the man says they're out of chickens."

"They can't be out of chickens," A.Z. says. "I mean, my boyfriend works there, and he's been talking about killing a bunch of chickens." She feels self-conscious saying "boyfriend," like the word obviously announces that they've just had sex.

"I don't know," Thu says. "The man says there's no chicken. But I read in the paper they still have chicken to hook that alligator. Maybe they wasted too many on that? It's like Vietnam during the war. Always shortages, and then the army sprayed poison on the rice fields."

Thu never talks about the war. A.Z. usually forgets she lived through an actual one that had barely ended, but was also totally unreal, by the time A.Z. was born.

"And then I told your dad, and he just get very upset and said, 'It's my fault,' but I don't see what he has to do with chickens."

Despite being sleep-deprived and distracted, A.Z. is piecing things together. Unless Chuck Chicken has really run out of all the chickens in the area—which seems doubtful—the First-First Southern Baptists must be pressuring him not to sell Chuck Chickens to Thu because she's responsible for summoning Satanic Chinese alligators. And her dad must have missed his deadline, which means his crocodile clarification hasn't come out yet.

"It's going to be OK," A.Z. says. "I mean, it'll be better after the paper comes out today or whenever." She's feeling like she's being very reassuring and mature. More mature. That makes sense. "And in the meantime, maybe you could use pork instead?"

"Pork doesn't taste like alligator," Thu says authoritatively, as if she's recently eaten several alligators.

Right after A.Z. gets off work, Kristoff pedals into the parking lot wearing bright-red jean shorts that he must have dyed himself. The red makes his legs look amazing—all ropey muscle and scars on tanned skin and long dark hairs—but not gross, hairy hairs; nice hairs. This is her boyfriend who she had sex with, and even though thinking this freaks her out, she isn't as shy about it as she thought she'd be.

"Hey," she says.

"Hey." He grins at her. "I'm starving. Wanna get ice cream?"

"Yeah," she says, even though she isn't hungry. She just wants to do something normal—to not admit that she told her mom like a scared kid, even though she deserved to be scared.

The sign at Tastee Twirl says 2 For 1: ALLIGATOR FLOATS, and the line stretches the length of the parking lot.

"Yuck," she says. "Pretty soon all the food in town is going to be green."

"St. Alligatricks Day!" Kristoff says.

"It's really St. Crocodile's Day," A.Z. says. "Remember?"

"Oh yeah," Kristoff says. "What about that place downtown?"

When they get to Creamy Days, Liz is making waffle cones and Larsley is scooping. She's saying, "Would you like a taste?" and "Single or double?" and only someone who knows her as well as A.Z. used to would realize she's smiling sarcastically wide.

"Whoa," she says, doing a double take that makes A.Z. wonder again if it's totally visible that she and Kristoff had sex. "What are you guys doing down here?"

"Getting ice cream," A.Z. says, feeling relieved but also a little disappointed. She wishes Kristoff would put his arm around her or do something to show they extra belong together now.

"I just got here; I overslept," Larsley says loudly—like she's trying to point out to the pilgrims how flakey she is. She tightens the rubber band on top of her head and hands a pilgrim a waffle cone with strawberry dribbling down. "I'm quitting, anyway."

"You are?"

"Yeah, I'm sick of serving stupid pilgrims. Hey, did Greg give you any foot jerky?"

A.Z. can't help laughing. Larsley is acting super normal, like she and A.Z. are still friends. Maybe they sort of are. Maybe the rules are different now, like the world is a giant hourglass that's gotten turned over.

But then A.Z. realizes it's weird to be talking about another guy in front of Kristoff, so she says to him, "You know that guy who shot himself in the foot? He's got this dumb joke about squirrel jerky."

"Yum," Kristoff says. "I'd try squirrel jerky. Squirrel jerky ice cream."

The people in line behind them are probably not thrilled about this—or Larsley leaning against the counter, like she's forgotten she's working. "He's got a total crush on A.Z."

"No he doesn't," A.Z. says. She looks at Kristoff, who is reading the menu board and doesn't seem jealous, which he shouldn't be, but could be, a little.

"I'd go for two hot dogs with extra mustard," he says. "And a large strawberry shake."

"Strawberry?" A.Z. says. "I thought you liked chocolate."

"Whatever. It's all ice cream."

A.Z. is still full of stir-fry noodles, which have settled into one of those famous rubber band balls in her stomach. She's hoping this is why she feels bloated and maybe pregnant. But Larsley insists on giving her a scoop of the new cookie dough flavor, which tastes good, like butter and vanilla. She gives them a crazy discount, so everything comes to $2.05. A.Z. pays because Kristoff won't get paid 'til next Friday.

"Tell me about it," Larsley says. "I don't get paid for two weeks. Except tips." She says this loudly so the customers, who probably aren't going to tip her anyway, are sure to hear. The guy behind them clears his throat and then goes ahead and orders two waffle cones: one chocolate and chocolate chip, and one with low-fat lemon sherbet.

"You know the waffle cones have tons of fat in them; they're like 250 calories each," Larsley tells the woman with him. "If you're trying to watch calories."

"Just a little scoop," the woman says.

Larsley scoops an extra giant scoop of lemon sherbet. "Scotty's been playing basketball this summer," she says, looking at Kristoff.

"Kristoff doesn't play," A.Z. says. "Not all tall people play basketball."

"We played dunk-the-chicken last night," Kristoff says. "My boss-hole turned the stunner down, so chickens kept missing the blade. We had to take the really mangled ones off the line, and Steve-o started trying to dunk them in the basketball hoop out back. I creamed everyone."

A.Z. is pretty sure—or at least she's hoping—that he's just joking.

"Wow," Larsley says, sounding impressed. "I'll have to tell Scotty."

A.Z. and Kristoff take their ice cream outside where it's less crowded and sit on the curb.

"Have you figured out where you're going to live?" she asks nervously.

"Yeah," Kristoff says. "Gerald says we can stay with him for a while. Hey, I worked on the mast a little this morning. I biked out there because I couldn't sleep."

She realizes she hasn't actually thought about the boat all day. "Really?" She's feeling really relieved. Kristoff isn't leaving the state; he's working on their mast. "I couldn't sleep either." And then she feels strangely shy—imagining them both not sleeping and thinking of each other.

"Did you ever send messages in bottles?" Kristoff asks.

"Yeah. Of course. Did you?"

"I sent a balloon once."

"A balloon?"

"I climbed to the top of our apartment in Miami and let go of this balloon with a letter to my dad tied on. I was reading some book about the Middle Ages where they delivered messages by carrier pigeon. I was a dumb kid."

"That's not dumb." She pictures Kristoff—who she can only imagine exactly like now, but shorter—waiting on the roof for his dad's response. It's like her mom waiting in the desert for her dad to return from the war. But at least her mom knew her dad; Kristoff has never even seen a picture. His mom said it was just a bad one-night stand, although A.Z. is sure he must have been cool, probably also an artist.

"When I was little, I wrote these letters to people in China and India and Australia and places and sent them in bottles," she says. "Once, one of them washed back up on Mud Beach, and I found it and thought it was an answer." She's never told anyone this; it makes her sad to remember how excited she was, and how confused that someone else had written back the exact same thing she'd written.

"You were a dumb kid, too," Kristoff says. "We were both dumb kids."

19

"Hiya," Kristoff says when she comes through the swinging doors of the library on Sunday. He's sitting on the reference table like he does. He's supposed to be at the trailer packing, so it takes A.Z. a minute to believe he's really here with her mom.

Her mom has been acting super normal since A.Z. told her about having sex, which is like when a dog is quiet just before it bites you. A.Z. read that in one of the old books she was reshelving. Barking is actually safer.

"I thought you were packing," A.Z. says.

"I ran out of boxes, so I drove over to get some."

"You *drove* over?" Of course: Kristoff is a year and a half older. But they've never talked about driver's licenses. She's just assumed they both knew bikes and boats were cooler.

"Hi, honey," her mom says. Then she looks at Kristoff: "You can take all these magazines, too. And I was thinking you could use the cot we have in the garage if Gerald doesn't have an extra bed for you."

"What cot?" A.Z. says. She feels embarrassed—like her mom is treating Kristoff like some charity case, or like she's about to say, "for you to have sex on once you get birth control."

Instead, she says, "We used it for camping trips when Catherine was little. The first two years we lived in Arizona, I actually slept on a cot in that awful house with the red walls. I'd never seen a roach in my life, and they were in all the cupboards."

"We used to have roaches," Kristoff says.

"In the trailer?" A.Z. says.

"No, in Miami. These huge ones. They'd hang out inside the phone on the wall. You know, with their feelers sticking out at you when you tried to dial." Kristoff is spinning the globe like he doesn't have any intention of picking up boxes or leaving. A.Z. usually loves the globe—because it shows really clearly that the world is more water than land—but right now it reminds her of everything she and Kristoff haven't researched.

"We had tarantulas, too," her mom says, "and one night I was walking across the room, and I stepped on one. I thought it was a rubber band with hair stuck to it, so I reached down to pick it up. I was terrified when I realized what I was holding."

Kristoff laughs and stops the globe with his index finger. "Gerald just found one of Thing One's hamsters in the recliner. It was all soupy and flat. I guess it had been there all week."

"What?" A.Z. says.

"His twins," Kristoff says. "Thing One and Thing Two. They're shitheads."

A.Z.'s mom doesn't like cursing because it shows a lack of imaginative vocabulary, but she doesn't say anything, maybe because A.Z.'s dad appears just then through the swinging door.

"The Chuck Chicken pullets have been out all night again," he says. "All day. All night. All day. And the alligator won't eat them. Reverend Bicks says it's more definitive proof that the alligator is

Satan; no other creature would turn down Chuck Chicken. And now the Baptists have put up a huge new sign about the Leviathan by the highway, and they're stopping cars to tell pilgrims not to go near the Sea. I need more books."

"On what?" A.Z.'s mom says.

"I don't know," A.Z.'s dad says. "Anorexic alligators?"

"It's a crocodile. Remember?" A.Z. says.

"I can't print that." Her dad runs his hands back and forth through his hair and takes a second pen from his pocket. "Nell has already made brochures, and she said I shouldn't change the species of a sign from God based on supposition."

"It's not supposition," A.Z. says. "It's a different species. It's science."

"We don't know for sure," her dad says. "We don't know anything for sure."

The next morning, A.Z. wakes in a sweat. She's just dreamed she was swimming alone in the Sea. She wanted to call to Kristoff to come meet her, but then she saw the crocodile—its snout just bobbing at the surface like a log, but obviously not a log, because it had eyes: green and slitted like a cat's, only much more terrifying. She screamed, but Kristoff didn't hear, so she tried to swim toward shore, but her body was heavy and strange—like it wouldn't float. And then Sahara appeared, waving a protest sign and calling, "Someone has to help her; she's pregnant!"

Lying awake now in bed, A.Z. tries not to panic. Her abdomen feels weird: squishy and soft, like fat, but not like fat, like something—a baby—pressing against her bladder. It's Monday, which means her period is at least a whole day late.

Finally, she realizes she needs to pee.

When she goes downstairs, her mom is in the kitchen, cracking eggs into a bowl. This strikes A.Z. as really irritating—like her mom has found out about her nightmare and gotten up to feed her.

"I'm not hungry," she says.

"I wasn't making them for you," her mom says. "Your father is leaving early to get pictures of the new Leviathan sign. Of course, he'll probably decide he can't use them." She sighs. "There are plenty of eggs if you decide you want some."

"I won't," A.Z. says. "I'm already all huge and bloated. Why is everyone always eating all the time?"

"You're bloated and in a bad mood because you're premenstrual," her mom says in that awful rational way.

"I'm not in a bad mood," A.Z. says crossly.

"Stress can keep you from menstruating. If you relax, your period is more likely to start."

"Who said my period hasn't started?" A.Z. says, stalking into the bathroom. She feels a little better once she pees but she doesn't admit this.

"I went ahead and scheduled you an appointment at Planned Parenthood next Monday," her mom says when A.Z. returns and stands in the doorway brooding. Her mom is talking at a normal volume, like they're just discussing breakfast. Hopefully A.Z.'s dad is in the shower or something.

Her mom slides the eggs onto a plate. They actually look good, all fluffy and topped with black pepper, but A.Z. won't admit this either. She's furious with herself for telling her mom about having sex and also furious with her mom for somehow making it so A.Z. had to tell her.

A.Z. is furious all day at work, too. She washes dishes furiously and eats one egg roll furiously and gets off work furiously and rides furiously toward Kristoff's house instead of the library.

She's furious most of all at her awful pregnancy cramps, which double her over as she gets off her bike. It's like they were folded up as she was riding, but now there's an origami gnome with a pitchfork stabbing the soft flesh inside her abdomen. She leans her bike against the cement block steps of Kristoff's trailer and knocks. Then she knocks again.

Finally Kristoff answers. His hair is standing up like he's been taking a nap. "Hey," he says, smiling. "You're just in time. I was just going to pack some stuff."

A.Z. had pictured that most of the packing would be done, but everything looks pretty much untouched—the same piles of dusty junk mail and magazines and cups on the coffee table.

"Don't you have to start moving everything to Gerald's?" she says.

"Yeah." Kristoff walks down the hall and sits on his bed, throwing a pillow onto a pile of stuff he's apparently dragged out from underneath. A.Z. tries not to think about the condom that used to be in that pile. He leans over and starts putting empty Mountain Dew bottles into a box.

"Are you saving those for extra flotation?" she says. She thinks about their boat still sitting in the bushes where they dragged it—in less-than-dry dock. Sailless. All the stupid time that's passing.

"Whatever." Kristoff puts a pair of ripped-up Converse she's never seen him wear on top of the bottles and seals the not-totally-full box with duct tape he rips with his teeth.

A.Z. picks up a pile of clothes from the corner and stuffs them in the laundry hamper. "Those were clean," Kristoff says.

"They were on the floor," A.Z. says.

"Yeah, the clean part of the floor."

A.Z. isn't sure what to say. She wants to say something about being scared she's pregnant but she's too scared to even say the word.

"I can't wait to not sleep on this stupid bed. It's way too short," Kristoff says, sitting down on the bed.

A.Z. keeps forgetting most of the bigger furniture came with the trailer; at least that's less stuff to pack. "I bet the cot my mom has is even shorter. Doesn't Gerald have a couch or something?"

She's having another round of cramps, zigzaggy like a lightning storm, and she wants to sit, but Kristoff isn't packing anything, and she feels anxious—like she needs to be doing something.

Kristoff shrugs, leaning back like he has all the time in the world. "The dog sleeps on it. And Thing One and Thing Two have the bedroom. I'm going to sleep in the laundry room."

"Are you serious?" In her abdomen, something like the metal bars of the recliner that squished Thing One's hamster fold in on themselves. She winces, but Kristoff doesn't notice. He pulls a T-shirt out from under the bed and shakes it, fluffing loose grey dust and chicken feathers.

A.Z. thinks about pointing out that the good thing about sleeping in a laundry room is that he'll be closer to the washing machine.

Surely he and his mom won't live with Gerald and his kids for long; they'll find an apartment—maybe even in Compolodo. If they move before school starts, he and A.Z. could be at the same school and meet at her locker for lunch every day, unless of course she's pregnant and has an abortion with awful complications and has to drop out.

"I don't feel very good today," she says, as sort of a hint, sitting down beside him.

"Yeah. My mom's sick, too. Some lung infection. She's switched to Menthol Lights." He laughs and stuffs the cow skull into a pillow-case.

"I thought you were going to paint that," A.Z. says.

"Yeah, I used all my paints on that big sea monster sign."

"What sea monster sign?"

"That one on the highway that your dad was talking about the other day."

"You painted the Leviathan sign for the crazy Baptists?" Obviously, this is some dumb joke that he's trying to make her fall for.

"Yeah, that preacher dude saw me painting in the yard and said he'd give me twenty dollars for more supplies. It was super easy, except the tail."

A.Z. understands about Kristoff needing extra money, but she really doesn't understand why he would paint Baptist propaganda to make Thu go out of business and ruin her own life even worse than it's already ruined by being pregnant and not on the Sea doing research.

"You can't be serious," she says crossly. "Reverend Bicks is crazy. He once tried to get all the books except the Bible banned from the library. And they're being racist. It's completely nuts to say Thu is responsible for a Satanic crocodile when everyone knows the crocodile came from the Ark Park. They're just jealous because nothing like the Sea ever happened in Greenville."

"We have that closed-down water slide," Kristoff says. "And Wal-Mart."

"Right," A.Z. says.

"If Gerald's sucks, I was thinking I could move into a tent in Wal-Mart and live with the mannequins. Kim Cattrall was pretty hot."

"Who?"

"You know, in that movie where she was the mannequin that came to life."

A.Z. didn't see *Mannequin*, but she remembers posters of a skinny blond woman in a tight pink dress and heels that made her legs look all perfect and muscled. The image makes her even more furious and weirdly jealous. She's helping Kristoff pack so he can go live in a tent in Wal-Mart with a mannequin.

Now that she thinks about it, Kristoff hasn't said she's beautiful since they had sex; maybe he doesn't think she's beautiful. He doesn't even care about her or understand what it means to be a not-plastic woman stuck on land with pregnancy cramps. He's purposefully doing everything slowly so they'll never get out on the water.

"I heard that movie was really stupid," she says, standing up to show that she's leaving. But then she looks at Kristoff's bed where she's been sitting. There's a little spot of blood, that isn't chicken blood, on the comforter. She sits back down because she's not sure what else to do.

"I can't believe you really painted the stupid sea monster," she says.

"Seas need sea monsters," Kristoff says, grinning at her.

20

"If they really believed God was on their side, they wouldn't need to stop cars," her mom says, braking. "Of course, if the whole Sea dried up tomorrow, the Bickses would still find some reason to hate the Gordings. You'd think they would have accepted by now that pilgrims just want to eat ice cream and get skin cancer. Did you put on sunscreen?"

"Yeah," A.Z. says, even though she forgot. She spent too long changing shirts, worrying a tank top would look slutty and anti-abortion protesters would yell things at her. She's heard from Angie they do that sometimes. She can feel her arm, resting on the window sill, burning.

"I hope Kristoff is being supportive of your appointment," her mom says. "It's important for both partners to take responsibility for their sex life."

A.Z. can feel her face flushing, so she stares at the sign Kristoff made, about twenty feet in front of them. Even though she wishes it weren't there, it's actually sort of cool-looking: a super abstract sea monster coiling under waves, with some brownish-red speckles that are maybe supposed to be fish. She wonders if her mom knows Kristoff painted it.

"Of course, men didn't use to take any sort of responsibility," her mom says. "I was married to Curtis for fifteen years, and I never had a single orgasm. He didn't even think to ask me if I was satisfied, and I just thought that's how sex was supposed to be. I hope Kristoff thinks about how you're feeling."

A.Z. blushes again and tries hard not to think of any real answers. "Uh, yeah," she says, pretending to be distracted by the three kids in the station wagon in front of them. They're squirming and fighting, and occasionally one head disappears, and then one turns around and sticks his tongue against the glass. A.Z. sort of wants to stick out her tongue back but of course she doesn't.

"Good," her mom says. "I would expect him to be. Artists tend to be more sensitive." She leans her head out, looking at the traffic. "Are you nervous about your appointment?"

"No," A.Z. lies. She tries not to think about the crampy metal thing.

"They always say it doesn't hurt," Angie told her once. "But it totally cramps."

Fortunately, a man in a blue polyester suit is walking toward them. It's the first time A.Z. has ever been relieved to see a First-First Southern Baptist.

"Good morning," he says, smiling as he leans toward her mom's open window. "I hope you're having a blessed day. I just wanted to take a moment of your time to talk to you about your eternal salvation. Now some people will tell you that there's an alligator in that water, but that is no natural creature. We have seen proof for two full weeks that it will not eat our blessed Chuck Chicken pullets. And the Bible tells us that only the Leviathan itself—the coiling, demon monster of the Sea—cannot be hooked. The Bible says, *only* 'The LORD will punish with his sword, his fierce, great and powerful sword, Leviathan the gliding serpent, Leviathan the coiling serpent; he will slay the monster of the sea.'" The guy closes his eyes as he says this last part, like he's not sure he has it memorized.

"Crocodiles don't coil," her mom says. "And I hope Nell Gording appreciates all the free publicity she's getting from you. It's a long-proven principle that any press is good press. That's why banned books usually end up on the bestseller list."

"Excuse me, ma'am?" He wipes the sweat off his forehead. A.Z. wonders if he'd be less worried about Hell if he'd take off his polyester suit.

"We're on our way to Fayetteville," her mom says. "We're not going to the beach."

"Well, praise the Lord." He smiles again and hurries to the next car.

"People have too much time on their hands," her mom says. "When I was growing up, people didn't stop cars unless they thought your physical life was in danger. When my mother was driving us to Arizona after my father died, we passed through Elizabethtown, Kentucky. It had been snowing all afternoon, and a police officer stopped us and said there was no way we could make it up the hill. I'm sure he was worried about a woman by herself with two young children out on icy roads. But my mother told the officer she was from northern New York, and she knew how to drive. The officer said, 'Really, ma'am, there's no way you're making it over there,' and she said, 'Watch me,' and the officer actually did. He stood there on the side of the road as she drove up the hill and down the other side."

A.Z. has always liked this story. It's one of her mom's only stories in which it's good to do whatever you want to—provided, of course, that you actually know how to do it.

There aren't any protesters outside Planned Parenthood, and the building is weirdly normal, like a dentist's office. A.Z.'s mom doesn't want to leave the groceries in the heat, so she carries two paper sacks with celery and a loaf of bread sticking out, like she and A.Z. are planning to make sandwiches while they wait.

"We have an appointment at noon. For Anastasia McKinney," her mom tells the woman, who is behind what might be bulletproof glass.

"You're a new patient, right?" the woman says.

"*She* is," A.Z.'s mom says, gesturing at A.Z. with the hand next to the celery.

The woman smiles, and A.Z. smiles back as naturally as she can. She feels suddenly really young—like maybe the woman assumed she wasn't the patient because she doesn't look old enough. "Make sure to fill out both sides of menstrual history," the woman says. She lifts the sheet to show the back, as though A.Z. might not be able to find it otherwise.

A.Z. fills out the first form with her name and address, and then the menstrual history form, which is also pretty easy. She writes down that her period first started when she was thirteen, and counts up how many days her period lasts, and tries to decide whether to mark "moderate" or "severe" for her cramps. There's also a "none" option, which must be a joke. Then she fills in a row of "no" checkmarks on gynecological history because she's never heard of the diseases.

The next section, sexual history, is harder, particularly with her mom sitting beside her. A.Z. doesn't trust her. Her mom is good at reading *National Geographic* and paying attention to other things at the same time.

One of the questions—"Do you have any concerns about sex?"— has just a little "yes" or "no" checkbox. A.Z. isn't sure what to mark because of course she has concerns—like if bleeding the first time is normal, and how to give a blow job, and if that's a good idea, and if Kristoff meant the things he said when they had sex. Finally, she checks "no" in case her mom is watching, and so she won't have to talk about any of this.

When she returns the form, a couple is checking in—a red-haired girl with a bunch of piercings and a guy with a backward baseball cap who keeps glancing out the window. A.Z. sort of wishes she were here with Kristoff, but she also can't quite imagine him talking about the void while she filled out her forms.

She's just picked up a copy of *Seventeen* with a really skinny blond girl with a perfectly flat stomach and a flowery bikini on the cover, when a nurse calls her.

"Do you want me to come in with you?" her mom asks. She reaches for the grocery bags.

"No," A.Z. says quickly. "Thanks."

The nurse is middle-aged and plump, and her nametag says Barbara.

"I see you're here for an exam and birth control," she says. A.Z. is scared she's going to ask questions about why, when, and where, but instead she says, "I just need your right arm to check your blood pressure." She velcros a black strap around A.Z.'s arm and pumps a little plastic ball. Inside a dial that reminds A.Z. of a compass, a needle moves past numbers, hovering, then moving back down.

"Good," Barbara says. "Step up on the scale." She gestures at one of those awful doctor's scales that wobble when you step on them, like you're so heavy you're making the ground unstable. She ratchets the metal weight to the right and then back, which is a good sign, and then further to the right, even though A.Z. swears the scale was about to balance.

"One hundred and twenty-three point five," Barbara says, writing down, in ink, this awful number. "Do you need to urinate?"

"Sort of." A.Z. realizes that could be half a pound, which means, minus the half pound Barbara added, 122.5, which is only two and a half pounds heavier than she wants to be and probably fifteen pounds heavier than that model on *Seventeen,* who never has to worry about her stomach pooching.

"You can take this cup to the bathroom and leave a urine sample," Barbara says, handing A.Z. a plastic cup with a ridged red cap. "After you take care of the sample, come back here and get undressed. Panties and bra, too. The opening goes in front. You tie it here." She points to a piece of stringy paper, flimsier than the tabs for the paper dolls that A.Z.'s mom gave her instead of Barbies when she was little. "And here's a sheet for your legs."

In the bathroom, A.Z. reads the instructions on the wall twice about the alcohol wipe and cup, which she's supposed to somehow hold without peeing on her hand. This is so awkward she can't pee, but finally she does. She screws the lid on the cup, which is warmer than she would have imagined, and slides it through the little window. Then she hurries back to the room and strips quickly without looking at her body, and ties the white paper string, but the gown gaps anyway and she has to hold it closed. That means she can't read a magazine, so she sits there—cold and papery on the crinkly paper of the examining table. There's a glass jar of cotton balls on the desk and another jar of long Q-tips that she hopes aren't going to be stuck inside her, and a poster of birth control pills, which are green and peach and remind her of those candy bracelets kids used to wear in elementary school.

Finally, someone knocks. "Hello," a woman's voice says. The door opens. "I'm Dr. O'Farrell." She's tall and thin and younger than A.Z. was expecting—with straight blond hair pulled back in a ponytail. "Anastasia," she says. "That's a nice name. Are you Russian?"

"No. My mom's a librarian. She named me for a book."

Dr. O'Farrell nods, like this is normal, even though it's not. "Compolodo," she says, reading the chart. "I keep wanting to go over and see the alligator. That must be big excitement."

"Yeah. It's pretty crazy. It's actually a crocodile."

"Interesting," Dr. O'Farrell says, still reading as she talks. "I heard they're trying to catch it with a hook?" She flips the page over.

"Yeah, and chickens."

Dr. O'Farrell nods again, like she knows all about crocodiles, in addition to knowing—now—all about A.Z.'s sexual history.

"So you've been sexually active for a little over a week? With just one partner?"

"Yes." She's embarrassed that Dr. O'Farrell would consider that she'd had multiple partners in a week.

"And, to the best of your knowledge, he hasn't had other partners either?"

"No. I mean, yes, he hasn't had other partners." She really doesn't like the wording "to the best of your knowledge."

"And you've been using condoms?"

"Yes. Well, we've actually just had sex once and we used a condom, but it tore. But I'm not pregnant. I mean, I just had my period. I don't think I'm pregnant."

"We'll know for sure from your urine test." Dr. O'Farrell smiles. A.Z. wonders if Dr. O'Farrell, all cheerful with her ponytail and little star-shaped earrings, is going to personally study her cup of urine. "And you want to start on birth control pills?"

"Yes," A.Z. says.

"Great. As a woman, that will give you more control because you won't have to rely on your partner to remember." She raises her eyebrows a little as she says this—as if to suggest she's sharing an inside womanly problem. Then she rolls her stool toward the door and calls to Barbara. "Barbara will assist with the exam now, and then we'll get you set up. We'll just start by checking the breasts."

It's sort of comforting that Dr. O'Farrell talks about body parts as if they're not really attached to A.Z. But in another way, it makes A.Z. feel like she's a specimen, a drop of water in someone else's refractometer.

She sort of wishes her mom were here squeezing her hand, the way she did at the dentist the time A.Z. got a filling, but of course, she doesn't really want her mom here while Dr. O'Farrell presses latex-gloved fingers in circles around her breasts. A.Z. has never really touched her own breasts—except maybe once in the bathtub—and Kristoff has only touched them a few times, and she feels weird about having breasts right now, and it being someone's job to touch them.

"OK, now put your feet up on these," Dr. O'Farrell says, gesturing to some sort of metal-stirrup-looking things at the end of the table. "And then just lie back down and scoot this way. Farther." A.Z. scrunches her papery self down the papery table, with the gown bunching up under her. "A little farther."

A.Z. scrunches farther. She sort of feels like crying.

"Now just a little more," Dr. O'Farrell says. "There. Now let your knees fall open. This will feel a little strange the first time. But you'll get used to it."

A.Z. closes her eyes—not that she can see anything that's going on beyond her knees and the paper sheet. She can feel the cool air-conditioned air between her legs. She's never felt so naked. "This is just my finger. This may cramp a little bit. And then I'll be using the speculum."

"Aah," A.Z. says, even though she can't feel anything yet.

"It's OK," Barbara says. A.Z. doesn't trust her. She isn't sure she trusts Dr. O'Farrell either, who is jamming something—cold and metal and wrong—between her legs, so her abdomen cramps in tightening, concentric, scrapey circles.

She bites her lip. She tells herself to recite the names of all the ships she can think of—which used to help when she was scared as a little kid—the *QE2* and the *Endurance*. The *Titanic. Ra. Kon-Tiki. Great Western. Mount Hood. Fram. Elissa. Bounty. Mayflower. Niña. Pinta. Santa Maria. Sea Eagle. Savannah. Andrea Doria*—which has a cool woman's name—the *Arizona, Calypso, Cutty Sark . . .*

"Great," Dr. O'Farrell says. "Now just the swab. OK . . . and we're done." The crampy thing slides out, although A.Z.'s abdomen still feels bruised inside. "Everything looks fine so far; we'll call you with the results. You can get dressed, and I'll be right back in."

Even though it's nice to have her clothes back on, A.Z. still feels naked and leaky—like her body isn't totally put back together right, or maybe something is stuck inside her, or something fell out.

She sits on the edge of the table and waits again, and then Dr. O'Farrell comes back carrying a white paper bag. "Good news," she says. "You're not pregnant. We can start you on Ortho Novum 777. These tend to work well for most young women." She snaps open the case to reveal a ring of shaded peach and green pills on a silver disk, like the ones on the wall.

"You take a peach one every day at the same time. And then during your period, you take a green blank each day. And then you start a new pack. The important thing is not to miss a day. If you do, take that pill immediately, but if you miss more than that one, you'll need to use condoms for the rest of that cycle. Does that make sense?"

"Yeah," A.Z. says, although she isn't really sure, and she's distracted by the news that she definitely isn't pregnant and the fact that the pills are tiny, like they couldn't possibly have enough power to stop her from getting pregnant in the future.

"You'll need to use condoms this month. I've put some in here, too. The pill won't take effect for thirty days. After that, provided that you take it faithfully, it's more than 95 percent effective." She's talking faster, like she needs to get to another appointment. "Did you have any questions?"

"The condoms you're giving me shouldn't break?" A.Z. asks, feeling nervous about bringing this up again. "I mean, the other one broke, so I just get worried."

"I'll include a pamphlet," Dr. O'Farrell says. "If your partner isn't very experienced, then the condom probably broke because of the way he put it on or a lack of lubrication. Let me give you some lube." She opens a desk drawer and gets out two little silver packets that remind A.Z. of the to-go soy sauce at Seven Happiness. "This can help if you're not wet enough; that's common the first time."

"OK," A.Z. says, feeling like she should be writing down all the details. She wonders if she'll have to remind herself to take the pills or if it will become sort of natural.

"Have a great rest of your day," Dr. O'Farrell says. She shakes A.Z.'s hand. "Good luck with the alligator."

Her mom wants to drop the cot by Gerald's on their way back to town, which is nice because it means A.Z. gets to see Kristoff right away, but also awkward to show up straight from Planned Parenthood. What if she and Kristoff want to talk in private so she can show him the birth control pills and so he can hug her in that way that will make her feel like she's in the right non-inside-out body again?

For the first fifteen miles, her mom asks more awkward questions, but then an NPR show about *The Satanic Verses* comes on, and her mom starts listening. Her mom has kept *The Satanic Verses* behind the counter all year, waiting for someone to ask to check it out, but no one has—not even Dragonfly. A.Z. hasn't read *The Satanic Verses* either, but she's relieved to listen to commentators talking about *fatwa*, which is a cool term that means some sort of death price. She thinks about laughing with Kristoff and telling him, *There's a crocodile fatwa.*

Gerald's house is a little wider than a mobile home but the same sort of rectangle—with white siding and a bunch of stuff on the porch, including an old washing machine and two Big Wheels. There's also a limp kiddie pool in the front yard—the inflatable one Kristoff's mom bought that immediately sprung a leak because Gerald's kids were playing with knives in it.

The front door is open, and they can see through the screen, but A.Z.'s mom rings the doorbell.

"Yeah?" Gerald says. He comes to the other side of the screen but doesn't open it.

"Hi," A.Z. says. "I'm A.Z. We met that time at Pizza Hut. And this is my mom, Sophie. We brought something for Kristoff." She's holding the folded-up cot, which is so wood-rickety she's sure it's going to collapse the first time Kristoff tries to lie on it. It makes her think anxiously about their mast, which they need to be sanding, and which will have to withstand a lot more than Kristoff's hundred and fifty pounds.

"Jack!" Gerald yells. "Beanpole!" He opens the door. The room smells menthol-smoky just like Kristoff's old trailer and looks pretty much the same.

"Hi," A.Z. says to Kristoff's mom, who is watching some show where a woman is crying in a dramatic way that matches the music. "Are you feeling better?"

"I feel like shit," Kristoff's mom said. "It's living with these two assholes."

"Beanpole!" Gerald yells. "Get your head out of your ass."

"This is my mom, Sophie," A.Z. says, praying Kristoff appears so this will all be over.

"Hi," A.Z.'s mom says to Kristoff's mom. She actually doesn't seem fazed.

"Hey," Kristoff says; he's come out of the dark hallway and sits on the floor and yawns.

"I been there," Gerald says, nodding toward A.Z. It takes her a minute to realize he means the Eiffel Tower on her T-shirt. "We had a layover there on the way to the war. We climbed all the way up that tower."

A.Z. can't really imagine Gerald being in a war and she's going to ask which war, but before she can, Kristoff's mom says, "You're too fat to climb anywhere."

"I wasn't fat then," Gerald says. "I could do three hundred push-ups. I wasn't no beanpole like him." Then he laughs. Kristoff's mom laughs, too.

A.Z. feels herself turning red, but the room is dim, so probably no one notices. She's scared Gerald is going to bring up Kristoff's dick again.

"Where should I put this?" she asks, glancing down at the cot she's still awkwardly holding.

"He doesn't need any more crap," Kristoff's mom says. "He doesn't take care of the stuff he's got." She turns from the TV and glares at Kristoff, who is wearing his cool ripped-up jean shorts with the safety pins and one of his bloodier shirts, which used to be blue but is kind of brown now. A.Z. secretly agrees he could take better care of his clothes, like wash them sometimes, though probably it's hard to sleep on the floor next to the sloshing.

"Shut up," Kristoff says, standing up and walking back down the hall. A.Z. feels kind of weird leaving her mom, but she needs to give him the cot and she also really wants to be alone with him, so she follows, almost tripping over a couple of rubber balls on the dark hall floor.

"We weren't using the cot," she can hear her mom saying, "and we thought it might come in handy. When I lived in Arizona . . ."

When A.Z. gets to the kitchen, Kristoff is already standing in front of the open fridge eating fried chicken out of a box. A.Z.'s mom hates open refrigerators because she grew up with iceboxes that people had to fill with real ice. A.Z. doesn't mean to feel stressed about the refrigerator, too, but she sort of wants to close it.

"Is that the laundry room?" she says. She can see the washing machine in a little closet to the left of the stove, but the room isn't even a real room. It's more of a storage pantry—too small for Kristoff to sleep in.

"Yeah," Kristoff says. A.Z. is hoping he'll say something more—like ask how her appointment went—maybe lift her up like he does and spin her around.

Instead he takes a bite of chicken. "They should leave their heads on," he says. "It's a lie. People buy this and they don't even think that they're eating something that used to squawk and flap around. Squawk!"

"Yeah," A.Z. says. She understands, but also she can't help thinking about her own body—which Kristoff still hasn't asked about—laid out on the table at Planned Parenthood, like some kind of dissection. She didn't even really want to know all the parts of herself. But of course you have to. That's what it means to do research.

Kristoff takes an exaggerated bite of chicken, including the bone, so it's hanging out of his mouth. "Ozzy Osbourne had the right idea," he says.

It takes her a minute. "About the bat?"

"No, the dove. He was meeting some guys from a record company and he was going to release these doves as a sign of peace, but he was so drunk, he bit the head off one instead."

Kristoff spits the bone back in the box and stands there with the fridge still open. "Crunch!" he says in a weird, exaggerated voice that doesn't make A.Z. feel comforted or put back together at all. "I'm going to start a new school of hyperrealism. Crunch! Squawk! Squawk!"

21

"I guess you heard about the boat?" Greg says, limping toward A.Z. down the P.M./A.M. aisle with his foot in one of those weird black boot things.

"What boat?" A.Z. says. She closes the cold case and stands there holding her can of Mountain Dew, trying to breathe and not sound anxious. Greg has finally found her boat. He's really commandeering it before she ever gets to sail.

"The motorboat we're getting from Springfield next Friday. We gotta catch this gator for good before school starts."

"Oh," A.Z. says, exhaling. "But it's sacrilegious to take boats on the Sea."

"Used to be," Greg says, "but Nell says that God wants us to take this boat out. It's His will that everyone see the gator in all its glory."

The Gordings must be really worried about pissed-off pilgrims going somewhere else on vacation—somewhere they can actually swim instead of getting lectured about Hell—but it isn't fair the Gordings are changing their own rules to get a boat. She already has a boat. Not that she's going to volunteer herself to Greg or Nell or anyone. What would she say? *I've been planning to find the scientific origins of your miraculous Sea and secretly working on a sailboat while trespassing on your land except when I've been helping Kristoff pack and going to Planned Parenthood and talking about Ozzy Osbourne and chickens.*

"It's a crocodile," she says. "And I bet it's already dead. That would explain why no one's seen it."

"It's not," Greg says, lowering his voice and trying to sound mysterious. "It's out there. We found part of a bloody seagull floating in the water this morning. That gator just doesn't like Chuck Chicken." He laughs, and she can smell a gust of wintergreen breath. "I bet you Chuck Chuck let the alligator loose because he's mad we took his dumb chickens from the beach to the Ark Park."

"Maybe," A.Z. says. She hates to admit to herself how logical this is. She pictures Chuck Chuck with the pullets in the ice chest—waiting for his photo op as the hero who baited the crocodile that he maybe let out so he could bait it. In which case, the First-First Southern Baptists would be protesting themselves, which doesn't seem that unlikely.

"So you're really taking a boat out to look for the crocodile? I mean, way out on the water?" She thinks about a motorboat churning up all the ecosystems she hasn't had a chance to study yet. A motorboat speeding past the shore where her boat still doesn't have a finished mast or rigging.

"Yeah," Greg says. "We've got a secret weapon, this special underwater heat sensor."

A.Z. wants to say, *I know*, but she doesn't. She also wants to point out that it's not really a secret weapon if Greg just told her.

"You should tell that hippie girl she can't stop us either." Sahara is in their same class in school, with twenty-seven other people, so it's not like Greg doesn't know her name. Maybe he's been reading some Gording Foundation pamphlet on how to pretend to be a security guard. "She's handing out flyers about barricading the highway to stop the boat. It's a private beach. We can do whatever we want with it."

A.Z. really doesn't like the words "private beach." But then she thinks about all the rest of the Sea, which is technically private, too, but which she and Kristoff could finally explore if everyone else were really distracted by a barricade and a motorboat. Now that she thinks about it, Nell will need to be down at the beach Friday night, too. Everyone will.

"Friday?" she says.

"Yeah," Greg says. "Sy's going to drive up to Bass Pro during the Miracle Play and bring the boat down. And then I'm in charge of the mission to get the gator."

"Have you seen the vials?" A.Z. calls, taking a break from sanding one of her new wooden cleats and rummaging again through the tackle box. The box is full of extra grommets and rope she's measured for the rigging and new tubes of paint Kristoff bought with the money from Reverend Bicks, and with which he painted *The Evol Taob* on the bow: white on white so it's there but invisible, which is really romantic but also won't help the boat actually sail in just seventy-two hours.

"No," Kristoff calls. He wipes sweat off his face with his shirt, which is inside out today, and just as splotchy inside with something paint- or blood-like. She tries not to think about this. She isn't sure she's a fan of hyperrealism.

She checks her backpack pockets and then the ground around the boat where she's been gathering rocks to anchor the vials—anchors that could, admittedly, slip away or smash the glass. She's worried about adding weight to the boat, but of course she can't get deep-water samples if her vials stay on the surface. What she needs is one of those cool acoustic release devices she read about in *Discover*—which send your vials into deep water and then remotely call them back—but of course those probably cost more than even going to Sea Camp.

Deep water—way out in the center of the Sea where no one has gone—is definitely her best hope for good data and a big discovery: like the saline in the center is higher because it isn't near outlets, or the Sea has similar salinity patterns to a more famous, larger ocean—maybe the Baltic.

What she and Kristoff need is one clear, huge discovery that will convince the oceanographers at Sea Camp to accept them as a research team. She's been thinking about this a lot since the other night in Gerald's kitchen: Kristoff should definitely apply to Sea Camp with her. It'd be good for him to focus on living things for a while.

"I swear the vials were right here," she says.

"There are lots of bottles over there," Kristoff says. "Big Bob found a dead mouse in one of them."

He nods toward the junk pile and the mushroomy mattress where he's been sleeping the past few nights because he says it's more comfortable than the cot at Gerald's.

She suddenly imagines Big Bob coming for sensor supplies and Kristoff telling him their plan. Big Bob telling Nell. "Big Bob wasn't down here lately, was he? He doesn't know about Friday night, does he?"

Even saying "Friday night" makes her anxious. It's not really a night; it's an hour or two after Kristoff gets off work and she leaves the Boat Barricade, which she dumbly promised Sahara she'd come to, and before Sy gets past the barricade and down to Mud Beach and fills the boat with gas, or whatever you do with motorboats, and drags it out in the water.

"No," Kristoff says. "He hasn't been here since yesterday."

"That's lately," she says. "And we can't use those gross bottles; they've got all kinds of stuff in them."

"Yeah," Kristoff says. He's sanding the mast, which he's made from a skinny pine tree slightly taller than he is. Even with the sanding, the nubs where the branches were sawed off still look more lumpy than aerodynamic. Not that A.Z. can criticize; her plywood leeboard looks maybe not fully hydrodynamic either, and she's worried it won't provide enough lateral resistance to the wind, and they'll capsize or the hull will split or the oar will be hard to steer with.

"He was testing the sensor," Kristoff says. "It's really cool. We sensed this huge school of fish we couldn't see."

A.Z. really doesn't like the idea of Big Bob in their cove with a sensor. "How do you know the fish were there if you didn't see them?" she says.

"The sensor picked up their heat."

"Fish are ectothermic," A.Z. says. "They're cold-blooded. I mean, even if the sensor worked, wouldn't it just be picking up the temperature of the water?" Now that she thinks about it, a sensor that picked up variations in water temperature might be useful for another study, but she's not going to say this. "Crocodiles are ectothermic, too," she says. "It's not like he's trying to find a manatee or something."

She feels relieved about this; at least no large marine mammals will be endangered by the motorboat—which she realizes is just one motorboat but in her mind has sort of turned into a chainsaw heading toward her to cut apart everything in the Sea if she doesn't finish in time to study it.

A.Z. has all day Wednesday to work on the boat, which would be good except that it means Seven Happiness has been so slow Thu doesn't need her for the lunch shift. Apparently pilgrims keep complaining that there's no alligator in the alligator chow mein and no chicken in the chicken chow mein.

Thu hasn't turned in the paperwork to bring her brothers over, and it's sitting on the shelf above the stove with the Buddha, getting crinkly and grease-splattered.

"The delivery man still said they don't have any chicken," she told A.Z. yesterday, stirring bamboo shoots in the one wok she had going. "Your boyfriend can get me some?"

"I doubt it," A.Z. said, feeling bad for Thu—who Chuck Chuck and Reverend Bicks really should thank for starting the whole alligator-meat craze—but also worried about her own savings. With all the boat repairs she's back down to $225—the $150 her parents gave her as a start plus a little summer savings—barely enough to maybe fly to Florida.

Now she's had to buy more nails so Kristoff can attach the mast to the thwart—which he's currently doing—and she's apparently going to have to buy new vials, which weren't in her room when she checked last night.

Maybe they got pushed to the back of the cave when she and Kristoff finished the sail yesterday and ended up lying down on it and having sex to celebrate—very carefully, with the condom plus the pills she's been taking every single night, because she's very organized.

But she checks again, and the vials are still nowhere.

"This is so weird," she calls, double-checking the rest of her supply list, and marking off rope for the halyard. "I still can't figure out where the vials went. You're sure you haven't seen them?"

"Yeah," Kristoff says. "I put scrambled messages in them and sent them across the Sea."

"What?"

"Yeah, I told you the other day."

"No you didn't. You said you hadn't seen them."

"That other day," Kristoff says. "When we were talking about balloons and stuff."

"You didn't say you sent my vials across the Sea with messages," A.Z. says. "You just asked if *I'd* ever sent messages. That's not the same thing at all."

Sometimes it seems as if Kristoff only tells her one piece of information at a time and only if she asks the exact right question. Although, in another way, that's sort of the scientific method: you have to know what to ask.

"Didn't you know we were going to use them?"

Kristoff shrugs. "They were the right size for the void."

"The Sea isn't really the void," she says, feeling sort of frustrated. "Once we're able to get data to understand its salinity, which affects the currents and what can live in it and everything, it's going to be like the opposite of the void."

"Maybe we'll hear back," Kristoff says, looking out at the water in a way that makes A.Z. feel kind of weirdly hopeful despite herself—as if the Sea itself is going to write back to them.

"We needed those vials for our data," she says. "So we'll have a good application for Sea Camp."

"We could make some data up," Kristoff says.

"We can't make it up," she says. "That's the whole point of research. And the oceanographers would know."

"Yeah," Kristoff says. He grins, like he's agreeing with her, and starts hammering again in a way that sounds simultaneously really echoey loud and not very sturdy.

Then he leans back, letting go of the mast and looking up at it sort of the way he looked at A.Z. that one night in the darkness. Like the mast isn't like other masts.

But also, it *is* like other masts. It's suddenly standing on its own, like a mast in a drawing in one of A.Z.'s books, and it sort of makes her breathless to look at it. She imagines a photo of it taped into their Sea Camp application: this mast and the sail they're about to rig to it. She's pretty sure that at least they'll be the only research team that's had to build their own boat.

"Boats are barbaric," Sahara calls through a cardboard megaphone. She's trying to get everyone to chant louder to drown out the First-First Southern Baptists down the highway, who are stopping the few passing cars that haven't already gone to the Miracle Play. "Boats are barbaric!"

A.Z. isn't sure that "boats are barbaric" is very good karma to say right now. Not that she believes in karma. She's a little worried—even though she practiced yesterday—about raising the sail in the dark, and whether there will be enough wind tonight to carry them, and whether Kristoff will remember the new vials he helpfully bought at Wal-Mart and forgot yesterday but has promised to bring.

"What do you call an alligator in a vest?" Josh says. He's been telling alligator jokes while playing hacky sack by himself, which means—since they're part of a human chain, like Hands Across America, or at least hands across Highway 62—he keeps twisting A.Z.'s arm.

"I don't know," she says because she sort of has to.

"An investigator," Josh says, laughing.

The longer A.Z. stands here, the more she feels contradictorily stretched and puffy, like she's melting and swelling, maybe from some side effect of the pill magnified by humidity. It's one of those late summer days that seems determined to fit in as much heat as possible before fall, so the air feels almost indistinguishable from water. Not the nice seawater she's going to be gliding over in only another two hours, but a muggy, mosquito-swarming swamp.

After what A.Z.'s watch says is forty-eight minutes, but feels like several achy-armed, puffy-stretched, raw-throated hours, the Woods arrive with their six homeschooled kids. They're New Ark Traditionalists, who don't believe the Sea should be touched for any reason, even swimming. It's weird to be on their side, but their addition means the barricade finally stretches across the highway, so people can take breaks, and A.Z. can finally lower her arms, which have a weird dull pulse, like a dial tone, running through them.

She drinks some water and sits on the gravel shoulder to eat chicken chow mein with no chicken, which is fine because she's having trouble eating meat lately anyway.

She's chewing, wondering if the barricade will be a better alibi if she sneaks away right after she eats or if she rejoins the protest, when her dad shows up. His shirt pocket has so many pens she can't count them.

"It's over," he says, agitatedly. "It's finished. It's finally, finally finished."

"They caught the crocodile? But the boat isn't even here yet."

"No," her dad says, sitting on the gravel beside her. "Nell is furious." He unfolds a copy of the latest special edition. The paper has been coming out on random days because there's so much strange news, and also her dad has quit sleeping much or looking at his calendar.

Below the headline "Foundation Finally Finished" is a picture of the vaguely starfish-shaped foundation at the Starfish Inn. Even though that's where she first saw Kristoff, A.Z. has forgotten about the Starfish. Probably everyone has.

"What does Nell have to do with the Starfish?"

"If someone just reads the headline," her dad says, anxiously. "'Foundation Finally Finished.'" He spaces the words out, as if he's setting them in larger print than the rest of his speech. "I should have thought of it. It sounds like the Gording Foundation is over. Nell already thinks Chuck Chuck is trying to shut down the Sea with the alligator, and now she thinks I'm siding with them. She says she'll put out her own paper. Her own paper!" He looks as if he's about to cry. "I'm driving out to the beach to see her."

"That's ridiculous," A.Z. says, "and you can't get to the beach. We're barricading the road."

"You are?" He glances at the line of people—like he's just now noticing.

"Um, yeah," A.Z. says. "Maybe you should go get some sleep. I mean, and wait for some of this to blow over."

"It's too late," her dad says. "All the pilgrims are tired of waiting for an alligator appearance, and Chuck Chuck figured out that All-American-Asian Food is the same as Chinese, and now I've gotten Nell mad at me. 'Now would I give a thousand furlongs of sea for an acre of barren ground.'"

He stands up without using his hands, that way he learned when he was an Indian in some play, and walks toward the road to Mud Beach and out of sight.

A.Z. is looking at her dad's car—which would be useful for her to duck behind and head for the woods herself—when she hears sirens.

"Stand your ground," Sahara calls through the megaphone as Officer Gibbs—lights swirling and siren blaring—brakes to a stop in front of them. He gets out, dispatch radio pressed against his hearing aid, and stands where the dotted yellow line would be if the highway department had ever painted one.

Officer Gibbs is semi-deaf and semi-retired but he's Compolodo's whole police force and Nell Gording's cousin, and right now he looks pissed.

"This is an illegal traffic violation," he bellows. "This foundation is not finished. And you are ordered to get out of Sy Gording's way. We got a boat coming through."

Sure enough—when A.Z. stands up she sees, down the high-way—stuck in a circle of Baptists—Sy's pickup. She can't see the boat from this angle, but she can imagine it: awful and hulking and fiber-glass.

She checks her watch. Sy is more than two hours early, which is really, really bad. Best case, if the chicken stunner hasn't jammed, Kristoff is just now biking toward her.

"We are not a traffic violation," Sahara yells hoarsely. "The traffic is violating us."

"I am ordering you to get out of the highway," Officer Gibbs yells.

"You cannot make us leave," Sahara calls. "We're peacefully assembled."

A.Z. is pretty sure that Officer Gibbs *can* make them leave, and she's not feeling peacefully assembled. Her head is swirling—as if the red and blue lights from the police car are spinning everything inside her around, illuminating it. How she's going to get away, how they'll get out on the water before Sy, if she's going to get arrested right here on the stupid landlocked highway.

Then the passenger door to Officer Gibbs's car opens. In the flash-ing near-dark, A.Z. hasn't been able to see through the windshield. And it's like that part in *The Purple Rose of Cairo*, which A.Z. always thought was dumb but her parents like, when Jeff Bridges or Daniels, or whoever, climbs out of the screen.

A.Z. hasn't seen Nell for years—but also she's sort of seen her every opening night up on stage at the Miracle Play, an actress lip-syncing for Nell. And even though the actress is younger than this real Nell, there's enough of the same short-cropped hair and serious but sort of delicate jaw. Like maybe right now they're all in a deleted scene: the original protesters that got cut out of the story of the 1950s. And here's Nell, like always, to say, "God has chosen us!"

But the real Nell doesn't say anything. She stands there looking oddly regal, even though she's wearing some sort of aviator-style pantsuit.

"The foundation is not finished," Officer Gibbs says again.

For a strange flashing second, A.Z. considers trying to explain that her father never meant that, that no one thinks the Gording Foundation is finished. But of course she can't call attention to herself. She has to get away now, before Nell and Officer Gibbs arrest the protesters.

She ducks, as fast as she can, behind her dad's Oldsmobile and dives toward the woods. She doesn't dare turn on the bike light she's using as a flashlight until she's far below the highway, so she's running almost blind, branches scraping her legs as she scrambles down the hillside toward the valley that connects to the valley that connects to the shore. Finally, she turns the light on—the beam flickering and pooling on the underbrush and dark lumps of cedars.

Even though she's breathing hard, anxiously, she feels relieved. For once, she knows for sure that Nell isn't at her house and Sy won't be searching the shore. If she and Kristoff can just work fast enough, no one will be anywhere nearby to see them.

She's just above the cave, skidding down the hill, when she hears Kristoff's voice. He's gotten off early. He's maybe already raised the sail to surprise her and is calling to her.

But then she hears another voice—baritone—the splash of waves. She switches off her light and takes another step. No voice. Just splashing, and a seagull's squawk. Maybe she imagined the birds were voices?

But then she hears laughter and again, clearly, voices.

Big Bob saying, "Got it. Oh shit, didn't get it."

Kristoff saying, "That way," and more squawking.

Then silence, with the creak of a few trees in the wind, and Big Bob saying something like "Old salt, Sayonara," and Kristoff calling

"Sayonara" back, and then a crunching of leaves as Big Bob heads up
the hill.

Inside her, she can feel a rising tide, a Bay of Fundy swell of disbelief and anger. Although it's like the disbelief is belief, which makes
it worse, like she expected Big Bob to be here exactly where she told
Kristoff she didn't want him. Big Bob getting some stupid last supplies for the stupid heat sensor that can't really sense anything, ready
to go out on the stupid motorboat.

She scrambles the rest of the way with her light off. In the darkness, Kristoff is a tall silhouette standing on shore—which, she realizes when she gets closer, isn't shore at all, but the water. "What's
going on?" she calls. "What was Big Bob doing here?"

"Hey," Kristoff says cheerfully. "The stunner jammed completely,
so I got off early."

"Why didn't you come get me? The motorboat is already up on
the highway. They got here really, really early."

She presses her light on again, its incandescent stream grazing
Kristoff, who is knee-deep in the Sea beside their boat that he's
dragged, helpfully, from the cedars where they've been hiding it.

For a second, she sees what she's imagined seeing: the triangle of
the off-white, slightly paint-splattered sail in relief against the glossy
black water. But then it's like she's seeing through the sail—like an
afterimage of the water's bright darkness has supplanted it. And she
realizes she isn't seeing the sail at all. There's nothing above the boat
but air and the empty black space of the Sea.

Something like a wave taller than any wave she's ever imagined
rises in her chest, sucks down hard against her ribs.

"Where's the mast?" she yells, running down the hill, not even
caring that she's scratching her legs. "What happened to our sail?"

"I was trying to rig it up," Kristoff says, "but then we saw this
seagull, and Big Bob thought maybe we could net it."

"What?" A.Z. says.

"With the sail. I guess he used to do that in Costa Rica."

"Are you joking?" A.Z. says. "You have to be fucking joking. You used the sail I spent a million hours sewing as a net?" She realizes she's digging her nails into her used-to-be-bike-wrecked palm. It feels good, the pain just barely holding her together.

"Yeah," Kristoff says. "That didn't really work. And I guess the seagull sank before we could finish clubbing it."

"What?" She walks closer, her shoulders shaking, not wanting to see her sail draped over the side of the boat—like that old encyclopedia picture of the skin of the mythic selkie. Only this isn't mythology. It's her rigging in the water. Her mast, snapped off, cracked, leaning like stupid deadfall against another tree. "What happened to the mast? What'd you do to the mast?"

"The seagull was harder to club with the oar than we thought," Kristoff says, kind of hollowly and quietly. "It kept squawking and squawking, and then I slipped and the boat turned over, and I guess the mast hit that tree."

"What?" A.Z. says. She's feeling dizzy, like the air itself is unraveling around her. "You knocked our boat over clubbing a seagull with the oar?"

"Yeah," Kristoff says, "We wanted dinner. And besides, birds suck."

"What are you talking about?" she yells. "Birds don't suck."

"Yes, they do," Kristoff says. "Yves Klein said they tore holes in the sky, his most beautiful creation."

"Yves Klein didn't create the sky!" A.Z. says. "I don't care if he signed it and jumped into it and whatever. And now you've destroyed *our* most beautiful creation that we'd worked and worked on. I don't understand! This can't be happening! How am I ever getting into Sea Camp? How are either of us ever getting anywhere?"

She's crying now, and everything is blurring, but it's also like she can see it all more clearly: the mast, the sail, the split oar that was going to be their rudder, and Kristoff standing there in the water with a few feathers floating around him. "I can't believe you ruined our boat to kill a seagull," she yells.

"Seagulls suck," Kristoff says.

"Stop saying that," she says. "Seagulls are amazing. They're totally different from Chuck chickens. They fly way over the water where *we* were going to go."

"Not really," Kristoff says. "Seagulls are basically just big chickens. They come through the line sometimes."

"What?"

"You know, they get picked up with the chickens when they blow off the trucks. But they don't fit in the machines right, and blood sprays everywhere. That's probably what actually jammed the stunner."

"Oh my god. That's horrible!" She imagines pilgrims loading plates with kung pao alligator, which was really kung pao chicken, but might really have been kung pao seagull.

"It's hyperrealism," Kristoff says. "We're all just blood and guts."

"I don't care about stupid hyperrealism," A.Z. yells louder—not caring where her voice carries. "I care about going out on the water. I care about all the work we've done. What we were going to finally get to do. And now you've ruined everything." She's digging her fingernails harder into her palm; she's crying harder.

Kristoff is still looking out at the water and maybe he's crying, too. She can see his shoulders curl in, like some kind of mollusk. She doesn't feel sorry for him.

Across the water, she can hear the awful roar of a motor churning to life.

22

When A.Z. wakes up, the phone is ringing, and her head is on a pile of papers on the couch in her dad's office. She stumbles to the desk, crunching more papers as she reaches for the phone.

"Is your father there?" her mom says.

"What?" A.Z. says. "I must have fallen asleep here."

"Apparently," her mom says. "Is Kristoff there?"

"No. Why would he be here?" For a second, she feels embarrassed that her mom would think she and Kristoff were alone in her dad's office, and then she thinks how wonderful this would be, but then she remembers. She was just dreaming about Kristoff: he had pecan shells glued to his teeth and was wearing pink sweatpants.

"I don't know," her mom says.

"I haven't seen anyone since the barricade earlier," A.Z. says. "Dad left to look for Nell, and then the barricade got broken up, so I came back here to wait for a ride home, and I guess I fell asleep." She's hoping the barricade actually got broken up so this makes sense. Also, she doesn't care. Nothing makes sense any more.

Her mom sighs. "It's 3 a.m. I'm going to come get you. I just realized neither of you were home when Dragonfly called. I can't believe Nell Gording actually had Sahara arrested. Everyone is taking leave of their senses in this town."

At the house, A.Z.'s mom pours milk and molasses and vanilla into a pan and heats it up. It's way too hot and late for molasses milk, but it's what she used to drink as a kid in New York, and it's what she used to give A.Z. when she was little and scared. Even though A.Z. doesn't want hot milk, she doesn't argue when her mom hands her the cup—the top creamy and slightly wrinkled like those dogs old ladies sometimes have.

"Did I ever tell you about the walrus?" her mom says.

"What?" A.Z. says, staring at the milk, which is maybe also the color of a walrus.

"Your great-grandfather was a pharmacist when I was young, but before that, he'd been a soda jerk. Drug stores were like that then. They all had soda fountains, in addition to selling medicine and toiletries and things. And one day, he was working behind the counter, and a man sat down and said, 'I'd like a glass of walrus.' And my grandfather said, 'What?' He thought the man was crazy. But then he looked down and realized that the taps on the soda fountain were Walrus brand. He'd touched them for decades but never actually read what they said."

"Oh." A.Z. isn't sure why her mom is telling this story right now, but she also wants her mom to keep talking, to put all the words in order like the Dewey Decimal System.

But her mom has stopped and there's just the awful loud-quiet of the kitchen, like that Rothko quote Kristoff read once: "Silence is so accurate."

A.Z. didn't understand that then. But she sort of does now. It has to do with mastless, sailless boats, and water that is also walrus, and research vials full of nothing, and Kristoff standing there silently by her ruined boat as she walked away. The Sea she's known her entire life without getting more than a few drops of water closer to understanding it.

"What are you crying about?" her mom says.

"I'm not," she says. For a second, she's crying and she's not crying. They're both true, and that just makes her cry harder.

"It's not another pregnancy scare is it?"

"No," A.Z. says crossly. "Of course not."

"Your father hasn't been home all night," her mom says. "He's beside himself about that Starfish article. He should not be letting Nell Gording intimidate him with her inability to read past the headline. He came to the library tonight to borrow *The Tempest*."

"*The Tempest*?" A.Z. finally looks up, wiping her nose on her hand. She thinks about that weird thing her dad said about the acre of barren ground. "What for?"

"Lord knows," her mom says, looking for once as if she really doesn't.

When A.Z. gets to her dad's office later that morning, he's sitting on the floor, surrounded by papers. He's holding a glue stick between his teeth. Even in the dim light, she can see the circles under his eyes—puffy and extra dark, like the newsprint he sometimes gets on his hands.

"How's it going?" A.Z. says, out of habit. She's barely slept either.

"'Bravely, my diligence,'" her dad says. "'Bravely.'" He glues down a picture and puts the glue stick back between his teeth to shuffle papers. "Sahara is out of jail and protesting outside it. And Kristoff is at the Sand Muffin." The words come out garbled around the glue. "He came in looking for you. 'Come into these yellow sands, and then take hands. Curtsied when you have kissed the wild waves whist. And, sweet sprites, the burden bear.'"

"What?" A.Z. says.

Her dad takes the glue from his mouth. "It's the new shop. It's actually owned by some First-First Southern Baptists, but I'm not saying that. I'm not saying that at all. I'm not even writing about it. But they offered me free samples, and Kristoff was hungry. They have holey muffins."

"Holy muffins?"

"Yeah, like donuts. But muffins. Muffins with holes."

"Oh," A.Z. says, feeling pissed that Kristoff is eating her dad's free muffins. "Did you see Nell last night?"

"'What's past is prologue,'" her dad says, gluing an ad for a two-for-one egg roll special at the bottom of the front page that says "Miracle Motorboat!"

"Were you just reciting *The Tempest*?"

"Kristoff really liked the first act. He thought I was particularly good at Prospero."

"You recited *The Tempest* to Kristoff this morning?"

"'To every article, I boarded the king's ship,'" her dad says, which makes her want to burst out crying.

"Is there a production of *The Tempest* going on or something?"

"There might be," her dad says. "It's possibly probable."

The Sand Muffin is in the narrow space that used to be vacant beside High Tidey Laundry, and Kristoff is at the first table, wearing his inside-out shirt that's super bloody on both sides. He has a big bag of muffins in front of him. As soon as she sees him, A.Z. isn't sure why she's come.

"Hey," he says, way too normally, biting into a chocolate muffin. "This isn't cooked."

"You should tell them." She glances at the woman behind the counter, sprinkling sugar onto a pan of muffin rings.

"I like it."

She can't think of anything else she's willing to say, so she stands there, listening to what sounds like a Christian radio station.

Kristoff takes another bite of muffin, crumbling crumbs onto a library paperback that's open by his plate. "Do you ever see waterfalls of blood when you close your eyes?"

"What? No."

"It's kind of freaky." He's set the muffin down and he really does look freaked out—like maybe right now he's seeing blood pouring from somewhere above the table.

"You need to quit Chuck Chicken," A.Z. says crossly. "It's messing you up."

"Yeah," Kristoff says, "after I get Thu some chickens."

"What?"

"I went by Seven Happiness earlier looking for you, and she said, 'You're A.Z.'s boyfriend who works at Chuck Chicken?'" A.Z. can hear Thu saying this—as if A.Z. has a lot of boyfriends who work at a lot of different places, which right now she wishes were true. "She asked if I could get her chickens, and I said I'd just killed two hundred last night before the stunner jammed."

"I didn't come here to talk about dead chickens," A.Z. says. She's not sure why she's actually come.

"I've been grokking things totally wrong," Kristoff says.

"Grokking? What the hell are you talking about?"

Kristoff nods toward the book. "It's Robert Heinlein. It's like deeper understanding. You join completely with whatever you observe. He says it's religion and science and what color means to the blind, all at the same time, but we can't really get it as Earthlings. This book is great. This alien comes to Earth and seduces all these women."

"That sounds stupid," A.Z. says, even though the idea of grokking sounds sort of cool—like understanding the Sea by going out into its center, by joining yourself with water samples, which no one, including Kristoff, has even tried to do.

She lowers her voice so hopefully the Baptist muffin lady can't hear: "I can't believe you and Big Bob took down our sail and then cracked our mast and ruined everything. I've been waiting all summer to get those samples that prove something about the center of the Sea, and that was our perfect chance. I don't even know why I'm talking to you."

Kristoff doesn't say anything. Instead, he unzips his backpack and pushes two vials across the table. New glass vials with stoppers, full of sort of clear and sort of brown-green seawater. She'd recognize it anywhere.

"What's that?" she says anyway.

"Water. Before we screwed the sail up, Big Bob was testing out the sensor by swimming out and dragging it around the bottom, and I asked him to stick these on it. I thought you'd like some samples from down there."

"Oh," A.Z. says. She pictures Big Bob with his dumb sensor with her vials tied to it. Big Bob knowing about her research. Big Bob ruining her boat. Big Bob trying to net a seagull. Big Bob unfortunately not getting eaten by the crocodile he was crazy enough to swim with.

But she also thinks of Kristoff thinking to get her deeper-water samples. Kristoff doing research without her.

She stares at the bottles on the bakery's little fake wood table; they're murky with floating debris, but also kind of beautiful.

Kristoff lays his head in his arms by the bottles. "I'm sorry I fucked things up."

"Yeah," A.Z. says. "You really, really did."

"I wasn't thinking." He lifts his head. His eyes have that far-away look they get, as if he's climbed someplace deep inside himself, and she's just seeing the shell. "I keep having that dream."

"The chicken one?" She imagines Kristoff awake all night with the squawking of undying chickens, lying on Gerald's kitchen floor with blood waterfalling above him. She'd be grokking everything wrong, too.

"I really think you need a new job," she says. "What about Creamy Days, if Larsley's really quitting?"

"Yeah. I could go for some ice cream." He takes another bite of muffin, which collapses around its little hole. "I'll fix the mast or cut a new one or whatever. We'll still go out there."

"They're patrolling in the motorboat now. They could see you. And anyway, they've already gone out on the water." It makes her feel sort of sick to say it. Not like a motorboat can really change the saline levels, but maybe it can a little. Now there are oils and things that should never have been there.

"I'll work on it at night," Kristoff says. "I don't sleep, anyway." Then, more cheerfully, "Hey, your dad invited me to your house for dinner. He wants to recite the start of Act Two."

"Oh," A.Z. says. Kristoff has never been to her house and it's weird that her dad invited him now. She pictures being with Kristoff in her room, looking at her fish and the photo of the fireworks on the beach the day she was born, making plans for re-rigging their boat.

And when she thinks of rigging, she feels it, too: the ropes she wouldn't know how to begin to untangle between them, all the knots she doesn't even know the names of. The way it hurts to look at Kristoff in his bloody shirt, and also makes her feel as if some sail deep inside her is catching the first real open-water wind she's ever found.

While Kristoff bikes downtown to buy a new T-shirt and stop at Creamy Days for an application, A.Z. bikes home and puts away her plastic seagull and then gets it out and then puts it away and then worries it's dumb to have R.E.M. tacked beside Jacques Cousteau. Kristoff doesn't have posters on his ceiling, although of course right now he barely has a ceiling.

She dusts her dresser and bedside table, then gets out a couple of mixtapes Angie gave her, with cool U2 and Pink Floyd songs, and lays them casually on her bedside table with the refractometer and the water Kristoff gave her.

She's helping her mom mince garlic for garlic bread when Kristoff and her dad show up.

"Guess who's going to be the new ice cream reaper," Kristoff says. He's wearing a T-shirt that says SEA THE SEE! which is maybe a joke or a typo. Shore Shirts sometimes misspells stuff, which drives A.Z.'s mom crazy.

"'Beseech you sir; be merry. You have cause,'" her dad says, bowing. He still has newsprint on his hands and dark-circled eyes, but he looks more cheerful.

"Really?" A.Z. says to Kristoff. "You got the job?"

"Marie liked me," Kristoff says, leaning against the counter and eating grated cheese that's supposed to go in the lasagna. "I said I was really fast at slitting throats."

A.Z. is suddenly anxious that Kristoff is going to mention clubbing seagulls. "So she gave you the job?"

"She said she'd talk to me about it tomorrow."

"I can give Marie a call. We've known each other for years," A.Z.'s mom says, spreading sauce across the noodles. "Creamy Days will be so much better for the school year. Howard Chuck should not be hiring school-age people to begin with."

"Yeah," Kristoff says, absently picking, with the same cheese-eating hand, at some of the blood that A.Z. notices is still on his shorts. Hopefully Marie thought it was paint or something.

"I'm sure you're excited about art classes starting," her mom says, as if she's thinking this, too.

"There are art classes?" Kristoff says.

"At school," her mom says.

"Oh, yeah," Kristoff says, as if he hasn't really thought about school starting in just a week. Of course, A.Z. *has* been thinking about this—and worrying about Mrs. Reuter failing her on her independent study and about the Sea Camp application, which has to be postmarked on September first, one day less than three weeks.

It's not like she can explain in her personal statement that she tried to gather data but couldn't because her boat was never seaworthy, and a crocodile appeared, and everyone got endlessly distracted, and her boyfriend ruined her sails and mast, but now he's fixing them, only really right now he's watching her mom make lasagna.

Then she pictures Kristoff at Greenville High School and that makes her anxious in a different way, like they're in *Grease* or a lot of other movies where the couple goes back to different schools and everything ends up not at all like you imagined in the summer.

"I've never been very artistic," her mom says, "but Arthur and I did design some beautiful brands. We used to practice drawing what we'd have for our own ranch someday." She turns over the recipe card and draws crisscrossing squiggles, sort of like a snowflake "This was mine, for Sophie Simons—my maiden name. And Arthur's was *A* with the *C* for Connor." She cups a *C* below an *A*. "The *C* was supposed to be like a good-luck horseshoe." She sighs.

"Cool," Kristoff says, peering at the brands as if he's imagining his own. A.Z. pictures their initials together: *AZM* and *KS*. Kristoff doesn't have a middle name because his mom didn't want to think of one.

A.Z. sort of wishes Kristoff would design them a brand right now, but she's also worried she won't have any time alone with him to test the water, and he won't get to see her room or anything. "Kristoff and I have some research to do," she says. "Can we run up to my room?"

When they climb the stairs A.Z. has climbed a million times, the staircase feels shorter than usual, the ceiling at the top of the landing lower.

"Leave your door open," her mom calls, embarrassingly, like they'd do anything with a closed door.

Kristoff sits on her bed, not looking around at the fish or the picture of the fireworks or the tapes. Instead, he leans back on his elbows, staring up at the ceiling fan. "That could totally chop up a chicken," he says. "Hey, did you know those guys from R.E.M. are up there?"

"Yeah." She knew she should have taken them down. Even though R.E.M. is the best band, it's sort of cheesy to have Michael Stipe, Peter Buck, Mike Mills, and Bill Berry posing in a grey landscape that isn't even a landscape. "They're sort of standing in the void," she says.

"Yeah," Kristoff says. "The void is stupid."

He rolls onto his side and pulls her toward him, and it's hard not to slide sideways onto the bed, too, their feet dangling into space, the comforter silky cool-warm, almost the color of the Sea on bright days. It's hard not to kiss him, even with the door open, their legs tangled, their faces so close there isn't a poster above or parents below.

But of course there are. She pulls herself away finally—sort of sweating and dizzy. "We should test the water. I hope there's enough light still."

"It's clear." Kristoff holds up one of the vials. "Well, actually, it's not." He leans on one elbow, squinting at it.

A.Z. takes the refractometer out of its case, wiping the prism carefully with a clean cloth. She's been trying to take extra good care of it all summer not only to get the right results but because she wants to prove to Mrs. Reuter that she's very responsible with equipment, in case Mrs. Reuter ever gets an acoustic release device or some other real oceanographic equipment for the school. "Do you want me to show you how to calibrate this?"

She drops freshwater from her squeeze bottle onto the prism, counts down fifteen seconds and lifts it toward the window to show him. "You put freshwater on first, and wait a few seconds for the temperature to adjust, and then hold it up to the light. What it's measuring is the speed of light through the liquid. You have to use the refractometer because saltwater is a solution; you know, you can't see the salt particles with your eyes because they're too dissolved into the water. They're part of it."

She's feeling kind of geeky for explaining all of this, but also excited to tell Kristoff. She holds the eyepiece to his eye. "You adjust this screw to calibrate. Look at that line there, where the dark and light meet. That tells you the refractive index, which is also expressed as parts per thousand."

Kristoff looks, a few long curls hanging out of his green bandana. He looks really good right now—like someone who dips ice cream for a living, who calibrates refractometers, and makes salinity charts, and takes classes at Sea Camp.

"And next we put a drop of the seawater on," she says. "The salt will slow the light, so there will be a higher refractive index than the freshwater." She angles the refractometer to the light again. Then she takes it from her eye and wipes the lens off with her cloth and shakes another drop on and tries again.

"What's up?" Kristoff asks, looking interested.

"Something's wrong. The reading isn't changing. Are you sure you got this from the Sea?" She should have thought of this; it's the sort of not-funny joke Kristoff might play.

"Yeah, from down near the bottom. Big Bob was underwater for a long time. He used to be a Navy Seal."

"No, he didn't," A.Z. says. "He was a conscientious objector."

"Yeah," Kristoff says, as if this isn't contradictory.

"Maybe the refractometer got damaged from the heat or humidity?" A.Z. says, trying to stay calm. "Or maybe there's too much mud or some other kinds of minerals counteracting the salt?" She doesn't want to sound ungrateful for the water, but something is obviously wrong with the reading. "This isn't even registering as saltwater."

23

Technically, the first day of geometry should probably focus on math, but Coach W. is writing a grid of categories on the chalkboard. He loves *Jeopardy*, and last year in algebra, the class played at least three days a week.

"I heard Thu isn't selling chicken because of her religion," Larsley says. Coach W. has assigned her to sit in front of A.Z. because he forgot about the flaming hairspray or found out they're not friends anymore. Despite this, Larsley is twisted around, resting her elbows on the notebook where A.Z. is re-recopying her saline data. It's all she can do until she gets to see Mrs. Reuter during fourth period.

"No. Where'd you hear that?"

"I don't know. That's just what people are saying."

"That's dumb," A.Z. says. Before she can say anything else, someone knocks on the classroom door and then opens it.

Even though A.Z. just walked outside ten minutes ago, she's surprised by how bright it is—a wedge of non-fluorescent sun pouring in along with Principal Oakens, who has sweat stains on his dress shirt.

He glances at the board and smiles, his chin folding down. "Big cats," he says. "I wish I could hear that category." Principal Oakens loves cats, and the main office is decorated with posters of kittens clinging to cliffs and ceilings below words like HANG IN THERE.

"Stay and play with us," Coach W. says. "We're just about to get started."

"I wish I could," Principal Oakens says, "but I have to get around to all the classes to announce two important schedule changes." He takes a wheezy breath and mops at his brow with his handkerchief. "First, the pep rally today is going to be during fifth and sixth periods instead of just sixth. We want to send those alligators off with style."

"The what?" A.Z. says, sort of involuntarily.

"Didn't you hear?" Larsley says, "Coach is renaming the team."

"It's a crocodile," A.Z. whispers, "and they haven't even found it yet."

Larsley shrugs. "Scotty says they're going to chomp some flatland ass this year."

"Alligators aren't even marine," A.Z. says.

Coach W. raises his eyebrows at her for talking. She doesn't really care if she gets moved away from Larsley, but it seems bad to get in trouble on the first day of school, with the principal right there in the doorway saying, "And then—this is important for all of you—tomorrow, not only the juniors and seniors, but also the sophomores are going to get to take the ASVAB test."

"The ASS-VAB?" Bobby says, grinning.

"The ASVAB," Principal Oakens says. "You'll be meeting in the cafeteria starting in fourth period tomorrow. Fourth, fifth, and sixth periods you'll be in the cafeteria. It's a standardized test that will help you identify your vocational aptitude."

A.Z. already knows her vocational aptitude, which is why she really needs to be in biology talking to Mrs. Reuter right now, and also not missing biology tomorrow. For a second, when Jeopardy starts, she tells herself she's not going to answer a single question. She's just going to sit there and brood.

But then people keep saying, "Come on, you know you know the answer, Librarian," and it's easier to answer than be begged to, which is why her side—the Destroyers—wins by two points against the Sea Tigers, which is Bobby's dumb idea for a team name.

As soon as they get to biology, Mrs. Reuter starts prepping them for dissections. Apparently she got a discount on frogs from some summer-school program in Springdale and she needs to get them off the ice and cut apart before they rot.

A.Z. has always liked dissection—because it's super scientific and tells you exactly what a thing is made of—but when Mrs. Reuter starts talking about formaldehyde and scalpels, she pictures seagulls with blood spraying from their necks and her own body like a crampy frog on the table at Planned Parenthood. And when Mrs. Reuter asks if anyone isn't dissecting—which Sahara never is, even though dissection is sort of necessary for vet school—A.Z. raises her hand. Mrs. Reuter looks at her quizzically.

"They're going to be dissecting alligators next," Sahara says when she and A.Z. move to the back to start tracing the textbook's frog picture. "It's so cruel."

"It's a crocodile," A.Z. says.

"Yeah," Sahara says. "I've been trying to sneak the trap down to the water, but Officer Gibbs has been watching me. Did you sign the petition about police brutality?"

"No," A.Z. says. "Did they really keep you in jail overnight?"

"Yeah," Sahara says. "It was like being in a chicken cage. Now I know how they feel."

The bell is already ringing—early, so everyone will have time to get to the pep rally. A.Z. is worried that Mrs. Reuter will leave right away, too, but she's still at the front of the room dumping formaldehyde on the frog bodies. Up close, they smell nauseating.

"Mrs. Reuter," A.Z. says nervously. "Do you have a minute to talk?"

"Sure," Mrs. Reuter says. She closes the ice chest and sits on the edge of her desk. She doesn't look like she's in a hurry to get to the pep rally either.

"I'm sort of worried about the refractometer," A.Z. says. "I mean, I've been doing my research, but my data doesn't make sense. I think maybe the humidity or heat has affected the calibration. I really tried to keep it cool and clean and everything in my backpack." She can feel her voice shaking. She really doesn't want to admit that she's maybe messed up Mrs. Reuter's equipment and doesn't even have a hypothesis.

Mrs. Reuter smiles. "I'm glad you stuck with your project all summer," she says. She pushes her hair back from her face; it's greying but only in the front, like a frame. She looks more tanned and somehow younger than last year.

"I didn't get as many samples as I wanted," A.Z. says. She can't explain, of course, what she was trying to do, or about wanting to apply with Kristoff. "But I've charted some patterns; the salinity has been low most of the summer, but my last reading doesn't make any sense. There has to be something wrong. It can't be all the way down to 0.5 ppt. That's freshwater."

"Maybe it's a seasonal variation?" Mrs. Reuter says. "It's almost fall." She glances unconvincingly toward the window, where the air-conditioner is on high, rattling in its metal frame. "Maybe this is something you can talk to the scientists at Sea Camp about."

"But I can't get into Sea Camp if I don't have a project that makes any sense," A.Z. says. "I need to be able to prove something about the Sea's salinity."

Mrs. Reuter smiles in that way adults sometimes do, like they've been trained to tell you everything is going to work out. "I wouldn't worry too much," she says. "Sometimes strange data leads to big discoveries. You know the writer Isaac Asimov? He said, 'The most exciting phrase to hear in science, the one that heralds new discoveries, is not *Eureka* but *That's funny.*' I've always liked that."

"But I can't just write down 'that's funny' on my Sea Camp application. I mean, my research needs to show something."

"Yes," Mrs. Reuter says, "but there are a lot of different things you could show. You know, water was never really my specialty. But I know some inland seas are very salty, and some are less salty than certain lakes—like the Great Salt Lake, for instance."

"Yeah," A.Z. says, "but inland seas are still saline, except the Sea of Galilee, which isn't even a sea. But real seas like the Caspian. I mean, parts of it are closer to freshwater because of the Volga River, but overall, it's saline." She could usually quote the ppt, but right now her brain is formaldehyde-refractometer scrambled. She's not quite sure what Mrs. Reuter's point is.

"And you've checked it against a pure saltwater solution?" Mrs. Reuter says. "I know that's what I learned to do for the aquarium."

"No," A.Z. says. She feels super dumb suddenly; she missed this part.

"You can make a saltwater solution at home from iodized salt," Mrs. Reuter says, "but I maybe still have a bottle." She goes to one of the locked cabinets, which have bones and microscopes and things that always seem extra valuable because Mrs. Reuter has to unlock them, and rummages around on a shelf. She pulls out what looks like a very ordinary plastic squeeze bottle and checks its label. "Here," she says. "You might give it a shake."

A.Z. feels like her hands are also shaking as she shakes the bottle, which is labeled, "3.65 weight percent solution NaCl." She wipes off the prism of the refractometer and calibrates to thirty-five: standard saltwater. The line, which should not line up if the refractometer is broken, lines up perfectly when she holds it to the light.

"It looks like it's working," she says.

"That's funny," Mrs. Reuter says, smiling at her own sort-of joke.

"'The masters of some merchant and the merchant have just our theme of woe,'" A.Z.'s dad says, driving fast around the curves to the beach after school. "I don't think town really needs another magician."

Apparently Dr. Grulkey finally found the crocodile's former owner through vet records. He's a magician in Branson who used the crocodile in his show and has offered—for a fee—to come to Compolodo and make it reappear.

"We don't have a magician," A.Z. says. She's worrying about filling her vials without the lifeguard noticing. Collecting Mud Beach swimming lagoon water isn't a huge advancement for her data, but now that she knows the refractometer is working—and probably the samples Big Bob and Kristoff got were just contaminated or something—she's hoping she can at least get some end-of-summer samples to compare to the start of summer.

"'I'll break my staff and bury it certain fathoms in the Earth,'" her dad says. He turns into the Mud Beach lot, which is mostly empty. The only living things on the beach are four parents, six kids, and a couple of seagulls. A.Z. looks at the gulls closely to make sure neither of them looks recently clubbed, but they seem totally healthy. The good news about the beach only having two families on it—trying to build sandcastles out of dry sand this side of the caution tape—is that the lifeguard isn't even in his stand.

Across the water—distant, but roaring—she can hear the motorboat. She imagines Greg and Sy out there, trailing the sensor, waiting for the cold-blooded crocodile to surface.

"I'm going to walk down the beach," she says, taking off fast so hopefully her dad will take the hint and wait for Sy. But her dad doesn't have anything to do, so he follows her. "I need to get some water for my independent study," she says finally.

"Great," her dad says. "'And deeper than did ever plummet sound.'"

For a second, A.Z. feels paranoid her dad knows about the deep-water samples she was trying to get, but this is probably just the next line. *The Tempest* has a lot of sea lines, which is what makes it kind of cool.

Having her dad with her is actually handy. If the lifeguard appears and catches her crossing the caution tape, she can say she's on official journalistic business. And her dad can hold the vials after she fills them.

It's high tide, so the water is lapping almost to the stakes holding the tape, and once she's stepped across, she doesn't have to reach very far to skim each vial below the surface—trying to keep it high enough to avoid sand or other debris.

She hands the first one to her dad, who props it on his steno pad, spotting the tan cover. She's waiting for water to gurgle into the second when she sees the boat sweeping around the edge of the woods, where her dad saw the turtle. She screws the cap on and steps over the caution tape—not super subtly—just as Greg calls, "We sensed something in the east quadrant."

"East quadrant," her dad calls back, jotting this down—as if it's an actual mapped place and not some weird military name Greg and Sy made up.

"Yeah," Greg says, standing on the prow in his hunting vest as Sy kills the motor. "Something big." He grins. He's not helping Sy drag the boat onto the beach, maybe because he still can't get his foot wet. Instead, he stands there, rocking and grinning. "We're gonna go back out and find that gator."

Her dad looks relieved—as if, with the crocodile found, everyone will be reunited.

A.Z. is doubtful. She can't imagine the First-First Southern Baptists and New Arkers uniting over anything—especially once the crocodile is stuffed and put in the Miracle Museum, like some Noah's Ark taxidermy.

"I'm going back to the car," she says. "I've got homework to do."

"School just started," Greg says.

"Yeah. I know." She's happy Greg is stuck in the boat and can't follow her—even though, in another way, she feels dumb being the one on land.

While her dad talks to Sy, A.Z. lays the vials out on the hood of her dad's car. She's calibrated the refractometer and placed a drop of water from the first vial on the prism when the families of pilgrims from the beach show up, shaking sand off their towels.

"They should add the alligator to the Miracle Play," one of the moms says. "It's so beautiful that God is still sending wonders."

"They ought to wall off an area for swimming," the other mom says. She's tall, with a bad red sunburn down both arms. "It's just not the same if you can't be in the water. And with my psoriasis." She glances at A.Z.'s vials. "I just wish I had some of that holy water."

A.Z. has the sudden urge to throw herself across the vials. Did the pilgrims watch her get the samples? Are they going to report her? She stuffs them hurriedly into her backpack before holding the refractometer up to the light—pretending she hasn't noticed them. Scientists can't let themselves be distracted.

Except she *is* distracted. The refractometer is reading 0.5 ppt.

"Good data?" her dad says, driving a little more in his own lane back to town.

"No," A.Z. says. She doesn't want to explain, but also she does. "Something's wrong with the refractometer. I mean, Mrs. Reuter says it's working, but obviously it isn't. The humidity has been really bad all summer; maybe it's gotten wet inside or something."

"'Good wombs have borne bad sons,'" her dad says in one of the female voices. Then, in his own: "Do you want to use my computer? You could type up your notes. Things always make more sense when they're typed up." Then he sighs. "That's not true," he says. "Not true at all."

A.Z. has only used her dad's computer once, so when they get to his office, he opens a new file for her. Then he checks his voicemail messages and hurries back out because the Ark Park has apparently just gotten an armadillo.

A.Z. decides to title the file "Research Results," and for a second she feels hopeful, as if she has real results, as if her fingers are going to figure out how to make sense of all the numbers without her mind even having to. But when she types the column of data—35.1, 36, 18, 15, all the way down to 0.5 and 0.5—the numbers seem even less significant, like the time she saved that huge jar of pennies and it only added up to $2.45. The only truly saline samples are from Mud Beach at the start of the summer.

Finally, she types *alligator is crocodile*, and then she deletes that because it doesn't really have to do with her main research. Then she types *saline definitely decreasing. New samples freshwater.* She deletes that, too. The backspace is sort of comforting, sweeping into the past, erasing even the facts, the way you don't usually get to do in real life.

For a second, she wishes she'd given the vials to the pilgrim woman—let her carry them around as stupid holy water, splash them on her skin and wait for something to happen.

Caspian Sea, she types, *freshwater near Volga River.* She did a report on this in junior high. *Baltic Sea, stratified.* But of course she doesn't have any data to prove inlets or outlets or stratification. *More than seasonal variation.*

She imagines the other Sea Camp applicants—girls like the model on *Seventeen* who wear bikinis to their oceanography classes that just started, that they already have As in.

She sits, staring at the blinking cursor. She has no idea how her dad comes up with words to follow it every day. It winks at her: green and slitted, like the eye of the crocodile in that dream, waiting to eat her.

24

By the time she walks to Creamy Days, it's almost 6 p.m., but there's still a long line of pilgrims. Kristoff doesn't notice her. He's busy dipping—his ropey arm muscles extra visible.

Behind him Liz is making waffle cones: pouring batter onto the griddle and bouncing her head to her headphones and looking blond and pinched-faced in that way a lot of guys think is pretty but isn't. A.Z. should have thought of this. A lot more girls work and eat in ice cream shops than chicken processing plants.

A.Z. gets in line and waits between a pilgrim couple and a family with four kids who keep talking about snow cones, even though Creamy Days doesn't have a machine. She's looking out the smudgy plate glass window to the street when Sahara waves and comes inside.

"Dr. Grulkey just heard from the exotic animal dealer in Florida who sold the alligator to the magician," she says, standing by A.Z. and gesturing with a handful of flyers. She has a roll of masking tape like a bangle around her wrist, so she must be posting them on telephone poles. "We've almost traced the alligator back to its home in the wild."

A.Z. isn't sure how tracing the crocodile's home is supposed to help, but she nods. "It's a crocodile," she says. "Alligators don't have salt-processing glands."

"No," Sahara says. "It's definitely an American alligator. He has paperwork."

"So it's already died," A.Z. says. "Alligators don't live in saltwater."

Sahara shrugs. "I guess this one does." She hands A.Z. a flyer. "We want the pilgrims to boycott the Miracle Play until it's humanely caught and returned to its natural habitat. Could you hand these out in line?" She thrusts a handful into A.Z.'s hand before she can say anything.

A.Z. looks down at the stack of flyers, which right now seem like some photocopied nightmare: duplicate after duplicate of the wrong word, *alligator*. It isn't possible. If the crocodile is an American alligator, then the rest of the Sea isn't any more saline than her recent samples. But obviously, the Sea is saltwater; she's applying to Sea Camp, not stupid Lake Camp.

Unless, of course, the alligator died weeks ago like she originally thought. In that case, her dad saw a turtle, and Greg saw bloody seagulls that Kristoff and Big Bob were killing, and everyone just thought it was the alligator because that's what they wanted to see.

Maybe, if she can find the alligator decomposing somewhere on the Sea floor, she can dissect it and prove it died of osmotic shock. Finding the alligator seems like sort of a long shot, but also like it'd be really useful. She sort of wishes she hadn't gotten out of dissecting the frogs.

She's thinking about this when she finally reaches the front of the line.

"Hey," Kristoff says, grinning.

"Hey," she says. She wasn't planning to eat any ice cream, but she's waited this long, and the peach chunks look all fresh and delicious and comforting. "How's the peach?"

"The ear wax?" Kristoff takes a bite of the chocolate he's just dipped and licks some off his arm, which is kind of sexy and kind of against health regulations.

"Ear wax?"

"Look at it."

Through the smudgy glass, it's true; the peach pieces are the color of earwax.

"The squished roach is good, too." Kristoff scoops black cherry on top of the chocolate. A.Z. has never thought about how much the flattened cherry pieces look like roaches. "Mmm," he says, taking a bite. "I'm going to replace all the labels: Vomit. Turd Trail. Irish Spring." He waves the metal scooper at the key lime. "Or I might just switch all the names. I want to see if people still think chocolate tastes like chocolate if it's really vanilla."

"Cool," she says. "Maybe I'll just try a little scoop of vanilla."

"You mean the albino alligator?"

Kristoff dips the next customer a sugar cone of mint chip, which he's calling strawberry, and A.Z. sits at one of the little marble tables by the old-fashioned metal cash register that's really electric and eats her vanilla, which tastes a lot like vanilla. Finally, the line dies down, and Kristoff comes and sits with her. He's brought one of the receipt pads to brainstorm: *Fresh Blood* for raspberry, *Pencil Shavings* for cookies and cream.

"I'm having a really weird day," she says, glancing around to make sure no one is listening. "Sahara just told me the alligator is definitely an alligator. But that would mean it's been dead since right when it got to the Sea. And Mrs. Reuter says the refractometer is working, but I just came from Mud Beach, and it obviously still isn't. The new samples aren't testing as any more salty." She leaves out going to her dad's office because it just makes her feel more depressed.

"The world of common sense is violently opposed to the imagination," Kristoff says. "Rothko said so."

"Yeah," A.Z. says. Maybe this is true. Maybe she needs to have more imagination, but she's not sure exactly how or about what. "I don't even have biology tomorrow to talk to Mrs. Reuter because we've got this stupid vocational test. Do you have to take that?"

Kristoff shrugs. "I didn't go."

"To the test?"

"To school."

"But it was the first day." A.Z. has never heard of anyone not going to the first day of class, unless they're moving or something.

"Yeah, I was down at the cave working on the figurehead."

"What figurehead?" A.Z. says. She glances around again. "I thought you were fixing the mast."

"Yeah," Kristoff says.

"You really skipped school?"

"Yeah. Yves Klein didn't go to school."

"Yes he did. You told me he went to a French conservatory."

Kristoff shrugs and writes another flavor. A.Z. isn't really sure he should be changing labels during his first week at the job but she doesn't say so. That's what's hard about being an artist's girlfriend. If Yves Klein's girlfriend had told him not to paint everything blue, the void would never have existed.

"Your mom dropped out when she was a junior," Kristoff says.

"That was different. That was back in the '50s, and her boyfriend had just died and her mom had transferred her to a new boarding school before finals, so she was going to have to retake a whole semester and she already knew all the stuff." She realizes that she's starting to retell one of her mom's stories. But the story is sort of comforting right now. It's weird in an expected way, like a word problem you can actually work out the answer to.

"Yeah. Boarding school sounds boring."

"Seriously," A.Z. says. "We need good grades to apply to Sea Camp. And saline data that makes sense."

"Maybe Big Bob forgot to put the salt in," Kristoff says.

"Yeah, right," A.Z. says, as Kristoff crosses off *milk chocolate* and writes *Turd Wipe*.

A.Z. finds a seat at a table as far as she can from the kitchen, but the cafeteria still smells like tater tots and mop water, which someone should tell the Arkansas Standardized Vocational Test Board distracts from intelligent thoughts.

She didn't sleep very much last night because she kept waking up worried about her data, so now she's going to have to try extra hard to focus if she wants to get a good score on the ASVAB. She's decided that if the results come back in time, a vocational aptitude test may be her best proof that she's really good at oceanography, even if she doesn't exactly have a completed independent study with a hypothesis.

Fortunately, the first question—which she flips to the minute that Mr. Finley says to turn their booklets over—is pretty easy:

How many degrees would you need to rotate Gear A in order to make it connect to Gear B to turn the turbine if the smaller gear is three inches smaller than the larger?

She doesn't have a lot of experience with gears, but it's sort of like figuring the total wind force and drag for a sail—how all the rigging attaches, how the leeboard provides lateral resistance. Maybe this is the exact sort of evidence of oceanographic logistics Sea Camp is looking for.

She finishes the gear section in seventeen minutes and then moves onto Word Knowledge, which is even easier because she pretty much grew up with all the words in the county surrounding her. Mathematics is also easy, despite Coach W. never teaching math, and so are the next sections: Paragraph Comprehension and General Science.

One of the science questions is so obvious that she feels—for the first time in days—truly hopeful.

Water is an example of:

A. crystal.

B. solid.

C. gas.

D. liquid.

D, she bubbles in happily, before speeding carefully through the rest of the sections and then flipping back to double-check everything just in case there were trick questions. She's the last person out, one minute before Mr. Finley calls time.

"That was dumb," Angie calls from the stairs by the gym when A.Z. appears. "I filled in *C* for every answer. Larsley's lucky she didn't have to take it."

"Is she sick?"

"No, she's home crying. Didn't you hear? Scotty broke up with her last night."

"Really? What happened?"

"He won't even answer her calls. She didn't go with him to the cross country meet because she was looking at cars with her mom, and Scotty was flirting with some girl on the Greenville team. When Larsley heard, he said that he thought he should be with someone who really understood running and that Larsley was holding him back from greatness."

"Jesus," A.Z. says. She feels bad for Larsley—crying in her room and watching endless MTV videos—but also like Scotty was always a dumb jock, and Larsley should have realized that.

"Yeah," Angie says. "It sucks. I'm going to go see her after I drop off my brother." She glances toward the gym where her brother, who is in junior high, and therefore doesn't have to take a vocational aptitude test, must still be in PE.

A.Z. is turning the lock on her locker when Dragonfly and Sahara come out of Principal Oakens's office.

"You didn't just take that test, did you?" Dragonfly asks.

"Yeah. We all did."

"Sahara didn't. She walked out as soon as she saw what they were asking her to do. It's inexcusable, the school making you take a military recruiting test without notifying the parents. My theory is that they purposefully had the test this week so there wouldn't be time to tell us. I'm going to call all the parents to sign a petition not to send the results."

A.Z. stares hard at her lock, like she's forgotten the combination, which she has. She didn't notice Sahara leaving. And she didn't actually read the cover of the test. She assumed ASVAB was *Arkansas Standardized Vocational* something-something.

"It's unconscionable," Sahara says, using one of the words from the week's vocab list. She's always practicing in case she goes to law school in addition to vet school.

"The school should be educating you," Dragonfly says, "not getting you ready to be sent off and killed. I suspect the military is offering new uniforms or something for the Alligators."

"You're done with the Armed Services Vocational Aptitude Battery?" her mom asks when A.Z. gets to the library. Apparently Dragonfly has already called in the time it's taken A.Z. to bike to Creamy Days looking for Kristoff, who strangely wasn't there.

"I didn't realize what it was," A.Z. says. She doesn't, of course, admit how excited she was about proving her vocational aptitude, which is now some dumb military aptitude that won't help her get into Sea Camp.

"The name was right on the test," her mom says, as if she was in the cafeteria, too.

"They didn't tell us," A.Z. says.

When she was little, she used to think the navy sounded cool: living on a ship and going places in the South Pacific or hundreds of feet underwater. But then her mom pointed out that even though regular ships are dangerous enough, at least they don't usually blow apart with hundreds of fatalities, including the people you most love. A.Z. can tell her mom is about to say something about this now. She's looking at A.Z. as if her accidentally taking a recruiting test is somehow retroactively responsible for her grandfather getting drafted and dying.

Her mom sighs. "I hope Kristoff didn't have to take it in Greenville. He's exactly the kind of boy the military tries to prey on."

A.Z. doesn't explain that Kristoff probably didn't take the test because he probably didn't go to school, and he also wasn't at work. When she looked through the smudgy plate glass, Liz and, strangely, Marie herself were working.

"Kristoff wouldn't go into the military," A.Z. says. "Has he come in today?"

"No. I imagine he went right to Creamy Days after school." Her mom looks at her oddly through her bifocals. "I guess you heard about the alligator?"

"Yeah, Sahara told me yesterday. If it's really an alligator, that means it died weeks ago, and everyone has been making a huge deal out of nothing."

"Well, it's dead now," her mom says. "I hope your father didn't get a speeding ticket on the way out there. They haven't found the body yet."

"What body?"

"The alligator. I thought news had probably made it to school. Greg just shot it."

"What? In the hour since he left the ASVAB? But that would mean it was alive until then."

"Yes," her mom says, sighing. "It was a lucky break. It surfaced right outside the swimming lagoon. I guess he got it squarely, but then it sank. They're dredging for it right now."

"But it can't have been alive," A.Z. says, taking hold of the rolling reshelving cart to steady herself.

A.Z. has never ridden so fast toward the cave. She's shaking, anxious from having to ride on the shoulder beside the speeding tour buses and cars—everyone suddenly in a hurry to see the dead alligator.

But in a way, too, it's like she isn't even pedaling—like she's caught in a storm that's swirling her thoughts like the wave and sky around the Raft of the Medusa. Everything closing in around her one little sail.

You know the writer Isaac Asimov? she can hear Mrs. Reuter saying.

But it isn't funny. None of it is funny. Not Mrs. Reuter and her dumb broken refractometer. Not the ASVAB and her independent study that proved nothing. Not Kristoff ruining their mast so she never got the samples from the center she needs. Definitely not the dead-and-therefore-recently-alive alligator swimming around the Sea with its glands that didn't evolve to process salt.

She wants Kristoff to hug her and tell her this will all make sense or that nothing makes sense. She wants to finish fixing the rigging and sail out while everyone is at Mud Beach distracted by the dead alligator that should have already been dead.

She's on Gording Way, pedaling hard down the dirt road, gripping the handlebars, willing her bike to stay upright and steady in the potholes when she sees a car; a car that seems, in the heat and dust and distance, at first like a mirage. A spot of the Sea drifting in the pasture. Or a big shiny blue Buick coming from the direction of Nell's house.

There's a barbed wire fence between A.Z. and the field, but she can't keep riding toward the car, so she rides into the shallow ditch by the road, jettisoning her bike and climbing—her hands on either side of the barbs, her feet on the lowest wire. She can hear the car coming closer, slowing by her bike, grinding on over gravel. Whoever it is has definitely seen her.

The problem with panicking is that she's on the wrong side of the road to get to the cave. She stays close to the fence until she's sure the car is far out of sight, then climbs quickly back over and hurries across the road.

She's swinging her leg over the fence on the other side when she sees Kristoff riding his bike through the high grass toward her. This seems unreal—like she's hallucinating Kristoff because she wants to see him. "What are you doing here?" she calls. "What's your bike doing on that side of the fence?"

"I finished the mast and was coming to look for you. Cool timing that you showed up."

"You finished the mast?" A.Z. says. She's feeling a little calmer already. "So we just need to get the sail rigged up. But we have to hurry while the motorboat is definitely at Mud Beach. Apparently Greg just shot the alligator, and they're dredging for it."

Kristoff laughs and takes a long drink of Mountain Dew, the

green-yellow tipping and balancing like a level. "Greg just shot the alligator?"

"Yeah." She has the knee-jerk reaction to correct Kristoff and say "crocodile," even though she's just said "alligator," too. And even though this shouldn't make her start crying, it does.

"It can't be an alligator," she says. "Alligators don't live in saltwater."

She bites her lip to stop crying. This is all going to make sense once she gets on the water, the water, the water. She can do this. Even if the ASVAB won't help her get into Sea Camp, she's proven she can figure out unlikely logistics—like Ballard, who discovered how whole ecosystems survive in deep-sea trenches without energy from the sun.

"We need to hurry," she says again. "Someone in a car just saw me crossing the road, and I think it was probably Nell. They didn't see you, did they?"

"No," Kristoff says, starting to walk his bike toward the woods. "I haven't seen anyone all day."

"All day? Didn't you have school? And work?"

Kristoff shrugs. "Ice cream just lies there. It's boring."

"Yeah," A.Z. says, "but at least you don't have to kill it. And you were making those cool labels." But then she realizes. "Marie didn't fire you because of the labels, did she?" She feels suddenly sure this is why Kristoff isn't at Creamy Days. "My mom just helped you get that job."

"Maybe I don't need so much help."

A.Z. wants to point out the waterfalls of blood and the beaten-up seagull—all the ways that Kristoff *does* seem like he needs help. But right now she needs help, too. And she's not sure regular work matters. Maybe neither of them needs help. Maybe once they rig the boat, they'll sail along shore until they find the freshwater outlet where the alligator survived. Then they'll sail all the way to Florida and live on the beach, rearrange all the signs from DISNEY WORLD to LEWD DINO, start everything over.

They're at the edge of the woods now, and the wind coming from across the Sea is gusty, good for sailing. It smells like woodsmoke, heavy and fallish.

"Do you smell smoke?" A.Z. says. "It's super hot for someone to be using a woodstove."

"No," Kristoff says.

"Are you sure?" A.Z. suddenly pictures Big Bob down at the shore, roasting seagulls.

"Yeah," Kristoff says. But then he stops. "Shit," he says. He's looking toward the Sea, where a haze of smoke, like mosquito netting, is visible now, about twenty-five degrees to the west through the trees. "I didn't think the brand was so hot."

"What brand?"

"On the manatee." He's walking faster now, crunching through brush.

"What are you talking about?" A.Z. says, hurrying behind him. She pictures a soft, pug-nosed manatee, its grey skin scorching. But that's impossible. Unless the Ark Park got a manatee. But manatees don't live on land. And alligators don't live in saltwater.

She's feeling kind of light-headed, like maybe from almost running or the smoke, which is getting stronger.

"The figurehead," Kristoff says.

For a second, she's imagining a cute wooden manatee on the prow of the *Evol Taob* with its new, repaired mast. But then Kristoff says, "I was branding scars on it to go with the blood. You know, from the motorboats. But the blood was sort of attracting flies."

"You were branding a manatee figurehead with blood on it?" Then, even before Kristoff says, "It was looking really cool on the boat," she puts it all together, like Gear A terribly turning Gear B until Gear C grinds to a stop in her brain.

"The boat?" she says. "You left a brand on the boat? The boat isn't on fire, is it?"

Kristoff has jumped off the ledge of the cave and is walking even faster toward the shore now, and she jumps off and follows him—not even thinking about nails in the junk pile. Not even looking where she's running. The smoke is thicker down here, and her eyes are stinging, like she's crying again even before she's crying.

The dry, hot wind blowing toward them doesn't feel like any Arkansas wind she's ever felt. It feels like all the moisture has evaporated from the world.

"I was trying to surprise you," Kristoff says somewhere beside her but also far away, through layers of gauze. "I wanted to make the manatee hyperrealistic with propeller scars to show pain is reality."

"What are you talking about?" A.Z. says. "What the hell are you talking about?" Just down the shore, by the stand of purple-red pokeweed where they first found the boat, she can see not only smoke but flames: a bonfire, a pyre. She wants to run toward it, drag her boat into the water, throw herself in, run from the woods, but she can't. She's frozen: a stuck compass needle.

And then she's moving without really feeling like she's moving—like those stories about people surged with sudden bursts of adrenaline who lift cars. She's throwing aside tin cans, burners, rusted wire, a little legless cow statue—running to the Sea to fill the few cans without holes, throwing the water on the boat, sizzling and useless. The flames are spiring higher toward the trees. The white paint. The crooked mast. The leeboard she sanded. The ropes. The grommets she sewed and sewed. The charred nub of what must have been a manatee. The invisible *Evol Taob*. The wood glue. The wood she sistered so carefully.

"Art isn't supposed to be permanent," Kristoff says, flatly, like he's explaining something that has nothing to do with them. He's filling a tin can now, too, but he looks as if he's moving in slow motion.

"It isn't art," A.Z. yells, wiping back her tears and throwing more water as the flames keep rising. "This isn't some dumb hyperrealism or concept or whatever. This was my last chance to go out on the real Sea to get real data for the Sea Camp application that has to be mailed in a week and a half. That's a *real* time, and I have to go to the *real* post office and mail it with *real* information about the *real* salinity that I can't get because the *real* boat is burning!"

She's crying so hard now she can hardly see, but she keeps throwing water anyway—the can-fulls sputtering against the fire. She's scared the trees are going to catch, that she and Kristoff are going to catch fire. She almost doesn't care.

Maybe Kristoff doesn't care either. He sits down on the ground like he does with his knees against his chest, so he looks almost like a kid, rocking back and forth. "I told you I was fucked up," he says.

"Yeah," A.Z. says. "You keep saying that and then doing more fucked-up stuff. You've been doing this all summer. And I keep making excuses for you. I keep thinking it's your job or your mom or something. And then you keep fucking everything up. You and that stupid alligator."

"Yeah," Kristoff says. "I was going to paint it pink but then it got away too fast."

"What? You saw the alligator?"

"When it came out of its cage. I didn't think they moved so fast."

"You let the alligator out of its cage?"

"Yeah," Kristoff says.

"This whole time, you're the one who let it out? You let the alligator out and watched it ruin everyone's summer? My dad is going crazy, and Thu is about to go out of business, and no one has gotten to swim, and I haven't gotten any good data from Mud Beach or the center of the Sea, and everything is all fucked up, and you never told me?"

Kristoff is still rocking, like that first night on the beach. Only there are no waves under them. There never have been.

Then he rocks over onto his side, holding himself in a fetal position, making a sound that is sort of a whimpering. A.Z. suddenly, very clearly, imagines herself kicking him.

"I thought it might be better in the Sea," he says. "Like the Jungle Cruise."

"It's not some dumb Jungle Cruise," A.Z. says, feeling like her throat, her head, her whole body have actually caught on fire, too—like the fire is Christo's pink fabric spreading out and out but also blazing into one red, impossible crumple. "It's our lives. It's the Sea. It's everything I've ever wanted to do."

"Me, too," Kristoff says.

"What is?"

"I don't know," Kristoff says, crying harder, rocking, balled up there on the ground.

"You can go to hell," A.Z. yells, "for all I care. I don't care. I don't care at all. I wish I'd never met you."

She takes off running. She's crying so hard she can't even see where she's going, but it doesn't matter. She runs until her legs hurt and her head is throbbing, and she feels dizzy, and then she folds over—her body doubling on itself like a piece of slack rope—and hangs there, her head pounding, and the water pounding against the shore, and the fire burning.

25

When A.Z. closes her eyes, she's drowning. There's saltwater on her face and skin, in her mouth, in her throat. But it isn't saltwater. It's freshwater. Then it isn't water at all. It's ashes.

She's running with her eyes closed. She's hyperventilating. She's running with her eyes open. She's on Nell's road, pulling her bike from the ditch, riding shakily and sobbing so hard she can't see anyway. It doesn't matter if she sees or not. There's nothing in the world.

But also, there are sirens. She can hear them—not the mythical sirens that call sailors to the sea rocks but fire truck sirens—like the day the trash barrel exploded. She turns onto the highway, riding fast down the other side as a fire truck races past, its lights flashing, those sirens blaring backward through her mind.

Kristoff is saying—a million years ago, earlier this summer— *Anything can be art. If someone says a paperclip is art, then it is.*

But he lied to her. He lied to her about everything. She can't say the Sea is salty when it's not. She can't say she's an oceanographer when she's a fucking void.

She's at the intersection of Shell and the highway. She's waiting to cross, or waiting to stop existing, when an old white Mustang with a dented hood pulls over.

"Hey," Larsley says, leaning across the seat and blowing a bubble with her gum, pressing it flat with her hand the way she always does.

A.Z. doesn't say anything. She doesn't exist. Neither does Larsley. Or her car.

"Did you hear about the alligator? I bet Greg can't wait to make you alligator jerky." Larsley smiles, but A.Z. can tell she's been crying, too. Her eyes are puffy, and she's wearing way too much makeup. "I'm going to the beach. You can stick your bike out of the trunk; it doesn't really close anyway because of that stupid telephone pole I hit last night."

The inside of the car is big and dimmer than should be possible on such a sunny day. The seats are shiny burgundy leather and smell like furniture polish, like someone's grandmother's car. A.Z. finds it strangely comforting in the way that apparently nonexistent things can be comforting. She looks out across the long hood and listens to Larsley humming along to the Violent Femmes. She's driving fast, one hand on the wheel because she's pressing the other one against another bubble.

"My dad says I can't drive because I got into another wreck this morning," Larsley says. "But they both got called to this fire out on Nell's land, so I left. I'm not going to sit around the house like a prisoner." She glances over at A.Z. "What are you crying about?"

"Nothing," A.Z. says. She wants to ask about the fire but she doesn't. She doesn't know why she's gotten into the car with Larsley. She doesn't know why anything is anything.

"Men suck," Larsley says, blowing another bubble and then spitting the gum out the window, like she's trying to spit out the whole idea of men.

The beach is crowded—a sea of people blocking the real Sea—everyone holding up cameras and binoculars, and putting their kids on their shoulders, and shielding their eyes to scan the waves. Sahara is waving a sign about stopping alligator genocide. Greg is standing by the lifeguard stand, getting his picture taken.

"He probably aimed at his foot," Larsley says.

A.Z. wonders why Larsley is here. She wonders why she's here. She follows Larsley down the beach, where Larsley stops to talk to Liz and Tammy. A.Z. sort of listens, but she listens more to the roaring coming closer and then farther on the water. She feels like her nerves are on the wrong side of her skin.

"Sy's having a party tonight to celebrate," Liz is saying somewhere far away, where people say words to each other and people listen and care. "I know he's gross, but they're getting a keg. He has a hot tub, too. I think it's at his uncle's place or something."

"Cool," Larsley says. "I can drive us. Hey, did you hear the Gordings' woods are on fire? Apparently Sahara was trying to burn the woods down to save the alligator."

"Wow," Liz says.

"That doesn't make sense—" A.Z. starts to say, but then she catches herself. Nothing makes sense. She can't let Sahara get arrested, but also, what other people think isn't her fault.

When Liz and Tammy walk away, Larsley puts her hand up to shield her eyes, scanning the beach. "There's your dad," she says. "Down by the water."

A.Z. should have thought about this. She doesn't want to see her dad. She doesn't want to see anyone.

But her dad has already seen them. He's walking toward her.

"Sy thinks the body might wash up here any minute," he says. "It was such an amazing shot. A synchronous shot. Greg says he was inspired by taking the ASVAB. I want to interview him, but there's a fire over by Nell's, and she says she saw a girl climbing the fence to start it, but Sahara has an alibi. An alligator alibi. She was at my office dropping off information about the original owner." Her dad is talking really fast. He's holding four Bic pens as if he's going to write a bunch of different stories at once.

A.Z. really wishes everyone would stop saying "fire," stop saying anything at all. She sees Kristoff curled on the ground, the flames maybe spreading out toward him, like a tide, but not like a tide. Like fire.

"Cool," Larsley says. "Sy is having people over later to celebrate. A.Z. and I are going."

"What?" A.Z. tries to say. But she doesn't get the word out fast enough.

Larsley smiles her sweet, convincing smile she uses when she's trying to get something—the smile A.Z.'s mom never trusted. "I'll drive her home in the morning. I got a car."

"Nice," A.Z.'s dad says, writing with one pen with the other ones still sticking out at weird angles from his hand. "Amazing aim. Astounding assassination."

"I'm not going to the party," A.Z. says when they get back up to the parking lot. She's pissed, not only that Larsley told her dad about the party but that Larsley and her dad have decided she's going without even asking her. She's not celebrating anything ever.

"Parents like to feel informed," Larsley says, starting the engine.

"And if you admit where you're going, they assume it can't be a real party with a keg and stuff. It's reverse psychology. It's way better than that dumb thing we used to say about Jacques Cousteau."

A.Z. always thought their Jacques Cousteau story was pretty smart, and she feels kind of hurt even though she doesn't care. "Whatever," she says. "You can drop me off."

"Fine," Larsley says. She's leaning across and rummaging in the glove compartment. She's not going that fast though, because there's a lot of traffic. "I just thought it would be fun. Like old times. God, we were so young back then."

A.Z. still isn't going to the party. She's just hanging out at Larsley's house for a couple of hours. Then she's going to sit in her room and stare at her speckled trout and cry for the rest of her life. But she can't quite figure out how to start the process of leaving. She's sitting on the blue carpet in Larsley's room, and it's like she's sunk into water. Warm, fuzzy water she can't step out of. Larsley turns on MTV and goes downstairs to her parents' liquor cabinet and comes back with a bottle of rum.

"It prevents scurvy," she says. "That's why pirates drink it."

A.Z. knows that vitamin C prevents scurvy and rum probably doesn't contain any, but Larsley is already pouring two glasses. "Yo-ho, yo-ho," she says. She drinks her whole glass in one gulp. "Do you still think about going out on the Sea?"

"No," A.Z. says. "The Sea sucks." She looks at the rum she's holding; it's a weird blue color because of the blue plastic glass. Sort of like pool water but darker. She drinks it.

"Yeah," Larsley says. "This town is lame." She lies on the carpet by A.Z., and they watch a dumb giveaway contest for tickets to see the

Bangles, and then "Eternal Flame" comes on, and A.Z. has to bite her lip really hard to not start bawling.

Finally, she gets up and goes to the bathroom and leans against the counter, breathing hard, forcing herself to breathe. And when she comes back out, "Express Yourself" is on, and Larsley has poured more rum, and A.Z. drinks it and sits there, feeling sort of safe, like the rest of the world is on some other island really far away and all she has to face is the muffled carpet and smell of microwave food and air freshener.

The hot tub isn't really a hot tub. It's one of those big plastic jet tubs in the bathroom. And A.Z. doesn't have a swimsuit, so she's wearing her T-shirt and jean shorts. Larsley said she should just wear her bra and underwear, but A.Z. isn't going to.

"It's like a bikini," Larsley said. "Bikini bingo."

Larsley is saying random stuff because she's drunk. Earlier, she called Scotty a "dickheaded cock," which Liz and Tammy thought was really funny. A.Z. has lost her sense of humor, but it doesn't matter. She's sitting with her eyes closed, and the hot chlorine is swirling around her and making her dizzy, and she isn't really in her body at all. Larsley is probably right; it doesn't matter what she's wearing. It doesn't matter. Doesn't matter. She's saying this to herself. She hasn't told her mother where she is. She's going to be grounded for the rest of her life, or maybe longer, but it doesn't matter. It doesn't matter.

Greg has been telling everyone about the alligator surfacing. It was right by the boat, and he saw its eyes, just barely above the water, watching him.

"We locked eyes," Greg says, "and then I pulled the trigger, and *boom*, he was gone, right into the water. He's one dead gator."

It strikes A.Z. again that until the body is found, no one will know for sure if Greg shot the alligator. And it doesn't matter.

"Right there," Greg is saying. "And there was blood in the water." He points between his own eyes. "*Boom.*"

"He must have had a death wish," someone says. Someone else says, "Or he thought Greg couldn't hit him." And someone else says, "Can't wait 'til they drag it out."

There are a lot of someones standing around the hot tub. It's popular because it's full of girls in their bras and underwear, or at least five girls, all of whom except A.Z. are in their bras and underwear. Not that this is super visible because the water is swirling and steaming and chloriney, and the lights are on underwater, making everything smoky, topazy grey-gold. And there are plastic cups of beer, which keep appearing—keep getting handed in by someone or taken away by someone—and A.Z. is dizzy and should sit up on the edge, but she'd be really visible there and really wet, and Sy is climbing into the hot tub in his boxers and orange John Deere cap, and everyone jostles closer, so Larsley is beside A.Z. with her eyes closed.

Sy is saying, "This is my kind of bath," and someone is laughing, and someone else has a gun—a hunting rifle. And he's walking through the room with it up on his shoulder like a military salute.

It's Gus—Sy and Greg's cousin who runs the Ark Park. He's aiming at the ceiling and yelling, "I'm gonna get you, gator." And someone is cheering.

And A.Z. says before she hears herself saying it, "Is it loaded?"

And Sy says, "Yeah, but Gus is good with guns. He has to shoot the sick animals."

A.Z. feels really anxious—not so dizzy anymore—but like her whole body is super awake, guarding against whatever is going to happen. Like she knows that something terrible is going to happen, and it's probably in one of her mom's stories, although maybe it isn't.

Maybe she's outside all of her mom's stories. Maybe she's vanished into other stories where people drink Bud Light in hot tub bathtubs and aim guns at the ceiling, which is that bumpy white stuff they use in cheap houses, which would feel terrible if you were lying on it, although of course why would you be lying on the ceiling?

Apparently she's said some part of this out loud because Larsley is singing "Dancing on the Ceiling" and laughing. She's still got her eyes closed and has floated closer to Sy, who is grinning from under his cap. A.Z. should pull Larsley back because of course Larsley doesn't want to be close to Sy, but she doesn't.

Tammy is saying, "My uncle took me hunting when I was ten, and I almost shot a deer."

"A doe?" Sy says.

"Yeah," Tammy says. "But it got away right when I fired."

"Then you didn't almost get it," Greg says. He's barefoot, and apparently his foot is healed because the bullet wound, which looks like a dark red scar, isn't bandaged or anything. He's climbing into the hot tub in his jeans and T-shirt, which is kind of weird and kind of exactly what A.Z. has done.

"You want some alligator jerky?" It's the first thing he's said to her all night because he's been busy telling his story about locking eyes with the alligator and watching it slip away in the bloody waves. She doesn't answer because of course it isn't a real question; it's pretty much just like saying hi.

"I'm gonna get you," Gus yells. And then he throws his beer cup into the hot tub and spins around like he's going to shoot something behind him.

A.Z. wants to get out but she doesn't know where she'd go; she's too far away to walk home, and she's kind of drunk, so she has to wait for Larsley to leave, which isn't going to happen because Larsley is drunk, too. Besides, she's probably safer sitting really still like that guy in her mom's story with the rattlesnake on his chest, only not like that—like a girl in a hot tub bathtub in a room full of hick guys, one of whom has a gun.

"We're not returning the boat rental 'til we find the gator's body," Greg says to her. "I could take you out in it if you want."

"What?" A.Z. says, even though she's heard him. Gus's beer cup is floating in the hot tub, and no one else seems worried about the gun, which Gus is swiveling at the air just over their heads now. "Are you sure he isn't going to shoot someone?"

"Ah, Gus," Greg says. "Probably not." He calls to Gus, "You oughtta go look for alligators outside, Gus. I think there's some in the bushes."

Gus staggers to the door.

"He's gonna go pass out," Greg says. "He always does that."

Larsley has her eyes open now and she's sitting in Sy's lap. Greg is sitting next to A.Z., leaning back against the tub. He smells like Skoal up close, disgusting and fungusy and wintergreeny, and also weirdly nice—like moss, and wet woods, and the swimming dock.

"I'm not supposed to take anyone out, but I know you like boats and stuff."

"Sort of," A.Z. says. "Where were you when you killed the alligator?"

"Way out there," Greg says. "By these rocks. You know, sort of this island."

"An island?" A.Z. says. She should be feeling calmer now that Gus has gone, but she still feels really anxious, like a clock is wound up tight inside her and is ticking toward something.

"You still hanging out with that tall guy?" Greg says.

"No," A.Z. says. "He's gone." She doesn't mean to say this.

"Gone?" Greg says. He grins. "Like the alligator." Then he says to Sy, "You shoulda seen it, that gator was a goner."

But Sy doesn't answer because he's kissing Larsley, which should not be happening, and A.Z. therefore pretends isn't because there isn't room in her mind, which is crowded and swirling and no bigger than this hot tub that is probably made for four people and has seven in it.

"I finished this big case for the gator," Greg says. "It's gonna be in the museum right next to that old boat."

"Yeah?" A.Z. says. Greg's knee is against her knee—wet denim against her skin, and maybe because she's also wearing wet jean shorts, she somehow feels as if she knows what it feels like for Greg to be sitting there in those jeans, and she imagines Greg out on the boat in the middle of the Sea. "I can't believe you've been out on the Sea," she says.

"Yeah," Greg says. "You should go out with me." He grins at her, and it's nothing like Kristoff's grin. She doesn't even think he's cute, not really. Disgusting Greg with his Skoal-breath and his pale blue eyes, too pale to be ocean water, like early morning sky. And if she existed. If this mattered. If she were still herself. She would not have kissed him.

26

When A.Z. opens her eyes, it's Wednesday morning, and she's lying on Larsley's carpet. For a minute she imagines that she imagined the whole night—that they never left; they drank rum and watched MTV. But her skin smells like chlorine. Chlorine and Skoal.

She realizes she's shivering. She's wearing a pair of Larsley's pajamas. She's drowning in the dry blue fire of the carpet. It's Wednesday morning, and she's not at school, and Larsley isn't at school either; she's lying on her comforter in her clothes, snoring.

A.Z. can't stand up. The air is too far above her. She crawls to the bathroom—pulling herself like Robert Smith in that muddy cave. He was right all along: love is being a dying fish flopping around in the mud. Love is the most terrible thing ever.

She turns on the hot water in the bathtub and then she leans over it, swirling the water with her hand, the chloriney tap water steaming against her more chloriney skin. And then she drags herself into the tub, like dragging herself up onto the boat that first time when she and Kristoff had just found it, when they were going to fix the oars and go everywhere. She's crying and burning in the hot water and shivering. She's back in the hot tub. She can feel it churning. She can feel Greg's skin. She can feel her skin—dirty with Skoal and chlorine and ashes. No matter how much soap she uses they'll never wash away.

Twice, she leans over the edge and dry-heaves above the bathmat. Her stomach is in a million mis-tied knots, and her mind is all knotted, too, so one minute she's seeing Gus walk past the tub with the gun and she's hearing Greg say, "You oughtta look for alligators outside," or "You should come out on the boat with me," and the next minute she's seeing Kristoff's eyes, which are nothing like Greg's. Eyes that are dark and full of layers, and shine when he laughs, like sunlight rippling over the Sea. Then she's yelling at Kristoff; she's telling him he's ruined everything. But she also ruined everything. She kissed Greg in a hot tub in front of Sy and Larsley and Tammy and Liz and everyone, who will always know she's an idiot and doesn't deserve to sail or explore the Sea that's probably really a lake anyway that an alligator could survive in forever if someone didn't shoot it.

She sinks under water with the tap still running—a sound like a waterfall thundering at her feet: a waterfall of blood, a waterfall of fire, a waterfall of freshwater. Maybe she'll drown right here in Larsley's bathtub and never have to face anyone again. She has her eyes closed, she's holding her breath, she's letting the water and the flowery soap-Skoal-chlorine smell have her when she hears Larsley's mom's voice—distant through the rushing water—but also kind of close, like in the doorway.

Larsley's mom is still in her paramedic clothes, which makes sense because A.Z. is obviously dying. "I guess you girls had a little too much fun at the party last night," she says. She smiles and takes a bite of a shiny pink Pop-Tart. "It's a good thing they closed school today."

"What?" A.Z. says. She's feeling exposed, on account of being naked in a bathtub, but Larsley's mom doesn't seem fazed. A.Z. wishes she could really sink under—feet and feet under to some deep-sea trench. She'd live on reflected sunlight and cold. She wouldn't live at all.

"Officer Gibbs checked out all the threats, and I don't think there's any reason for people to think the Baptists are going to try to burn the rest of town down," Larsley's mom says, "but that was an amazing blaze. The firefighters were at it all night. Nell's lucky they saved her house and a few trees. It could have been much worse."

"The Baptists?" A.Z. says. She thinks of all the trees burning, everything burning, Kristoff maybe burning.

Larsley's mom nods, wiping Pop-Tart crumbs from her mouth and sitting on the edge of the sink. "Reverend Bicks is up at the highway preaching about the fires of Hell consuming Compolodo, so it's pretty clear they set the fire. Nell thinks it was his daughter Stacy who climbed over her fence."

"Oh my god," A.Z. says.

"Your father is working frantically on the story; I said I'd drop you off. Then I have to get some sleep." Larsley's mom yawns.

"Drop me off where?" A.Z. pictures her mom, her mom staring at her through her bifocals—everything A.Z. has really done magnified and magnified.

"Home," Larsley's mom says. "I'll be downstairs on the couch. If I'm asleep, just wake me."

When A.Z. opens her eyes, her mom is holding a thermometer above her like an icicle. She shakes it and sighs.

"One hundred three," she says. "I hope you realize that your father failing to tell you not to go to that party does not constitute a lack of responsibility on your part. You knew very well you weren't allowed to spend the night with Larsley or go to Sy Gording's. And if you ever go to another party with drinking and boys who have already graduated and should not still be hanging out with high school girls, you're not going to Sea Camp until you're out of the house and on your own."

A.Z. doesn't bother pointing out that only Sy and Gus have graduated and just last year. It doesn't matter. There is no Sea Camp.

"You're just lucky you lived through riding with Larsley," her mom says. "Between that and your father's smoke inhalation, this family is a mess. Of course he's working anyway. The Baptists are livid about the accusations, although Nell is positive it was Stacy." Her mother looks at her. "I can't imagine a milquetoast girl like her having half the courage to climb onto Nell's land and set a fire, can you?"

"No," A.Z. plans to say. But then she rearranges and adds letters in her head, and what she says is, "I don't know."

"But of course it'd be a good strategy," her mom says. "No one is really going to arrest the minister's underage daughter."

A.Z. closes her eyes again and has a dream that she's Nell Gording. *It's before the Miracle, when Nell was so sick with that fever. And when A.Z.-Nell stands up to walk, she's so weak she has to drag herself along the barbed wire fence, like in the play, but with real barbs, so her hands are bleeding. Then there's an alligator in the pasture, which is the dried-up space that used to be the Sea.*

When A.Z. opens her eyes again, her mom is reading by her bed. Apparently she's closed the library for the first time in the history of her being its librarian. Her mom looks her right in the eyes. "Were you and Kristoff anywhere near Nell Gording's land?"

"No," A.Z. says. "Of course not."

"Did you and Kristoff have a fight?"

"No."

"Right," her mom says.

When A.Z. closes her eyes again, she sees her boat. She hears Mrs. Ward saying, *Fire symbolizes rebirth,* but she's lying.

On Thursday, A.Z.'s dad is at his office all day, but he calls her. "I found a file called 'Research Results' on my computer," he says. "Should I print it for you?"

"No," A.Z. says.

"Really? There are a lot of numbers." She can imagine him squinting at them, those little green numbers against his black screen. She can hear him typing at the same time.

"Yeah," she says. "Write 'the Sea of Santiago sucks.'" She doesn't usually say "sucks" to her parents but she doesn't care. Language sucks.

"OK," her dad says. "The paper is late. Out, out, damned deadline."

A.Z. is pretty sure that's not even the right play, but nothing is, so she doesn't say so.

She quits taking birth control pills because she can't remember to, and anyway, she's not going to get pregnant. Days don't matter. It's August thirtieth.

It's September second. Her Sea Camp application is an unwritten pile of ashes.

The fire inside her is a high tide that sweeps over her until she drowns somewhere in herself. She sees Kristoff's body: charred, disfigured like the figurehead, curled on the ground. He was just trying to surprise her with a manatee—a scarred, surviving manatee—because he knows she loves them. Not like Greg, who doesn't know anything about her. And she told Kristoff to go to hell. Maybe she killed him. Maybe he just killed her boat. Later that night, or maybe it's another night, the phone rings. It's a man's voice she doesn't recognize. "I'm calling for Anastasia McKinney. Is she at home?"

"Yes," she says. "This is her."

"Very pleased to meet you, Miss McKinney," the man says. "This is Lieutenant Scowers from the United States Navy. We don't usually call people who still have several years to go before recruitment age, but we wanted to compliment you on your very promising ASVAB scores. In fact, the U.S. Navy is looking for just your sort of talent."

"What?" A.Z. says.

"I know it's a lot to think about," the recruiter says. "And the good thing is that you have the next two and a half years, if your parents are willing to sign a waiver so you can enlist at seventeen. We just wanted you to know a career in the U.S. Navy could be waiting for you. It's very rare to get a perfect score on more than half the sections and a 97 percent or higher on the others. That's better than most juniors or seniors, which is why we've identified you as someone with a real aptitude for this career. We'll be sending some literature in the mail soon, and I hope you'll take the time to read it."

"Really?" A.Z. says. As soon as she finishes dying, she's going to get a fake ID, run away to the navy, spend the rest of her life on a ship, and never come back. She's going to go to a real sea. Or she's not going to do that because she hates water. She hates boats.

"Was that your father?" her mom says, coming upstairs with a glass of orange juice.

"No," A.Z. says.

Her mom stands there, the orange juice glowing like some weird liquid flame; it reminds A.Z. of Mountain Dew or a light bulb that won't turn off, burning inside her. "Was it Kristoff?"

"No." She doesn't want to tell her mom, but it's too hard to think of a lie. "It was someone from the navy."

Her mom sighs and sets the juice down. "It's a luxury of peace time that they're even concerned about aptitude," she says. "When my father was drafted, all they wanted were warm bodies." She sits by A.Z.'s bed and looks out the window. "Do you know where Kristoff is?"

"No," A.Z. says.

27

On Friday, A.Z.'s fever breaks. She's drenched in sweat, her sheets are drenched; the whole world is liquid.

On Monday, she goes back to school because her mom makes her. By now, everyone will have heard about her and Greg: the Librarian and Shop Guy. Wet bookmarks. She doesn't even want to think about the jokes.

When her mom drops her off in the parking lot, she imagines walking all the way down the hallway and out the other end where she'll keep walking until she finds a pay phone and calls a navy recruiter and lies about her age and enlists.

Instead, she ends up in geometry because Sahara runs into her in the hall and drags her over, talking excitedly about plans to create a memorial for the trees that died in the fire. When A.Z. gets to her seat, Scotty leans over and whispers that he's been failing the quizzes in English, so he's glad she's back. Larsley is back, too, on the other side of the room; she must have said she couldn't see the board from her seat, so she'd get moved away from Scotty.

A.Z. thinks about telling Coach W. that she can't see the board at all because she's gone suddenly blind, but that would just attract attention. She stares at her desk, like Stephen does, and wishes she had his greasy, stringy hair to hide her face. She carefully avoids seeing the third row, where Greg is sitting or maybe not sitting; she doesn't know because she doesn't look.

Before Jeopardy, Coach W. has a long discussion with his runners about whether they're still going to rename the team the Alligators now that the alligator is supposedly dead. Apparently they've been trying to decide this for days. Of course, there are also a lot of dead whales in the world, which no one, including A.Z., brings up.

Coach W. ends up erasing one of the categories and writing *Alligators*, and everyone says Greg is bound to cream this, which doesn't make sense because shooting something doesn't mean you know anything about it. Then someone says A.Z. will cream it because she's practically a scientist or something, and then someone else says, "Greg versus A.Z.," and several people giggle, and A.Z. almost runs out of the room, like Kim did that time in kindergarten when someone pointed out she had toilet paper hanging out of her shorts.

But she doesn't. Instead, she vows to herself that this time—for real—she isn't going to help her team win. And she doesn't—not even when Scotty says, "Come on, Librarian. Something got your tongue? *Someone* got it?"

She's almost to history class when Greg calls, "Hey." She doesn't turn around.

"This is top secret, but we detected heat from the body," Greg says. "I thought you might want to know."

"Why would I want to know?" She still isn't looking at Greg. She's still walking toward history, but he's following her because that's his next class, too. That's the problem with having only twenty-nine people in your entire class.

"I'm going out by myself to make sure and then Sy is going to come help drag it out." He lowers his voice. "Nell trusts me to do this last exploratory mission." The way Greg says "exploratory mission" sounds really creepy. For a second, A.Z. can feel wet denim against her skin. She wants to run from school, to take a shower, a million showers.

"I'm not interested in your dumb exploratory mission," she says. "I'm not interested in anything about you."

"Nell isn't happy that it's taking so long, you know?" Greg says, as if he isn't listening. "It costs a lot to pay for gas for the boat and everything, and people are anxious to swim. And we're way behind on the salting."

"What?" A.Z. says, but she has her back to Greg so she's not 1,000 percent sure that's really what he's said. Instead she rushes ahead of him through the door, bumping into the last people coming out.

Mr. Hummer reads aloud all hour about the Civil War. He reads the same sentences over and over, like always, so everyone can copy them: "The Battle of Pea Ridge, also known as the Battle of Elkhorn Tavern, was fought here in northwest Arkansas. The Battle of Pea Ridge. That's p-e-a like the vegetable. Also known as the Battle of Elkhorn Tavern, was fought here in northwest Arkansas. New sentence. Although Confederate troops outnumbered the Union, the Union won the battle. Although Confederate troops outnumbered the Union, the Union won . . ."

A.Z. doesn't take notes. Instead, she writes a list of ways to die. She pictures herself like Edna Pontellier in *The Awakening*, walking off into the ocean until she drowned. Only she won't be walking into an ocean. She'll be walking into a stupid salted lake. She'll wear a long white Victorian dress or maybe her jean shorts and the T-shirt that Sahara pointed out is inside out—the picture of the Eiffel Tower on the inside, which is fine, because Paris doesn't exist.

As soon as the bell rings for biology, she hurries out the door to the parking lot.

There's a long line of cars on Miracle Way because apparently everyone is still hoping to see the dead alligator, which is probably rotting by now with no formaldehyde to preserve it in the lake water. Or maybe Greg—with his too-soft lips and his tongue that tastes like Skoal and watery beer—has left school early, too, and found its body. He's dragged it up the beach, just like they'll drag A.Z.'s corpse tomorrow. Only they won't build a display case for her.

She pays the guy at the gate three dollars, which is the price for hoping to see the dead alligator—or for coming to kill yourself—but it doesn't matter because she isn't saving money for anything.

Maybe this is all her feeling connected to the Sea has ever meant: this terrible, sad moment when she's going to sink into the water, not grokking it, because grokking is stupid science fiction, but drowning, which can happen in any kind of water, which is what she's thinking as she walks across the parking lot crying, so everything and everyone is so smeary she can't tell who they are. And of course it doesn't matter; all the sounds are muffled, as if the car doors and voices are miles away, and she can only faintly, faintly hear the voice that says, "Anastasia Zoe McKinney, where do you think you're going?"

And because the voice is miles away and doesn't really exist except in the wave-washed recesses of A.Z.'s mind, she says, "I'm going to die."

And the voice says, "No you're not. We need to go get your father before Nell has him arrested." A.Z. should keep walking. If she were really Edna Pontellier, she would keep walking. But the voice, which is of course attached to a hand that is now on A.Z.'s shoulder, says, "Are you running a fever again?"

"What?" A.Z. says.

"Have you been drinking again?" Her mom steps ahead of her

and turns to face her—looking right into her eyes like she does—only A.Z. is still too tear-blurry to really see her.

"No," A.Z. says. "You won't have to worry about me anymore. I'm going to die. I'm walking into the water."

"You're not walking into the Sea. And you wouldn't drown anyway. It's not deep enough."

"It's not even a sea," A.Z. says. She starts to cry again, harder. Her mom doesn't say anything. Instead she puts her arm around A.Z., and they walk like that. Her mom smells faintly of old books and dust and dry land, which is better right now than salt or sunscreen or fish, although A.Z. would never admit this.

The beach is crowded with people watching the motorboat, which is out past the swimming dock. The thickest crowd is past the lifeguard stand, where A.Z.'s mom steers them.

A.Z. can hear her father before she sees him; he's shouting above the waves and the motorboat, "'My brave spirit! Who was so firm, so constant, that his coil would not infect his reason?'" and a few people are clapping.

A.Z. isn't really sure why her mom is trying to stop her dad from reciting *The Tempest*. It's sort of cool, as much as anything can be cool when you're supposed to be dead. Her dad obviously has it mostly memorized, and he's playing all the parts: doing different voices, waving his Bic pen like a wand, and flapping his arms like wings for Ariel. A.Z. kind of wants to sink onto the sand and watch him. She is, she realizes, incredibly tired, and it's soothing to listen to the waves washing up around her dad's feet, and his voice, higher now for Ariel, saying, "'Not a soul but felt a fever of the mad and play'd some tricks of desperation. All but the mariners plunged in the foaming brine and quit the vessel.'" It's like the world has already ended in shipwrecks and foaming brine and desperation, and Shakespeare and her father understand.

"'Then all afire with me. The king's son, Ferdinand,'" her dad cries, "'with hair up-staring—then, like reeds, not hair—was the first man that leaped, cried, *Hell is empty and all the devils are here.*'"

A.Z.'s mom lets go of A.Z. and pushes into the crowd. "James," she says.

"'Why that's my spirit! But was not this nigh shore?'" A.Z.'s dad says, like he's trying to figure out which character she is but can't since he's all of the characters himself.

"He's better than that boring Miracle Play," one of the pilgrims says.

And then an older woman says, "The Miracle Play was just beautiful. It was God's perfect word."

"'Close by, my master,'" A.Z.'s dad says, flapping his wings and glancing at his notes.

"James," her mom says again. "Sy says security is going to have to remove you if you won't leave the beach. Nell is still being unreasonable."

"'But are they, Ariel, safe?'" A.Z.'s dad says, meekly, not really in character.

A.Z.'s mom picks up the notepad from the sand and closes it. For a second, A.Z. imagines pushing through the crowd and taking the pad back and refusing to leave. She and her dad will stage a protest version of *The Tempest* until a real tempest blows in and the waves come and wash them away.

But A.Z.'s dad is walking away with her mom, and people are clapping, and people are laughing, and the crowd is dispersing down the beach toward the motorboat, which is circling the dock now, slowly. A.Z. shouldn't be following her parents. She should be running into the water. But what if Sy and Greg come save her?

Her father is smiling but he also looks kind of like he's going to cry. His hair is standing up in that wispy way, and he has ink leaked all over his right hand from holding the pen upside down as a wand.

"That was good," A.Z. says to him. "You should have kept going."

"He can keep going at the house," her mom says. "I hate to cave to Nell Gording's machinations, but she owns the beach. She isn't bright enough to appreciate Shakespeare, anyway." She opens the passenger's door of her car for him. "We'll come back for your car later."

"'O heaven, O earth, bear witness to this sound,'" A.Z.'s dad says. He climbs into the passenger side but doesn't fasten his seat belt. A.Z. wonders if her mom is going to lean over and do it for him, like she used to when A.Z. was younger, but she doesn't.

"I hope Howard Chuck reimburses him for photocopying all the special sightings sheets now that he's quit," A.Z.'s mom says, backing up. "I'm not concerned about the money, but in principle, he should be recognized for how hard he's worked for those crazy people."

"He quit?" A.Z. says. "You quit the paper?" But her dad doesn't answer. He's leaning his head against the window.

"If hollowly invert what best is boded me to mischief," he says softly. This doesn't sound like a real line, and A.Z. wonders if he's starting to mix stuff up. She feels awful for him; she wishes she knew some lines to say back so maybe they could have a conversation. What if her dad never talks in real sentences again? What if he never alliterates anything?

"I don't think Howard will hold him to it," her mom says. "There's no way he'll find anyone else with his writing abilities to do that thankless job. And besides, you can't imagine how much the Baptists are celebrating. They think he's finally come over to their side."

"What?" A.Z. says.

"He was racing to make the deadline, and I guess some files got mixed up. Obviously he would never purposefully write 'the Sea of

Santiago sucks' in the middle of an article about the fire. Of course, Nell thinks the Baptists put him up to it, and she wants him to print a retraction *and* start putting out a paper that doesn't include Greenville."

A.Z. suddenly feels really feverish and light-headed. Maybe she isn't really better. Maybe she's going to die. She ought to die. Her dad actually typed what she said. This is all her fault: wanting to know the truth about the Sea, and falling in love with Kristoff, and making stupid sails that took forever, and kissing Greg, and now her dad going crazy. But also, it's all Kristoff's fault.

Her mom glances at her in the rearview mirror. "All your father does is boost their business with these pieces about the alligator and potlucks and chickens and all sorts of fluff that wouldn't get half the attention if he didn't write about it. He's ruining his own health for them, and they're not even noticing. Of course that's so common. When my father worked in a sawmill before the war, the workers didn't have masks, and everyone developed asthma."

"'And for your sake am I this patient log-man,'" A.Z.'s father says louder now, sitting up and looking at A.Z.'s mom as he starts to cry. She puts her hand on his arm and sighs.

When they get home, A.Z.'s mom makes her dad molasses milk, and A.Z. goes to her room and watches her fish and thinks about drowning and worries about her dad, who has maybe lost his mind forever because of that stupid thing she told him to type.

Although, in a way, maybe he's lucky he doesn't have to think of new words. He can just say his lines and even if they don't make sense, that isn't his problem. It's someone else's script. But at the same time, he chose it; it's no one else's news.

Just after eight, the phone rings, and A.Z. answers expecting it to be the military recruiter, who called again last night—and to whom A.Z.'s mom told the whole story of her father's ship exploding, and told never to call again, although he probably will anyway. "Hello?" she says.

"Hey," Kristoff says.

It's like the tide rushing back in: Kristoff's voice, his aliveness, rushing into the phone line, her room.

"Oh," she says. "Where are you?"

"Florida."

For a second, A.Z. pictures him sailing there. But then she remembers the boat burned, and anyway, the stupid Lake of Santiago probably doesn't connect to anything. "How'd you get there?"

"I flew. It sucks here."

"It can't suck as bad as here." Then, before she realizes she's saying it: "My dad has had some kind of breakdown and is only speaking in lines from *The Tempest*, and I've been super sick, and I missed the Sea Camp deadline, and the boat is gone, and you just ran away from everything." She almost tells him about Greg but she doesn't know how to.

"Yeah," Kristoff says. "It was sort of conceptual."

"What was?"

"Leaving. I had the concept, and then I cashed my last check from Chuck Chicken and went."

"Oh," A.Z. says again. This isn't really what she thought conceptual meant. And then she starts to cry: rough, jagged sobs that come out of nowhere.

"I feel like shit, too," Kristoff says. "I'm out of money and I've been sleeping on the beach."

"What beach?"

"I don't know. I've been moving around. And I was in jail for a while."

"In jail?"

"Yeah, I peed on the beach. There aren't any public restrooms."

"Oh." She feels strangely disappointed.

"Yeah. I was going to call, but I had to use my one call in jail so Kara could get me."

"What? Who's Kara?"

"This girl who's been sleeping on the beach, too. She had some money she stole from her parents."

For a second, A.Z. has the impulse to hang up. It's like the gravity between the phone in her hand and its cradle is getting stronger.

"I had this crazy dream the other night about the boat," Kristoff says. "It showed up down here. It was underwater, like a submarine, but you could sail in it anyway. You know, I pushed it into the water after you left. I mean, what was left of it."

A.Z. pictures her boat burning, floating out onto the water—Kristoff braving the fire to try to save it. She wonders how long he stayed in the woods, if he tried to put the fire out.

"They think the Baptists started the fire," she says. "To try to sabotage Nell or burn the alligator up or whatever."

"Yeah," Kristoff says. "It's in the backpack."

"What?"

"Nothing. I was talking to Kara. Hey, sorry, the quarter's about to run out."

"Yeah," A.Z. says. And before she can say anything else, the line goes dead—a dull buzzing—like maybe Kristoff never really called at all.

28

A.Z.'s mom comes into her room at nine, which feels like six minutes after A.Z. finally cried herself to sleep, saying, "Rise and shine."

A.Z. pulls the pillow over her head. In her dreams, she was in the hot tub with Greg, which was also a beach where Kristoff and some girl with a backpack were making a sand castle. And then she looked out at the Sea, and Big Bob, in pink sweatpants, was floating there with a huge saltshaker.

"How's Kristoff?" her mom says. A.Z. can hear her opening a window. Her mom believes in fresh air and probably, in another universe, today is one of those crisp fall mornings that smell like sun and dry leaves and persimmons.

A.Z. doesn't even ask how her mom knows he called. She doesn't take her head out from under the pillow where her face is all swollen from crying. She doesn't want to explain because there's no way to explain everything, which keeps getting turned back over and mixed up with itself like the seawater when the ice melts in the spring.

"Where is he?"

"Florida."

"Oh. Did you make up?"

"It doesn't matter."

"Kristoff has a lot to work out," her mom says. "And his mother certainly isn't going to help. I finally got in touch with her yesterday, and she says she's saving money by his not being there. If he needs money to get home, tell him I'd be willing to loan him some."

"He has money," A.Z. says, "from some girl named Kara." She's about to say, "She loaned him some to get out of jail," but she catches herself. Not like her mom cares. Arthur went to jail, too, although of course he was desperate and forged a check. He didn't just pee on a public beach and lie about letting the alligator out and everything else in the world.

"It's hard to be entirely on your own," her mom says.

"He wasn't on his own." A.Z. yanks the pillow off her face. "I was there with him. I was with him all summer trying to help him. You don't even understand. You're always taking his side, and you wanted me to date him, and you don't even know what he's like."

"Your dating Kristoff is *not* my responsibility," her mom says. "And I'm not siding with him. I'm trying to help you, too. Last I heard you were in love with him."

"I don't need your help."

"No? In case you don't remember, you were walking to the Sea to drown yourself yesterday."

A.Z. almost says, *That-had-nothing-to-do-with-Kristoff-I-kissed-Greg-and-everyone-knows-and-my-boat-caught-on-fire-and-the-Sea-was-never-even-a-real-Sea-and-I-keep-thinking-about-the-way-Kristoff-and-I-used-to-come-up-with-the-funniest-ideas-and-the-way-he'd-look-at-me-which-is-probably-exactly-like-he's-looking-at-Kara-now-because-he-probably-doesn't-love-me-which-doesn't-matter-because-I-hate-him-because-he-lied-to-me-about-everything-and-ruined-my-life-and-now-*

I'll-never-be-an-oceanographer, but fortunately, she's too exhausted. Instead, she says, "It doesn't matter."

"Of course it matters." Her mom takes her bifocals off, and A.Z. realizes she's wiping her eyes. "Your father is still talking in the voice of Ariel," she says.

"Is he going to be OK?"

Her mother sighs and puts her bifocals back on. "When people get overwhelmed by reality, it's not such an uncommon reaction to disassociate briefly. One of Curtis's friends who was in World War II, the pilot with the burned eyelashes, spent a whole month after the war not speaking. Even the doctors thought he'd lost the ability to speak, and then one day he just started talking again." She sighs again and looks A.Z. right in the eyes. "It's been a hard couple of weeks for everyone."

"Is your dad OK?" Sahara asks when A.Z. gets to school. A.Z. doesn't want to talk to Sahara, but she can't pretend she didn't hear because their lockers are next to each other. "I heard the Gordings aren't allowing him on the beach. It's completely illegal to ban journalists. It's totalitarian repression."

"My mom thinks he's just in shock," A.Z. says. She doesn't admit that this is partly her fault, like everything.

"It's unjust," Sahara says. "Freedom of the press is a First Amendment right. I'm pretty sure the Gordings started the fire themselves to try to frame me and then the Baptists. We need a journalist to uncover the truth." She links her arm through A.Z.'s and pulls her toward geometry, where they actually have to do math for some reason. The answers are in the key in the back of the book, though, so everyone copies them—even A.Z.

Fourth period, she's planning to skip biology again and leave school or hide in the locker room, but Mrs. Reuter sees her in the hall.

"Can you clean the aquarium?" she says. She's obviously trying to get A.Z. to come to class for the first time in more than a week. "It's filthy, and the class is doing a quiz about their dissections." She's acting nonchalant, but it's not the good kind of acting like A.Z.'s dad, but the "the world isn't ending" kind that no one believes.

A.Z. wants to think of an excuse, but she's too tired.

She's scrubbing algae off the filter when Mrs. Reuter comes from the classroom into the lab. "I guess you're excited to hear back about your application?" she says. "Maybe October? I imagine they'll make the decisions fairly early so you can get ready for December. It'll be amazing to be in Florida over Christmas break. I know I'm jealous."

A.Z. pretends she didn't hear Mrs. Reuter, but of course they're the only two people—besides the skeleton on the metal stand—in the room. She stares hard at the algae, scrubbing until the little bristle brush makes a soft *shrring* sound on the glass.

"Is everything all right?" Mrs. Reuter says. "I know you didn't feel as if your research data was as good as it could have been, and you're a little behind on turning your essay in to me, but I'm sure your application was still great." She smiles and measures hydrogen peroxide into a beaker. "We're going to talk about solutions next."

For a second, A.Z. thinks she means solutions—like how to fix A.Z. never going to Sea Camp and everything else that is super fucked up in the world—but then she realizes that Mrs. Reuter means solutions like hydrogen peroxide and water, with that extra oxygen atom: H_2O_2.

"Everything's fine," A.Z. lies. She's not going to tell Mrs. Reuter she's a failure and the Sea's a failure, and she never even finished her application, and anyway there's nothing for her to go away and learn about and come back and study. She runs the filter under the water in the sink and puts it back in the tank, even though she hates fish.

After school, Sahara insists A.Z. come with her to the library, where A.Z.'s mom is at her desk, on the phone with someone, explaining about A.Z.'s dad. "He's really good at the different voices," she says. "My father used to be wonderful at doing the comics: Dick Tracy and Krazy Kat and Little Orphan Annie. He'd read them aloud to us every Sunday until he got drafted."

"Hi, sweetie," she says when she hangs up. "Hi, Sahara. I've been wondering if everyone thought the library was closed. You're the first two people I've seen all day."

"People just don't like to read," A.Z. says. "And anyway, you always tell them stories so they don't have a chance to." It's not a nice thing to say, especially in front of Sahara, but it's not actually A.Z.'s fault that Sahara is there, or she is, or her mom is.

Her mom raises her eyebrows. "People come in because they like my stories," she says. "There aren't many people in this county with perspective that extends beyond 1955, their own bank accounts, or the Bible."

"I'm so sorry about Mr. McKinney," Sahara interjects, like she's trying to change the subject. "It's completely unjust. I'm working on posters calling for the return of the Compolodo free press."

A.Z.'s mom sighs. "The paper has never been free. You can't run a free press with the county's main employer controlling it and the other main employer generating most of the rest of the advertising revenue."

"It's a travesty," Sahara says, using another vocab word. "We have to have the free press or else we'll all be brainwashed."

"A free press is a beautiful idea," A.Z.'s mom says. She takes her glasses off and cleans them on her dress. Maybe she's been crying, or her eyes just look smaller than A.Z. remembers, softer and more vulnerable, like the underside of a turtle. A.Z. feels kind of bad for what she said.

"Of course, since their inception in the 1700s, the papers in this country have been as much about gossip and inciting people to war and profit as objective reporting. If Nell Gording had ever spent as much time thinking through the ramifications of a Sea as she spends advertising it, none of this mess would have happened. A living body of water is going to attract alligators and journalists and protesters and all kinds of things. If she'd stuck with a cathedral like they did in Spain, all she'd need to do is repair the mortar, although, of course, and this is exactly the point, it's hard to charge as much for visiting a cathedral."

A.Z. doesn't say it, but she thinks that it's kind of cool that her mom just called the Sea "a living body of water," which it is, factually, no matter how salty it is or isn't.

"They're building a cathedral?" Sahara says. She's looking at the shelf of law books and obviously hasn't been listening.

"No," A.Z.'s mom says. "The medieval bishops in Spain built a cathedral in response to a strikingly similar miracle that occurred there. And people walk for hundreds of miles across France and Spain to kiss a stone and receive a certificate. Some of them—and you'll like this, Anastasia—walk all the way to the Atlantic, which is another fifty miles, and throw their shoes in to signify the end of the journey."

A.Z. hasn't heard the part about the pilgrimage before, and it sounds like kind of an amazing idea, although she doesn't say so. For a second, she imagines walking all the way from Compolodo to the Atlantic Coast. Not Florida. Farther up. South Carolina or somewhere.

"Most of the pilgrims here wouldn't walk farther than the nearest buffet table," her mom continues. "Not that excessive devotion to an imaginary being is any better."

"We should have a march," Sahara says, as though she's missed the part about people not liking to walk. "A free speech march. We can do it after the pep rally on Friday."

A.Z. is really doubtful that people are going to march to protest the lack of free speech. Most people in high school don't even read the paper. Or their textbooks. She doesn't either anymore. She spent most of English—after that quiz on "The Most Dangerous Game"— working on a letter to Kristoff that she wouldn't send even if she knew where to send it:

Kristoff—

I don't see why you bothered to call me if you were just going to get off the phone for another girl and not really apologize for ruining the boat and everything.* None of this would have happened if you hadn't let the alligator loose, which was really ridiculous and ruined everything for everyone. And also, not that it's any of your business, but I kissed Greg the other night in a hot tub. I don't even know why I did it. Maybe you're right about that. Nothing makes any sense.

*Unless when you said "sorry" at the end that was supposed to be some kind of lame apology, but I think you were just saying you were sorry that you had to go, which was good because I didn't want to talk to you anyway.

A.Z.

When they get back to the house, A.Z.'s dad looks more relaxed than she's ever seen him. He doesn't have any pens in his pocket, and he doesn't have to write stories, or edit stories, or plan stories, or worry about angry calls, because A.Z.'s mom has been leaving the ringer off. She's convinced that every day he spends without hearing Nell or Chuck or Reverend Bicks's voice is a day closer to recovery.

"Those people," she says again as A.Z. washes dishes and her dad eats soup and recites Act Four. "Did I tell you that Vera called the library? I'm sure Howard put her up to it. She said she wanted me to tell your father how much she's going to miss the weekly recipe. And I told her that a lot of people are going to miss a lot of things. Of course, they're trying to get your father to take his job back, which he should *not* do without a formal apology from both Howard and Nell for alternately berating him. Is Sahara still planning to bring the march into the library?"

"Yeah," A.Z. says. She doesn't care about the march, but it will give her something to do while she figures out how to run away and join the navy, which, the more that she thinks about it, isn't the most practical plan because she definitely looks like she's fourteen and a half, not eighteen, and she doesn't have a fake ID, and the navy already has a record of her age.

"Good. Dragonfly's interlibrary loan came in, and I wanted to give it to her," her mom says. "The book on Yves Klein finally came in, but I can't imagine anyone except Kristoff would be interested."

"No," A.Z. says. She feels suddenly really sad—like the book has somehow brought the void closer, not a huge abstract space, but a hole inside her where her boat and Kristoff and everything, even the Sea, has vanished.

Fortunately, there's no biology on Friday because of the extra-long pep rally. Despite all the "Gators, Gators, shake your tails!" cheers, and the talk about how fast alligators run on land, A.Z. still isn't convinced the name change is going to happen because it's dumb and sad to name the team after an animal that got let loose from a run-down zoo as some dumb conceptual art project.

Or maybe the name change doesn't seem real because A.Z.'s dad isn't there, clapping and stomping and taking notes, and there won't be an article next Wednesday announcing it with a blurry picture of something.

At the end of the cheers—which include the gloved caterpillar, which Angie turns around and rolls her eyes about, which is the one kind of normal moment—Principal Oakens lets Sahara announce her Free the Press March.

By Sahara standards, a decent crowd forms—maybe twenty peo-ple—including Mrs. Ward, who teaches English so she has to care about words; Mr. Gibson, who teaches shop but has a crush on Mrs. Ward even though she's married; of course Josh and Sahara's friends; Dragonfly and Abe; A.Z.; Coach W. and his runners, who don't really mean to be part of the march but have started jogging at the same time in their new green do-rags; and Larsley, who won't look at Scotty, but who is walking that way, too, because apparently she wrecked her car again yesterday.

Sahara's idea is to march to the newspaper office and hang a sign and then make a loop to as many newspaper stands as possible. A.Z. is pretty sure most people aren't going to walk that far, and before they can even start, there's a delay because Josh has forgotten tape, so they have to borrow some from Dennis's Videos, which is next door to the paper, and then Sahara tapes up a poster that says FREEDOM OF THE PRESS SHOULD BE FREE! and Thu comes out of Seven Happiness.

"Is your dad in there?" she says to A.Z.

"No. He's still sick."

"I left egg rolls for him yesterday. You think that fat man Dennis ate them all?"

"Yeah. Probably."

"Your dad's still going to run my new ad?" Thu asks.

"I don't know," A.Z. says. "I don't think there's going to be a paper anymore."

"Of course there's going to be a paper," Dragonfly says, putting her hand on A.Z.'s shoulder. "We're not going to give in to the bullying of Chuck Chicken *or* the Gording Foundation. We'll raise the money to make the paper free of financial and religious ties."

The march loses a couple of people at Whale Tail grocery and then gains Dan, the taxi man. A.Z. drops behind the marchers, walking slowly so she won't have to talk to anyone, or chant, or anything.

Everyone is stopped at the newspaper box outside the post office, on the corner of Ahoy and Main, when a red-haired man—maybe in his twenties—walks up. He's wearing a backpack and khaki pants, the kind explorers wear on nature specials, with a lot of pockets, and a long-sleeved shirt, also with pockets, and even though this is geeky, it seems useful and interesting and it's what A.Z. notices first. Useful pockets. He has a camera around his neck, too: not a dumb tourist camera but the kind with a long zoom lens—the kind A.Z.'s dad used to wish he had.

"This is really dumb," the guy says to A.Z.—and she thinks he means the protest, and she's starting to agree, but also feeling offended for her dad, when he says, "but I've lost my car. I parked by the library and must have gotten turned around somehow."

He has this slow smile and a slight accent—maybe British—so the words sound better than they usually would, like this ordinary sentence is full of interesting currents. For some reason, A.Z. is sure he isn't a usual pilgrim, or if he's a pilgrim, he's like the ones in Spain her mom was talking about who walk for hundreds or even thousands of miles. Maybe he's walked across the ocean from somewhere. Although, of course, he just told her that he has a car.

"Oh," A.Z. says. "Yeah, that's easy to do. I mean, the streets are all kind of winding, and some of them have a couple of names." She gestures up at the sign. "They renamed them after the Miracle, but people got confused, so they kept both names, which is more confusing."

The guy looks at the Ahoy/Oak sign and rubs the stubble on his chin and smiles. "Yeah. That's probably the problem."

"You're really close to the library, though. It's another three blocks on the left." She points north, where Sahara and Josh are marching up the middle of the street, chanting, "Free the press, free the press," as though A.Z.'s dad is being held in jail somewhere.

"Thanks, mate," the guy says. "So what happened to the press?"

"The one journalist quit. My dad. I mean, he was the reporter and editor and he got really stressed out because all this weird stuff has been happening with an alligator and these crazy Baptists and the Sea and stuff. It's kind of a long story."

The guy nods. "This place is something else."

He's started walking with A.Z., since they're going to the same place. And even though A.Z. doesn't want to talk to anyone, she's sort of glad the march is moving slowly.

"I mean, the Sea alone." He lets out this whistle that obviously means he can't find the words for how great, or something, the Sea is.

"Yeah?" A.Z. says. "You've been out there?"

"All day. Until I came back here, obviously, and lost my car. I do better with birds. Cities confuse me." He laughs, this sort of self-deprecating, soft laugh.

"What do you do with birds?" It sounds sort of dumb as she says it.

"Well, usually I study sea eagles on Rotamah Island. That's Australia. But the researcher I'm working with specializes in gulls, and he heard about your Sea during the whole alligator uproar and sent me over here to do some preliminary studies."

"Yeah?" She's feeling the good kind of light-headed. "You heard about the alligator in Australia?"

The guy laughs. "We keep track of our *Crocodilia*," he says. "Actually, I think we got lucky and someone was vacationing over here and brought the story back. But in any case, it made a bit of a splash. I was expecting to see heaps of Aussies here."

A.Z. isn't sure whether Aussie is a person from Australia or some kind of bird or fish, but she's not going to admit this. The way he says it sounds also a little bit like her name, only blurred. "So you're over here studying the birds?"

"Yeah," the guy says. "The gulls and their adaptation to an inland sea environment. We're on the lakes at Rotamah. Interesting situation. The water used to be part of the bay, but the dunes closed it off. So we're a sort of inland island, accessible only by boat." He smiles. "This is probably really boring. And that's my car." He nods at a silver sedan. "Well, it's not mine. I picked it up from the airport in Fayetteville. Do you realize that people here drive on the wrong side? I'm not so good with that either. I'm better with boats."

"Oh," A.Z. says. "Yeah." She wants to say something else—something better and smarter—but her mind is kind of cloudy, like there's water from Australian lakes and the Sea churning together, and she would feel really dumb except the guy is smiling at her. "You're on inland lakes that used to be part of a sea?" she says.

"Yeah," the guy says.

"Wow," A.Z. says. "I used to do some research on the Sea and stuff. I'm really into science."

"That's ace," the guy says. "Inland seas are fascinating, huh? You never know what you'll find."

"Yeah," A.Z. says. Her heart is beating really fast; there's a researcher, a real researcher, here from across the world to study the Sea that is maybe a lake that is maybe part of a sea anyway.

The guy turns toward his car, but then he turns back. "I'm Warfe. It's my last name but that's what everyone calls me." He holds out his hand to shake hers.

"A.Z." A.Z. says. His hand feels strong but not in that squishing-oppressive way that adult guys' hands sometimes are, but like her hand is also strong, because people need strong hands to do research and sail, or row to all the places in the world that are only accessible by water.

When Warfe gets into his car and A.Z. runs up the stairs to the library and opens the door, she sees the marchers—more people than have ever been in the library at once—standing at the foot of the stairs to the loft.

They're looking up at her dad, who is at the railing saying, "'The sky it seems would pour down stinking pitch, but that the sea, mounting to th' welkin's cheek, dashes the fire out,'" and Dragonfly is clapping softly like people sometimes do if they get excited, even in the middle of a scene.

"He's wonderful," she whispers to A.Z.

A.Z. glances over at the counter, but her mom isn't there. And then she realizes she's standing over by Sahara and Josh. She's wearing her bifocals and one of her button-up dresses with the little cloth belt around the waist, but for some reason, A.Z. sees her in the fringed leather skirt and cat-eye glasses she was supposedly wearing the first time that A.Z.'s dad came into the library and sang her "Marian the Librarian." She sees her dad looking down at her mom, and at the crowd, at everyone watching him say the lines he was destined to say, here on the stage of this library, where obviously her mother has brought him, hoping this would happen. And A.Z. starts clapping, too, even though her dad is in the middle of a line. And even though it's probably just part of Ferdinand's role at this moment, it seems as if he smiles at her and sort of bows.

29

The phone rings at 8 a.m. Apparently A.Z.'s mom forgot to turn the ringer off after Mrs. Ward called at 6:30 a.m. and woke them all up the first time to see if A.Z.'s dad knew *Julius Caesar* or *Romeo and Juliet*, which she teaches because they're boring plays where people give long speeches and die a lot.

A.Z. has always thought *The Tempest* is better because everyone who has been magically imprisoned ends up free, and the storm and shipwreck turn out to be really synchronous.

A.Z. answers. It's a reflex; her body gets out of bed before she consciously realizes what's happening. She's been dreaming that she's at a research station that is also a floating dock, and she's counting birds.

"May I speak to James McKinney?" a woman says.

"What?" A.Z. says.

"This is the McKinney residence, right?"

A.Z. is still sleepily counting birds, which are sort of chickens, but also sort of sea eagles, which she's never seen, but should definitely be the national bird. She wonders if Warfe is technically a biologist or an ornithologist, and where you go to study that sort of thing, which seems really interesting and adaptable: like you could study birds on any kind of water. Maybe there's a camp in Australia or somewhere.

But then the voice on the other end says, "This is Nell Gording calling."

Oh my god, A.Z. thinks, through the wings flapping in her brain. *She's found out it was me on her road. She's finally calling to arrest me.*

"Hello?" Nell says after a few seconds, as if she thinks the connection has been dropped, which it sort of has been, because A.Z. still hasn't said anything.

"I'm here," A.Z. says finally, trying to breathe calmly.

"Good," Nell says. "I've been trying to reach you since last night but the phone seems to have been off the hook. I wanted to tell your father that Officer Gibbs has investigated and we know exactly what happened."

"It was an accident," A.Z. says before she means to be speaking. "He didn't mean to set the fire. He was trying to burn propeller scars in a wooden manatee as a present for me because I love manatees, and he wanted to symbolize pain and realism, but that just created this awful realism and pain, which were sort of conceptual and sort of reality."

She's not even sure she's saying the words as she says them; they just spill around her, like the words themselves form the existential void Kristoff told her about one time, like she's standing in the middle of nothing forever, but also, that nothing is everything she's ever done or known.

"Whatever are you talking about?" Nell says. "Is this James's daughter? Can you get me your father?"

"Yes," A.Z. says, hearing, even as she says it, her own voice in her head saying, *No, it isn't*. She's just confessed—or maybe turned Kristoff in—but Nell doesn't even know who she is, which means she wasn't calling for a confession. "I mean, I don't think my dad can talk; he just talks in *The Tempest*."

"I've noticed," Nell says. "But I was hoping he'd get over that and come out to the Sea. There's been a new miracle. It's very urgent. And he is, after all, the only one who knows how to get the paper written and published quickly. Officer Gibbs has filed his report that Chuck Chuck inserted that awful comment about the Sea into the paper *after* your father wrote the article. We know how the Baptists operate."

"Oh," A.Z. says. She's trembling. Nell wasn't even really listening. She was calling about a new miracle, which somehow in A.Z.'s scrambled mind is maybe another sea. A real sea. A saltwater sea that has appeared where the old sea was. But that doesn't really make scientific sense, and probably someone has just finally dredged up the alligator.

"I'll see if my dad's here," she says. She calls downstairs and checks the kitchen and their bedroom, but neither of her parents is there or anywhere else in the house.

"He's not home," she says when she gets back, halfway expecting Nell to not be there either. "But I'll tell him you called."

"Thank you," Nell says. "Tell him I'll be out at Mud Beach. And again, this is urgent. We'll need a full-page ad and a front-page story."

A.Z. is taking a shower to try to wash her mind back into her body or her body back out of the void when she hears a car pull up. She rinses her hair quickly and wraps in a towel, stepping out of the bathroom just as her mother comes in the side door with a grocery sack.

"I wanted to make pancakes for your father," her mom says. "He was talking about them in his sleep."

"He was talking about pancakes?" A.Z. is pretty sure there aren't any pancakes in *The Tempest*.

"Yes. He was quoting from that article you helped him write at the start of the summer about the Anchor's Away Buffet. He kept saying, 'light and lofty.'" Her mom sighs. But then she smiles. "Those must have been lemon, right?"

"Yes," A.Z. says. "Of course. But I don't think he's here."

Her mom furrows her brow. "He was in the shower when I left." She goes through the dining room to their bedroom and opens the bathroom door. Then she opens the back door.

"Yeah. I was looking for him," A.Z. says when her mom comes back. "Nell Gording called. She has some huge news about a new miracle."

"I've got some news for that woman," her mom says. She gets a mixing bowl out from under the counter, but then she just stands there staring at it as if she's waiting for it to fill itself. "Do you think he went to the buffet?"

"I have no idea," A.Z. says. Her mom doesn't usually ask this kind of question because she usually knows everything. "I was sleeping."

Her mom goes into the dining room and dials someone, and A.Z. is expecting to hear her reprimanding Nell Gording for having the nerve to call the house, but instead her mom hangs back up. "The line at his office is busy. He must be there."

"Maybe that's a good sign?"

"Maybe," her mom says. "Would you help me juice the lemons?"

It's only 9:30 a.m., so Thu shouldn't be at Seven Happiness, but she is, and A.Z. is, too, or at least she's in the parking lot while her mom runs into her dad's office to see if he's there. Thu is standing by the front door, staring at the doormat, the green one she got from Coastal Dry Goods with the alligator on it.

"What are you doing?" A.Z. says.

"A big, big miracle occurred," Thu says, smiling.

"Oh," A.Z. says. This must be what Nell was calling about.

"Sam saw this morning when he came to get the paper," Thu says. "Somebody left four dead chickens outside the door. Right here on the doormat." She points at her feet. "I'm just checking to see if any more arrived."

"Someone left dead chickens on the doormat?" A.Z. feels sort of sick suddenly, like she's looking at dead chickens circled with flies, even though there aren't any chickens or flies.

"Yes." Thu beams. "I'm making all the chicken dishes again today. Chicken chow mein. Chicken wonton. Maybe now that the alligator is dead, they have more chicken again?"

"Maybe," A.Z. says. "They were just lying on the doormat?" She's pretty sure it isn't legal to serve dead things that appear on your doormat. And she can only think of one person who would leave dead chickens, but of course that's impossible.

"Yes," Thu says. "Right here. In a pillowcase."

"In a pillowcase?"

"Yes. Very nice. I just finished plucking. I'll make you a special lunch if you like."

A.Z. and her mom haven't driven out to the Sea together since A.Z. was a little girl and liked to go feed the gulls. Her mom looks determined as she drives, as if delivering pancakes is a moral necessity.

A.Z.'s dad wasn't at his office, and although he might be anywhere, her mom has decided the beach is most likely. "He's going to tire himself out," she says, signaling to pass a truck.

It's a chicken truck, which seems to A.Z. like a cosmic joke. It's stacked with cages—crowded, terrible boxes with feathers stuck to the mesh and flying onto their windshield. The road is too winding to pass, but her mom leaves her signal on and keeps easing to the left.

"I hate to be late to the library," her mom says, "but at this rate, we won't even be out to the Sea by ten. The least Nell could have done was put it in town."

"The Sea?"

"Yes. But I suppose people don't have control over miracles."

A.Z. is pretty sure she's being sarcastic, but it's a little hard to tell. "Do you think they found the alligator?" she says. "That must be the miracle Nell called about, right?"

"Maybe," her mom says. "Though I'm not 100 percent sure that Greg Cabbot even killed it." She looks at A.Z.—right in the eyes— even though, somehow, she's also still watching the road. "You know him better than I do. What do you think?"

A.Z. tries to not think about the hot tub, to not look embar-rassed. "He takes hunting really seriously," she says. "I don't think he'd make it up."

"Right. You may find that teenage boys make up all kinds of things if they think it will get a girl to like them." Her mom looks as if she's about to launch into a story but she doesn't. Instead, she eases into the left lane, guns the engine, and passes the chicken truck, pull-ing back in just as a red Honda comes toward them.

"Right," A.Z. says. She's thinking about the dead alligator but she's also thinking about chickens. Four dead chickens in Thu's doorway. Ordinary Arkansas chickens. And sea eagles. The Sea of Santiago's reputation lapping all the way across the world to Australia as a place with living animals worth studying.

The sun is mid-morning bright in the cloudless sky, and some of the leaves are pale gold, and her mom is slowing for the curve that Bobby's older brother flew off that time when he was drunk and smashed his car and almost died. And there's a scientist counting gulls on the beach.

All of it real. Not hyperreal. Not conceptual. Just ordinary beautiful and terrible and strange and real.

At Mud Beach, A.Z.'s mom parks in the farther lot, although the main lot isn't full. "Don't forget the pancakes," she says, even though A.Z. is holding them. A.Z. kind of doubts her dad wants lukewarm pancakes out of a plastic bag, but she doesn't say this.

The guy selling tickets tells them it's $3.50 each to see the new miracle. A.Z. doesn't recognize him; he's maybe a couple of years older and pug-nosed and freckled.

"We're just going in for a minute," her mom says. "And Nell Gording should pay us for the trouble of coming all the way out here. You can tell her that when you see her."

A.Z. hasn't noticed this before, but her mom seems really natural walking on sand, maybe from all the time in the desert. When they get to the edge of the parking lot, she cuts right toward the Sea without looking down or kicking sand out of her shoes like pilgrims tend to.

The motorboat is beached a few feet up by the lifeguard stand, and a crowd of people, including Sy, standing with his back to them and wearing his orange hunting cap, are leaning in toward something.

A.Z. doesn't want to stand by Sy, so she goes toward the water, which is when she sees her dad. He's beside Warfe, who is taking pictures with his long-lensed camera—aiming at the center of the circle. When A.Z. gets closer, she sees what everyone is looking at. It isn't the alligator. It's a white sheet, like a carpet or a shroud, and set on that is something that looks like one of her research vials with a little piece of paper curled beside it.

Nell, in a skirt suit and pearls, is kneeling on the sheet, posing for the picture. She lifts the paper, holding it between her fingers like a tiny white flag. "It's a message in tongues," she explains, sounding both reverent and scripted, as if she's already said this to several groups of pilgrims this morning. "God sent it to us from the Sea last night. *'Adroco sive wotinon poseto matim thellis esne mondop lyn fotheig.'*"

"Reverend Bicks will have a field day with this one," A.Z.'s mom says.

"'*Adroco sive wotinon.*' God says we are his chosen children," Nell says, standing now and circling through the crowd, looking down at the paper as if it's translating itself in front of her. She enunciates the words slowly, as if they're still floating in water rather than air.

A.Z. can already imagine the words floating from the speakers at next year's Miracle Play. She suddenly feels somewhere right between laughing and crying: that point when you've done so much of one it might be the other. It suddenly strikes her how easy it is to let simple things get scrambled, to not even want to unscramble them.

Her mother looks at Nell and sighs. Then she looks at A.Z.'s dad, who's jotting notes. "I made you pancakes."

"Perfect," he says. "I hurried out here to work on my new column, the 'Daily Drama.'" He takes a pancake from the bag and holds it, flapping slightly against the steno pad as he writes. "I thought of it in the middle of the night. It'll come out weekly, and everything will be in dialogue in case someone wants to act it out. I was working on the first one at the office when Nell called."

"You're not going to write two separate papers for Nell and Chuck Chuck, are you?" A.Z. asks. She says it softly, even though Nell has moved further out into the clapping crowd, pressing the little piece of paper against her breast like in the Miracle Play when the young Nell walks around in those rain boots talking about the flood.

Her dad shakes his head. "Subscriptions have substantially increased since the article accident. Better bad publicity than no publicity. I'm still trying to figure out if I should give the alligator a speaking part." He takes a bite of pancake. He still looks more relaxed, like he did last night after bowing, smiling and sort of tired, the way people look when they've been in the sun at the beach all day.

A.Z.'s mom sighs again but she doesn't really look sad. She fishes a pancake out of the bag for herself, looking back toward the parking lot like she's thinking about opening the library.

"'*Poseto matim thellis*,'" Nell says, raising her voice. "He says the Sea is safe to swim in again. '*Esne mondop lyn fotheig.*' He says that we should all go out in the boat to see His wonder up close."

"What?" A.Z. says involuntarily. For a second, Nell's regular words sound just as strange as the mixed-up ones.

"I get to go on the inaugural ride," her dad says. "This nice man has been taking pictures for me with his zoom lens, and says he'll loan me his camera. There are going to be fireworks. Festive fireworks."

Warfe shrugs and smiles. "The fireworks will scare the birds off anyway," he says.

"Pilgrims have been asking to go out since we rented the boat," Greg says, appearing from somewhere in the crowd and standing way too close to A.Z. "Now we can take them for fifteen dollars. It's a blessing that God sent this." He grins at her. "Did you hear I'm the one who found the message? It was radiating heat so the sensor picked it up. That's one way—that and the tongues—we know it's from God."

A piece of paper doesn't radiate heat, A.Z. wants to say. *If you felt any heat, it was from the sun on the glass or the water itself—the algae and living bacteria. And the vial is just a vial, a research vial. Out of all the things in the Sea of Santiago, you just happened to find it with the dumb motorboat instead of finding the alligator, instead of burned boards from my boat, instead of anything else. And then you made it say what you wanted it to.*

But she doesn't. She's looking past Greg and her dad and everyone at the water, which is glimmering silver-blue in the morning light like it always has, oblivious to all the words written across it. She doesn't need a boat to see that.

Somewhere out there is maybe the dead body of the alligator. Or even the living alligator drinking the unsalted water. And plants adjusting to growing in lower saline or that maybe have already adjusted. And maybe another research vial like the one that Nell is lifting now—like that Cartesian Diver experiment Mrs. Reuter did back in seventh grade where the eyedropper in the pop bottle full of water floats to the top. And then you squeeze the bottle and it sinks; and you release the bottle and it floats again.

It's basic, ancient science—how the air inside the dropper expands and contracts like the water can't; how a single object can keep switching between buoyant and heavy; how the slightest change of pressure can make what you thought you knew reverse itself. Even if you know exactly how it works, it sort of looks like magic.

And right there, with Nell speaking in tongues, and A.Z.'s dad taking notes, and everyone around her on the beach, A.Z. bends down and unlaces her Converse. And even though it's probably illegal, she walks to the edge of the water and throws them—watching one lace and then the other churn up and vanish.

She doesn't even think about how she's going to walk back across the parking lot. The waves are rippling over her feet, swirling with sand. And a few seagulls are screaming and skimming for fish, splashing, reeling back, sailing, and diving again. And toward the woods, five new chickens have taken up residence, nesting and squawking in the shallows. She stands there, seeing how it feels to have arrived, barefoot, boatless, glorious, at the shore of this water.

Acknowledgments

I am beyond grateful for the careful reading, patience, belief, and generosity of my friends, family, and colleagues during the almost decade of writing and revising. Thanks first to my San Francisco writing group: Jen Sullivan-Brych, Cindy Slates, and Rob McLaughlin, who kept me going and asked so many good questions to help A.Z. and Kristoff find their way. And my Moscow writing group: Joy Passanante, Jeff Jones, Mary Clearman Blew, and Rochelle Smith, whose key questions changed an entire religion. So many thanks to Kristin Elgersma and my sister Beth Reaves for their reading and encouragement, and to Stacy Isenbarger and Alisa Messer for belief and questions, and Jennifer Ladino, Erin James, and Jodie Nicotra for listening as we ran through the Palouse. Abigail Ulman for wonderful conversations across a much bigger sea and in person: thank you for helping me not lie down in the castle grass. Annie Lampman: you've been such a vital part of this process, and I can't imagine this book without our many walks and talks and hours of library revising. To my stepmother, Bonnie, for her great reading, insights, encouragement, and advice, and my father, Raymond, for all those in abundance, plus careful, repeated copyedits. Eternal gratitude to my encouraging, fantastic agent Brent Taylor, and my brilliant editor, Chelsey Emmelhainz, for spot-on edits and steering this project so beautifully these last months. I am so lucky that you both wanted to work with me and this world! And thank you to everyone at Skyhorse for your beautiful and careful work on this book. And finally, to Dylan Champagne, who has listened to every page more times than I can count and been a beyond phenomenal, generous partner; thank you for the edits, questions, advice, laughter, ideas, patience, and love, and for first suggesting we do NaNoWriMo (even if it turned out to stand for nine-year-novel-writing). While the story and characters are inventions, I could not have invented this world without the teenage years I spent in the Ozark Mountains of Arkansas—an area and people I deeply love, and for which I wish only good stories.